Johanna Lindsey's **"wickedly witty, lusciously sensual"** (*Booklist*) storytelling has captivated millions!

The crowning glory of a remarkable career . . . her stunning 50th novel

ONE HEART TO WIN

"Delightful and entertaining. . . . This extraordinary author never fails to bring a new, exciting story."

—*Fresh Fiction*

"With that special touch of Lindsey humor and sexual tension, she wins her fans' hearts."

Thrill to the **"potent, sexy chemistry"** (*Booklist*) that shimmers in all of her beloved bestsellers!

LET LOVE FIND YOU

"Filled with Lindsey's trademark humor, sensuality, and emotional intensity. . . . Lindsey knows what readers want and makes us believe in love."

—*RT Book Reviews*, Top Pick (4½ stars)

JAN 2018

SF

JOHANNA LINDSEY

STORMY PERSUASION

POCKET BOOKS

New York   London   Toronto   Sydney   New Delhi

Pocket Books
A Division of Simon & Schuster, Inc.
1230 Avenue of the Americas
New York, NY 10020

This book is a work of fiction. Any references to historical events, real people, or real places are used fictitiously. Other names, characters, places, and events are products of the author's imagination, and any resemblance to actual events or places or persons, living or dead, is entirely coincidental.

First Pocket Books paperback edition March 2015

POCKET and colophon are registered trademarks of Simon & Schuster, Inc.

For information about special discounts for bulk purchases, please contact Simon & Schuster Special Sales at 1-866-506-1949 or business@simonandschuster.com.

The Simon & Schuster Speakers Bureau can bring authors to your live event. For more information or to book an event, contact the Simon & Schuster Speakers Bureau at 1-866-248-3049 or visit our website at www.simonspeakers.com.

Cover design by Lisa Litwack
Cover illustration by Alan Ayers

Manufactured in the United States of America

10   9   8   7   6   5

ISBN 978-1-4767-1429-5
ISBN 978-1-4767-1431-8 (ebook)

STORMY
PERSUASION

Chapter One

JUDITH MALORY KNELT IN front of the window in the bedroom she shared with her cousin Jacqueline, both staring at the ruined house behind the Duke of Wrighton's mansion and formal gardens. Although Judith was the older of the two young women by a few months, Jack, as her father had named her just to annoy his American brothers-in-law, had always been the leader—actually, instigator was more like it. Jack said that she was going to be a rake, just like her father, James Malory. Jack said she was going to be a pirate, just like her father. Jack said she was going to be a superlative pugilist.... The list went on. Judith had once asked her why she didn't have any goals to be like her mother, and Jack had promptly replied, "But *that* wouldn't be exciting."

Judith disagreed. She wanted to be a wife and a mother, in that order. And it was no longer a faraway goal. She and Jacqueline were both turning eighteen this year. She'd had her birthday last week, and Jacqueline would have hers in a couple months. So they were both going to have their first Season come summer, but Jacqueline's debut was going to take place in America instead of London, and Judith didn't think she could bear not being able to share this occasion with her best friend. But Judith still had a couple of weeks to figure out how she could change this disagreeable arrangement.

The daughters of the two younger Malory brothers, James and Anthony, the girls had been inseparable for as long as they could remember. And every time their mothers brought them to visit their cousins Brandon and Cheryl at the duke's ancestral estate in Hampshire, they'd spend hours at this window hoping to see a light glowing eerily in the ruins again. The night they'd first seen it had been so exciting, they couldn't help themselves.

They'd only seen the light on two other occasions since then. But by the time they'd grabbed lanterns and run across the extensive lawn to reach the old, abandoned house on the neighboring property, the light had been gone.

They'd had to tell their cousin Brandon Malory about it, of course. He was a year younger than they were, but it was his home they were visiting, after all. The Duke of Wrighton's title and estate had passed to him through his mother, Kelsey, who had married the girls' cousin Derek. His parents had elected to move into it when Brandon was born, so he would grow up aware of his stature and consequence. Luckily, being a duke hadn't spoiled him rotten.

But Brandon had never actually seen the light himself, so he wasn't the least bit interested in the vigil tonight or any other night. He was currently on the other side of the room engrossed in teaching Judith's younger sister, Jaime, to play whist. Besides, having just turned seventeen, Brandon looked more like a man than a boy, and not surprisingly, he was now much more interested in girls than ghosts.

"Am I old enough *now* to be told the Secret?" Brandon's younger sister, Cheryl, asked from the open doorway to her cousins' room.

Jaime Malory leapt up from the little card table and ran over to Cheryl, grabbing her hand and pulling her forward before turning to her older sister, Judith. "She is. I was her age when you told me."

But it was Jacqueline who answered, scoffing at her younger cousin, "That was just last year, puss. And unlike you, Cheryl actually lives here. Tell her, Brand. She's your sister. She'd have to promise never to go investigating on her own and you'd have to make sure she keeps the promise."

"Investigate?" Cheryl looked at her two older cousins, who'd been refusing for years to tell her their secret. "How can I make a promise if I don't know what I'm promising?"

"This is no time for logic, puss," Judith said, concurring with Jacqueline. "Promise first. Jaime had to, and she doesn't even live here. But you do, and without the promise, we'd end up worrying about you. You don't want that, d'you?"

Cheryl gave that a moment's thought before she shook her head. "I promise."

Judith nudged Jacqueline to do the honors, and Jack didn't disappoint, saying baldly, "You've got a ghost for a neighbor. He lives next door."

Cheryl burst into giggles but stopped when she noticed Judy and Jack weren't laughing. Wide-eyed, she asked, "Really? You've seen it?"

"About five years ago, we did," Judith said.

"Judy even spoke to it," Jacqueline added.

"But Jack saw the light first, from this very window. So

we just had to go have a look. We'd always thought that old house must be haunted. And we were right!"

Cheryl walked forward slowly and joined them at the window to take a quick peek at the old eyesore her parents had complained about more'n once. She let out a relieved breath when she didn't see any light. She wasn't nearly as brave as her cousins were. But in the moonlight she could see a clear outline of the large, old manor house that had fallen to ruin long before any of them were born, a big, dark, scary outline. With a shudder, she turned and hurried over to her brother for protection.

"You didn't actually go inside that house, did you?" Cheryl asked.

"Of course we did," Jack said.

"But we've all been warned not to!"

"Only because it's dangerous with so many broken floor-boards, crumbling walls, and a lot of the roof caved in. And cobwebs. There's cobwebs everywhere. It took Judy and me forever to get them out of our hair that night."

Eyes flaring a little wider, Cheryl said, "I can't believe you actually went inside, and at night."

"Well, how else were we to find out who was trespassing? We didn't know it was a ghost yet."

"You should have just told my father you saw the light," Cheryl said.

"But that's no fun," Jack pointed out.

"Fun? You don't need to pretend to be so courageous just because your fathers are." When the two older girls started laughing, Cheryl said, "So you're just pulling my leg? I should have known!"

Jacqueline grinned at her. "D'you really think we'd keep the Secret from you all these years just to pull your leg? You wanted to know and now we're finally telling you. It was incredibly exciting."

"And only a little frightening," Judith added.

"And foolhardy," Cheryl insisted.

Jack snorted. "If we let things like that stop us, we'd have no fun a'tall. And we had weapons. I grabbed a shovel from the garden."

"And I took my scissors along," Judith added.

Cheryl had always wished she was as brave as these two. Now she was glad she wasn't. They'd thought they'd find a vagrant, but they'd found a ghost instead. It was a wonder their hair hadn't turned white that night, but Judy's gold hair was still streaked with copper, not gray, and Jack was still as blond as her father was.

"We couldn't tell where the light was coming from when we stepped inside the house that night," Jack was saying. "So we split up."

"I found him first," Judy said, continuing the story. "I'm not even sure which room he was in. I didn't notice the light until I opened a door. And there he was, floating in the middle of the room. And none too pleased to see me. I promptly told him he was trespassing. He told me I was the trespasser, that the house was his. I told him ghosts can't own houses. He just stretched his arm out, pointing behind me, and told me to get out. He was a bit harsh. He seemed to growl at me so I did turn about to leave."

"And that's when I arrived," Jack said. "Only to see his back as he floated away. I asked him to wait, but he didn't. He just bellowed, 'Get out, both of you!'—so loud it shook the rafters, or what's left of them. We did, ran right out of there. But we were only halfway back to the mansion when we realized he couldn't really hurt us. And we were missing the opportunity to help him move on. So we went back and searched every room, but he'd already faded away."

"You wanted to help him?" Cheryl asked incredulously.

"Well, Judy did."

Cheryl stared at the slightly older of the two cousins. "Why?"

Judith shrugged evasively, saying, "He was a handsome young man. Must've been only twenty or so when he died. And he seemed so sad when I first spotted him, before he noticed me and got belligerent and protective of his crumbling ruin of a house."

"And because she fell in love with a ghost that night," Jack added with a snicker.

Judith gasped. "I did not!"

"You did!" Jack teased.

"I'd just like to know what caused him to become a ghost. It must have been something quite tragic and frightening, if his hair turned white before he died."

"White hair?" Cheryl said with owlish eyes. "Then he must be old."

"Don't be silly, puss," Jacqueline admonished. "My sister-in-law Danny has white hair, doesn't she? And she was as young as we are now when she met Jeremy."

"True," Cheryl allowed, then asked Judith, "Was he really handsome then?"

"Very, and tall, and with lovely dark green eyes that glowed like emeralds—and don't you dare go looking for him without us," Judy added, sounding almost jealous.

Cheryl huffed, "I'm not daring or curious like you two. I have no desire to meet a ghost, thank you very much."

"Good, because he seems to have magical powers, too, or haven't you noticed that the roof's been repaired?"

Cheryl gasped. "By a ghost?"

"Who else?"

"No, I didn't notice. My room's on the other side of the house."

"I noticed," Brandon spoke up. "And I've never seen workers there to account for it, but the roof has definitely been repaired recently."

"I hope you didn't point that out to your father?" Jacqueline said.

"No, if I did, I'd have to tell him the Secret, and I'm not breaking the promise."

Jacqueline beamed at him. "I knew we could count on you, Brand."

"Besides, Father grumbles anytime someone mentions that old place. He's annoyed that he can't get rid of it. He's tried to buy it so he could tear it down, but the last owner of record was a woman named Mildred Winstock, and she merely inherited it, she never lived in it. And no wonder, with a ghost in residence. It's actually been empty since my great-great-grandfather's day, which would explain its crumbling condition. But then I told you why he built it and who he gave it to."

"Who?" Cheryl asked.

"That's not for your young ears," Brandon replied.

"His mistress?" Cheryl guessed.

Judith rolled her eyes at her precocious cousin and changed the subject. "It's amazing this place didn't fall to ruin, too, being empty for five generations as well."

"Not quite empty," Brandon replied. "The ducal estate has paid to maintain a minimal staff here to keep that from happening. But Father could find no record of who Miss Winstock left the ruin to when she died, so we're stuck with it mucking up our backyard."

Derek had planted trees and thick shrubbery along the property line, though, to block the crumbling, old house from view so people could enjoy the ducal gardens without having to look at that eyesore. But the trees didn't block the view of the old house from the upper floors of the ducal mansion.

Judith sighed as she moved away from the window. "All right, Cousins, time for Judy and me to get to bed, so you probably should, too. We return to London in the morning."

As soon as their cousins left the room, Jacqueline said, "What did you expect? They haven't seen the ghost like we have."

Judith sighed. "Oh, Cheryl's lack of an adventurous nature doesn't surprise me. Derek and Kelsey keep her too sheltered here, while you and I've grown up in London."

"Ah, so that sigh was because we didn't see the light on this visit? We can go search through the ruin tonight if you'd like."

"No, the ghost only revealed himself to us once. I'm quite sure he hides now when we invade his domain. More's the pity," Judith said with another sigh.

Jacqueline threw a pillow at her. "Stop mooning over a ghost. You *do* realize he's not the marrying sort?"

Judith burst out laughing. "Yes, I've had no trouble figuring that out."

"Good, because it'd be quite difficult to get a kiss out of him, much less a nice tumble."

Judith raised a brow. "Tumble? I thought you scratched being a rake off your list last year?"

"Bite your tongue. I'm just going to take a leaf from our cousin Amy's book and not take no for an answer—when

I find the chap for me. And when I do, heaven help him. The man won't know what hit him," Jacqueline added with a roguish grin.

"Just don't find him too soon. And do *not* find him in America."

There it was again, Jacqueline's voyage looming in front of them. The first time Jacqueline had sailed off to America with her parents, Judith had been distraught and inconsolable the entire two months of Jack's absence. The girls had sworn then never to be more'n a carriage ride away from each other ever again, so Judy got to go along the second time Jack visited America. But the girls hadn't known at the time about the promise James Malory had made to the Anderson brothers when Jack was born. Her American uncles had agreed that Jacqueline could be raised exclusively in England as long as she had her come-out in America, because *they* hoped she'd marry an American. At least be given the chance to.

When asked why he would agree to something so out of character for him, James had said, "It kept me from having to kill them, which would have made George quite annoyed with me."

True, they were George's brothers, after all, and James hadn't actually been joking, either, about killing them. George was Jacqueline's mother, Georgina to be exact, but James insisted on calling his wife George because he knew her brothers would hate it, but truth be known, even her five older brothers called her that now on occasion. But that promise James had made had kept an unspoken truce in effect all these years with his five American brothers-in-law. Which had been needed, considering they'd once tried to hang James Malory.

"I'm not going to marry until you do," Jacqueline assured her cousin, "so don't *you* be in a hurry to either. We don't need to be following the pack and getting married our first Season, even if our mothers are expecting us to. This year is for fun, next year can be for marriage."

"That's not going to stop you from sailing off without me," Judith said forlornly.

"No, but we still have a couple of weeks to come up with a solution. We'll talk to our parents as soon as we get back to London. It's *your* parents that have to be convinced. My father would be glad to have you along, but when Uncle Tony said no, Father had to side with him. Brothers, you know, and those two in particular, always stick together. But if I tell them that I won't go to America if you can't come with me, they'll see reason. And why *did* your father say no? It's not as if he's looking forward to your come-out. He's been a veritable ogre with it approaching."

Judith giggled. "My father is never an ogre. A bit terse and snappish lately, yes, but—you're right, he'd be quite happy if I never marry."

"Exactly, so he should have jumped at the chance to send you off with me, prolonging the inevitable."

"But is marriage inevitable, with fathers like ours?"

Jacqueline laughed. "You're thinking of Cousin Regina's being raised by the four Malory elders after their sister Melissa died, and how none of them could agree on a man good enough for their niece, and she had to go through numerous Seasons because of it. Poor Reggie. But, remember, back then, the Malory brothers didn't have wives who could put their feet down as they do now. D'you really think *our* mothers won't do exactly that when love shows up for us? Wait a minute, that's it, isn't it? It was Aunt Roslynn who said you couldn't go and Uncle Tony just agreed with her to keep the peace?"

Judith winced as she nodded. "She's *so* been looking forward to my come-out here, much more'n I am. She's even got her hopes set on one man in particular she thinks will be perfect for me."

"Who?"

"Lord Cullen, the son of one of her Scottish friends," Judith replied.

"Have you met him?"

"I haven't seen him since we were children, but she has. She's assured me he's rich, handsome, a great catch by all accounts."

"I suppose he lives in Scotland?"

"Yes, of course."

"Then *he* won't do! What's your mother thinking, to pair you with a man who'll take you away from us?"

Judith laughed. "Probably that she'll buy us a house in London to live in."

Jack snorted. "We don't take chances like that, especially with Scots, who can be stubborn. Wait a minute, is *he* why she won't bend?"

"She *is* worried he'll get snatched up by someone else if I'm not here at the start of the Season. So, yes, I wouldn't be surprised if that's the real reason she's refusing to let me delay my debut for a trip to America."

Jacqueline rolled her eyes. "You silly. We just haven't tackled this together yet. We're much stronger when we do. Mark my words, you'll be sailing with me. I never had the slightest doubt."

Chapter Two

JUDITH LAY IN BED with her eyes wide-open. Jacqueline had promptly fallen asleep, but Judith remained awake because she'd realized she might be married the next time she visited her cousins in Hampshire. Not to Ian Cullen, but to a man she simply couldn't resist. Although she and Jacqueline didn't want to fall in love right away, certainly not this year, Judith had seen what had happened to her older Malory cousins. Love had a way of interfering with the best-laid plans. And as soon as she married, she'd probably forget about her ghost.

That was a sad thought. Whimsically, she didn't want to forget such an exciting encounter or never see her ghost again. Which was when she got it in her mind that the ghost might reveal himself to her if she entered his house alone, and *that* thought wouldn't let her sleep.

She finally gave in to temptation, donned a hooded cloak and slippers, headed downstairs to find a lantern, then ran across the back lawn. But when she reached the dark, old house and tried to get in the front door as she'd done before, she found it locked. Not stuck, actually locked. Had Derek done that? But why, when many of the windows were missing their glass and were easy enough to slip through?

She set her lantern on the floor inside one window and climbed through. She'd seen no light from outside, but still headed straight for the room where she'd found the ghost before. Boards creaked under her feet. If he was in there, he'd hear her coming—and disappear again.

She thought to call out, "Don't hide from me. I know you're here. Reveal yourself."

Of course he didn't. She chided herself for thinking a ghost would do her bidding. She'd surprised him last time. And she'd foolishly lost the element of surprise this time. Nonetheless, she was determined to check that room again before she gave up and went back to bed.

She opened the door. It didn't squeak this time. Had it been oiled? She held her lantern high to light the room. It looked different. A lot different. The cobwebs were gone. The old sofa was no longer dusty. And a cot was in the corner of the room with a pillow and a crumpled blanket. Was someone other than the ghost staying here? A real trespasser now? Even the windows in this room were covered with blankets, so the light of her lantern wouldn't be seen from outside—and was why they hadn't seen the ghost's light in so long. He was probably furious that some vagrant had moved into his house and he'd been unable to scare him away.

But the vagrant wasn't here now. Maybe the ghost still was. She was about to tell her invisible friend that she could help with his vagrant problem when a hand slipped over her mouth and an arm around her waist. She was surprised enough to drop her lantern. It didn't break, but it did roll across the floor—and extinguish itself. No! Utter blackness and a very real man with his hands on her.

She was about to faint when he whispered by her ear, "You picked a lousy place to do your trysting, wench. Is your lover in the house, too? Is that who you were talking to? Just shake or nod your head."

She did both.

He made a sound of frustration. "If I let go of your mouth so you can answer, I don't want to hear any screaming. Scream and I'll gag you and tie you up and leave you to rot in the cellar. Do we have an understanding?"

Being bound and gagged didn't frighten her so much and was even preferable to anything else he might do to her. Jack would find her in the morning because she would guess exactly where she'd disappeared to. So she nodded. He removed his hand from her mouth, but his arm still held her tightly to him so she couldn't run. Screaming was still an option. . . .

"So how soon before the other half of this tryst shows up?"

"I wasn't meeting anyone," she assured him without thinking. Why hadn't she said "Any minute now" instead?! Then he'd leave—or would he?

"Then why are you here and how did you get in? I locked the bleedin' door."

"*You* did? But what was the point of that when some of the windows are open?"

"Because a locked door makes a statement. It clearly says you aren't welcome."

She humphed. "Neither are you. Don't you know this place is haunted?"

"Is it? I'm just passing by. If there are any ghosts here, they haven't made an appearance yet."

"Passing by when you keep a cot here?" she snorted.

"You're lying. And you weren't here a moment ago. Did you come out of the wall? Is there a hidden room connected to this one?"

He laughed, but it sounded forced. She had a feeling she'd guessed accurately. And why hadn't she and Jack thought of that before? Even the ducal mansion had hidden rooms and passageways.

But he placed his chin on her shoulder. "Quite the imagination you have, darlin'. How about you answer the questions instead? What are you doing here in the middle of the night if you're not meeting a lover?"

"I came to visit the resident ghost."

"That nonsense again?" he scoffed. "There are no such things."

It would be *so* nice if her ghost would show up to prove him wrong right then. The vagrant would be distracted long enough for her to escape and bring Derek back to get rid of him. But then she realized the room was too dark for her to see the ghost even if he did show up. Frustrated that this trespasser was ruining her last chance to see the ghost again, she just wanted to go back to bed. She tried to pull away from him but he tightened his hold on her.

"Stop wiggling, or I'm going to think you want some attention of a different sort. Do you, darlin'? I'll be happy to oblige." She sucked in her breath and stood perfectly still. "Now that's disappointing." He actually did sound it. "You smell good. You feel good. I was hoping to find out if you taste good, too."

She stiffened. "I'm ugly as sin, with boils and warts."

He chuckled. "Now why don't I believe that?"

"Relight the lantern and you'll see."

"No, the dark suits us. I'll call your warts and boils and

raise you a lusty appetite. I think I'm going to win this hand."

Despite the warning, and warning it was, she still wasn't expecting to be flipped around so fast and kissed before she could stop it from happening. She didn't gag. His breath actually smelled of brandy. And for a first kiss it might not have been so bad if she'd wanted to explore it. But she didn't. Her hand swung wildly in the dark but she got lucky with her aim. It cracked against his cheek and got her released.

He merely laughed. "What? It was just one quick kiss I stole. Nothing for you to get violent over."

"I'm leaving now, and you will, too, if you know what's good for you."

A sigh. "Yes, I've already figured that out. But let me get you out of here safely. I don't want it on my conscience if you fall through the floor and break your neck."

"No! Wait!" she cried as he picked her up in his arms. "I know this house better than you do!"

"I doubt that," he muttered, and carried her out of the room and across the main room to the nearest window, which he shoved her through. "Say nothing about seeing me here and I'll be gone before morning."

"I didn't *see* you. You made sure of that."

And she still couldn't. A little moonlight was on the porch, but he stepped away from the window as soon as he released her, disappearing into the blackness inside the house. She didn't wait for a response if he'd even heard her, just ran all the way back to the ducal mansion and up to her room.

She almost woke Jacqueline to tell her about her little

misadventure but decided it could wait until morning. It still nagged at her, how a poor vagrant could afford French brandy. The tariff on it was so high, only the rich could afford it. That was why it was the prime cargo of smugglers. . . .

Chapter Three

"**W**HY DO *YOU* LOOK like *I'm* in trouble?" Boyd Anderson wondered aloud as he entered the dining room to join his sister, Georgina, for lunch.

His voice was teasing, his grin engaging, but he was quite serious given the frown he saw on her face. Brother and sister both had identical dark brown eyes, but his brown hair was shades lighter than hers. She was dressed today to receive company in a pretty coral gown, but she wore her hair down, as she often did when she only expected to entertain family.

Boyd was the youngest of Georgina's five brothers, and the only one who lived permanently in London. It had been his decision, and a good one since he was the third Anderson to marry into the Malory clan. His wife, Katey, was Anthony Malory's illegitimate daughter, a daughter that Anthony hadn't even known he had until Boyd began to pursue her. Newly discovered as Katey was, the Malorys, and there were many of them, would have been quite up in arms if Boyd had tried to sail off to America with her despite her having been raised there.

Georgina tried to give Boyd a reassuring smile, but

didn't quite manage it. "Sit." She pointed at the chair across from her. "I've asked the cook to prepare your favorite dish. It wasn't easy to find white clams."

"Bribery? Never mind, don't answer that. It's Jacqueline's trip, isn't it? What's wrong? Did something happen with the boys?"

"No, they're happy to stay at school. They're not interested in their sister's come-out."

"I thought you were in agreement that she could go?"

"I am. I know you and our brothers only want the best for Jack. And this momentous trip has kept the peace in my family—even if it was forced down our throats."

Boyd winced. "Must you put it like that?"

"Yes, I must, since it's true."

He sighed. "I know we were rather emphatic when we insisted she have her come-out in America—"

"Very."

"—and, yes, I know we're all more often in England these days than in Connecticut as we were back then. But there's another more important reason for her to go to America for her come-out." He paused to glance at the door before he added in a near whisper, "Your husband is absent from the house, I hope? I wouldn't want him walking in on this conversation."

"Yes, James has gone to the dock to make sure all the provisions have been delivered for the trip. But I wouldn't be surprised if he drags Tony to Knighton's first."

"Damn, I wish they'd let me know when they do that. I do so enjoy watching fights of that caliber."

"You wouldn't today. James is rather annoyed, so it's bound to be brutal."

"All the better! No, wait. Why is *he* annoyed? Because you're upset—with someone?"

"I'm not upset with anyone, just worried. It's Jack who's having the bloody fit."

"About the trip?"

"In a roundabout manner."

"But I thought she wanted to go."

"Oh, she did, but she thought that Judy would get to go with her. But that's not happening. And now Jack refuses to go without her."

Boyd laughed. "Now, why doesn't that surprise me? They've always been inseparable, those two. Everyone knows it. So why can't Judy go?"

"Her mother won't allow it. Roslynn has been preparing for the Season here for months, has been looking forward to it even more than our daughters are. She already knows who will be hosting what parties and balls, has promises of invitations for them all. She already knows who the most eligibles are, including a Scotsman she favors for Judy because he is the son of a close friend of hers. She's leaving nothing to chance and thinks that Judy might miss a significant event if she sails with us."

Boyd cast his eyes toward the ceiling. "But they will be back in time for the Season here, might only miss a week or two of it. They'll still have the rest of the summer here. That *is* why we're leaving now, in the spring."

"But missing the beginning is what's turned Judith's mother stubborn, and she can be very stubborn. And I even understand her reasoning, since the very beginning of a Season *is* when attractions first spark, pairings get made, courting starts. To arrive even a week late can make a world of difference, with all the best catches already taken.

Of course she's most concerned about that Scotsman. She doesn't want another girl to snare Lord Cullen. So she's making sure Judy will be here when he is, right at the start of the Season."

"Do you really think that will matter for the two prettiest debutantes this year?"

"It won't matter for Jack. She'll go after who she wants as soon as she claps eyes on him, consequences be damned, this side of the ocean or the other."

"For God's sake, Georgie, you're talking about your daughter, not one of the Malory rakes."

She raised a brow at him, a habit she'd gotten into soon after marrying James Malory. "You're surprised she'd take after her father?"

"Too much after him, obviously," Boyd mumbled, adding the complaint "And that should've been nipped in the bud."

She chuckled at him. "There's no nipping an influence that strong. But that's beside the point. Unlike Jack, who occasionally acts before she thinks, Judith is too kindhearted and considerate of others to even come close to stepping on toes. And Roslynn knows that about her daughter. Which is why she won't budge on Judy's not missing the first ball of the Season here. I'm afraid if we can't change Roslynn's mind, we won't be sailing. Jack has simply *and* furiously declined to have a Season without her best friend beside her."

"Damnit, Georgie, we're three days away from sailing. It's too late to cancel. Katey has been looking forward to the trip."

"D'you think I like this situation? We're already packed. *The Maiden George* has been brought up from her dock in the south and a full crew hired. She's anchored in the Thames as we speak. We've been browbeating and cajoling

Roslynn for months, and now we're down to the last few days and she's still saying no."

"But our brothers are all on their way to Bridgeport. And Amy will be there soon to oversee the preparations. She sailed with Warren last week. They will all think something horrible has happened if we don't show up as expected!"

"James would sail anyway to let them know what's happened, if it comes to that. They won't be left to worry. I'm sorry, Boyd. I know you and our brothers have been looking forward to this. I just don't want all of you to be angry if James doesn't keep his promise. It's *not* his fault."

Boyd gave Georgina a pointed look. "Since when does Jack rule the roost? I'll get her on the ship myself if you and James are reluctant to insist."

"You're missing the point, Boyd. There *is* no point to this trip if my daughter spends the entire time miserable. None of us expected Roslynn's opposition. We've all tried to change her mind. But she won't budge. She's a Scot, you know, and she's lost her temper more'n once, with all of us trying to change her mind."

"Then don't count on Jack's ever marrying," Boyd said flatly.

Georgina shot to her feet. "Excuse me? You take that back, Boyd Anderson!"

He rose as well, his brow as furrowed as hers. "I will not. I told you there is another even more important reason for Jack to have her come-out in America. You know she's going to have a much better chance of finding love with a man who isn't familiar with your husband's reputation. The young men here are going to be scared to death to approach her because of him."

Georgina dropped back into her chair but was still bristling on her husband's behalf. "Jack isn't worried about that happening and neither are we."

"Then you're deluding yourselves, because it's human nature. There isn't a man who knows him, or who has even merely heard the rumors about him, that would risk having James Malory for a father-in-law—that's *if* James doesn't kill him before they get to the altar."

Georgina gasped, even sputtered before she said furiously, "I now agree with Jack. In fact, I'm not going either. I wouldn't be able to bear weeks at sea with someone as pigheaded as you!"

Boyd lost his own temper, snarling on the way out of the room, "I won't let my niece throw away a golden opportunity just because *you* don't know when to put your foot down!"

"How dare you!" Georgina yelled, and threw a plate at him.

The plate missed and shattered in the hall. The front door opened before Boyd reached it, and Jacqueline remarked wide-eyed, "Is she breaking dishes on you again?"

Boyd snorted and took Jack's arm to lead her back out of the house. "She never did have good aim." And then sternly: "Do you know how much trouble you're causing?"

Jack grinned cheekily, not the least bit repentant. "It's all part of my plan."

"To drive us crazy?"

"To get Judy on the ship with us."

"I've a better idea. Come on, we're going to find a certain Scotsman and arrange a little accident for him."

"Really?!"

"I'm definitely in the mood to, but I suppose we can try to reason with him first."

"Reason with a Scotsman?" Jack started laughing.

Boyd tsked. "Just tell me he's in town. I don't want to kill a horse riding to Scotland and back in three days."

"He is here on business, actually. Arrived a few days ago and has been calling on Judy each day. I've had a devil of a time making sure she's not home to receive him, hoping he'll get the hint and just go away. But Aunt Ros guessed what I've been up to after Judy found the nerve to tell her that she'll have no Season a'tall if she can't have one on each side of the ocean."

"Did that work?"

"No, not yet, but it has to eventually. For now, Aunt Ros is sure Judy will come around once our ship sails without her. She is calling me a bad influence, though," Jack ended with a grin, rather proud to be called that.

"So Judy hasn't even met Lord Cullen to know whether she would like him or not?"

"Not since he was a boy. He, on the other hand, has seen her in recent years and is quite besotted. But she's in no hurry to find out what the man is like. She's supposed to be meeting him right now in the park. Roslynn was taking her. But Judy's going to pretend to be sick."

"Then let's meet him instead. We can use his infatuation to good purpose, tell him he'll be doing Judy a favor if he cooperates and claims he's had an accident that will prevent him from joining the Season for a few weeks. As long as he agrees to assure Roslynn of it, so she'll no longer have a reason to object to Judy's coming with us, I won't actually have to break any bones."

Jacqueline grinned. "You realize you sound like my father?"

"Bite your tongue, Jack."

Chapter Four

"HAVE YOU THOUGHT OF something yet? We're down to two days before we sail, and now neither Jack nor George intends to join us thanks to your wife's intransigence," James said as he landed a hard jab to Anthony's chin that moved his brother back a step.

Word had spread fast in the neighborhood when the Malory brothers were seen going into Knighton's Hall together. The seats around the ring were already filled as if this fight had been scheduled. A crowd was at the door fighting to get in. Knighton had thrown up his hands and stopped trying to prevent access. Anthony, the youngest Malory brother, had been coming to Knighton's for most of his life for exercise in the ring, but his fights weren't very exciting since he never lost—unless his brother James stepped into the ring with him. No one ever knew which brother would win, and thus bets were flying about the hall today.

Anthony's black brows narrowed on his brother. "No, and you can stop taking your frustration out on me."

"But who better?" James said drily, and another hard right landed. "What about now?"

"Blister it, James, it ain't my bloody fault."

"Of course it is, dear boy. You are the only one capable of talking your wife around. Lost your touch? Good God, you have, haven't you?"

Anthony got in a solid punch to James's midsection for that slur, followed by an uppercut. Neither one moved James Malory, who had been likened to a brick wall more'n once by men who had tried to defeat him, his brothers included. But Anthony was knocked off his feet with James's next blow, deciding the matter of his giving up this round. Bloody hell. James won too easily when *he* was annoyed. But Anthony was saved from having to concede when his driver climbed up on the side of the ring and waved for his attention. Seeing the man as well, James stepped back.

Anthony got up to fetch the note his man was waving at him, reading it as he returned to James in the middle of the ring. He snorted before he told James, "Judy suggests I save my face a bruising today and come home to pack. Apparently, Ros has given in."

James started to laugh at the good news, which is how Anthony caught him off guard with a punch that landed his older brother on his arse. But James's own annoyance was completely gone now with the unexpected news, so he merely raised a golden brow from his position on the floor to inquire, "Then what was that for?"

"Because now I'm no doubt in the doghouse," Anthony grumbled, though he offered James a hand up. "I don't know who changed her mind or how they did it, but I know I'll end up catching her anger for it."

"Then it's just as well you'll be sailing with us and your wife will be staying home. She will have more'n enough time to calm down before we return."

Both men knew that Roslynn wouldn't sail with them

because of her seasickness. She and Anthony's younger daughter, Jaime, suffered from the same malady, so even if Roslynn was willing to endure the discomfort for Judy's sake, she wouldn't subject Jaime to it again. Nor would she leave Jaime at home alone for the two months they expected to be gone.

But James noted that his remark didn't seem to ease his brother's concern. "Come on, old man, don't tell me London's most notorious rake can't redirect a lady's anger into passion of another sort," James said as he leaned forward to take his brother's proffered hand.

Anthony abruptly withdrew it. "It's against my code of honor to hit a man when he's down, but I *could* make an exception just for you."

James chuckled as he rose to his feet. "I'll pass on that favor. Don't want Judy to think her message didn't get to you in good time."

In the middle of the Atlantic, *The Nereus* was making good headway toward Bridgeport, Connecticut. While the Andersons' family business, Skylark Shipping, had many ships in its fleet, each sibling also had one of his or her own, and *The Nereus* was owned and captained by Warren, the second-oldest Anderson brother and Amy Malory's adoring husband. The couple spent half of the year at sea, along with their children, Eric, and the twins, Glorianna and Stuart, and of course the children's tutors. The other half of the year they spent in their house in London so their children could get to know their large family.

Amy was basking in the spring sun on deck, despite the wind's being nippy. As the only woman in the Anderson family who had experienced a successful social Season in

London, she'd been asked by the Anderson brothers to plan the social events for Jacqueline's two-week visit to Bridgeport. Of course, Drew Anderson's wife, Gabby, had had a London social debut, but it had been cut short and turned into a scandalous disaster by Drew, so she couldn't offer much advice about come-out parties. Amy wasn't simply relying on her own experience. She had conferred with her cousin Regina, the Malory family's expert in social events.

Amy had to get the Anderson family home ready for these events. She had to plan the menus and send out the invitations. Warren would help her with the invitations since he knew whom to include. Although Amy had been to Bridgeport with him dozens of times over the years and had met many of the Andersons' friends and acquaintances, she couldn't be expected to remember them all. Yet everything had to be perfect before Jacqueline and her parents arrived.

Her own children were more excited about this trip than she was, since they were going to get to attend each event. In England they'd have to wait until they were eighteen to be included among the adults, but in America rules like that didn't apply. Amy was too frazzled to be excited. So many things to do, so many lists to make.

With so much on her mind, she almost didn't notice the feeling that started to intrude, and then she did, doubling over from it, as if she'd received a blow to her stomach. Warren, approaching her from behind, noticed and was instantly alarmed.

He put his hands gently on her back. "What sort of pain is it, sweetheart?"

"No pain."

"Then . . . ?"

"Something—bad—is going to happen."

Warren immediately looked up at the sky for an approaching storm that might cripple them, but not a dark cloud was in sight. "When?"

"I don't know."

"What?"

"I don't know!"

He sighed. "If you're going to have these feelings, I really wish you could interpret them more specifically."

"You always say that. And it never helps because I can't. We have to go back, Warren."

He tsked, helped her straighten, and turned her around so he could hold her in his arms. "You're not thinking clearly. We'd miss half the family that are already heading this way. Even James and Georgie will have departed with Jack long before we could get back."

"I wish there was a faster way to travel," she growled in frustration against his wide chest.

He chuckled. "That's never going to happen, but we don't sail with cannons anymore—"

"You still acquired a full cargo that's weighing us down."

"Of course I did, that's my job. And despite the cargo, we're making damn good time. Another week, give or take a day or so, and we'll be in Bridgeport."

"If the wind holds," she mumbled.

"Naturally. But you know, no matter what your feeling portends, you can lessen the blow and make sure it isn't devastating. Do it now. Say something to relieve your mind, sweetheart. Make a bet. You know you always win."

She glanced up at him and gave him a loving smile for

the reminder. "I bet nothing is going to happen that my family can't handle."

"Are you sure you want to be that vague?"

"I wasn't vague. That covers everyone in my family, everyone in your family, all wives, husbands, and children."

Chapter Five

THE HOLDING CELL, ONE of many, was the only one currently in use. The cell wasn't in a jail or a prison, although it certainly felt as if it were to the men detained there. Underground, no windows, the prisoners would have no light at all if a single lantern weren't kept burning day and night. That light was for the guard, not the prisoners.

The revenue base had been built toward the end of the last century when the Crown got more aggressive in patrolling her southern waters, mainly along the Cornish coast. The base had started out as no more than a dock and a barracks halfway between Dorset and Devon. As it had expanded over the years, a community had grown up around it. Shops, a stable, taverns, but the main business was still the apprehension of smugglers, and they were dealt with severely. Sent to the colonies in Australia or hanged. One or the other with trials that were a mockery.

Nathan Tremayne had wished more than once that he'd been born in the last century, before the revenue men got organized. Then, smuggled cargoes could be unloaded right on the docks of a village with everyone helping. Even the local nabobs would turn a blind eye on the illegal activities as long as they got their case of brandy or tea. It had been a simple way to get around exorbitant taxes, and the long expanse of rocky Cornish coastline made that section of England ideal for bringing in rum, brandy, tea, and even tobacco to otherwise law-abiding citizens at reasonable prices. With so few revenue men patrolling back then, the smugglers faced little risk. Not so anymore.

These days the few smugglers still operating were running out of places to hide their cargoes. Even the tunnels built into the cliffs were slowly being discovered and watched by the revenuers. Smugglers had resorted to storing their cargoes farther inland, away from the revenuers, before their cargoes could be distributed. But the goods still had to be unloaded onto shore for transport—or loaded back onto a ship if a smuggler suspected his hiding place had been discovered by a meddlesome wench who would likely inform the authorities. That's how Nathan had been caught last week. His crew had gotten away, scattering like rats in a sewer. He and his ship hadn't.

It had been a setup. The revenuers had been lying in wait. He just couldn't prove it unless he could escape. But that wasn't happening from a cellblock such as this. Chained hand and foot with the chains spiked to the wall behind him, he could barely stand or reach the man chained next to him. Four in the cell were in a similar position. He didn't know them, didn't bother to talk to them. An old man had been left unbound. His task was to pass out the tin bowls of gruel to the rest of them. If he was awake. If waking him didn't get him angry. Nathan had already missed a few meals because of that old man's temper.

Nathan was asleep when they came for him, unchaining him from the wall, dragging him out of there. The last man to be removed from the cell had gone out screaming about his innocence and hadn't returned. Nathan didn't say a word, but a slow-burning anger was inside him. He'd had other choices, other kinds of work, other goals, too. He might have stuck to that path if his father, Jory, hadn't died. But one thing had led to another, a long chain of events, and now here he was about to be hung or sent off to prison for life.

The two guards dragging him didn't even give him an opportunity to walk. That would have been too slow for them, with the chains still on his ankles, and they weren't removing those. He couldn't even shield his eyes from the daylight that blinded him when they got aboveground.

He was taken into a large office and shoved directly into a hardback chair in front of a desk. The fancy room had more the look of a parlor with expensive furnishings, indicating that the man behind the desk was important. The man who, Nathan guessed, was maybe five years older than he was, which would put him around thirty, wore a spotless uniform with gleaming buttons, and had curious blue eyes. He had the look of an aristocrat. A common practice was for second sons to work for the government in some capacity.

The guards were dismissed before the man said, "I'm Arnold Burdis, Commander Burdis to be exact."

Nathan was surprised he'd been left completely alone with the officer. Did they think a week of nothing but gruel in a bricked and barred hole had made him weak? The office might be in the middle of a base crawling with revenuers, but still, it wouldn't take too much effort for Nathan to overpower this man.

He'd immediately spotted the old dueling pistol on the desk, which was there for obvious reasons. Nathan eyed it for a few moments, debating his chances of getting to it before the commander did. The likelihood that it had only one bullet in it decided the matter because he would need at least two, one for the commander and one for the chain between his feet in order to escape. Unless he wanted to take the commander hostage . . .

"Would you like a brandy?"

The man was pouring one for himself, and two glasses were actually on the desk in front of him. "One of my own bottles?" Nathan asked.

Burdis's mouth quirked up slightly. "A sense of humor despite your dire straits, how novel."

The commander poured the brandy for him anyway and slid the glass across the desk. The rattle of his chains as he raised it to his lips screamed of those dire straits, but sarcasm wasn't humor. And he only took a sip to wet his dry mouth. If the man intended to get him drunk to loosen his tongue, he would be disappointed.

"You are quite the catch, Tremayne. But it was just a matter of time. You were getting sloppy, or was it too bold for your own good?"

"Try desperate?"

"Were you really? Dare I take credit?"

"For dogged persistence, if you like. I prefer to blame a wench."

Burdis actually chuckled. "Don't we all from time to time. But my informant wasn't wearing skirts."

"Care to share his name?" Nathan tossed out the question, then held his breath.

But the man wasn't simply conversing with him or distracted enough to reflexively reply to a quick question. He was cordial for a reason; Nathan just couldn't imagine what it was. But he was beginning to think he was being toyed with. A nabob's perverse pleasure, for whatever reason, and he wanted no more of it.

"Do I even get a trial?" he demanded.

The commander swirled his brandy and sniffed it before he looked up curiously and asked, "Do you have a defense?"

"I'll think of something."

A tsk. "You're far too glib for your situation. Admirable, I suppose, but unnecessary. Has it not occurred to you that I hold your life in my hands? I would think you would want to rein in that sarcasm, at least until you find out why I've summoned you."

A carrot? It almost sounded as if he wasn't going to be hanged today. But it raised his suspicion again. If this wasn't his trial, the commander his judge and jury, then what the hell was it? And he'd been caught red-handed. He had no defense and they both knew it.

He sat back. "By all means, continue."

"I am successful in this job because I make a point of finding out all there is to know about my quarries, and you are something of an anomaly."

"There's nothing peculiar about me, Commander."

"On the contrary. I know you've been involved in other lines of work. Lawful ones. Quite a few actually, and you mastered each one, which is an amazing feat for someone your age. Couldn't make up your mind what to do with your life?"

Nathan shrugged. "My father died and left me his ship and crew. That made up my mind for me."

Burdis smiled. "So you think smuggling is in your blood? I beg to differ. I already know about you, Tremayne, more than I expected to learn. Privilege of rank, access to old records."

"Then you probably know more'n I do."

"Possibly, but I doubt it. Moved quite far down the proverbial social ladder, haven't you? Did all the women in your family marry badly, or just your mother?"

Every chain rattled as Nathan stood up and leaned across the desk to snarl, "Do you have a death wish?"

The commander immediately reached for his pistol, cocked it, and pointed it at Nathan's chest. "Sit down, before I call the guards."

"Do you really think one bullet would stop me before I break your neck?"

Burdis let out a nervous chuckle. "Yes, you're a strapping behemoth, I get the point. But you have an earl in your bloodline, so it was a logical question."

"But none of your bleedin' business."

"Quite right. And I meant no offense. I just found it a fascinating tidbit, who your ancestors are, a bit far back in the tree, but still . . . D'you even realize that you could be sitting in a chair like mine, instead of the one you're in? It boggled my mind when I realized it. Why did you never take advantage of who you are?"

"Because that isn't who I am. And you ask too many questions of a man you've already caught."

"Curiosity is my bane, I readily admit it. Now *do* sit down, before I change my mind about you and send you back to your cell."

There was that carrot again, alluding to a different outcome to his capture than the obvious one. Nathan drained the brandy in front of him before he dropped back in his chair. He could handle at least one glass without losing his wits. Bleedin' nabob. Nathan still suspected he was being toyed with, and now he guessed why. His lordly ancestor probably ranked higher than the commander's did. Why else would the man want to sit there and gloat?

"Are you going to tell me who your informant was?" Nathan asked once more.

"He was just a lackey, but can't you guess who he works for? I have it on good authority that you've been searching for the man yourself. He must have thought you were getting too close to finding him."

Nathan stiffened. "Hammett Grigg?"

"Yes, I thought that might be clue enough for you. The same man suspected of killing your father."

"Not just suspected. There was a witness."

"An old grudge finally settled between the two men, was the way I heard it."

"My father was unarmed. It was murder."

"And is that what you had in mind for Grigg?"

"I want to kill him, yes, but in a fair fight—with my bare hands."

Burdis actually laughed. "Look at yourself, man. D'you really think that would be a fair fight? I've nothing against revenge. I feel the need for it m'self occasionally. But I'll have Mr. Grigg caught and hung long before you can get your hands on him. He is my next quarry, after all."

"And I'll be dead before you catch him."

Burdis refilled Nathan's glass before he replied, "You misunderstand why I've brought you before me. I'm going to give you the opportunity to thank me one day."

"For what?"

The commander opened a drawer to retrieve a clean, unfolded piece of paper that he set in front of him. He tapped it. "This is a full pardon already signed, an opportunity for you to start over with a clean slate. But it's conditional, of course."

Nathan's eyes narrowed. "Is this some joke?"

"Not a'tall. This document will remain with me until you fulfill the terms, but it's a legitimate offer."

"You want me to catch Grigg for you without killing him? You really think I could resist the temptation if I get my hands on him?"

"Forget about Grigg! I told you, *assure* you, I'll see him hanged for you."

For the first time, Arnold Burdis didn't look or sound so cordial. Nathan was done with second-guessing him, other than to say, "You sound angry."

"I am. My man guarding your ship was killed, left floating in the water where your *Pearl* should have been."

"You've lost my ship!?"

"I didn't *lose* it," Burdis growled. "It was stolen, and, no, not by Hammett Grigg. We caught one of the thieves. Nicked as they were sailing away, he fell into the water and was recovered. We gave chase, of course, probably would have caught them, too, if we'd known their direction. We searched up and down the coast, while they did the unthinkable, sailing straight out to sea and beyond."

"Who were they?"

"They're not Englishmen, but they've been stealing English ships for some ten years now, just so sporadically, and never from the same harbors, that no one linked the thefts. At first they were just taking the vessels offshore and sinking them, but then they decided to have their revenge and make a profit at it."

"Revenge?"

"It's a couple of Americans who bear a grudge against us for the last war we had with their country, which orphaned them. They were just children at the time, which is why they only got around to getting some payback a decade ago." A folded note was tossed at Nathan. "Those are the particulars I got out of their man. My superiors don't give a rat's ass about this crime ring targeting our harbors. They only want you and your ilk. But I don't like having my toes stepped on, and these thieves did that when they killed one of my men and stole *my* prize right off my docks."

Nathan raised a brow. *His* prize? "Tell me you're not asking me to bring my ship back to you."

"No, if you can recover *The Pearl*, she's yours again, but good luck with that. They refit them with new paint, new names, then auction them off to their unsuspecting countrymen, who actually think they are legitimate shipbuilders. And they've gotten away with this for years. But you're going to end it. It won't be easy getting the Yanks to do you any favors, but you'll need to figure out a way to get the authorities over there to work with you in closing down that operation. That's my condition. I want a letter from an American official stating that the thieves have been arrested and put out of business."

"That's all?" Nathan rejoined drily.

The commander's eyes narrowed with the warning. "Don't even think of running away once I give you your freedom for this task. As I mentioned, I found out more'n I expected to about you, including that you have guardianship of your two remaining relatives. I would hate to see your nieces end up paying for their uncle's crimes. So do you agree to my terms?"

"For my freedom, did you even need to ask?"

Chapter Six

IN GROSVENOR SQUARE, AT the home of Edward and Charlotte Malory, most of the extensive Malory family in England and a few close friends were gathered for a send-off party for Jack and Judy, who would be sailing in the morning for America. The crew was already aboard *The Maiden George*, the trunks had already been delivered. It only remained for the seven members of the family bound for America to row out to the ship at dawn, too early to expect good-byes at the dock, thus the party tonight.

Glancing about the room, Judith was looking for Brandon so she could ask him what had happened with the vagrant. She'd told him that she suspected the vagrant was a smuggler, and Brandon had assured her he and his father would send the man packing. But it appeared her cousins from Hampshire weren't going to make it tonight. She wasn't surprised, when she and Jacqueline had visited them so recently and they had already given Jack their good wishes for the trip.

Derek had even told Judith, "I bet your mum will change her mind, so I'm going to wish you a wonderful voyage, too."

"I wish *Amy* were saying that," Judith had replied, and she hadn't been joking.

Derek had laughed. "Yes, that would guarantee your sailing to America, wouldn't it?"

It would indeed. Amy never lost a wager. Judith realized she should have asked Amy to bet on it before she'd sailed with Warren. Maybe Amy had and *that's* why Judith was going now.

Jacqueline came up beside her and said in an annoyed tone, "*He* shouldn't be here when he's not a close friend of the family and only your mother knows him."

Judith followed her cousin's gaze and saw Roslynn fussing over Lord Cullen. "But now we all know him, and besides, my mother is right. It was quite thoughtful and gallant of him to come here tonight to wish me well on my voyage when he must be in pain from his injury."

"He's here because he's got his heart set on you and your mother's got her heart set on him *for* you. Tell me your heart's not getting set here, too, when you and I swore not to marry this year."

Judith grinned and teased, "Now that I've met him again after all these years, I have to admit he turned out rather handsome, don't you think?"

"If you like dark red hair and pretty blue eyes. Flirt all you want, just no falling in love yet."

"Stop fretting. I'm not eager to get back here because of him when we haven't even left yet."

In a corner of the room, Boyd joined James and Anthony, who were looking at the Scotsman, too. Anthony was saying, "Ros should've confessed what she was up to, trying to match him with Judy. But I'm not complaining when he managed to bring peace to the family by getting himself laid up. But if it weren't so obvious that my baby ain't interested in him, I bloody well would."

"Noticed that," James agreed.

"He's head over heels for her, though," Boyd put in.

"And how would you know anything about it, Yank?" Anthony asked.

"Because as a last resort, Jack and I tracked him down and asked him to feign an injury to help Judy convince her mother to let her go to America."

"That splint on his leg is wrapped up rather tight for a fake," James remarked.

"It's not a fake," Boyd said with a grin. "The man is as clumsy as an ox. He got so excited by the scheme he really did fall off his horse and break his leg."

James rolled his eyes.

Anthony said, "I see I'm going to have to have a word or two with Roslynn, after all. What the deuce could she be thinking, matchmaking our daughter with such a bungler?"

"It was a brilliant plan, though, you have to admit," James said. "The broken-limb part. You should have thought of it, Tony."

"I didn't even know about *him*, so how could I?"

"Just remember you owe me one, both of you, the next time you lay into me," Boyd said before quickly walking off.

"Did he just goad you?" Anthony said with an incredulous laugh. "And with a smirk, too!"

James shrugged. "He should know by now that I have a faulty memory when I find it convenient. And my memory will definitely be faulty when it comes to being beholden to an Anderson—wife excluded, of course."

Lord Cullen didn't stay long, shouldn't have come at all when his doctor had ordered him to stay off his feet for three months. After Judith thanked him again for coming and wished him a swift recovery, Jacqueline steered her toward their mothers.

"D'you feel the excitement?" Jack asked. "We're going to have a grand time, you know. I feel it, I'm bubbling with it."

"You're bubbling with triumph, not excitement. Note the difference."

"Pooh, whatever it is, let's go share some of it with your mother. She might have given in when she learned the Scot won't be here for the start of the Season either, but she's still not happy about it or what she termed our 'collective tantrum.' And if she's not happy, then Uncle Tony won't be getting a nice good-bye from her tonight, and he'll be in a rotten mood the whole trip."

Judith blushed at that statement as Jacqueline dragged her across the room to their mothers. Despite how brazen Jack could be at times and how used to it Judith was, she believed some things just shouldn't be mentioned or even alluded to, and what their parents did behind closed doors was definitely one of those things.

Both girls walked up to Roslynn and put an arm around her waist. Judith was now as tall as her mother at five feet four inches and had the same sun-gold hair streaked with copper, but her father's exotic cobalt-blue eyes, a stunning combination, or so her family liked to remind her. But Judith's features also resembled her mother's. She had a heart-shaped face and finely molded cheekbones, a small, tapered nose, even the same generous full lips. Jacqueline, on the other hand, looked nothing like her mother. She didn't inherit Georgina's diminutive height. She was taller at five feet six inches and had James Malory's blond hair and green eyes, but her features were uniquely her own: a pert nose, high cheekbones, a stubborn chin, and a mouth far too sensual for a woman.

Her lips were turned up now in a smile meant to melt hearts. Few people were immune to it, and Roslynn wasn't one of them, but she still admonished her niece, "None of that now. You won't be cajoling me out of this snit."

"Are you sure?" Jacqueline asked. "I haven't heard your Scot's brogue yet to prove you're in a snit. But Judy won't take my word for it, so a little reassurance from you before we sail is in order." Then, in one of her more serious tones: "Don't make her suffer because there's been a little dent—"

Georgina cut in with a gasp. "Jacqueline Malory! Not another word!"

Jacqueline merely met her mother's eyes with a steady look that offered no apology. She was protective of family, always had been, and most particularly of Judith. It wasn't the first time she had stepped up to be Judy's champion, and Roslynn loved her all the more for it.

"It's all right, George," Roslynn said, and then to Jack, "You've made your point, sweetheart. And I wasn't going to let my darling leave without my best wishes." Roslynn leaned her head toward Judith's. "You can have fun. In fact, I want you to enjoy every minute of your trip." But her tone turned stern when she added, "But don't you dare come back in love. You will wait and fall in love here. And that's the last I'm going to say about it." But Roslynn ended that with a smile.

Jack still leaned forward around Roslynn and said to Judith, "You didn't tell her?"

"Tell me what?" Roslynn asked.

Jacqueline chuckled. "We're not getting married this year. Next year maybe, or even the year after that. We're in no hurry to. Really we aren't."

"It's true, Mother," Judith confirmed. "The fun is going to be in the trying, not the doing."

As the girls moved off to circulate about the room, Roslynn remarked to Georgina, "That was no doubt word for word from *your* daughter."

"I quite agree," Georgina said.

"But they can't be that naive. When it happens, it's going to happen, and there's not a bloody thing they can do to stop it."

"I know, but still, I wish Jack had let her father know that was her intention. James has been masking it very well, but he's been a powder keg since the beginning of this year, with the thought of Jack getting married by the end of it. He's not going to deal gracefully with her falling in love, you know."

"You think Tony is? He used to only visit Knighton's Hall a few times a week, but it's been daily for several months now. He wants to stop time from advancing but he can't, and he's extremely frustrated because of it. Truth be told, that's why I didn't want to delay Judith's Season here and hoped she would favor young Cullen before it even began. The sooner Judy gets married, the sooner my family can get back to normal—until Jaime comes of age."

Georgina laughed. "You *really* should have owned up to that sooner, m'dear."

"Prob'ly." Roslynn sighed. "I swear, our husbands were never meant to have daughters. Sons and more sons would've been fine, but daughters! It was just asking for trouble. I fear for their suitors, I really do. Our men don't have the temperament to just stand back and let nature take its course."

Chapter Seven

JUDITH TRIED TO MASK her smile when she and Jack moved away from their mothers. She was starting to feel some of the excitement that had infected Jacqueline. And her cousin was so proud of having been right, she might as well have been crowing with it. To keep her from bragging with an "I told you so," which would have annoyed Judith because she'd heard it so often, she put a finger to Jacqueline's mouth when she started to open it.

"Don't say it. Let me. You were right—as usual. My mother is not angry at me for the way this turned out, so the burden is gone and now I can fully enjoy the trip."

"I wasn't going to mention *that*," Jacqueline replied, and turned Judith around to face the parlor's double doors. "Who's that and why does he look familiar?"

Judith saw the man then, a stranger, elegantly clad if not quite in an English style. He wasn't wearing a greatcoat, but a cloak edged with black ermine. The frock coat underneath it was a bit too full skirted to be fashionable. And was that a sword poking out from under the cloak? He appeared to be a foreigner, but Jacqueline was right, he did look familiar. And they weren't the only ones who thought so.

Their uncle Edward put his finger on it, taking a step forward to say in his typically jovial tone, "Another long-lost relative? Come in!"

Everyone more or less turned in unison to see whom Edward was talking about. The young man at the door seemed embarrassed now that he was the center of attention, and perhaps a little overwhelmed, with so many people in the room. Even though Judith doubted that the tall, handsome young man was related to them, she didn't think her uncle had been joking. But then, when did her uncle ever joke about family?

And the stranger didn't dispute her uncle's conclusion. In fact he appeared rather amazed when he replied, "How did you know?"

Judith's cousin Regina stepped forward, grinning. Jack's brother, Jeremy, stepped forward, grinning. Anthony just stepped forward. They all resembled the stranger with their exotically slanted, cobalt-blue eyes and raven-black hair.

"Another Malory," James stated the obvious in his drollest tone.

The young man looked directly at James and, not seeming the least bit intimidated by him as most men were, said, "No, sir, I am not a Malory. I am Count Andrássy Benedek, of Hungary."

"Are you now? A blood relation nonetheless. Tell us, which Stephanoff you are descended from?"

"Maria—apparently."

"Our grandmother Anastasia's grandmother?" Anthony remarked. "You don't sound too sure."

"I obtained the information from my great-grandfather's journal, which is only a memory now."

Anthony began to laugh. "Another journal?" At Andrássy's curious look, he added, "We found one, too, some ten years back, written by my grandmother Anastasia Stephanoff. Prior to that, it was only rumored that Gypsy blood ran in our family."

Andrássy nodded. "I had never heard of this Stephanoff ancestor. I don't believe my late father was aware of her either. Gypsy bands pass through Hungary, never staying long. I have never met one myself. So for me, there was no rumor or other clue until I found the journal. Ironically, I might never have known of it, or had a chance to read it, if my stepsister hadn't found it in our attic while she was hiding there during one of her tantrums, but that is some unpleasantness I don't need to burden you with."

"Another time, perhaps," Edward said as he stepped forward to lead Andrássy into the room. "What happened to your ancestor's journal? Why don't you have it anymore?"

"It perished in the fire that destroyed my home and all my family heirlooms."

"How awful," more than one person said.

"You're destitute?" Edward asked.

"No, not at all. My father might have distrusted banks, but I never shared that sentiment. I had an inheritance from my mother. May we speak in private?"

"No need, m'boy," Edward said. "Everyone in this room is a member of our family."

That rendered the young man speechless, but then all four of the eldest set of Malory brothers were present: Jason, the third Marquis of Haverston and the oldest, Edward, the second oldest, and James and Anthony. Their wives were present, too, and most of their children, including their children's spouses and a few of their older grandchildren. More than twenty Malorys had shown up for Jack and Judy's send-off, and the young count was obviously overwhelmed.

"I had no idea," Andrássy said, his blue eyes moving slowly about the room, a little glazed with emotion. "I had hoped I would be able to track down one or two of Maria's descendants, but . . . never this many. And you don't even seem surprised by me."

Edward chuckled. "You aren't the first member of this family to show up full grown, my boy, albeit one more distant than we might have expected. And I am sure we are all interested in hearing what you read in the journal about our great-great-grandmother Maria Stephanoff."

Anthony handed Andrássy a drink, which he merely held as he spoke. "The journal belonged to my great-grandfather Karl Benedek, Maria's son. Karl's father, understandably, didn't want to speak of his indiscretion with a Gypsy woman, and he didn't until the night he thought he was dying. Maria's caravan was merely passing through and he allowed them to spend one night on his land. She came to him and offered herself in payment. She was young and pretty, but he still refused her, until she said a son would come of it. He had no children, even after going through four wives trying to obtain one. He was desperate enough to believe her that night, but come morning he was angry over what he guessed was a deception."

"But it wasn't a lie?"

"No, it wasn't. Somehow Maria knew and swore she would bring him the boy when he was born. He still didn't believe she was carrying his child, but just in case, he refused to let her leave. He kept her a prisoner until exactly nine months later when she gave birth to a son. He let her go, but he kept his son, whom he named Karl. Maria said the boy would be able to find her if he ever needed her, no matter where in the world she was. Such an odd thing to say. My great-great-grandfather never saw her again and did not tell his son, his only heir, about her until the night he thought he was dying."

"Did he die that night?" James asked curiously.

"No, not for another ten years, and he and Karl never spoke of his strange tale again. But when my great-great-grandfather did die, Karl went in search of his mother, Maria. He found her in England, still traveling with her band of wandering Gypsies. Her granddaughter, Anastasia, had just married an English marquis."

"Wait," Jason spoke up with a frown. "That can't be all that Karl wrote about Anastasia's husband. Merely that he was a marquis from this country?"

"No, Christopher, Marquis of Haverston, was the name written in the journal. I went to Haverston first, only to be told the current marquis was in London. I was given this address, but I almost didn't come here tonight since I am only passing through England on my way to America to search for my stepsister Catherine's real father. I had planned to get her settled and out of my life before I tried to find any descendants of Maria's here. I simply couldn't resist the chance to meet at least one of you before I left England."

James guessed, "I'm beginning to suspect we don't want to meet your stepsister?"

Andrássy sighed. "No, you don't."

"Not to worry, dear boy," Edward said. "My brother James deals remarkably well with difficulties that arise in the family, so we've learned to leave such things to him, trivial or otherwise."

By the young count's expression he had obviously taken offense. "I didn't come here for help. I am capable of dealing with my responsibilities and she—"

"Yes, yes, she's your albatross, we get that," Anthony said, putting an arm around Andrássy's shoulder. "But you haven't heard my brother complaining about being your champion, have you?"

James raised a golden brow. "Give me a moment," he said, but was ignored.

Anthony continued, "As luck would have it—ours, yours, who knows—we happen to be sailing for America in the morning. You're welcome to join us. No need to say another word about your sister if you'd rather not. Think of it as giving us a chance to get to know you a little better, and vice versa. You might want to consider it fate that led you here tonight."

Andrássy didn't agree, but he didn't decline, either. And before he decided either way, the rest of the family wanted a chance to speak with him. James and Anthony stood aside, watching how readily the family took to him. Jack and Judy had him cornered now.

"They're going to talk his ear off," Anthony remarked.

"Jack will," James agreed. "She's rather good at that. And if she thinks he ought to come with us, the matter is as good as settled."

"You don't doubt he's one of us, d'you?" Anthony inquired thoughtfully. "You weren't exactly throwing open those beefy arms in welcome."

"There's no harm in checking into his background," James replied. "I'll ask Jeremy to see what he can find out about him while we're away. But considering we're heading into Anderson territory, it might not hurt to have another

Malory relative, however remote, on our side." James paused a moment. "On the other hand, I'm not so sure it's a good idea to stick him on a ship with us. Once he gets to know us, he might want to run in the opposite direction."

"Speak for yourself, old man."

"Regardless, it's been known to happen. And on a ship, there's nowhere to run."

Anthony chuckled. "Do we need to wake up Knighton tonight? Get rid of all our aggression before we sail? Might work for a week or so."

"No need. I had a ring installed in *The Maiden George*'s hold for us. I do like to plan ahead."

Chapter Eight

~⸻⸽⸻~

"YOU SURE YOU WANT to do this, Cap'n?" Corky Menadue asked hesitantly as he stood with Nathan on the London dock.

Nathan smiled. "Get my ship back? Damned right I do."

"I meant work your way over to the colonies."

"I believe they call them states now."

"But it ain't like you couldn't pay for passage instead," Corky said, and not for the first time.

Nathan looked down at his first mate. He had inherited Corky when he'd inherited *The Pearl*, but he'd known the older man most of his life. Corky had been Jory Tremayne's first mate, and Nathan had pretty much grown up on his father's ship—until Jory had kicked him off it. Such impotent rage he'd felt back then, but nothing he'd said or done would change Jory's mind. It was for his own protection, Jory insisted, as if Nathan couldn't protect himself. And he was haunted by the thought that his father might still be alive if he *had* been there the night his father was shot.

"Forget about Grigg! I told you, assure *you, I'll see him hanged for you."* Not if Nathan could find him before Commander Burdis did. But he had a ship to find first.

Nathan reminded his old friend, "The other vessels aren't leaving for another week and they're not bound for Connecticut, which is where I need to go. This one is actually going about fifty miles west of my destination. Damned lucky, and about time some luck came my way. Besides, time isn't on our side even if I wanted to waste the coin on passage, which I don't. *The Pearl* will be sold if we don't get there soon."

"I'm just worried about your temper. Last captain you took orders from was your father and that was five years ago. D'you even remember how?"

Nathan barked a laugh, but Corky added, "And this captain is some kind of nabob, if you can go by the high wage he's paying us. And I know how you feel about nabobs."

"You don't have to come along, you know," Nathan told his curly-haired friend.

"And what else would I be doing until you come back with *The Pearl*?"

After Burdis had released Nathan, he'd found Corky and most of his crew in the haunt they frequented in Southampton, where Nathan had settled after leaving Cornwall. At first they'd been shocked to see him and then quite rowdy in expressing their relief that Nathan was a free man. After he'd been captured by the revenuers, they hadn't expected to ever see him again. He didn't begrudge them their escape the night his ship and cargo had been confiscated. In fact, he was fiercely glad they had escaped because they wouldn't have been handed the boon he'd been given. He still couldn't quite believe he was walking free again.

Burdis turned out to be not such a bad sort—for a nabob. He'd arranged for Nathan to have a bath, a good meal, and his personal belongings returned to him, even his pistol. Then they'd transported him to his home port of Southampton.

After telling his men what had happened and what he had to do now, they'd wanted to snatch a ship for him that very night. He'd been tempted, but with the commander's terms still fresh in his mind, he'd had to tell them no, that he needed legitimate passage.

"If you steal a ship other than your own, our deal is off," Burdis had said. "No more breaking laws of any sort for you, Captain Tremayne."

Too many bleedin' conditions, but he was going to abide by them since it meant a shot at getting his ship back.

When he'd elected to follow in his father's footsteps, he'd known it wouldn't be easy. Still, he'd enjoyed the challenge of smuggling, enjoyed thumbing his nose at the revenuers when they gave chase. They never came close to catching him when he was in the Channel. But constantly having to find new places to store his cargoes had taxed his patience and caused him no end of frustration.

He'd thought he'd finally solved that problem a few months ago when he'd figured out the perfect hiding place: the abandoned house a little ways inland in Hampshire. The house had an extra advantage as its closest neighbor was the Duke of Wrighton. No revenuers would dare snoop around there. But he hadn't counted on the duke's having nosy servants. If that wench hadn't come ghost hunting or meeting up with her lover, which is what he suspected she'd really been doing, he wouldn't have been forced to move the cargo so soon and wouldn't have gotten caught because of it.

After he'd sent word to his crew in Southampton to bring the ship to their usual unloading cove, so it could be reloaded, one of his crew must have mentioned the plan to someone in Grigg's crew. Or maybe someone in Grigg's crew had heard his men talking about it. It wouldn't be the first time the two crews had ended up in the same tavern. He preferred to think that than that he had a traitor in his crew. But the ghost-hunting wench was still ultimately to blame.

He hadn't been joking when he'd told Burdis he blamed a woman for his capture. He should have put more effort into securing her silence. A kiss usually softened them up, but not her. He'd gambled that he'd be able to get her feeling friendly and agreeable toward him, so she'd keep his presence a secret. Maybe he should have lit her lantern so she could see whom she was dealing with. One of his smiles tended to work wonders on wenches, too. But kissing her hadn't yielded the result he'd hoped for, and he had ended up insulting her instead. He hadn't needed to see her to tell she was bristling from it.

"We've time for a pint and a quick tumble, Cap'n. You game?"

"Thought I asked you to stop calling me that? I'm not your captain for this trip."

Nathan *was* bored, though, just standing around waiting for wagons to show up. He glanced around the London dock, but the last wagon had left ten minutes ago and no others could be seen heading their way. There would probably be more, though, and he didn't want to risk a delay in sailing to America by getting fired because he wasn't there to unload wagons. Every day mattered with *The Pearl* on her way to being altered and sold. It was annoying enough that the ship he'd signed on to in Southampton was making this short detour to London to pick up passengers.

"Come on," Corky cajoled. "We were told to wait, but no one said we couldn't do that waiting in yonder tavern. Watch from the door for the next wagon if you've a mind to, but the rowboat ain't even back from the ship yet to carry another load. And it's going to be a long voyage. One more wench to see me off is all I'm interested in tonight."

Nathan snorted. "You just enjoyed the company of a wench three nights ago in Southampton. Were you too drunk to remember?"

"Oh, yeah." Corky grinned. "But that was then and this is our last night on land. Three weeks at sea is a bleedin' long time."

"The voyage could be as quick as two weeks and besides, *you* don't need to be here. You can still head back to Southampton to wait for my return."

"And leave you without a first mate for the return trip? It's a shame we heard about this ship too late to get the rest of our boys on her."

"I wouldn't have known that her captain was hiring a crew at all if I didn't stop by to tell Alf and Peggy I'd be gone for a few months."

Old Alf was the caretaker of a cottage a few miles up the coast from Southampton. Nathan had been steered to the couple when he'd been looking for someone to care for his nieces while he was away on *The Pearl*. It had proven to be a nicer arrangement than he'd first thought, since the cottage had its own private dock, and Alf let him use it as a berth for *The Pearl*.

Alf had been generous in that after his wife, Peggy, had agreed to watch the girls for Nathan. He hadn't even charged Nathan a fee, merely laid down the rule that no cargo was ever to be unloaded there, since he knew what business Nathan had got into. Alf refused to say much about the bigger vessel at his dock, or why she sat empty, and Nathan was in no position to pry when the elderly couple was doing him such a big favor.

"At least you got me on her with you," Corky said.

"Only because they still needed a carpenter and I bargained to have you included. Alf even hesitated to mention the job, since he knows I no longer practice carpentry. It was his wife, Peggy, who brought it up. Every time I visit the girls, she nags me to go back to work that won't land me in prison. The old gal worries about me."

"She's fond of your nieces and worries they will be left without a guardian again. And she's right, you know. Look how close you came to fulfilling her fears this time. Are you sure you even want your ship back?"

"Are you going to nag now, too?"

"Is that pint of ale suddenly sounding like a good idea?" Corky countered.

Chapter Nine

NATHAN CHUCKLED AND GAVE in, steering his friend across the docks. The tavern Corky had his eye on stood between a warehouse and a ticket office. Nathan didn't know London at all, had never been there before, and had never heard anything good about it either. But taverns were taverns, and this one looked no different from the ones he'd find at home in Southampton. While Nathan had no interest himself in a woman his last night on land because he had too much on his mind to spare any thoughts on a wench, a pint of ale would indeed be welcome.

He'd never asked for them, but now he had responsibilities that he didn't have last year when he would have been the one to suggest a quick tumble. Not anymore. Not since his sister died and he was the only one left in their family who could care for her two children. Not that he hadn't had an agenda before that happened. He just hadn't been in a hurry to achieve his goals.

His nieces, Clarissa and Abbie, were darling girls. He never expected to get so attached to them so quickly, but each time he visited, it was getting harder to say good-bye. At seven years of age Clarissa was the younger and the more exuberant of the two. She never failed to throw herself into his arms with a happy squeal when he arrived. Abbie was more reserved at nine years of age. Poor thing was still trying to emulate her father's snobby family, thinking that's how she ought to behave. But she was starting to come around. She expressed delight now when she saw him and he'd even felt dampness on her cheek when she'd hugged him good-bye a few days ago. My God, that had been difficult, walking away from them this time.

They didn't deserve to live in poverty just because their parents had passed on. He had to do right by them, give them a home, a stable one. One way or another, he was going to provide them with the comfortable life they used to have.

The girls had been raised so differently from him, but then his sister, Angie, had married well. She'd had a fine house in Surrey and her daughters had had a governess, tutors, and fancy dresses. It was too bad it had all come with such disagreeable people for in-laws, the lot of them thinking they were grander than they were just because they held a minor title. Nathan hadn't liked Angie's husband because it had become apparent soon after the wedding that he had only married her because she was descended from an earl. Nathan hadn't even been able to visit her or her children without sneaking in to do it because his brother-in-law had found out Jory was a smuggler and assumed Nathan was one, too.

But everything his nieces had had was gone now, taken back by their father's family when he'd died, killing Angie with him, because he'd been foxed and driving his carriage too fast. Nathan hadn't thought it possible, but he'd come to hate the nobility even more than he already did when those heartless snobs turned their backs on their own granddaughters just because they'd never approved of Angie. All the girls had left were the fancy dresses that didn't even fit them anymore, and an uncle who only hoped to accomplish goals that a sane man would realize were impossible.

He ordered that pint, then another. He was starting to feel the anger that tended to show up when he thought about his situation too long. Maybe what he should be looking for this last night on land was a good fight.

Ale in hand, Nathan turned to glance about the room, looking for someone who might accommodate him, but the tavern was so crowded, he didn't doubt one punch would lead to a full-scale brawl. While it wouldn't be the first time he'd spent a night in jail for starting one, he couldn't afford for that to happen tonight if he wanted to get *The Pearl* back.

He started for the door, but turned about when five new customers stepped through it and he recognized one of them. What the hell? Hammett Grigg's men in London, of all places? The last time he'd seen Mr. Olivey, Hammett's first mate, who was the one he recognized, had been in Southampton five years ago. Grigg and a handful of his crew had tracked Nathan down to find out where Jory was holed up. Still furious with his father, he'd told them he didn't know and didn't care. They'd actually had him watched for a while, thinking he could lead them to Jory. But he never saw his father again, and Hammett and his men finally found Jory on their own. . . .

Was the Cornish smuggler actually crazy enough to deliver a load of untaxed goods to the biggest city in the country? Not using London docks, he couldn't. He had to be in London for some other reason, maybe to line up new buyers. But if his men were here on the docks, Grigg might be nearby, too. Could Nathan really get this lucky and find the man before Commander Burdis did?

Well, he'd wanted a fight. Trying to find out Grigg's whereabouts would definitely get him one, but he preferred that it take place outside if possible. Or he could just wait and follow them when they left. Would he have time for that?

He glanced behind him without turning. The five men were still by the door, looking about the room. There were no empty tables they could use. If they didn't leave, they'd be coming to the bar where Nathan was standing and that brawl would then be inevitable. . . .

Decision made, Nathan walked to the door and shouldered his way past them. Easy enough to do when he was taller and brawnier than them. And as expected, they followed him outside. Five of them against one of him would make them cocky. They just didn't know him well, and he'd like to keep it that way for a few minutes. Cocky men tended to have loose lips.

"Leaving without paying your respects, boyo?" Mr. Olivey said, grabbing Nathan's arm to stop him. "Thought we wouldn't recognize you?"

"Wot are ye doing 'ere, eh?" another asked. "Why ain't ye—? Heard ye got locked up."

"I heard you helped with that," Nathan replied. "Where's your boss? I'd like to thank him."

" 'Ere now, don't be blaming us 'cause you got careless, boyo."

"I bet 'e's plannin' to wield 'is 'ammer in London. Now the revs got 'is ship, wot else is there left for 'im?"

The men's chuckles were cut short when Nathan gripped the man's throat with one hand and pinned him to the tavern wall. "My business here is none of yours, but yours is certainly mine. I repeat, where's your boss?"

"You're in no position to ask," Olivey said behind him. "Or did you really think you could take us all on?"

"Let's find out." Nathan leapt to the side to position himself so that all five men were in front of him again.

Five against one might be lousy odds, but he had passion and purpose in his corner, while he guessed they just wanted to have some fun at his expense. He didn't have to wait long for the first swing to come his way. He blocked that one and threw one of his own. Two quick jabs at another had a second staggering back.

Blood pumping, Nathan had no doubt that he could do this, despite the odds, and get the answer he wanted before he was done. He just needed to leave one of them standing and able to talk.

The next sailor to come at him he knocked to the ground, but the man got back up too quickly, wiping blood from his mouth. "Should take to the ring, boyo, instead of wasting time with a hammer. You'd make a fortune."

Olivey's comment distracted Nathan a moment too long. Bleedin' hell. Both his arms were suddenly pulled forcefully behind him and Mr. Olivey stood in front of him laughing.

"Should have run while you had the chance. Should have left well enough alone, too. Hammett was done with your family—until he heard you were looking for him. Look where that got you, eh."

"Go to hell," Nathan spat out.

But suddenly his arms were freed and he heard the distinctive hollow sound of two heads cracking together. He didn't need to look behind him to guess that two of Grigg's men had just been hurt if not put out of commission. Then he was yanked aside, out of the way, and a strong arm fell over his shoulder. He tried to shrug it off, but the hold tightened enough to stop him. Blood *still* pumping, he was about to swing at whoever was holding him immobile until he got a look at him.

Tall and dark haired with shoulders as wide as Nathan's and wearing a fine greatcoat, the man could pass for a nabob except for one glaring fact. A member of the gentry wouldn't get involved in a street brawl, would he? No, he'd merely yell for the watch. Another man, too, a big, blond brute specimen unlike any Nathan had ever seen was pounding Hammett's sailors with his fists. Were they just a couple of rakehells out looking for trouble? Then they could add him to the count before they were done and he didn't think he'd walk away from that, could even miss his ship because of it. But right now he needed at least one of Hammett's sailors conscious so he could question him.

It was all he could do to sound reasonable when he said to the black-haired man, "Let go so I can help him." Stop him was more like it.

"Bite your tongue, youngun. That's not a snarl my brother is wearing, it's a grin." Then the man sighed because all five sailors were now sprawled on the ground. To his brother he complained, "Really, old boy, you could have dragged it out just a *little*."

The blond bruiser merely gave the black-haired man a bored look before he turned his piercing green eyes on Nathan. "Need a job? I could use a sparring partner."

Nathan choked back an impotent snarl. He'd just lost

his chance to get answers. He should have stopped the bruiser from knocking them all out, but the demolishing had happened so fast. And they actually thought they were being *helpful*.

He got out, "No thanks, I have a job."

The black-haired one who'd held him back let go of him now, saying, "No pearls of gratitude? Do we need to teach you some manners, youngun?" But then he added, "Behind you, James."

What happened next left no room for thought. It did flash through Nathan's mind that he had been left for last and was about to get the beating of his life. But he saw one of the sailors staggering to his feet. Nathan yelled, "Wait!"—but the man named James turned to the sailor, while the black-haired taller one put his steely arm around Nathan's shoulder again.

It was too much. Nathan swung, catching the black-haired man completely off guard and connecting with his chin, taking him down. He doubted he could do the same with the bruiser who was now staring at Nathan with a raised brow.

Nathan stiffened. He could probably bolt as the sailor was now doing, but he didn't want *this* one following him.

He broadened the distance between himself and the bruiser and, pointing to the fleeing sailor, quickly said, "I need answers that you and your friend are keeping me from getting."

"Then run along and get them. My brother's going to be in the mood for a fight now, but not to worry—"

Nathan didn't wait to hear the rest. With a nod, he ducked around the strange twosome's carriage, which had stopped in front of the tavern, and took off down the dock, chasing down the sailor. He thought he heard someone laughing behind him, but it was probably just someone in the tavern, and he didn't look back.

The sailor had ducked around a corner onto a wide street. It was dark, but not deserted. A good number of sailors were making their way back to their ships, some drunkenly. Nathan ran down the street, glancing at each man he passed. It took him a few minutes to spot Hammett's sailor just as the man turned another corner.

Swearing, Nathan reached the spot only to find a narrow alley filled with broken crates and other garbage. A dog barked to the left. He headed that way. He found the dog but the sailor was nowhere in sight. He could have entered any number of buildings through their rear doors. A light suddenly appeared in an upstairs window of one of them. He tried the door to that building and found it locked. He moved on to the next building. The door was unlocked and he slipped inside. The corridor he found himself in was dark—but not so dark he couldn't see the shadow crouched in it.

Nathan leapt forward and dragged the sailor outside before whoever had lit the lantern could come down to investigate why the dog was barking. He didn't stop until they rounded another corner and he shoved the sailor up against the side of a building.

"I distracted that bruiser so you could get away, but I'll be finishing you off m'self if you don't—"

"Wait!" the man pleaded. "I'll tell you what I know, just no more punches."

"Where is Grigg?"

"He ain't in town yet, but he'll be here tomorrow for the delivery."

"To who?"

"Man on the west side, runs a fancy tavern. The cap'n's been supplying him with brandy off and on for a year now."

"Who's the man? What's the name of the tavern?" Nathan tightened his grip on the man's shirt.

"Don't know. All I know is this is a big delivery, so the captain is coming to town himself for it. He's got quite a few establishments here eager for the finer stuff that he supplies now, those that cater to the gentry. Cuts them a deal they can't refuse."

"I need names."

"I don't know, I swear! Mr. Olivey does. You should be asking him—"

"He's not going to be answering anything tonight, but you aren't telling me anything useful either. That better change, and quickly."

"It *was* the captain who set you up. He had a man watching your crew in Southampton. You shouldn't be so predictable, boyo, always coming back to the same port."

Nathan ignored the gloating tone for the moment. "Is that how Grigg has managed to avoid me?"

"Aye, he never docks in the same place twice. But since you do, it was easy to set a spy on your crew when they were in Southampton. He was there when you sent your men that message that you needed to reload your cargo to move it to a safer spot. He even overheard where they were to meet you with your ship and when."

"How was that ambush arranged so quickly?"

"Because Captain Grigg was in town that night. He was told about your change in plans. He sent his spy to a revenue ship in the harbor, and the rest you know."

"What I need to know is where I can find him, *boyo*. So

if he doesn't have a base, why don't you tell me where he stores his cargo."

"I can't because he doesn't. D'you really not know how many men work for him? Half of them just drive the wagons and simply wait for him to beach, unload, and they cart the goods straight to the buyers. No hiding it like we used to. No giving the revenuers that patrol the waters a chance to find us. He arranges everything in advance and has been operating that way for years. There's nothing more I can tell you."

"Yes, there is," Nathan said in a quieter tone. "You can tell me why he killed my father."

"Well, your sis—you don't know?"

Nathan lifted the man a little off his feet to get his point across. "Tell me."

"I know nothing. Nothing!" The sailor's jaw was clenched, but he was shaking like a leaf. "I wasn't working for him back then."

Nathan pulled the man away from the wall and raised his fist warningly. "The tavern?" he growled. "Last chance to say something useful."

The sailor's eyes widened. "There's an alley behind it, that's all I ever see of it. The cap'n's of a mind that the less we know the better. Only Mr. Olivey gets told when, where, and who. But I heard him call the bloke we deliver to Bobby."

"The owner?"

"Don't know, never asked."

Nathan smashed his fist into the man's face. "Too little, too late," he muttered, but the man couldn't hear him.

Nathan hurried back to the tavern to rouse Mr. Olivey for more information, but he slowed as he approached.

The watch had found Grigg's defeated crewmen. All four of them were still unconscious, didn't even stir as they were lifted and placed in a wagon to be taken to jail. Nathan wasn't even surprised. The man who had laid waste to them really was a bruiser.

Nathan was disappointed, but if the sailor he'd questioned could be believed, and he probably could be, Nathan knew much more now than he had before. And if his new turn of luck held, Grigg wouldn't be caught by Burdis before Nathan returned to England.

Corky was in the small crowd gathered in front of the tavern, but he was nervously looking around for Nathan rather than watching what was going on. Nathan waved to draw his attention.

Corky ran over to him immediately. "We better get back to our post and quickly. The owners of the ship came by to see how the loading was going and got caught in a fist-fight. Someone actually knocked out one of them and he's furious."

"That's—unfortunate," Nathan said with a sinking feeling. "Did they board?"

"No, not tonight. Where did you take off to?"

He gave Corky the short of it, saying, "Grigg's men are in town. I had words with one of them."

"He's operating out of London? I know he's cagey, but I didn't take him for a loony."

"He only delivers here to a number of buyers, but I got a lead on one of them. It's the first clue I've had about Grigg's whereabouts since he killed Jory. And now I know where to look for him when we get back to England."

"Or you could send word about him to your commander friend."

"Hell no, and he's not my friend. He's just a revenuer using me to get himself a promotion. Our goals merely line up—temporarily."

Corky tsked. "Connections have their uses, particularly if they come with titles. It doesn't serve your best interests to hate all nabobs just because of your sister's in-laws."

"I don't hate them all. Only the ones I meet. Now it's late and we sail in the morning. We need some sleep. They can wake us if any more wagons show up."

"I'd agree, 'cept this one might be for us."

Corky was talking about an approaching coach, not a wagon. Yet it did stop and the driver called down, "Are you with *The Maiden George*? If so, I have passengers who want to board now."

Chapter Ten

LAST NIGHT, NATHAN HAD thought the couple were an odd pair, as he and Corky rowed them and an inordinate amount of heavy luggage out to *The Maiden George*. The man had introduced himself as Count Andrássy Benedek, a relative of the ship's captain. The woman's name hadn't been mentioned. They spoke English but the man had a foreign accent. And they didn't seem to like each other. Although the pair had been whispering to each other, Nathan had gotten the impression that they were bickering and didn't want to be overheard. The woman's pretty face had looked angry.

Nathan had felt sorry for the bloke, though. A henpecked man if he'd ever seen one, and he looked no older than twenty-five, his own age. Far too young to be stuck with a shrew for a wife, pretty or not, if that's who she was to him.

But this morning as the dawn sky brightened, Nathan was surprised to see Benedek joining him at the rail. Escaping the shrew? Nathan might have remarked on it, one man commiserating with another, if he didn't want to avoid drawing attention to himself on this trip. Besides, the man was titled.

Class distinctions didn't used to mean anything to Nathan. Having an earl for an ancestor probably accounted for his attitude, not that he'd ever mentioned that to anyone or ever would. It was galling that Burdis had found out. In fact, if someone called him gentry these days, he'd probably punch him in the face. He preferred to simply treat all men as equals whether they wanted to be or not, but most nabobs felt differently.

His reticence turned out to be a good decision because the count wasn't alone for long. His companion from the night before arrived a few moments later, saying, "You can't ignore me, Andrássy!"

"Can't I?" Benedek shot back. "Not another word about it, Catherine. I am *not* going to ask them for any more favors when I only just met them."

"But one of them could have the insight, could tell me if my father really is alive, or even where he is. You could at least ask."

"And have them think I'm crazy? The supposed magical abilities of Gypsies is just superstitious nonsense and trickery. That's what Gypsies do. They prey on the hopes and dreams of the gullible. They tell you what you want to hear and get paid for it. None of it is true and I'm not going to insult this branch of my family by mentioning these notions of yours. My God, do you listen to yourself, spouting such nonsense?"

"Of course I believe it, when I've seen you display the Gypsy gift occasionally. Deny it all you want, but you know it's true."

"All I have is the instinct of a tracker and luck. There's nothing mystical about that, Catherine. And I'll use those instincts to find your father, if just to be rid of you for good!"

"How dare you! You wouldn't even know about these relatives of yours if not for me! I found that journal that mentioned them. You owe me!"

"I owe you nothing, although I will honor the obligation my father saddled me with when he married your mother!"

"Perfect, luv. You really are a master of improvis—"

Nathan couldn't hear any more as the pair moved farther down the deck, but the woman's voice had changed to a purring tone there at the end, as if she really was offering praise.

But glad to be alone again at the rail, Nathan raised the spyglass he'd borrowed from Artie, the crusty, old first mate, for a closer view of the wharf. A longboat had been dispatched for the passengers because there were so many of them. Quite a crowd of well-dressed people were on the dock, waiting for it. But he wasn't interested in them.

He trained the eyepiece up and down the wharf as far as he could see. He was meticulous, stopping to peruse faces, making sure he didn't recognize any. He didn't expect to see any of Grigg's men this soon, but Grigg might show up himself looking for them. And if he spotted the man, he couldn't say if he would risk losing *The Pearl* to get his hands on him now.

Jory had decided to send Nathan away five years ago to protect him. Despite how angry Nathan had been because of it, he'd still loved the man. He felt angry to this day, but for a different reason: because he and his father had never made amends and it was too late to now. But that had been Jory's decision, too. No communication at all was to pass between them that could lead Grigg to Nathan, who could then be used against Jory. But settling that score for his father was *his* decision. And even with the ship soon to sail, he still had that on his mind.

As Nathan continued to scan the wharf with the spyglass, he found it a bit disconcerting to come across a fellow with a spyglass of his own trained right on Nathan. No one he recognized, well dressed in a greatcoat, a gentleman by all accounts. The man gestured to his head, as if tipping a hat to Nathan for having discovered him spying on *The Maiden George*. The man was even smiling before he put his spyglass away and got into a rowboat that took him out to one of the other ships.

Many ships were anchored in the river, unable to dock yet. Southampton's port was crowded, too, but nothing like London's. Weeks could go by before a ship could get a berth in this town, or so he'd been told.

"See anything interesting, Mr. Tremayne?"

Nathan glanced at the sailor who'd come up next to him. He'd said his name was Walter. Nathan knew him in passing from Southampton, but then the whole crew had been hired out of Southampton.

"No, just someone a little too interested in this ship. He actually had a spyglass trained on us."

Walter shrugged. "So? Just looking for someone."

"I suppose." Nathan glanced down at the stretch of water between the ship and the dock.

The longboat was halfway back to the ship, and it wasn't full of passengers after all, just four men and five ladies, not counting the sailors rowing them. He figured a few of those people could be ladies' maids and valets. Most of the people he'd seen on the dock must only have been there to see their family or friends off, because they were now getting back into carriages.

"There don't appear to be many passengers," he said.

"Well, it's a privately owned ship designed to accommodate family comfortably. The captain had her built to his specifications. All of the main cabins are like rooms in a fancy hotel."

Nathan knew how lavishly appointed the cabins were. He hadn't mentioned it to anyone, but he hadn't been able to resist inspecting *The Maiden George* when he'd been docking *The Pearl* next to it for the last year.

"You've sailed on her before?" Nathan asked Walter.

"A few times over the last decade, and I'm glad of it. I actually gave up the sea, but I'm always up for a voyage on *The Maiden George*. It pays too well to turn it down, and it's never boring. Did you not wonder why the purse was so high for this crossing?"

Nathan hedged. "Well, this is my first time across the Atlantic, so I had nothing to compare it to."

Walter chuckled. "It's triple the standard, mate. A pity she leaves her berth so rarely, or I'd be rich by now."

"If she doesn't get much use, why does the owner even keep her?"

"Because he can."

"Merely for convenience?" Nathan said. "That isn't normal, is it?"

"Not even close to normal. But then, neither is the captain. That's him there, Viscount Ryding, just one of many titles in his family."

Nathan followed Walter's gaze back to the approaching longboat. Now that the sky had brightened and the boat was closer, he could make out the occupants more clearly, but he looked no farther than the large man in the front of the boat. Blond, with broad shoulders under a greatcoat, he was the bruiser who'd rescued Nathan on a whim. And his dark-haired brother was in the boat, too.

Nathan's sinking feeling returned. He'd actually hoped when they hadn't boarded last night that the owners weren't going to sail with their ship. Many didn't, merely hired captains for them. But it looked as if his luck had just taken a swing for the worse, and now he was going to have to make himself scarce, at least until they got out to sea where it would be less likely that they'd toss him overboard. Up in the rigging would suffice before they boarded, and he might even stay up there for the duration of the trip down the river.

It didn't matter which of the two was the captain. They were both nabobs and he'd struck one of them. And even if he could somehow make it right with them, he was still going to hate working for a lord no matter how long the trip took. The nobility had a whole different way of thinking compared to ordinary men. As different as night and day. They could take offense at the simplest thing that wouldn't normally raise a brow. You wouldn't even *know* you were insulting them until it was too late.

Then the sun rose over a couple of buildings in the east to cast a beam along the water. Copper hair lit up like a flame in the sunlight and instantly drew his eyes. The young woman ought to have been wearing a bonnet to hide magnificent hair like that, but she wasn't. She was old enough—eighteen, nineteen?—to have her hair done up fancy, but it was simply tied back at her nape. Because it was so long, the wind still tossed it over her shoulders. Her clothing, though, was clearly that of a young lady, a blue velvet coat tied at the waist, a white fur cape that merely capped her shoulders, ending only halfway down her arms. But it was her beautiful heart-shaped face that tugged at a memory that wouldn't quite surface in his mind.

"The red-haired wench, she looks familiar."

He didn't realize he'd said it aloud until Walter admonished him, "I wouldn't be calling that one a wench if you don't want to end up in the ship's brig or worse. The cap'n's a fair man, but he can be a might touchy when it comes to family, and she's probably a member of his. Never seen him take on passengers who weren't related to him in one way or another."

A whole ship full of nabobs? Corky had been right. Bleedin' hell. But he assured the sailor, "I meant no disrespect."

"Was just a friendly warning, mate. You know how that family is. Very, *very* protective of their own."

"I wouldn't know. Never heard of the Malorys until I signed on and was told the captain's name."

"Really? Thought everyone knew who they are."

"So they're famous? Or notorious?"

"A little of both." Walter laughed as he walked away.

Nathan hightailed it over to the rigging and started climbing, determined to postpone his next meeting with the Malorys for as long as possible.

Chapter Eleven

"I HOPE *YOU* ARE NO' going tae prove as stubborn as your cousin," Nettie MacDonald said as she entered Judith's cabin to help her prepare for dinner.

Roslynn had insisted on sending her own maid on the trip to see to both girls' needs. Nettie was more a member of the family than a servant, so Judith was delighted that she was accompanying them. Nettie was the only maid aboard. Since *The Maiden George* didn't have an abundance of cabins Georgina and Katey, Judith's older sister, had elected to just hire maids when they reached Bridgeport, but then they both had husbands who could help them dress on the ship if they needed assistance.

"Jack is always stubborn," Judith replied with a grin. "But what's she being stubborn about tonight?"

"Wouldna let me touch her hair. Wasna going tae concede on wearing a dress either till I put m'foot down. Told her I wouldna be washing those breeches she loves sae much if she didna at least dress proper for your dinners."

Jacqueline had also had ship togs made for Judith, not that Judith planned to wear them if she didn't need to. She'd rather deal with her skirts whipping about in the wind than feel self-conscious in sailor's garb. But Judith had already braided her hair for tonight, quite in agreement with Jacqueline that putting her hair up in her usual coiffure on a ship was just asking for it to be blown apart by the wind. However, she moved straight to her little vanity and sat down, just to make Nettie happy, and the old girl did smile as she unbraided Judith's hair and started arranging it more fashionably.

Although Judith's cabin was a decent size, it was still rather cramped with a full-size bed, a wardrobe, and a comfortable reading chair, a little vanity, even a small, round table for two, and her trunks, which had been pushed up against one wall. But she didn't plan to spend that much time in her cabin. Today had been an exception. With most of the family unpacking and recovering from the party last night as well as the early-morning departure, she'd spent most of the day reading and resting. And getting her sea legs, as Jack called the adjustment to the constant motion of the ship.

Judith didn't mind that at all. In fact, she was exhilarated to be on a ship again. Possibly because she liked sailing even more than Jacqueline did. It was too bad Judith's mother and sister didn't, or she might have had more opportunities to sail with her uncle over the years.

She was looking forward to joining her family for dinner tonight in her uncle's much larger cabin and seeing their new cousin again—well, she assumed Andrássy and his stepsister would be invited to dinner. And Nettie made sure Judith looked as if she were going to a formal dinner at home. Her gown, sheer white over blue silk and embroidered with lilacs, wasn't new, but her new wardrobe for the Season hadn't yet been finished because her mother hadn't expected her to need it for another month. She'd still brought all of it along, which was why she had twice as many trunks as Jack did, clothes to wear on the ship and for the first few days in Bridgeport, and a full wardrobe that still needed a seamstress to put the finishing touches on it.

"There, you look lovely as always, lassie," Nettie said when she had finished putting up Judith's hair. "I'll get a sailor in here tomorrow to dig out your jewelry box. I'm no' sure why it's packed wi' the unfinished gowns."

"Because I didn't think I would need it until we get to America and I don't, not just for family dinners, so there's no need to unpack it." Judith hurried out of her cabin before Nettie disagreed with her.

Closing her door, she jumped in surprise when a woman behind her said much too sharply, "Move out of my way!"

Judith immediately stiffened and turned to see stormy gray eyes pinned on her. The woman's brown hair was bound up tightly, and the angry expression on her face prevented Judith from determining whether she was pretty or plain. The woman was angry because her way was blocked for mere moments? Judith couldn't imagine who she was, and then she did. Andrássy's stepsister, Catherine?

She opened her mouth to introduce herself, but Catherine was too impatient to let her get a word out. "Nearly knocked me over and now you just stand there gawking? I asked you to move!"

She was about to shove Judith aside when Jacqueline yanked her own door open behind them and snarled into the narrow corridor, "No screeching on the ship! Learn the bloody rules before you embark or get tossed overboard." And Jacqueline promptly slammed her door shut again.

Trust Jack to say something outlandish when she was

annoyed. The woman's face turned red. Judith had to get out of there before she burst out laughing, which would only make the situation worse. But poor Andrássy! He hadn't been joking last night when he said they didn't want to meet his stepsister, and now she knew why.

She squeezed past Catherine and ran upstairs to the deck before she did in fact giggle. She waited there a few minutes for Jacqueline to join her.

"I suppose that was the stepsister?" Jack said as she came up the stairs.

"That red velvet she was wearing doesn't bespeak a servant from the galley."

Jack huffed, "If she was heading to her cabin, let's hope she stays in it permanently. I heard every word. Rudeness like that—"

"Usually has a reason." Judith put her arm through her cousin's as they headed up to the quarterdeck. "Her face was pinched. It could have been from pain, rather than a horrible disposition."

Jacqueline tsked. "You always see the good in people."

Judith laughed and teased, "And you always try not to!"

"I do not! Besides, more often than not, first impressions are accurate. However, I'll reserve judgment this once, but only because I know you want me to."

A few minutes later they entered the captain's cabin. Accessed from the quarterdeck with only a few steps in front of the door that led down to it, they didn't knock. James and Georgina were on the sofa, his arm around her shoulders. Anthony and Katey were already present and sitting at the long dining table.

The large room resembled a parlor. A long sofa and stuffed chairs with two card tables were on one side, and a desk long enough to hold the charts was on the other side by the dining area. An intricately carved partition in one of the back corners closed off the bed from the rest of the room. The long bank of windows in the back had the drapes open, revealing the ocean behind the ship and the moon shining down on it.

That was Judith's favorite place on the ship. She loved to stand and gaze out of those windows. During the day the windows offered a wonderful windless view of the ocean, and at night, if the moon wasn't hidden behind clouds, the view was almost breathtaking.

After giving her father and sister quick kisses in greeting, she moved to the windows. She couldn't actually see the moon with the wind currently taking them on a southwesterly path, but its light was reflected on the waves.

Jacqueline had joined her parents on the sofa, and Georgina, glancing at the pale green gown Jack was wearing, teased her daughter, "I'm surprised you're not in breeches yet."

"The Scot wouldn't let me," Jack grumbled. "I've a mind to bar my door."

"Nettie means well, so why don't you try a reasonable approach instead."

"Reason with a Scot?" Jack said, looking directly at Anthony as she did.

Anthony burst out laughing. "Ros would box your ears for that slander if she were here."

"Only if she could catch me." Jacqueline grinned.

"I really wish Roslynn and Jaime were better sailors so they could have joined us." Anthony sighed, but his spirits were too high to dwell on it. "But with the Yank indisposed for a few days, I intend to make the most of this rare situation. After all, how often do I have my two eldest daughters to myself?" He raised his glass of brandy high. "Here's to seasickness!"

"That's not funny, Father," Katey said, quick to come to her husband Boyd's defense.

"I thought it was," James remarked.

Andrássy arrived a few minutes later. He knocked. James merely called out for him to come in. Their new cousin was formally dressed in black with a short cape with a pearl clasp and snowy cravat under it, and he was still wearing his sword. Even his greeting to everyone sounded a little too formal, or perhaps he was merely nervous.

With a smile, Georgina got up to lead him to one of the chairs, inquiring, "Is your sister coming?"

"No, she feels uncomfortable joining the family for dinner because she is not one of 'us' and doesn't want to interfere or be a burden. In fact, she insists on repaying you for your generosity in allowing her to travel with you by working for her passage. Perhaps in the galley or—"

"That's highly irregular and certainly not necessary," Georgina said.

"Actually, it is. Catherine can be quite mercurial"— Judith and Jacqueline looked at each other and rolled their eyes—"and she will be calmer if she keeps busy."

Was that really Catherine's idea, Judith wondered, or was it Andrássy's? If it was his, that might be why his stepsister was so angry tonight. Put her to work like a scullery maid?

Georgina must have had the same thought because she sounded a little annoyed when she replied, "She's not a servant and won't be treated as one."

"I tried to tell her exactly that," Andrássy said. "I just

worry if she is too idle—I wish we had thought to bring material she could work with on the ship. She's highly skilled with a needle, even makes all her own clothes, she loves sewing so much. So if any of you ladies need any clothes repaired, Catherine would be delighted to help in that regard at least."

"I could rip a few seams, I suppose," Georgina replied with a grin.

A few people laughed. Judith held her tongue and shook her head at Jack to keep her from mentioning that Judith could use a seamstress. She wasn't about to saddle herself with Catherine's company before she had a chance to form a better opinion of the young woman—if a better one could be had.

But the subject changed with the arrival of Artie and Henry announcing dinner. They got stuck in the doorway, both trying to enter at the same time. Which didn't surprise anyone other than Andrássy. Those two old sea dogs might be the best of friends, but a stranger wouldn't figure that out with all their bickering. Part of James's old crew from his ten years on the high seas, they had retired when James did to become his butlers, sharing that job and this one, too, both acting as his first mates for the voyage.

They all moved to the dining table as the many platters were brought in. Andrássy was quick to pull a chair out for Jack and then sit in the one next to her. A little too quick? Judith wondered if she was going to have something to tease Jack about later.

Judith wasn't hungry because she'd already had samples of tonight's fare when she'd visited the galley late that afternoon. She noticed that Katey, seated beside her, was also picking at her food, but for a different reason.

"Worried about Boyd?" Judith guessed.

Katey nodded. "I hate seeing him so miserable. You'd think after so many years at sea he would have conquered his seasickness by now."

"I don't think it can be conquered."

"I know." Katey sighed. "I just wish—you know he used to have his ship's surgeon make him sleeping drafts so he could just sleep through it. I offered to do the same for him, but he refuses because he wants to stay awake and talk to me. Yet he's usually too sick to say a word! So I end up sleeping too much, like I did today. I'm not going to be able to sleep tonight now, while that is the only time he *does* manage to sleep."

"At least his seasickness only lasts three to four days. But didn't you bring any books to read while you keep him company?"

"I didn't think to, no."

"I did and I just finished a very good one. I'll go fetch it for you in case you do have a sleepless night."

"Eat first," Katey insisted.

Judith grinned. "I did this afternoon."

Telling her father she'd be right back, Judith slipped out of the captain's cabin. A few lanterns were lit, but they weren't needed with the deck currently bathed in moonlight. She caught sight of the moon in the eastern sky and paused. She wished it were a full moon, but it was still lovely. After she got the book, she decided to go to the rail for an unobstructed view of the moon before returning to her family. But as she hurried back upstairs, she dropped her book when she slammed smack into a ghost. And not just any ghost, but the Ghost.

Chapter Twelve

ALL SHE COULD DO was stare at him as light from a lantern on deck illuminated him. Hair as white as she remembered and floating about his shoulders. His eyes a deeper green than she remembered. And tall. No, taller than she remembered she realized now that she was standing next to him, six feet at least. He was too close. She realized he'd grabbed her shoulders to keep her from tumbling backward down the stairs. But he should have let go of her now that she had steadied herself. Someone might come along and see them. Someone such as her father.

With that alarming thought, she stepped to the side, away from the stairs, and he let go of her. All she could think to say was "You're dead."

"No, I ain't, why would you say so?"

"You don't remember?"

"I think I'd remember dying."

"We met a few years ago in that old ruin in Hampshire, next to the Duke of Wrighton's estate. I thought you were a ghost when I found you there. What are you doing here?"

It took him a moment to connect the when and the

where, but when he did, he laughed. "So that's why you seem familiar to me. The trespassing child with sunset hair." A slow grin appeared as his emerald eyes roamed over her, up, down, and back up. "Not a child anymore, are you?"

The blush came quickly. No, she wasn't a child anymore, but did he have to look for the obvious evidence of it? She shouldn't have left her evening wrap in the cabin. Her ghost was a common sailor. She shouldn't be talking to a member of the crew for so long, either. Devil that, he was fascinating! She'd wanted to know everything there was to know about him when she'd thought him a ghost. She still wanted to.

To that end, she held out her hand to him but quickly pulled it back when he merely stared at it. A bit nervous now that he didn't know how to respond to her formal greeting, she stated, "I'm Judith Malory. My friends and family call me Judy. It would be all right if you do."

"We aren't friends."

"Not yet, but we could be. You can start by telling me your name?"

"And if I don't?"

"Surly for an ex-ghost, aren't you? Too unfriendly to be anyone's friend? Very well." She nodded. "Pardon me." She walked over to the railing. She gazed at the wavering reflection of the moon's light on the pitch-dark ocean. It was so dramatic and beautiful, but now she couldn't fully appreciate it because she was disappointed, much more than she should have been. She almost felt like crying, which was absurd—unless Jack had been right. Had she really fancied herself in love with a ghost? No, that was absurd, too. She'd merely been curious, amazed, and fascinated, thinking he was a ghost, that there really were such things. Even after Jack and she were older and admitted he couldn't *really* be a ghost, it had still been more fun and exciting to think of him that way. Yet here was the proof that he was a real man—flesh and blood and so nicely put together. Not as pale as she remembered. No, now his skin was deeply tanned. From working on ships? Who was he? A sailor, obviously. But what had he been doing in that old ruined house in the middle of the night all those years ago? The ghost had told her the house was his. But how could a sailor afford to own a house?

She was more curious about him than ever. Unanswered questions were going to drive her batty. She shouldn't have given up so easily on getting some answers. Jack wouldn't have. Maybe she could ask Uncle James . . .

"Nathan Tremayne," said a deep voice.

She grinned to herself and glanced at him for a moment. He was so tall and handsome with his long, white hair blowing in the sea breeze. He was standing several feet from her and staring at the moonlight on the ocean, too, so it didn't actually appear that he had spoken to her. But he had. Was he as intrigued with her as she was with him?

"How do you do, Nathan. Or do you prefer Nate?"

"Doesn't matter. D'you always talk to strange men like this?"

"You're strange?"

"A stranger to you," he clarified.

"Not a'tall. We are actually old acquaintances, you and I."

He chuckled. "Telling each other to get out of a house five years ago doesn't make us acquainted. And why were you trespassing that night?"

"My cousin Jack and I were investigating the light we saw in the house. That house has been abandoned for as long as anyone living can remember. No one should have been inside it. But we could see the light from our room in the ducal mansion."

"And so you thought you'd found a ghost?"

She blushed again, but they weren't looking at each other, so she doubted that he noticed. "When we saw you there, it was a reasonable assumption."

"Not a'tall, just the opposite." Was that amusement she heard in his tone? She took a quick peek. It was hard not to. And, yes, he was grinning as he added, "You drew a conclusion that no adult would have come to."

"Well, I wasn't grown yet. That *was* quite a few years ago. And you were holding your lantern so that its light only reached your upper body. It looked as if you were floating in the air."

He laughed again, such a pleasant sound, like a bass rumble. It shook a lock of hair loose over his wide brow. His hair wasn't pure white as she'd thought. She could see blond streaks in it.

"Very well. I can see how your imagination could've played tricks on you."

"So why were you there that night and looking so sad?"

"Sad?"

"Weren't you?"

"No, not sad, darlin'." But instead of explaining, he said, "Do you really believe in ghosts?"

She looked up and saw his mouth set in a half grin and the arched eyebrow. Was he teasing her? He was! She also noticed his green eyes were gazing at her intently. Quite bold for a common seaman if that's what he was. Quite bold for any man, actually, when they'd only just met—that first time didn't count.

In response to his teasing she said, "Jack and I admitted to ourselves a few years ago that we'd been mistaken that night. But we continued to refer to you as the Ghost because it amuses us. It was our special secret that we only shared with our younger cousins. It was much more fun to say we'd found a ghost than the new owner of the house. But you can't be the owner of the house. What were you doing there?"

"Maybe I like secrets as much as you do."

On the brink of discovery and of clearing up a mystery that had intrigued her for years, she was more than a little annoyed by his reply. "You really won't say?"

"You haven't tried convincing me yet, darlin'. A pretty smile might work. . . ."

Judith went very still. So still she thought she could hear her heart pounding. She couldn't believe what had just become crystal clear to her. She *knew* who he was. It was that second instance of his calling her *darlin'*. She'd been too flustered to pay much attention to it the first time he'd said it, but this time she remembered where she'd heard it before. A mere two weeks ago from a man who she suspected was far more dangerous than a vagrant.

The moment it had struck her that night of how odd it was for a vagrant to be drinking French brandy, she had known he wasn't what he'd first seemed to be. But that wasn't all. He claimed to know the abandoned house better than she did, so he'd either been staying there a long time or had visited it more than once. His putting a lock on a door that didn't belong to him. His coming out of a hidden room where he could have been storing smuggled or stolen goods. And his warning her to tell no one that she'd seen him there. All of it pointed to his being a criminal of one sort or another.

Of course she'd told Jacqueline about him in the morning, and of course Jack had agreed with her conclusion and suggested she tell Brandon, who could prevaricate a bit and warn his father without revealing that Judith had had a run-in with a criminal in the old ruin. Before they'd left for London, Brandon had told her he'd spoken to his father and assured her they'd catch the smuggler red-handed that very day. So what was he doing here, on *The Maiden George*?

He appeared to be waiting for her to answer him. She did that now, hissing, "You deserve to be in jail! Why aren't you?"

Chapter Thirteen

NATHAN WAS TAKEN ABACK by the girl's angry question. He almost laughed at how close to the mark it was, yet it didn't make sense. Nonetheless, the instinct for self-preservation kicked in, and quickly.

"You've mistaken me for someone else. But I'm not surprised. First you thought I was a ghost, then you took me for a landowner. Isn't it more obvious that I'm just a hard-working seaman trying to earn a living?"

"I don't believe you."

"Why not?"

"Because I'd never forget a face that's haunted me for five years, and now I recognize your voice, too."

"From five years ago? I doubt that's possible."

"From two weeks ago when you accosted me in that ruined house," she said hotly. "You're a criminal and I won't have you on board endangering my family."

So it was her, he thought, and not one of the duke's servants as he'd assumed that night. And maybe she was not quite a lady either, except in title. That was an intriguing thought and even likely, considering how he'd met her, both times, out and about alone at night. And now tonight.

"It seems to me you're the one guilty of criminal behavior, breaking into houses that don't belong to you. And more'n once? Tell me, darlin', does your family know about your late-night rendezvousing?"

She sucked in her breath. "Don't *even* go there. You know I spoke the truth about why I was there that night."

"If I wasn't there, how would I know? Or wait, were you there to see me again?" He grinned, suddenly beginning to enjoy himself. "Well, me in ghost form, but me nonetheless. And you already admitted you did that at least once."

She scoffed, "You're not turning the tables on me here, but nice try. There's simply no comparison to a smuggler, or is it a thief? Which one are you?"

"And why would I be either of those?"

"Because the facts add up precisely, and there's a long list of them. You even proved yourself to be a liar that night. You weren't just passing by, not with your own cot set up in that room."

"A criminal who carries a cot around with him? Do you realize how unlikely that is?"

"You put a lock on the door."

"If whoever you are talking about did that, I'd think he did it to keep pesky ghost hunters from waking him in the middle of the night. Didn't work, did it?"

"You think this is amusing?"

He smiled. "Did I say that?"

"You didn't have to when it's written all over your face," she snapped.

"Well, you have me there, darlin'. But it's not every day I get accused of criminal activities. I have to admit, I do find a certain humor in that."

"You were hiding illegal goods there and that put *my*

family at risk! My cousins could have been implicated. No one would believe they couldn't have known what was going on in their own backyard. The scandal would have touched my entire family!"

Enraged in defense of her family? Well, that at least he could understand. It just didn't alter that he needed to convince her she'd made a mistake.

So he chuckled. "Will you listen to yourself now? No one in their right mind would blame a duke for anything, much less something illegal."

"So you admit it? You came out of the hidden room, and I tasted brandy when you kissed me. You were *not* just a vagrant passing by as you claimed! I don't doubt you've even been using that ruined house to hide smuggled goods for five years, haven't you?"

He was hard-pressed not to laugh. She'd figured everything out and with amazing accuracy. Smart girl. Beauty *and* intelligence. When was the last time he had come across that combination? But she was merely making charges she hoped to hear him confirm. That wasn't going to happen. He did need to get her off the scent though. . . .

His voice dropped to a husky timbre, his smile broadened. "You know, darlin', if you and I had actually shared a kiss, that would be a pleasant memory I'd not soon forget. And now you make me wish it had happened. . . ."

She was staring at his mouth. As he'd hoped, he was distracting her. He just hadn't counted on his getting distracted, too. The pull was incredibly strong to kiss her again, right there on the deck in the moonlight. Utter madness.

But he was saved from finding out what might have happened next when he heard two of the crew talking, their voices getting louder as they approached. She heard them, too, glancing nervously beyond him.

"Good night, darlin'. I better fade away like a ghost. I'd hate for your family to learn of your predilection for late-night trysts."

Nathan walked away. The subtle threat plus the doubts he'd tried to put in her mind would hopefully be enough to keep her mouth shut for the time being. He was going to climb the mainmast again, but unable to resist the urge to look back, he merely moved into the main-mast's shadow. She was halfway to the quarterdeck before she turned to look back as well. Had she thought of more aspersions to cast on him? But he relaxed when he saw she wasn't looking for him, but for the book she'd dropped. She came back to retrieve it.

A few moments later he lost sight of her when she entered the captain's cabin, but her image was still in his mind. The woman was too beautiful—but she was trouble. He was going to have to come up with a better way to keep her from voicing her suspicions to other people. But that could wait for tomorrow.

Chapter Fourteen

In the morning, Nathan found Corky to discuss his newest problem—Judith Malory. But his friend had been tasked with swabbing the main deck, a chore so menial Corky couldn't stop grumbling about it long enough to offer any suggestions. Nathan still kept him company while he checked the railings for loose nails. It wasn't something he would have thought to do so early on the voyage if he hadn't seen Judith leaning against a rail last night.

"Watch out, Cap'n," Corky suddenly said behind him. "I think that trouble you were telling me about is coming your way."

Nathan turned to see Judith marching toward him and Corky quickly getting out of the way. She looked even more beautiful in daylight with the sun on her glorious red-gold hair, wearing a long velvet coat left open over an ice-blue dress trimmed with yellow-dyed lace—and the light of battle in her cobalt-blue eyes.

She'd lost a few hairpins last night, which he'd found on the deck after she'd gone, so he wasn't surprised to see she'd braided her hair today. Diamond-tipped pins. He'd thought about keeping them as a memento, but dug them out of his pocket now and handed them to her, hoping it would forestall another tirade. It didn't.

"I do *not* care for the way you threatened me last night!" she began.

He shrugged. "If you're going to make outlandish accusations about me, I can make a more realistic one about you—that you seem to have a habit of conducting nighttime trysts with strange men."

"When you put my family at risk, there is no comparison!" she said furiously. "I demand an explanation."

Nathan gnashed his teeth in frustration. He wasn't about to spill his guts to her and tell her about his unusual situation when he didn't know her and had no reason to trust her with the truth. Beautiful in the extreme, she was still a nabob. And he wasn't so sure she was going to spread her suspicions around either. If she was, why would she have come looking for him this morning to discuss them again? He just had to come up with a way to ensure her silence, or at least some explanation that she would believe so she could laugh off her damned conclusions. Or maybe another bit of truth would suffice. . . .

"Tremayne!" was suddenly bellowed from the quarterdeck.

Nathan hissed under his breath, "Bleedin' hell. I knew better than to talk to you when you've got relatives crawling all over this ship—including my captain."

"Why are you even aboard? Escaping a hangman's noose in England?"

In exasperation he said, "No, chasing down my ship, which was stolen."

"Yet another lie? Good God, do you ever say anything that's true?" Then she smirked, "But that was just my uncle's 'come here' voice, not his 'come here and die' voice. You'll hear the latter after I tell him who you really are, Nathan Tremayne."

He was out of time to talk her around, so he said, "Give me a chance to explain before you do anything we'll both regret. It's not what you think."

He left her with that, and hopefully enough doubt to keep her pretty mouth shut for the time being.

Nathan approached Captain Malory with a good deal of annoyance. The man's summons couldn't have come at a worse time, when he still had an ax hanging over his head from the man's niece. But he didn't think a few more minutes with Judith would remove that ax. She'd had two weeks to convince herself that her suspicions about him were accurate. He might need just as long to change her mind—if he could. And if he couldn't? If she spread her tale anyway?

He supposed he could jump the gun on her and make a full confession right now to her uncle—captain to captain. Like hell he would. That would only be a logical path if the man weren't a lord, too. Damned nabobs were too unpredictable. And he knew nothing about Judith Malory's uncle other than he was a rich lord with sledgehammers for fists—and he liked to fight. Nathan had definitely gotten that impression the other night.

At least he didn't think this Malory was the one he needed to avoid. He doubted the captain was going to want retribution for what had happened on the docks, not when he'd let him go after Hammett's sailor. However, as captain he was king of this ship for the duration, his word law, his dictates followed whether they were fair or not, and if Nathan had just gotten on his bad side because of a woman, Nathan was going to be furious—with himself.

He'd been so stupid last night, letting that pretty face dazzle him. Talking to her as if there could be no consequences for it, and then to forget that entirely after she made her accusations, which could bring even worse consequences. He should have walked away when he had the chance to, before she realized who he was.

It was laughable. This was supposed to be the easy part of this trip. The hard part wasn't supposed to start until they arrived in Connecticut and he had to convince the law-enforcing Yanks over there to help him, an Englishman, take down their own criminals. At the most he'd be giving them a good laugh over that. At the worst, they could toss him in jail instead for his audacity or run him out of town. But he still had a few weeks before he found out how strongly animosity still ran between the two countries that had gone to war with each other more'n once.

He didn't look behind him to see if the reason for his latest predicament had scurried off. He could still see her in his mind's eye, though, softly rounded, exquisite in every detail, lush, sensual lips, far too beautiful for any one woman to be. If he couldn't talk her around, maybe he could seduce her into keeping silent instead.

The moment the thought occurred to him, he made his decision. That's how he would handle Judith Malory. He hadn't felt so good about a decision in ages. So what if she was surrounded by family on this ship and the lot of them were aristocrats. He was used to living dangerously.

When Nathan approached James Malory, he saw him conversing with his first mate. Artie looked contrite, as if he'd just received a tongue-lashing.

"I didn't know you wanted it set up before we sailed . . ." Artie was saying.

The captain's back was turned toward Nathan, so he didn't intrude. Malory in a billowing white shirt open at the neck, tight, buff breeches, black, knee-high boots, and hair to his shoulders didn't look any more like a nabob now than he had the other night. Glancing around, Nathan realized he was the only member of the crew who was properly dressed. Like the captain, the other sailors had all stowed their jackets and were working more comfortably in their shirtsleeves. After all, it wasn't a military ship where the crew had to button up in uniforms.

Nathan was about to shrug out of his own coat when Malory turned and noticed him. "My brother has a bone to pick with you," he stated baldly.

Nathan winced. "I was hoping you wouldn't remember me from the other night."

"Forget hair like yours? Not bloody likely."

But the captain was grinning as if from a fond memory, prompting Nathan to ask cautiously, "You aren't angry that I punched your brother?"

"Not a'tall. Found it highly amusing, actually. Ain't often Tony gets taken by surprise like that. But he'll want a rematch, so you might want to avoid him for a few days. As it happens, the project I have for you will see to that nicely. I'm told you're my carpenter, but how experienced are you?"

Relieved he wasn't going to be questioned about the fight on the dock or be reprimanded for talking to the captain's niece, Nathan answered honestly, "Three years, sir. Two to master building and repairing, and then I spent a year branching out to furnishings. Before that I built chimneys. Before that, I tried my hand at painting and roofing."

"A jack-of-all-trades—for landlubbers? Then what are you doing on *The Maiden George*?"

"I inherited my father's ship a few years ago, but she was stolen last week. This group of thieves has been plaguing England for a good decade, but not so often that the authorities could piece together who they were or what they were doing with the ships."

"That doesn't answer my question, dear boy, but it does pose another. A captain reduced to ship's carpenter? Do you like the sea so much that you'll sail in any capacity?"

"Your destination is exactly where I need to go to get my ship back."

James chuckled. "Ah, there we have it, an ulterior motive. So your thieves are Yanks, are they? I find that particularly priceless, 'deed I do. Can't wait to mention it to my brother-in-law. But fess up, how did you figure that out?"

"I didn't. A Commander Burdis captured one of the thieves and he has an ax to grind with them because they killed one of his men. He agreed to tell me where to find the thieves and my ship if I agreed to put them out of business for him."

"So you're actually working for the government?"

"Unofficially."

"Of course, can't step on Yank toes without stirring up another war, can we," James said drily.

"Something like that was mentioned."

"Well, a captain you may be, but not on this voyage."

"I'll earn my way."

"You will indeed, and that begins now. My first mate remembered to load the materials for it, but now he tells me he forgot to inform *you* that I want an exercise ring built in my ship's hold. Fetch your tools and meet him below. He'll show you where to build it."

"An exercise ring?"

James had started to turn away but stopped and a frown formed. "Do *not* tell me you don't know what an exercise ring is."

Nathan stiffened, ready for battle. The man looked downright menacing when he frowned. But Nathan had to know what he was building in order to build it. The only rings he knew about were for pugilists. Surely that's not what the captain was talking about. Or was he?

"For fisticuffs?"

The frown vanished. "Splendid, so you do know."

"How large do you want it?"

"The size of the tarpaulin will determine the dimensions for the platform. A foot off the floor will suffice. I've been assured everything you will need for it is down there. And, Tremayne, don't take too long building it. I'm already feeling a need to make use of it."

"It shouldn't take more'n a day, Captain Malory."

"Excellent. Do a good job and you can test it out with me—yes, yes, I know I already offered you that job and you turned it down, but it sounds now like you might have some frustration to work off, lost ship and all, so you might want to reconsider. By the by, did you get your answers from that sailor the other night?"

"Yes."

"I suppose I should apologize for interfering in that little contretemps you were in. You didn't really look like you needed help. I just deplore passing up a spot of exercise when it presents itself so handily. But run along now. You've my ring to build."

Malory didn't seem to be a bad sort—for a captain. Nathan had told him nothing he didn't mind sharing. And the man was right, he could use an outlet for his frustration, just not for the reason he'd stated. But to spar with his captain, at sea, probably wouldn't be in his best interests. The man obviously didn't expect to lose, but what if he did? And ended up angry because of it?

No, the better course would be to avoid any further discourse with the captain altogether, which shouldn't be too hard. The first mate and the boatswain would be getting their orders from him. Those two had to deal with James Malory on this trip, Nathan didn't. Thank God.

Chapter Fifteen

As soon as Nathan had stepped up on the quarterdeck, Judith had moved to stand just below it, where she could hear what was being said without being seen. But what she heard just fueled her anger all the more. More and more lies. Did the man *ever* tell the truth? But he was going to have to. His "Give me a chance to explain before you do anything we'll both regret. It's not what you think" was the only reason she hadn't gone over to her uncle with him. Well, there was also the fact that James was the only member of her family who would just shrug at the news that a smuggler was on his ship.

It was her father she needed to inform, not his brother. Yet she didn't go in search of Anthony either. The smidgen of doubt that Nathan had planted in her mind held her back.

She went to Jacqueline's cabin instead to see if she was awake yet. Her cousin would never forgive her if she wasn't the first to know that their ex-ghost had been found and who he *really* was, but Judith hadn't had a chance to tell her yet. Last night after retrieving the book for Katey, her father had engaged her in a game of backgammon, which they had still been playing when Jack went off to bed.

But Jacqueline was still sound asleep now, and it only took Judith a moment to realize where she wanted to be. With Nathan Tremayne still firmly in her mind, she headed for where she knew she'd find him. But when she got there, she could hear him talking to Artie, so she went back on deck. She knew it was inappropriate for a lady to be alone with a member of the crew, and she didn't want Artie to mention to anyone that she'd sought Nathan out.

The moment Artie appeared back on deck, she headed down to the hold again. She peeked into the cargo deck before she took the last few steps down the stairway. Nathan was alone now. He was unpacking one of the crates so he didn't notice her approach. He'd removed his jacket and had even unfastened the top buttons of his shirt, which wasn't surprising because it was warmer in the hold than it was on deck. She couldn't take her eyes off him. He looked rather dashing like this. If Jack could see him, she would say he looked like a pirate—no, Judith reminded herself, like a smuggler.

The reminder got her eyes off him for a moment. She looked around the large cargo hold, which appeared almost empty because the ship wasn't carrying any cargo for sale. Provisions were stored along the sides in crates and barrels of various sizes. Toward the stern, pens contained farm animals that would be brought to the galley as needed. She could hear the clucking of a few chickens in the distance. Nathan was standing next to a pile of building materials, but otherwise, most of the space was empty, so there was plenty of room for the exercise ring he'd been tasked to build.

"Not exactly what you expected a ship's carpenter to have to do, is it?"

He stiffened at the sound of her voice, but he didn't

glance up. "Go away, trouble," he said in a grouchy tone. "We can continue our *debate* after I'm done working."

She ignored the unflattering name and the suggestion. "We need to clarify a few matters. And the sooner you accomplish your task, the sooner we can do that. I can help."

"The devil you can."

"You need to measure the tarpaulin before you begin building the ring, don't you? I can help you spread it out."

He turned to her. "So you were eavesdropping?"

She saw no reason to deny it. "I was just making sure that my uncle didn't kill you."

His eyes narrowed. "Spit it out. Are you joking about him or not?"

She shrugged. "That's a matter of perspective. To me he's the sweetest man, my best friend's loving father, my father's closest brother. Really, he's just a big, cuddly bear."

"But what about to people who aren't members of his family?"

"Some people do fear him, I suppose, but I can't imagine why."

Nathan grunted. "I can. I saw him make mince of four blokes in a matter of minutes the night before last. He's bleedin' well lethal with his fists."

"Well, everyone knows that. He and my father are both superlative pugilists. They have been for years. It's a skill they honed when they were London's most notorious rakes."

"D'you even know what you're talking about? Fighting and seducing women have nothing to do with each other."

"Course they do, when you consider how often they were challenged to duels by angry husbands. But they had no desire to kill a man just because the poor chap had an unfaithful wife, so they took a lot of those challenges to the ring instead. They still won either way."

Nathan took a step toward her. "I would think such worldly matters would be kept from tender ears like yours."

She backed up. Was it the subject matter that had turned his green eyes sensual? Her pulse began to race. She took a deep, steadying breath, but it sounded like a sigh even to her ears. So she blurted out, "It was common knowledge, not a family secret."

He kept moving toward her. "Does your family have secrets?"

She continued to step back, away from him. "There's a skeleton or two in most closets, but not as many as I suspect are in yours."

She thought only briefly about standing her ground. Was he trying to make her nervous about being alone with him down here? It might not have been the smartest move on her part when the man had his own secrets to hide and she was the only one who knew them.

She continued to back away from him, but something got in the way. Caught behind her knees, she abruptly sat down on a crate. He took a step back as if he'd just gotten the results he wanted and said with some amusement, "Stay out of the way if you're staying."

He'd done that deliberately!? Her hackles rose immediately as she watched him walk away. She was about to lambaste him for trying to frighten her when he stopped to add, "Unless you want that kiss I was thinking about." He glanced around. "Do you?"

He'd only been going to kiss her? Well, he could have made that clear! "Certainly not," she humphed.

He faced her again to say, "Don't get indignant, darlin'. I was just going to show you the difference."

"What difference?"

"Between your smuggler's kiss and mine. Thought it might be a more pleasant way to clear up the confusion for you."

"I doubt that would indicate anything a'tall."

He laughed. "He was that good?"

She raised a brow. "That implies you think you'd be better at it?"

He shrugged. "I don't get complaints, just the opposite. So you might want to think about the offer—instead of worrying that a smuggler might break your pretty neck to keep his secret. That *did* occur to you, didn't it?"

"Is that a not-so-subtle threat?"

"No, I would never threaten you. In fact, I think I'd protect you to my dying breath."

He'd managed to startle her. "Why?"

"Because only a few things are worth dying for, family, country—and the love of a beautiful woman."

Why would he even say that!? Merely to plant the seed that something romantic could develop between them if she kept his secret? But he didn't wait for her to reply. Instead he went about his work, ignoring her, taking the tarpaulin out of its crate and dropping it in the middle of the hold before he began unfolding it.

As she watched him, she saw how efficiently he worked. There wasn't a single pause to suggest he didn't know what he was doing, forcing her to conclude that he had really learned carpentry at some point. But had he worked at it for three years as he'd told James? When would he have had time to do that if he was smuggling five years ago? Very well, she conceded, maybe he hadn't been smuggling all that time, but definitely more recently. He'd admitted he owned his own ship—if what he'd told her uncle was true.

She couldn't take her eyes off him, fascinated by the way his muscles flexed as he staked out the four corners. He was far too muscular for a common seaman. She could see him captaining his own ship, though. Had he built the ship himself? Is that why he'd learned carpentry? Then who had taught him to sail it?

Good God, she had so many questions. One just led to another. Yet she still didn't ask him any, was even having trouble breathing when he removed his shirt and tossed it aside as he began hammering together the first side of the platform. His chest was already gleaming with sweat. She was feeling warm, too, so she shrugged out of her coat and draped it over the crate she was sitting on.

"Besides, I can think of much nicer things to do with your neck," he suddenly said, as if there had been no break in their conversation. And then: "No blush?"

She took her eyes off his chest and saw that he was looking at her again, had caught her staring at him. That brought on a blush. But had he actually been thinking about her neck all this time?

"There were more'n two rakes in my family, so there isn't much that can embarrass me."

"I seem to be having an easy time of it," he said with a chuckle.

"You're deliberately trying to embarrass me, so stop it."

"Not deliberately, or do you think I'm in the habit of talking to fine ladies like yourself? Believe me, the women of my acquaintance don't blush." He gave her a grin, then turned more serious. "What made you think you'd heard my voice before last night—aside from five years ago, which even you know is too long ago to remember something like that?"

"It wasn't your voice. It's what you keep calling me. 'Darling.' The smuggler called me that, too."

"You think sweet words aren't commonly used? That I'm really the only man to use that one?"

"If you're not a smuggler, what are you?"

"As has already been established, a shipowner and a carpenter. You should let it go at that."

"When you also said you were just here to earn a living?" she reminded him. "You realize one lie means everything you say is suspect."

He chuckled. "You're very suspicious for someone so young. A fine lady like you, how do you even know about smugglers and the like?"

"You'd be amazed what some of the members of my family have been involved in."

"Like?"

"I'm not sharing secrets, you are."

"Not while I'm working, I'm not."

She ignored that to ask, "Can you really finish this ring in a day as you told my uncle?"

"Yes, even if I had to cut the lumber, which I don't. Artie said he got all the materials from a man who builds rings for a living, so it's already cut to specifications and just needs to be put together. Are you worried I'll get on your uncle's bad side if I disappoint him?"

"No, when that happens, I doubt it will have anything to do with your carpentry job."

"It will if you keep distracting me," he retorted.

She suppressed a grin. "I *was* being quiet. You brought up necks."

He snorted but continued to hammer, even when he asked a few minutes later, "How often did your father and your uncle lose those challenges you mentioned?"

"They never did."

"Never? Even when they get taken by surprise?"

"Who would dare do that?"

He didn't appear to like her answer, but since he could apparently work and converse at the same time, she continued, taking a different tack. "I have to say, that was a very good excuse you came up with, instead of admitting that you're running from the law."

"What excuse?"

"That you're chasing a stolen ship. Did you build it yourself?"

"No, I inherited her from my father two years ago."

"So you've been smuggling for only two years?"

She slipped that in hoping to get him to tell the truth while he was distracted by his work, but it didn't happen.

He glanced her way. "I've told you how wrong you are, yet you do seem to be very curious about me, so why don't we make a deal. I'll answer your questions over the course of the voyage if you'll answer some of mine, and we'll agree to keep each other's secrets."

"I don't have any secrets that would land me in jail," she said pertly.

He shrugged. "Neither do I, but if you don't want to strike a bargain, so be it."

"Not so fast, I didn't say that. Let me be clear, you're offering to tell me your life story, the truthful version, if I agree to keep what you say to myself?"

"You'll have to do more'n that. You can tell no one that we've met before. That will have to be *our* secret."

"But my cousin Jack—"

"No one."

She snapped her mouth shut. She wasn't sure she could keep secrets from Jack and certainly didn't want to when they always shared everything. Annoyed, she said, "I seem to be getting the short end of the stick. I'll have to think of something else you can do for me to more evenly balance this agreement."

"Then we have one?"

"We do." She got up to shake hands on it, but heard her name being called. "I have to go. Jack's calling for me."

"That's a woman's voice."

"Yes, it is, but there's no time to explain."

"There's time for this."

She was already hurrying to the stairway and wasn't going to stop to find out what he meant. So she didn't see him put down his hammer and reach for her. But suddenly he was holding her quite intimately with one of his arms around her waist and the other halfway around her shoulders with his hand behind her neck. She was bent slightly back as his lips moved softly against hers.

Such a classic pose he had her in, romantic really, yet it did run through her mind that he was stealing kisses from her again. But this time she knew who was doing it, not some faceless rogue, but an incredibly handsome one. So when she did what she knew she was supposed to do and tried to push away from him, the merely halfhearted effort brought her hands sliding up his bare chest to his shoulders. And before she could try again, the pleasant way his lips were moving over hers caused such scintillating feelings to flutter inside her that she didn't want to pull away from him.

The foray was simply too sensual, the way he parted

her lips with his, sucking on her lower lip, nibbling at her upper lip, then running his tongue over both before flicking it teasingly at hers. His hold tightened and he deepened the kiss, sending her pulse thrumming erratically and a wave of heat over her whole body.

Utterly immersed in what he was doing to her, she was surprised when he let her go and she found herself standing there without his help. Her eyes flew open to find him giving her a curious look she couldn't fathom.

"Was there a difference?" he asked.

That's why he'd kissed her? "You already know there was a difference because you know how brief that other kiss was and that it ended like this."

She didn't slap him as hard as she'd done that night at the old house. Which was probably why he laughed. "I guess the bargain is off?"

"No, but I *will* think of something unpleasant for you to do to keep up your end of the bargain—besides giving me the truth."

"I doubt anything to do with you could be unpleasant, darlin'."

"Even if I keep you at my beck and call, subject to my whims?"

He grinned. "Sounds like the pot just got sweetened for me."

"I wouldn't be so sure," she huffed.

"Oh, I am. As long as it doesn't get me in trouble with the captain, I'm yours to command. Would you like to seal our bargain with another kiss?"

She didn't answer as she marched up the stairs. She'd amused him more than enough for one day. When they met again, she'd have the upper hand and she planned to keep it that way.

Chapter Sixteen

— ❧ —

"SHE LOOKS LONELY AND sad," Judith said to Jacqueline as she gazed at Catherine Benedek, who had just appeared on deck, her brown hair so tightly wound up the wind hadn't disturbed it yet.

"And why is that our business?" Jacqueline asked.

They were sitting on one of the steps between decks nibbling on pastries, far to the side so the sailors could navigate to and fro without having to ask them to move out of the way. Judith hadn't yet quite recovered from lying to Jack when she'd asked where Judith had been. And her cheeks had gone up in flames because of it. But Jacqueline had already grabbed her hand to lead her to the steps, so she hadn't noticed.

Oh, God, lying to Jack already. Before she'd gone topside, Judith had run to the galley for a couple of pastries. She'd needed an excuse for why Jack hadn't found her on deck. She'd handed Jack a pastry and said, "I went to the galley for these." Yet she was still agonizing. *How* was she going to be able to keep a secret from her dearest friend, when no one knew her better than Jack did?

But the mysterious Catherine Benedek was a useful distraction to get her mind off secrets and kisses and ex-ghosts, at least briefly. "Aren't you curious about her?"

"After the way she spoke to you last night outside our cabins, no."

"I am. Who yells like that for no reason?"

"Her."

Judith rolled her eyes. "Let's introduce ourselves."

"Fine. But if she screeches again, I'm going to toss her over the rail."

Jacqueline threw the rest of her pastry over the railing and dusted off her hands on her breeches as she stood up. She'd already donned her ship garb: baggy pants, a loose shirt, and a pink scarf over her head, which kept her long, blond hair securely bound up. And she didn't bother with shoes or boots, preferring to go barefoot. She'd had three sets of work clothes tailored for the voyage and three sets made for Judith, too, even though Judith had told her she wouldn't wear them. They both loved sailing, but Judith had no desire to help with the actual work of sailing, as Jack did.

"You barely touched that pastry," Judith said as she dusted crumbs from her hands, too. "Are you feeling all right?"

"I probably should have resisted the fresh milk Nettie brought me last night. I got too much sleep because of it and now I feel a bit sluggish, is all."

"Nettie brought me a glass as well, but it didn't cause me to oversleep, so I doubt it was the milk. Are you sure you haven't caught something? Are you feverish?"

Jacqueline swatted Judith's hand away when she tried to feel her brow. "Stop fussing, Mother. I'm fine."

Judith tsked. "Aunt George would send you back to bed. I only wanted to see if you have a fever."

"I don't. Now can we get our meeting with the harridan over with?"

They had nearly reached the elegantly clad woman, so Judith whispered, "Be nice," before she made the introductions.

A warm smile revealed the woman was quite pretty, after all. "I'm Catherine Benedek. It's a pleasure to meet you under better circumstances."

"So you aren't always so disagreeable?" Jacqueline asked baldly.

Taken aback, Catherine assured them, "No, only when I'm in pain, as I was yesterday. I had an excruciating headache. Caused by lack of sleep, I suppose. I was rushing to my cabin for some laudanum to help with it. I do apologize for being terse."

"You still have an American accent," Jacqueline noted. "You weren't in Europe very long?"

"I was." That sadness was back in Catherine's light gray eyes. "But my mother was American, so—"

"Was?" Jacqueline cut in.

"Yes, she died in the recent fire that took Andrássy's father, too."

That would certainly account for Catherine's sadness, Judith thought. "How awful. I'm sorry for your loss."

"You are kind. But I suppose I have my mother's accent. I'm surprised you would recognize it."

"Jacqueline's mother is American, and five of her uncles are, too," Judith explained. "That's why we're sailing to America. We're having a come-out in Connecticut to please the American side of her family. Then we'll have another one in England to please the other side. I was only able to get permission to go with her at the last minute. I'm actually quite unprepared. My entire new wardrobe still needs some finishing work, mostly just the hems."

Catherine's expression lit up. "So Andrássy told you that I love to sew? I would be delighted to assist you."

"It seems like an imposition."

"On the contrary, you would be doing *me* a favor by relieving my boredom. Say you will at least consider it."

Judith grinned. "Of course."

The smile remained on Catherine's lips, a little wider now. "How very accommodating of you to travel for such a reason. I, too, have family in America, though Andrássy doesn't think my father can still be alive after all these years."

"But you do?"

"Indeed. He was only assumed dead after his ship went down off the coast of Florida. But there were survivors of the shipwreck who returned to Savannah, which was where we lived. My father could have survived, too. Maybe he was injured and was recovering somewhere. That could have accounted for his not returning home. He might have come home much later and found us gone and had no idea where to look for us."

"Then you don't think your mother's marriage to Andrássy's father was even legal?" Jacqueline asked.

"No, I don't. God rest her soul, it was stupid and shameful of her to remarry so quickly. I hated her for many years for doing that."

"Really? Your own mother?"

Judith intervened before Jack turned the woman unpleasant again. "Anger can sometimes be mistaken for hate. It's understandable, though, that you would be angry at your mother for giving up on your father when you thought he could still be alive."

"Thank you for that." Catherine smiled at Judith. "Barely a month had passed before my mother packed our bags and took us to Europe. She told me that we were only going to visit an old friend of her mother's in Austria. But within three months of arriving there, she met the count, who was in the city on business, and married him. Three months! And then I was forced to live in that archaic country of his where English is barely spoken."

"I'm sorry—*we're* sorry," Judith said.

But Jack ruined it by adding, "Sounds exciting to me. A new life in a country that is so different from your own. Have you no sense of adventure a'tall?"

"Adventure? Are you joking?"

"I guess so," Jacqueline said drily.

Catherine didn't seem to notice Jacqueline's tone and changed the subject. "You two look nothing like Gypsies, as Andrássy does."

"You expected us to as far back in our ancestry as Anna Stephanoff was?" Jacqueline asked.

"You do have his eyes though, even the exotic shape."

"Only a few of us have the black hair and eyes you're referring to," Judith said.

"What about the gifts?"

Judith frowned. "What exactly are you—"

Jack interrupted with a laugh. "I think she means fortune-telling and other things Gypsies are renowned for."

Catherine suddenly looked quite excited. "Yes, indeed. Do you have any special abilities? Or does anyone in your family? I begged Andrássy to ask, but he doesn't believe in such things."

"Neither do we," Jacqueline said firmly.

The woman looked so disappointed, Judith took pity on

her. "Our family does have more than its fair share of luck, but no one would call it a Gypsy gift."

"Yet perhaps it is," Catherine said quickly. "Can you explain?"

Jack was glaring at her, but Judith continued, "Well, for instance, our uncle Edward is incredibly good with investments, but only some people call him lucky. Others view him as being very knowledgeable about financial matters. Our cousin Regina is rather good at matchmaking. The men and women she pairs up usually end up quite happy together. My father and Jack's brother, Jeremy, who take after the Gypsy side in looks, were always lucky with women, and now they're lucky with their wives, but again, that's hardly considered a gift. And—"

"—that's the extent of it," Jacqueline cut in to finish for Judith. "Now, it's your turn to tell us what you expected to hear and why?"

"Is it not obvious? I hoped for some help in finding my father. I plan to start my search in Savannah, but as I and my mother were his only ties to that city, it is unlikely he is still there. His trade routes were between there and the Caribbean, where he lived before he met my mother. It's daunting to think we might have to visit every port in the Caribbean to find him! I at least hoped for assurance that he's alive *somewhere*."

Jacqueline raised a brow.

Judith saw that Catherine was becoming distraught and quickly said, "I'd trust your instincts and start your search in Savannah. It really does seem the most logical place to start. No doubt you will find some new information about your father there. If you'll excuse us, we have some unpacking to do."

Jack dragged Judy away, mumbling under her breath, "Did we have to listen to her life's story?"

"We were being polite, and why did you interrupt me back there?"

"Because you were about to tell her about Amy, which is none of her bloody business."

Judith tsked. "We were just discussing luck, and Amy's *is* phenomenal, you'll have to admit."

"Yes, but that's all it is. Don't think for a minute that Catherine can be trusted, Judy. I don't fully trust Andrássy either, for that matter."

"Really?"

"You don't think it was a bit too convenient, him showing up the night before we leave and ending up on this ship with us? Just because he's got eyes like yours doesn't mean he is a relative."

Judith laughed. "You're forgetting he knows all about the Stephanoffs."

"From a journal that he could simply have found somewhere and decided to use the information in it for some nefarious end."

Judith laughed again. "You don't really believe that."

"All right, maybe not nefarious. And maybe he *is* related by blood. But that doesn't mean he isn't up to no good. So just watch what you say, to both of them. We don't need to spill family secrets just because he *seems* genuine."

Did Jacqueline *have* to mention secrets when Judith had such a big one of her own now?

Chapter Seventeen

"WHERE IS JACQUELINE?" ANDRÁSSY asked Judith when she arrived alone for dinner that night in the captain's cabin.

"She's coming. She's just a little off-kilter today. She overslept this morning, then overslept again from the nap she took this afternoon."

Georgina frowned. "She's not getting sick, is she?"

"She doesn't have a fever. I checked."

"Probably just too much excitement over the last few days," James guessed, and added for his wife, "I wouldn't worry, m'dear."

"Whatever you do, don't suggest she go back to bed," Judith said with a grin. "She's quite annoyed with herself for spending too much time in it today."

After that remark, only Andrássy still looked concerned. Judith wondered again if their new cousin might be a bit smitten by her best friend. But Jacqueline did arrive a few minutes later, eyes bright and wide-awake now, the picture of good health. Vivacious in her greetings, she arrived only a few minutes before Artie and Henry brought in the food, so they all took their seats at the table.

Andrássy had, unfortunately, been placed across from the girls, smack between James and Anthony, which didn't bode well for him. In fact, after what Jacqueline had confided to her after luncheon, Judith suspected Andrássy was in for quite a grilling. Jack had gloated that she wasn't the only one with reservations about Andrássy. She'd overheard their fathers discussing the same thing. Of course, it was *Jack's* father who shared her suspicions that Andrássy might not be who he claimed to be. But then when did James Malory ever take anything at face value? It was a throwback to his wild youth and ten years of raising hell on the high seas to be suspicious first and agreeable later—maybe.

Georgina inadvertently initiated the interrogation of Andrássy with the query "Your sister didn't want to join us for dinner again?"

"I didn't mention it to her."

Georgina glanced at the empty seat at the table. "Why not?"

Another innocent question. But then Georgina was completely trusting, unlike her husband. So James obviously hadn't shared his reservations with his wife yet, only with his brother.

"As I mentioned last night, Catherine has moods and isn't always pleasant company," Andrássy explained.

And he didn't want to subject his new family to that? Judith felt compelled to say, "I've seen her at her worst, but anyone with a severe headache can get snippy, myself included. Jack and I also had a nice conversation with her when she was feeling better."

"I wouldn't call it nice," Jack put in.

"It wasn't unpleasant," Judith insisted.

"Matter of opinion," Jack mumbled for just her ears.

James gave his daughter a quelling look before he said to Andrássy, "So you would describe your stepsister as hot-tempered? Many women are, including my Jack."

Jacqueline laughed, no doubt taking her father's comment as a compliment. But Andrássy said, "I never thought of it that way, merely that she can be moody. A new home, a new father when she wasn't reconciled to giving up finding her real father—it was a difficult time when she and her mother came to live with us."

"What happened to her father?" Katey asked.

Judith stopped listening as the conversation turned to what Catherine had already told her and Jack. She hoped Jacqueline was noting, though, that the pair did pretty much have the same story, which made it even more believable. Who could make up something like that? But Nathan Tremayne came quickly to mind. *He* could. He seemed to be quite adept at tall tales, making himself sound like a hero instead of the criminal he actually was.

She wondered if he had finished his job down in the hold. Likely no, since he probably wasn't *really* a carpenter. Any man could wield a hammer, but did he actually have the skills to build a proper ring? Oh, God, she hoped her uncle and her father didn't get hurt when they used the exercise ring and it fell apart beneath them.

Why didn't she just tell her father about the smuggler so Nathan would be spending the voyage in the brig where he belonged? She should never have agreed to a bargain with him, when it just gave him more time to get creative with his lies. Yet, if she didn't have to keep him a secret from Jack, would she be quite this uneasy about it? And why the deuce did she want to come up with an excuse to leave the table so she could go down to the hold to check on him?

She glanced across the table at Andrássy, who was saying, "It's why she ran away so often when she was a child. She was trying to get back to America where she grew up, so she could look for her father."

"Instead of traveling all over the world looking for someone who could be long dead, why don't you just marry her off?" Anthony suggested.

"I would if I thought it would make her happy. But until this matter of her missing father is settled, I doubt she will ever be happy in a marriage."

"So you're actually concerned about her happiness?" James asked.

"Of course." Andrássy seemed a little insulted to have been asked that. "The tantrums she had as a child were understandable. I don't even mind her temper. As you say, it's not something unique. Many women have one. It's merely embarrassing when it erupts in public. That is all I wanted to warn you about, so you wouldn't take offense if you witness any unpleasantness of that sort. Because of the fire, she has nothing and no one but me to depend on. But she is my burden, not yours."

"Are you going to rebuild?" Georgina asked.

"Perhaps someday, but my wish is to return to Austria where I was schooled and continue my studies there. I paint."

"An artist?"

"I dabble. I hope to do better one day. But I can do nothing with my life until I settle my stepsister's."

"A burden like the one you're shouldering can kill inspiration," James said thoughtfully. "What I don't understand is why you would go so far above and beyond when there isn't even a blood tie between you. Don't take offense, dear boy, but that smacks of coercion on her part. So I must ask, does she have some hold over you that you haven't mentioned?"

"James!" Georgina protested.

But Andrássy actually chuckled. "I am glad you feel you can speak so plainly with me. But consider, I am the last of the Benedek line, but not the last of Maria's line, and yet I would never have known that if Catherine hadn't found my great-grandfather's journal. So when she beseeched me to help her find her missing parent, I couldn't in good conscience deny her when I was about to embark on a similar search myself. For family." Andrássy looked around the table, a warm smile on his face. "You Malorys are so much more than I ever could have imagined. You've welcomed me without reservation." Only Jacqueline looked a little guilty over that comment. "But my father made Catherine a member of my immediate family. Despite the turmoil, he never regretted doing that because her mother made him happy."

"Is it as simple as that? Obligation, responsibility, and a debt you feel you owe?"

"Sounds like something that would rope you in, James," Georgina said with a pointed look. "Oh, wait, it already did, or aren't those the same reasons you agreed to help Gabrielle Brooks?"

He chuckled. "Guilty."

"Not to mention, ending up in a pirate's prison because of it."

"Point *taken*, George."

No one jumped in to explain that byplay to Andrássy, but then it was a touchy subject that the Andersons, wealthy shipbuilders and owners of a large merchant fleet, now had ex-pirates in the family on more than one shore. One long since retired (Georgina's husband, James) and the other turned treasure hunter (Drew's father-in-law, Nathan Brooks), but still, both guilty of wreaking havoc in their day.

Judith steered the conversation back to Andrássy's efforts to help his stepsister, telling him, "I think what you are doing is admirable. You've given Catherine hope, haven't you?"

"Yes, I believe so, but I fear she has yet to learn patience."

Jacqueline opened her mouth, but Judy pinched her under the table, knowing that her cousin was about to say that they'd already experienced the woman's impatience, and that she'd got it into her head that a Malory with Gypsy gifts could help her more than Andrássy could—which wasn't going to happen and didn't need to be discussed.

Judith said to Andrássy, "It may not be a quick undertaking, but you may find that it changes her for the better. You might consider pausing your journey in Bridgeport to allow your sister to have a little fun before you continue on." She stood up then. It was as good an opportunity as she was going to get to slip away before everyone else finished eating. "Now if you will all excuse me, I didn't get as much rest today as Jack did. I'm rather tired."

"Of course, poppet," Anthony said.

But before Judith left, she leaned down and whispered in Jacqueline's ear, "I got your foot out of your mouth. Don't put it back in as soon as I leave."

Jack merely snorted.

Chapter Eighteen

ONLY TWO LANTERNS WERE left burning in the hold, both by the exercise ring, but Judith didn't find Nathan there. The ring wasn't finished but the platform was. The tarpaulin had even been tacked to it, and two of the four posts were secured to the corners. It only needed the other two posts and the ropes strung between them, so Judith figured he thought he could finish that quickly in the morning before James came down to inspect it.

Judith was disappointed that Nathan had quit working for the day as this might well be her last chance to speak with him alone. She supposed she could ask him for instruction on some nautical matter during the voyage, maybe even get him up in the rigging where they *could* speak without being overheard. But then she'd have to wear those unflattering clothes Jack had had made for her, and besides, Jack would say that *she* could teach her anything she wanted to learn about sailing—unless Judith confessed her interest in Nathan. That wouldn't be giving away the secret, would it? Course it wouldn't. Once Jack got a look at the man, it would be blatantly obvious why Judy was interested in him.

She might as well turn in for the night, but she moved over to the ring to examine it first. She thought about climbing up on the platform to make sure its floor was as sturdy as it should be, but it was a bit too high off the floor for her, so she just pressed down on it with her palms.

"Couldn't stay away?"

She swung around with a gasp. Nathan was sitting on the floor between two crates, one of which still had her coat draped over it. He was leaning back against the bulkhead, holding a plate in one hand and a fork in the other.

She slowly walked over to him, noting that at least he had his shirt back on, and yet her heartbeat still accelerated. "I thought you'd gone."

"Only long enough to fetch some dinner. Damn fancy grub for a ship, too. Definitely not what we were served on the short trip from Hampshire to London."

"There probably wasn't an actual cook aboard yet. The one we have now isn't a seaman. My aunt and uncle sail with their own servants, most of whom boarded in London."

"All the luxuries of home, eh? But now I'm never going to be happy with my own cook again."

She smiled at his grumbling tone. "You actually have one? I thought smugglers only make short jaunts across the Channel and back, hardly long enough at sea to warrant needing a cook aboard."

"I wouldn't know. But I'll take your word for it, since you seem to know more about smuggling than I do. But have a seat. You can watch me eat while you tell me about my life."

Sarcasm, and quite blatant, too. Yet his tone was friendly, his lips even turned up in a grin. So he was merely teasing her again?

"I came for my coat," she said, though she sat down on top of it again anyway.

"I was going to return it to you."

She raised a brow. "How, without giving away that I was down here?"

"You don't think I could have found you alone?"

"Not when I'm with Jack most of the day and we're with our family in the evenings, so, no, I don't think so."

He chuckled. "I have a bed in the carpenter's store-room. Well, at the risk of stirring up a hornet's nest, I'll mention it's just a cot." He waited, but she wasn't going to address the cot issue again and merely snorted at his assumption that she would. So he continued, "But I've claimed it as my own for a little privacy. You're welcome to visit any night you feel like—"

"Stop it. You might find this all very amusing, but you should recall, you still have a noose hanging over your head."

"Breaking a bargain? Really? Thought you nobles had more honor than that."

"It was a silly bargain—"

"But it was struck—even sealed. Ah, there's that blush I remember so well."

"You are insufferable."

"No, I just have a lot on my plate, including you. And if your word is as wishy-washy as a mood, then it's not reliable, is it?"

"I'm keeping it, but only for the duration of the voyage as we agreed."

"That wasn't the stipulation."

"*That* was a foregone conclusion," she stressed, not giving in on that point. "But don't worry, you'll have time to disappear after we dock."

"Think you'll want me to by then?"

The question implied they were going to get much more intimately acquainted. His tone had even dropped to a husky timbre! It jarred her and brought all sorts of questions to mind that she should be asking herself, not him. She was *too* attracted to this man and out of her depth to deal with it. It had held her back from doing what she should have done the moment she realized who he was. It had impelled her to strike the Bargain. But she couldn't let that last question stand.

"You and I won't—"

His short laugh cut her off. "I merely meant, by the time we dock you'll be convinced that I'm innocent and not the blackguard you wrongly think I am."

Was she using her suspicion as an excuse to keep herself from giving in to this attraction? No, he was just good at stirring up doubt.

She reminded him pertly, "Our bargain was for the truth. Do you even know how to tell it?"

"Course I do, darlin'. But d'you know how to recognize it when you hear it?" Yet he didn't wait for an answer, not that there was one when his tactics were so evasive. Instead, he got back to the subject he didn't get to finish that morning. "So tell me how a woman gets a nickname like Jack?"

"Because it's not a nickname. It's the name her father gave her at birth."

"Really?"

"Of course the fact that her maternal uncles, who James doesn't like the least little bit, were all present at the birthing might have influenced his decision a tad, but he couldn't be swayed to change it."

"He's that stubborn?"

Judith smiled. "Depends on who you ask, but in this case, he was absolutely inflexible. However, Jack's mother, George, made sure—"

"Good God, another woman with a man's name?"

"No, Georgina is her real name. James just calls her George. Always has, always will. But she made sure Jacqueline appeared on her daughter's birth record. Nonetheless, among the family the name Jack had already stuck."

"I'm guessing that explains the odd name of this ship, *The Maiden George*?"

"Yes, James's original ship was named *The Maiden Anne*, but he sold her when he retired from the sea. This one he had built when Jack's mother wanted to take Jack to Connecticut to see where she was born. An unnecessary expense, really, when George and her brothers own Skylark Shipping, which is a very large fleet of American merchant ships, and at least one of them is docked in England at any given time. But as I mentioned, my uncle doesn't exactly like his five Anderson brothers-in-law. He refuses to sail on their vessels short of a dire emergency. And now it's my turn to ask a question."

He stood up abruptly at the noise suddenly coming from the animals down at the end of the hold. She looked in that direction, too. Probably just a rat scurrying past them, or a cat on the prowl for one. But Nathan set his plate down on the other crate and went to investigate anyway.

Not exactly adhering to the Bargain of tit for tat with questions, she noted with some annoyance, which she would point out when he came back. But he didn't come back. . . .

Chapter Nineteen

NATHAN DIDN'T EXPECT TO find anything in the back of the hold. He just didn't want to lose his advantage in this bout of verbal sparring with Judith, which would have happened if she started interrogating him again so soon. He preferred to keep her distracted from the facts as long as possible, or at least until he could better ascertain her reaction to them.

He hadn't decided if he should appeal to her sympathy—if she had any—with some truths he could share? Or admit everything, including that he owned the house in Hampshire and had a pardon waiting for him? Unfortunately, he didn't think she was likely to believe either. But if he told her too much and did convince her that he was innocent, their bargain would come to an end and he'd lose her company. And he liked her company. Liked teasing her, too. Liked the way her mouth pursed in annoyance. Liked the way her eyes could spark with anger or humor. Definitely liked the way she'd felt in his arms. Bleedin' hell, there was nothing about her that he didn't like—other than her stubborn insistence that he was a smuggler. *Why* was she so certain? What was he missing?

He was jumped the moment he passed the crate where the man had been crouched in hiding, and it was his own damn fault for having his mind filled with Judith instead of the matter at hand. And it was no scrawny runt either that tackled him to the floor. He was nearly as big as Nathan. In the brief glimpse he'd caught of him, he'd seen a young man with queued-back blond hair and dark eyes, who was barefoot but not poorly clad in a shirt made of fine linen and a fancy gold link chain at his neck. Nathan didn't recognize him as a member of the crew, and he doubted one of the servants Judith had mentioned would attack him.

The noise of their hard landing startled the chickens into squawking and set one of the pigs squealing. Nathan was only startled for a moment before instinct kicked in. He rolled, taking the man with him, and got in one solid punch before he was thrust back and the man scrambled to his feet. But he didn't run. He pulled a dagger from the back of his britches and took a swipe at Nathan just as Nathan got to his feet. He felt the sting of the blade on his chest, but didn't look down to check the damage. His anger kicked in full force because of it.

He'd never been in a knife fight before and had no weapon on him to counter it. He could have improvised with a hammer or a file, but his toolbox was too far away and he would likely get that dagger in his back if he ran for it. He positioned his arms instead to block the next swipe, but doubting that would be effective, he just tried to stay out of reach instead. But that wasn't going to be possible for much longer.

Weighing his options, he saw they were sorely lacking. Knock the dagger out of the man's hand so he could have a fair fight with him, which he knew he could win, or send Judith for help if she hadn't already run out of there. The second option didn't appeal to him in the least, and he would be dead before assistance arrived. Then a third option slid across the floor and stopped near his feet. His hammer.

The man spotted it, too, and quickly stepped forward with his dagger extended to move Nathan back from it. There was no time to think, but there was no way he was giving up the opportunity Judith had just given him. He turned his back on the man, dropped to the floor, and, bracing his hands on the floor, kicked backward. He didn't connect with his attacker, but it startled the man sufficiently to give Nathan the time he needed to grasp the hammer and rise to his feet, swinging it. He connected with the man's shoulder and the man stepped back. Nathan had the upper hand now and they both knew it.

He took the offensive with some steady swings. Sparks flew when the hammerhead struck the blade, but the blond man held fast to his dagger, although Nathan had him moving backward. He'd soon be out of room to maneuver with the animal pen behind him, but he might not know that yet.

With the advantage his now and not wanting to actually kill the man, Nathan said, "Give it up, man. Better than getting your head bashed in."

"Bugger off!" the man snarled, but desperation was in his expression, which warned Nathan the man was about to try something, and he did, flipping the dagger in his hand so he was holding it by the tip and raising his arm to throw it. Nathan only had a second to react, and the quickest way to get out of the path of that dagger or to stop it was to dive at the man.

He did, plowing them both into the fence of the animal pen, which broke with their combined weight. They hit the ground, animals scattering and raising a cacophony of panicked noises. But Nathan pressed his broad chest against his attacker's dagger arm so the man couldn't move his weapon, if indeed he still held it. Letting go of the hammer, Nathan smashed his fist into the man's face, once, twice, three times. Twice had been enough to knock him out.

Nathan took a deep breath and sat up. The dagger was still within his assailant's reach so Nathan shoved it out of the pen before he glanced down at his chest to see if he was wounded. The blade had sliced open his shirt and his skin stung. He'd been scratched, but not seriously enough to draw more than a few drops of blood.

"Are you all right?"

She was still there? He glanced up and saw how upset she looked and assured her, "I'm fine."

"But he attacked you. Why?!"

"Damned if I know." He got to his feet and dragged the man out of the pen before he added, "He's not a member of the crew, obviously."

She was frowning down at the man. "He's not a member of my uncle's kitchen staff either. I know them all."

"Must be a stowaway then."

"But stowaways don't try to kill people once they've been discovered."

She had a point. It was a minor crime that usually only got the culprit some time in the brig or forced labor until the ship reached land. Then most captains would simply let the stowaway go. The man's aggression didn't make much sense. He couldn't have been in the hold since they'd left London. Nathan was sure of that. The animals would have given him away sooner, and sailors who came down here several times a day for provisions would have noticed him. The man had to have been hiding somewhere else and snuck down here when Nathan went to fetch his dinner.

He grabbed a crate and used it to block the broken part of the fence so all the animals didn't get out before he could repair it.

Judith, watching him, suddenly gasped. "You're hurt!"

"No, it's nothing."

"Let me see."

She rushed over to him. He rolled his eyes at her, but she was too intent on opening the tear in his shirt wider so she could check his wound. But it gave him time to realize she was a little more concerned than she ought to be about someone she wanted to see in prison. Was she so compassionate that she'd help anyone in need?

She finally brought her eyes back to his. "It's just a scratch."

He smiled. "I know. You should have run the other way when the fight started, but I'm glad you didn't. The hammer tipped the scales in my favor. Clever of you to think of it."

She blushed. "I got angry that he wasn't fighting fairly. I *did* think about hitting him with a plank of lumber first, but I had no confidence that my swing would be effective."

He laughed at the image that brought up. He seemed to be doing a lot of that around her—yet another reason why he liked her company. "Never thought I would end up grateful for that temper of yours or have to thank you for it, but you definitely have my thanks, darlin'."

"You're welcome."

He bent down and hefted the unconscious man over his shoulder.

"Where are you taking him?"

"Your uncle needs to be informed about this, so take your coat and go before the commotion starts. He could order the entire ship searched tonight for more stowaways, and I doubt you want to be found down here."

"Quite right. I'm leaving now. No need to wait on me."

He still paused at the stairway to make sure Judith was safely out of there before he went up. The possibility that there was more than one stowaway would explain why the unconscious man had jumped Nathan instead of just giving himself up. Had he been distracting Nathan from finding his partner? When Nathan reached the main deck, he dropped his heavy load.

The man didn't stir even a little, but Nathan couldn't leave him there alone, so he simply yelled for the first mate. Only a few sailors were on deck at that time of night, but they came forward to investigate, one of them bringing a lantern.

"Cor, you decked one of the cap'n's London servants?" a sailor guessed. "Cap' won't be pleased."

"Fetch him and we'll find out," Nathan replied.

Artie arrived and peered down at the man. "He don't belong here. Where'd you find him, Mr. Tremayne?"

Nathan explained to Artie what had happened, then had to repeat it all when the captain joined them. If Malory was annoyed that someone would dare board his ship without permission, he hid it well. In fact, the man's face was without expression of any sort.

"He's not one of the crew, Cap'n, and from what Mr. Tremayne is telling us, he doesn't appear to be a typical stowaway, either," Artie pointed out.

"No, he doesn't." James stared down at the man and nudged him with the toe of his boot to see if he was close to coming round yet, but the man didn't move. "Did you have to hit him quite so hard, Mr. Tremayne?"

"I dropped my hammer first" was all Nathan said in his defense.

The slight quirk to the captain's lips was too brief to tell if it was amusement. "Our conclusion that he's not on board for the ride begs the question, what is he doing on my ship?" James said. "And why hasn't someone fetched water yet so we can bring him to and ascertain that?"

But the moment a sailor ran off for a bucket, Andrássy appeared with sword in hand, yelling, "How dare he endanger my family? I'll kill him!"

The count looked enraged enough to do just that as he ran down from the quarterdeck. Nathan leapt toward him to stop him.

Looking annoyed, James did, too, shoving Andrássy back. "What the devil d'you think you're doing?" James demanded ominously. "I need answers, not blood."

"But—are the women not in danger?" Andrássy asked, lowering his sword.

"Bloody hell," James snarled. "Just stay out of—"

"Cap'n!"

Nathan turned back and saw that the stowaway must have leapt to his feet, knocked down the only sailor still next to him, the one who'd just yelled, while they'd been distracted, and dived over the side of the ship. Nathan only saw the man's legs before he disappeared.

Incredulous, Nathan ran to the rail. "What the devil? Does he think he can swim back to England?"

The others had come to the rail, too. One sailor shouted, "Should we fish him out?"

"How?" the one with the lantern said in frustration as he held it over the rail. "Do you even see him down there? I don't."

Nathan couldn't spot the man either. Unlike last night when the sky had been clear, tonight a long bank of clouds covered the moon. More men arrived with more lanterns, but the light still didn't extend far enough for them to spot the stowaway. Nathan could hear the sounds of splashing, which indicated the stowaway was swimming away from the ship. And then he heard something else. . . .

"Oars," he said to James. "There's at least one rowboat nearby, so there must be a ship, too."

"Artie!" James started barking orders. "Get every man on deck armed in case this is a sneak attack. You two"—he pointed at the sailors—"get one of our smaller boats in the water and go after them. If it's not an attack, I want that bloody stowaway back. Henry, get the man in the crew with the best night vision and send him up in the rigging. I want to know what's happening down there."

Nathan ran to the other side of the ship, but he *still* couldn't see anything in the water. Moving around the ship, he did ascertain that the sound of the oars could only be heard on the side of the ship where the man had jumped. The sound was growing fainter, and finally it could only be heard from the stern.

He was on his way to inform James of that when Walter, the sailor with the best night vision, who hadn't needed to climb far to use it, called out, "Behind us, Captain!"

James moved to the stern immediately with the crew following him. Artie handed him his spyglass, but James didn't bother to use it. He glanced up at the thick clouds overhead instead and swore foully.

But Walter yelled down again: "Just one rowboat, moving swiftly back to the big ship. Our boat isn't close yet, Captain. Doesn't look like we can overtake it."

Then the clouds thinned, just enough for the moon to cast a dim light on the water. James quickly brought up the spyglass and said a moment later, "She's three masted and fully rigged—and pulling about to show off her cannon."

"To fire on us?" someone asked.

"No, she's not close enough. I'm guessing it's merely a maneuver to deter us from attempting to bring their man back for questioning. Artie, call our boat back. I'm not going to risk their lives if they don't have a chance of overtaking the other boat." Then James swore again as the light faded. "Bloody mysteries, I deplore them."

The comment hadn't been directed at any one of them in particular, but members of the crew tried to figure out what had just happened.

"Not piracy or they would have fired on us."

"Only one rowboat, so it wasn't a sneak raid," someone else said.

"For that rowboat to be halfway to *The Maiden George* when the man jumped means that a rendezvous had to be arranged for sometime tonight," Nathan speculated.

"Since I am doubtful of coincidences, I agree," James said. "But we have been at sea only two days. What could he have expected to accomplish in so little time?"

"Sabotage," Artie offered.

"To sink us?" James shook his head. "Too drastic and forfeits innocent lives."

"Perhaps they don't care," Artie said, "But I'll have the ship searched from top to bottom."

"If he was here for revenge, he might have been prepared to do the killing tonight and then jump ship."

"But you caught him first? I suppose that is possible, but my enemies tend to be impatient. The man would have tried to kill me by now if he wanted me dead. I suppose the crew can be questioned to find out if anyone else has a relentless enemy."

Nathan did, but Grigg wouldn't send a man on a suicide mission to kill him even if he had discovered Nathan was on this ship, so he didn't mention it. He suggested something not quite as nefarious instead.

"It could be that the stowaway was retrieving something that ended up on the ship by accident. He might have thought he could find it in a couple of days and maybe he did. He could have been waiting for me to leave the hold where he was hiding, but I found him instead."

"That possibility isn't wholly implausible, but it doesn't explain his immediately attacking you instead of trying to talk his way out of the hold. He could have claimed to be a crewman or a servant. No one but the first mates knows everyone aboard my ship."

Which was how the man could have gotten around on the ship without much notice, to eat and do whatever else he was there to do, Nathan thought. But he was done guessing when that's all they could do. It accomplished nothing.

"Do we turn about then, Cap'n?" one of the men asked.

"No, we're not giving chase, not with my family aboard," James said. "But I want constant surveillance of that ship that's trailing us. If it approaches, I want to know about it. And set up shifts of armed crewmen to patrol *The Maiden George* tonight."

"I'm beginning to hate mysteries m'self," Nathan mumbled.

James nodded and turned to his first mate. "I suspect this will go unsolved for the time being, but gather the rest of the crew and search the supplies for anything out of the ordinary. And every nook and cranny, for that matter, to make sure this wasn't a joint undertaking. Give me the results as soon as you're finished. I'm going back to my cabin." Then James paused to turn to Nathan again. "Did you finish my ring, Mr. Tremayne?"

"I'll have it done within the hour, Captain."

"It can wait until morning. You've done enough for one day."

Nathan nodded. "You said 'unsolved for the time being.' Do you think they'll continue to follow us if they didn't get what they were after?"

"Oh, I'm quite depending on it."

Chapter Twenty

JUDITH COULDN'T BELIEVE SHE was going to do this. Again. It was so against her nature to sneak about like this. There had to be another way to talk to Nathan without stirring up any curiosity about it. But she couldn't think of anything.

She hurried down to the lower level, aware that she had so little time she might as well not even bother. It was midmorning already. She hadn't meant to sleep this late and Jack would be looking for her soon if she didn't oversleep again, too. She might, though, after coming to Judith's cabin last night before she retired. Jack had had to share with her everything that she'd learned from her father about the stowaway, and Judith couldn't even admit she already knew half of it. Darned secrets . . .

She found Nathan putting his tools away. The exercise ring was finished. And he'd already repaired the animal pen. A few more minutes and she would have missed him.

He confirmed that, saying, "I was just leaving. Didn't think you were going to pay me a visit—and what the devil are you wearing?"

"Clothes that are easy to put on. My maid let me oversleep and I was too impatient to wait for her to come back. As it is, I don't have much time to spare."

The way he was staring at her britches brought on a blush. She'd tucked them into midcalf-high riding boots, but the britches weren't thick. Jack liked her clothes comfortable, which usually meant soft. So Judith didn't tuck in the long, white shirt, allowing it to fully cover her derriere instead, but she did belt it. She had no doubt she looked ridiculous, but that's not what his green eyes were saying.

"You're actually allowed to dress like that?"

"On board ship, yes. I wore breeches the last time I sailed years ago. My mother agreed. Better than a skirt flapping in the wind."

"For a child, maybe, but you're a woman now with curves that—"

"Stop looking!" she snapped.

He laughed. "There are some things a man just can't do, darlin'."

Her eyes narrowed. "Are you deliberately wasting what little time I have before Jack starts wondering where I am?"

His eyes came back to hers. "Doesn't work out well, you having me at your beck and call, does it? Not if you have to arrange it around your cousin."

She'd already figured that out but did he have to sound so amused about it? "If you have somewhere else to be, by all means—"

She didn't get to finish. He actually put his hands on her waist and set her on the crate next to him. It was a bit high for her to have chosen as a seat, leaving her feet dangling a few inches off the floor. But then he sat down on it next to her! It wasn't wide enough for two. Well, it was, but not without their thighs touching.

She might not even have noticed it if she were wearing a skirt and petticoats, but in the thin, black britches, she could feel every bit of his leg against hers and the warmth coming from it. She could feel the warmth of his upper arm, too, as it pressed against hers, since he wasn't wearing a jacket. The position was far too intimate, reminding her of how it had felt being pressed to his half-naked body yesterday when he'd kissed her. . . .

That pleasant fluttering she'd experienced yesterday showed up to fluster her further. She started to get down until she realized that sitting side by side, she wouldn't have to look at him and get snared by his handsome face and sensual eyes. If she could just ignore that they were touching. If she could not wonder if he had put them in proximity because he wanted to kiss her again. She groaned to herself. She was *never* going to get any answers from him if this attraction kept getting in the way.

"Where did you grow up?" she blurted out. There, one simple question he couldn't possibly evade.

He did. "Does it matter?"

Staring intently at the exercise ring in front of them, which was well lit with two lanterns hanging on its posts, she demanded, "Is this really how you're going to adhere to the Bargain?"

"Well, if I say where I was raised, you're just going to take it wrong."

"Oh, good grief, you grew up in Cornwall?" she guessed. "Yes, of course. The one place in England well-known for smugglers. Why did I bother to ask?"

"I warned you'd take it wrong. But Cornwall has everything every other shire has, including nabobs, so don't paint everyone who resides there with your suspicions."

"Point taken."

"Really?" he said in surprise. "You can actually be reasonable about something?"

"I favor logic, and that was a logical statement about a region."

He snorted. "I've given you lots of logic—"

"No, you haven't, not on matters that pertain to you personally. So did you learn carpentry before or after you took to the seas?"

"It's my turn."

"What? Oh, very well, ask away. I have no secrets to hide other than *you*."

"I rather like being your secret."

Why did that bring on a blush? Just because his tone dropped to a sensual level didn't mean he intended it to. Or it could mean he did. The man *could* be trying to deliberately discompose her. Or was he getting as caught up in this attraction as she was? The thought made her feel almost giddy. If he wasn't a criminal—but he was, and she had to keep that firmly in mind.

"Was that a question?" she asked.

He chuckled. "How big is your family?"

"Immediate? Both parents are hale and hearty. My sister, Jaime, is two years younger than I and doesn't take well to sailing, so she stayed home with my mother. My half sister, Katey, is much older and is aboard with her husband, Boyd."

"I meant the lot of you."

She suspected he didn't, but she answered anyway. "Don't think I've ever counted the number. My father is the youngest of four brothers. They've all got wives and children, even a few grandchildren, so if I had to guess offhand, there's more'n thirty of us."

It sounded as if he choked back a laugh. She was *not* going to glance his way to be sure. Keeping her eyes off him was working—somewhat. At least she'd stopped wondering if he was going to kiss her—oh, God, now she couldn't think of anything else. It had been thrilling, if a little overwhelming, but the feelings it had stirred in her had been too nice not to want to experience them again.

"—most of my life," he was saying.

"What?"

"Your previous question."

"But what did you just say?"

"Where *did* your mind wander off to?"

The humor in his tone made her wonder if he already knew, which made her blush even more. "Would you just start over, please?"

"When you ask so nicely, of course. I said that I was a sailor first, that I sailed with my father most of my life."

"Except for the three years you worked as a carpenter. You mentioned that to my uncle. Where and why did you learn that trade if you already had a job with your father?"

"No cheating, darlin'. That's three questions in a row you're asking."

She huffed, "I wouldn't have to if you would elaborate, instead of giving me terse answers that only lead to a dozen more questions."

He chuckled. "So you adhere to logic and exaggeration, oh, and let's not forget stubbornness. I'm starting a list."

"And you adhere to evasion. D'you really think that isn't obvious?"

"You know, I'm having a hard time keeping my hands off you."

She sucked in her breath, her eyes flying to his. His

expression said that he wasn't just trying to distract her. Blatant desire, poignant and sensual. It struck a chord, lit a flame. . . .

"Just thought you should know," he added, then looking away, asked, "Where did you grow up?"

Judith needed a moment to come back to earth. Actually, longer. As if he *had* touched her, her nipples still tingled from hardening, her pulse was still racing. She would like to think she would have stopped him from kissing her just then, but she knew she wouldn't have. Why didn't he!?

Oh, God, the man was more dangerous than she'd thought—to her senses. She jumped off the crate to put some distance between them. She was going to have to be more cautious of his tactics.

"London," she said, and said no more. Still watching him, she noticed when his mouth tightened just a little, but enough to guess he didn't like short answers either. "Annoying, isn't it, lack of elaboration?"

"I'll survive."

She snorted at his glib answer. "Well, since I'm usually more thorough, I'll add, I was born and raised in London, as well as tutored there. In fact, I rarely left the city except to visit family in other parts of England, such as Hampshire, where I first met you."

"And at least twice to America."

She smiled. "Before I comment on that, I require another answer from you. Why did you learn carpentry if you already were working with your father?"

He glanced at her again and laughed heartily. She liked the way humor disarmed him so thoroughly, his face, his mouth, his eyes, all revealed it. It said that he was getting used to her and wasn't the least bit afraid that she might land him in jail. Confidence that he could change her mind about him, or actual innocence? There was the rub. If she had that answer by now, then she wouldn't be here—or she would, just for a different reason.

He addressed her last question. "I had a row with my father that led to my leaving Cornwall for good when I was twenty. I ended up settling in Southampton, which is where I took up carpentry."

She repaid him in kind. "My first trip to America was with Jack, too, to visit her mother's hometown of Bridgeport. This trip is for her come-out there before we have another in London. It's unusual to have two, of course, but her American uncles insisted. If you don't know what a come-out entails—"

"I do. It's what you nabobs do to get yourselves a husband. So you're going on the marriage mart, are you? Somehow, I didn't expect you'd need to."

Had he just given her a compliment, but in a derogatory tone? "I don't *need* to. I've lost count of how many men have already petitioned my father for permission to court me this summer."

"So you've got a host of eager suitors waiting for you to return to England?"

"No, as it happens, my father threw all those hopeful gentlemen out of the house. He didn't appreciate the reminder that I was approaching a marriageable age."

"Good for him."

She raised a brow. "Really? Why would you side with him about that?"

"Because women don't need to get married as soon as they can."

"You're talking about someone you know personally, aren't you?" she guessed.

He nodded. "My sister. She should have waited for a better man who could have made her happy instead of accepting the first offer to come her way. It didn't turn out well."

Judith waited a moment for him to continue, but she heard the sound of approaching voices. She gasped. "That's my father and uncle."

"Bleedin' hell. Hide."

Chapter Twenty-One

THE TIMING WAS HORRIBLE on all accounts. Nathan had just opened up, answering questions without asking any of his own. That could have gone much further if they weren't interrupted. But Judith didn't need to be told to hide. She was hurrying toward the crates when Nathan's arm hooked around her waist and she was pretty much deposited on the floor behind one. At least she had room to hide there because none of the supplies were placed close to the hull since it needed to be checked regularly for leaks. It was one of Nathan's jobs as the ship's carpenter—when he wasn't being interrogated by the captain's niece.

She crouched down behind the crate with a few moments to spare before she could distinguish her father, just entering the hold, saying, ". . . answered too readily, without a single pause. Didn't have to think about it even once."

"And your point?" James replied.

"Thought that would convince you the lad is telling the truth."

"I never called him a liar, Tony. He can be exactly who he says he is and still have an agenda other than the simple one he claims. Telling us nothing but the truth doesn't mean he hasn't left out some pertinent details."

It almost sounded as if they were talking about Nathan, but Judith knew better. They were discussing Andrássy, although Nathan might not guess that. And why hadn't he left yet? She could still see him standing between the two crates by his tools, his back to the entrance, and less than two feet from her. He was providing her with more concealment, but she could tell from the aggressive set of his wide shoulders that he was tense. Did he expect a confrontation? Or just expect he might have to protect her from one? Decent of him, but she wouldn't let it come to that.

As if she weren't anxious enough, she felt dread when it occurred to her why her father and her uncle had come down here. To use the new ring. They wouldn't be leaving soon, which meant she couldn't leave either. It also meant they'd hear Jack calling for her when she didn't see her on deck, and that would be anytime now. She could even imagine her father initiating a search of the ship by everyone on board.

James's voice had sounded farther away, as if he'd already gotten into the ring. Judith didn't peek around the crate to find out for sure. But once they started sparring, they might be distracted enough for her to slip out of there. She'd have to crawl most of the way behind the supplies, but that would be easy enough to do in her britches.

"My nephew's wife has hair like yours," Anthony said in a deceptively affable tone.

Judith's eyes flared wide. It sounded as if her father was standing right in front of the crate she was hiding behind! But she knew he was talking to Nathan.

"Be a good chap and tell me you *aren't* related to the Hilary family."

"Never heard of them," Nathan replied cautiously.

"Good."

Judith didn't have to see it to know her father had just punched Nathan in the gut. The sound was unmistakable. But *why?* And not just once. She winced with each blow that followed. She knew how brutal her father could be when it came to landing punches. Was Nathan even trying to defend himself? She was afraid to look. She couldn't *not* look.

Nathan ducked the next blow. He'd maneuvered the fight so Anthony's back was to her. James was facing her from his position in the ring, but his eyes were on the two men below him and his tone was quite dry when he said, "You're allowed to fight back, Mr. Tremayne. My brother won't be satisfied unless you do."

Nathan blocked a blow to his face and followed it with a right jab that caught Anthony in the chin and snapped his head back slightly. She winced for her father now, yet she wondered if he wasn't secretly pleased that he wasn't going to win easily. He loved a good fight. There wasn't a Malory who didn't know it. But if he appreciated that Nathan *wasn't* flat on his back yet, he gave no indication of it. He continued to deliver blow after blow, concentrating on Nathan's midsection, while Nathan got in two more punches to Anthony's chin and cheek.

James finally said, "Enough, Tony. I don't want him damaging his hands on you. He needs them to do his job."

"Someone else can do his bloody job," Anthony replied in a snarl.

"Actually, they can't," James rejoined. "We only have one carpenter aboard."

"*He's* the one found your hidden miscreant last night?"

"Yes."

One more punch. "Very well, I'm done. I shall consider us even—Tremayne, is it? Unless you do something to tip the scales again."

"Your idea of *even* stinks—my lord."

Judith groaned to herself at that less than conciliatory answer, but Anthony merely seemed to be amused by it and quipped, "On the contrary, dear boy. You're still standing, aren't you?"

James offered magnanimously, "If you need to rest up after your exertions, Tony, I can wait another day to test out this ring."

"Bite your tongue, old man. That was just a warm-up." Anthony proved it by joining James in the ring.

Nathan should have left, but instead he sat on the crate that Judith was still hiding behind. She was sitting cross-legged now, facing the hull, her back against the crate. She assumed Nathan was just catching his breath, watching the action in the ring.

So she was surprised a few minutes later to hear him say in a low, if incredulous tone, "How does he do that at his age and after what I just meted out to him?"

He was talking about the punches her father and her uncle were doling out to each other in the ring. She whispered back, "Don't equate age with skill. My father has had years of conditioning, not to mention frequent matches with his brother like the one you're watching now."

Nathan snorted quietly. "I gave you the opportunity to leave—why didn't you?"

She didn't answer that and instead asked, "Did he hurt you?"

"What d'you think?"

"How badly?"

"I might survive."

She started to frown until she recognized the teasing note in his voice. There was something else she wanted to know. "What did you do to provoke his anger?"

"I have to be at fault?"

"I know my father. I can tell when he holds a grudge against someone. Why?"

"I might have knocked him out on the London docks before we sailed."

She gasped. "How? The only one he *ever* loses to is my uncle James."

"Caught him by surprise, you could say. But you heard him. We're even now."

She almost said, "Don't count on it," but she didn't want him to turn leery of talking to her because of her father. That might happen anyway now, but she wasn't going to help it along.

Then he added, "Go now while they're distracted. Stay low."

"You should leave as well."

"Not a chance. People have to pay to watch fights of this caliber. Besides, don't take it wrong, darlin', but I want to see your old man lose."

That infuriated her, enough to make her hiss, "You won't see it today. Mark my words, my uncle is going to *let* him win that bout."

"Why would he do a fool thing like that?" Nathan sounded surprised.

"Because those two are very close. It might not always seem like it, but they are. And because it will soothe ruffled feathers, even put my father in a good mood—which might help him to forget about you for the duration of the voyage. Just don't expect my uncle to do you that favor after we dock and you're no longer working for him."

Chapter Twenty-Two

$\sim$ ❧❧ $\sim$

"I PROB'LY SHOULD HAVE MENTIONED this sooner, but someone's caught my eye," Judith told her cousin.

They were sitting in the middle of the double bed in Jacqueline's cabin, both cross-legged, cards in hand, more cards on the blanket between them. Jack was barefoot and wearing her ship togs, which she would probably wear every day until they docked. Judith still preferred not to wear them and even more so after seeing Nathan's reaction to them. She was outfitted in a simple, blue day dress with short-capped sleeves.

They often played whist by themselves, despite its being a four-person game. They merely skirted the rules with each of them playing an extra hand. It was not as exciting with only one player to worry about instead of three, but it passed the time for them, and Judith found it more fun than a game of chess, which Jack *always* won.

But Jacqueline didn't even glance up at Judith after her statement, which Judith found rather disappointing because it had taken her several days to get up the nerve to make it. But she was still tense. Normally she'd be bubbling with excitement when she shared something like this, but she was too worried that she'd inadvertently reveal too much.

"In London?" Jack asked as she picked up her extra hand to play a card from it.

"No, on board."

That got Jack's immediate attention and a laugh. "Good God, not Andrássy! I know he's quite handsome, but he's our cousin."

Judith found the mistake amusing enough to point out, "Too distant to count, actually. What would you add to it, that he's our fifth cousin, sixth, tenth, when they usually stop adding numbers after second? But no, it's not Andrássy."

"Who then? There's no one else aboard except common sailors—oh, no, you don't!" Jack made a sound that was half gasp, half snort. "It's a good thing you mentioned it so we can nip this in the bud *right* now. Your parents will never let you go to a man who doesn't have at least *some* prospects!"

Judith rolled her eyes. "Are you forgetting what happened when I turned eighteen? Half my inheritance from my mother was turned over to me, more money than any one family could ever need. Prospects, I believe, won't be an issue."

"That's beside the bloody point and you know it," Jack was quick to stress.

"You're being a snob."

"I am not! Just realistic. Of course if you intend to elope instead of getting permission, then I won't say another word."

Judith started laughing, couldn't help it. This was not how she'd expected this conversation to go. But at least her tension was gone for the moment, thanks to Jacqueline's overprotective nature.

"You are getting *so* far ahead of yourself, Jack. I didn't say I've found my future husband. I'm just highly intrigued by this man and want to get to know him better, perhaps find a few moments alone with him when we could speak freely. And he's not just a common sailor, he's a carpenter." *And my ghost,* she wanted to add, but instead mentioned what Nathan had told James about his stolen ship.

Jack grinned, which brought forth her dimples. "Alone with him, eh? Are you sure you won't be too nervous to say a word, let alone have a conversation? You've never been alone with a man who isn't a relative."

"I think I can manage. And we're on a ship. It's not as if he can hie off with me or one of your father's sailors or servants wouldn't be within shouting distance."

Jack chuckled. "Point taken. And he does sound quite interesting. His name?"

"Nathan Tremayne."

Jack raised a golden brow so like her father's habit. "I even like the sound of it." But then she speculated aloud, "Judith Tremayne. Judy Tre—"

"I *told* you I'm not—"

"Yes, yes. And *we're* not getting married for at least a year. Doesn't mean you can't take that long to get to know this chap. Besides, options are good things to have, and you'll want lots before the time comes to choose a husband." Then Jack scooted off the bed, scattering their cards and pulling Judith with her.

"Where are we going?"

Jack tossed her some shoes, but didn't bother getting a

pair for herself. "I have to meet this young man of yours for myself. Let's go find him."

Judith wasn't about to protest when she hadn't actually seen Nathan for two days. And she'd looked for him each time she came on deck. But short of sneaking around and looking for him, which she had decided she was never going to do again, she hadn't been able to find him and had concluded that his job was keeping him busy elsewhere.

They found him in the first place Jacqueline looked, in the carpenter's storeroom. Jack knew exactly where it was, but then she'd explored every inch of this ship the last time they'd sailed on it. And learned every aspect of running it, too. Of course, she hadn't given up yet on her goal of being a pirate back then. She'd even tried to teach Judith everything she was learning, but Judith, not sharing the same interest, had only listened with half an ear.

The room was smaller than their cabins, but big enough for one man to work in. Materials weren't stored here, but in the hold. Only a long workbench and a wide assortment of tools were kept in the room. And the narrow cot Nathan had mentioned, replete with rumpled bedding to show he'd been using it.

He was standing at his bench twisting apart old ropes to make oakum from the fibers, which was typically applied between planks in the hull to keep them from leaking. Judith vaguely recalled Jack's mentioning the process. His white shirt was tucked in, half-unbuttoned and sweat stained, the sleeves rolled up. The door had been open, but the room was still hot. His hair wasn't quite long enough to club back, but he'd tied a bandanna across his brow to keep the sweat from his eyes. Some of his shorter locks had escaped it. It made him look roguish, and far too masculine.

Jacqueline, having pulled Judith into the room with her, was definitely caught by surprise, enough to whisper, "You forgot to mention he's a bloody Corinthian and so handsome it hurts the eyes."

Judith's cheeks lit up instantly, but Nathan didn't appear to have heard the whisper. As he turned toward them, he merely stated, "You must be Jack."

"Judy mentioned me? Yes, of course she did. And did she tell you that neither she nor I am getting married this year? Shopping, just not buying yet. Keep that in mind, Nate."

He laughed, that deep rumble Judith had missed hearing. "Has anyone ever told you that you're a little too outspoken for your age?"

"Wouldn't matter if they did," Jack retorted. "Malorys don't adhere to golden rules, we create our own."

He glanced at Judith. "Is that so?"

She rolled her eyes. "For some of us."

Jacqueline nodded toward the rope still in his hand. "That's something you could do on deck where it's cooler. Why aren't you?"

"Maybe I was avoiding meeting up with the two of you," Nathan replied with a slight grin.

"Why? I don't bite—without reason."

"He's just teasing, Jack. I'm beginning to recognize the signs."

Jacqueline glanced between them. "Just when did you two get so well acquainted?"

"We're not," Judith replied with only a slight blush. "We've only spoken a few times."

Jack nodded and told Judith, "I'm going to find Andrássy and see if he actually knows how to use that sword he carries. Don't be too long in joining us on deck." Then Jack actually smiled at Nathan. "It was a pleasure meeting you, Nate." But she ruined the cordial remark by adding, "Nothing inappropriate happens in this room or I'll have to gut you—if her father doesn't beat me to it."

Jack left as quickly as they'd arrived. Judith peeked around the door to make sure her cousin really was going up to the main deck.

"That was a little too direct," Nathan said.

Judith turned back to him. "That's just Jack being Jack. She's very protective of me, well, of everyone in the family, actually. It's a Malory trait we all share. But I think she's annoyed with me now that I didn't mention you sooner."

"You weren't supposed to mention me at all."

"No, your condition was to refrain from saying we'd met before and I've adhered to that. I told her nothing other than what you said to her father. But all that sneaking I was doing behind Jack's back was far too nerve-racking to continue. As you can see, it's no longer necessary."

"Yes, but how did you manage that?"

"By convincing her that I was interested in you."

He grinned. "That must have been hard to do."

"Yes, it was," she gritted out.

He abruptly tossed the rope in his hand on the work-bench and reached for her. She gasped, but he was just setting her on the bench. Deliberately disconcerting her again? He must have remembered how easy that was for him to do. It did put her closer to him, right in front of him actually, and he didn't move away to correct that.

Flustered, she demanded, "*Why* do you keep setting me down on things?"

"It's up, actually, and because you're a half-pint." But

he leaned a little closer to add, "And maybe because I like touching you."

She blushed and jumped down to put some distance between them, only to feel his hands on her waist again. He put her right back on the bench, he just didn't let go as quickly this time. His hands lingered on her waist. And those pleasant sensations were showing up again that had nothing to do with anything except him. She couldn't breathe, couldn't think, waited . . .

"So you like my touch, do you?"

"No—I—"

"Then maybe you'll stay put this time?"

She snapped her mouth shut. How bloody high-handed of him! And he did let go of her now, but too late. She was of a mind to leave but didn't doubt he was persuading her to do just that with his manhandling tactics. Had he hoped her interrogation was done when she didn't seek him out these last two days? Wanted to assure that it stayed that way? Too bad. She was too stubborn to let him manipulate her like that or to give up on getting at the truth.

She was angry now. Not because he didn't kiss her just then as she'd thought he was going to do, but because it appeared he was trying to renege on their agreement.

Not having seen him the last two days, she'd had plenty time to dwell on him and had realized that none of her questions to him had been about smuggling. She'd merely questioned him to satisfy her curiosity about his personal life. So she'd accomplished nothing so far other than to nearly get caught hiding in the hold. By her father no less.

"I've missed you."

She blinked. The anger simply drained away and too

quickly, making her realize he could be doing it again. Saying things designed to distract her.

And he wasn't done. "I thought I caught your scent a few times." Then he laughed at himself. "Kept glancing behind me, expecting to see you. I even opened a few doors I was so sure I could smell you nearby. Just wistfulness on my part, I guess."

Her brows narrowed suspiciously. "You know I don't believe a word of that."

He grinned. "I know."

He moved farther away, over to the cot to sit down. She was surprised he hadn't sat next to her again, but guessed the workbench wouldn't support their combined weight. She caught the wince, though, as he sat, making her wonder if he was still in pain from that fight with her father.

"Everything I say is going to be suspect," he continued. "Because you don't know me well enough to know when I'm telling you the truth. If you come over here and sit on my lap, maybe we can change that."

She snorted to herself. *That* didn't sound as if he were in pain. Or he simply knew she wouldn't be doing anything like that. It didn't even warrant a reply, it was such an outrageous suggestion.

Instead, she asked, "How bad was the bruising?"

"Black."

"Still?"

"I think he ruptured my stomach. I can't keep anything down."

Her eyes flared, but she quickly realized he had to be teasing. "Nonsense, you'd be dead by now if that was so." Then she smirked. "Maybe you're seasick. Now *that* would be hilarious, wouldn't it?"

He snorted. "No, just absurd."

"But you've never been at sea this long to know, have you?"

"I was just exaggerating, my way of letting you know what I think of your father."

"Oh."

A compliment to Anthony's prowess in the ring, or a slur? It was unusual to see someone at odds with her father. Her instinct was to defend her parent, but she held her tongue, recalling how rough that fight had been. She supposed Nathan was due a little grouching about it, at least until he was fully recovered, even though by the sound of it he'd started the animosity in the first place. Of course, she didn't know what that had been about. Yet.

"Now I'm craning my neck in the opposite direction," Nathan complained. "At least come sit over here." He patted the spot next to him on the cot.

"On a bed? With you? That's far beyond the pale of inappropriate and isn't happening."

"Close the door first. Who will know?"

Her eyes narrowed. "Stop trying to seduce me."

He shot off the bed and didn't stop until he was leaning into her. "But it's working, isn't it? If you're going to admit to anything, darlin', admit you want me as much as I want you."

Oh, God, did she? Is that what these feelings were? No wonder she was so confused and excited by him by turns. She'd never experienced desire before.

He'd pushed between her legs even though her skirt wasn't wide enough to allow him to get that close. She didn't know how he'd done it until she felt his hand on her outer thigh—against her skin. Steadily moving upward and bringing her skirt up with it.

Simple instinct moved her hand to his to stop its ascent. And it worked, he just didn't take his hand away, and she would remember later that she didn't either. She was too deep in the throes of anticipation. Yet the fear of discovery was present, too, with the door wide-open, when anyone could pass by and see them. But it didn't occur to her yet to simply push him away.

His cheek rasped across hers before he bent his head to breathe deeply by her neck. "There it is again." His lips brushed against her skin as he said the words, causing gooseflesh to spread, leaving a trail of tingling sensations across her shoulders and back. "The smell of ambrosia."

"Jasmine," she corrected breathlessly. "And vanilla . . . with a touch of cardamom . . ."

"Then it's just you that's ambrosia."

He leaned up, was suddenly staring deeply into her eyes. He did that for the longest moment. Such intensity! As if he were trying to see into her soul. Then he kissed her with such passion it took her breath away.

"I'm going to hate m'self for this moment of gallantry." His words brushed against her lips. "But if you don't leave this second, I'm going to carry you to that bed. That's a promise, darlin', not just a warning."

Sanity returned with a vengeance, crimson embarrassment with it. But he didn't move back so she could get down from the bench without sliding against him. She heard the groan as she did, just before she ran out of there.

She stopped at the end of the corridor near the stairs, and the trembling set in. She put her back against the wall and closed her eyes for a moment. Her cheeks were still scalding hot. What just happened?! But she knew, because once again she hadn't got a chance to ask a single pertinent question. He'd found the perfect way to avoid that. He was chasing her away with sex. And what would have happened if she hadn't left? Would he really have made love to her?

Oh, God, she wasn't even near him now and yet that single thought made her knees go weak.

Chapter Twenty-Three

NATHAN LEFT THE STOREROOM before he demolished it. What the bleedin' hell was wrong with him to let her go like that? She'd been his for the taking. He'd seen it in her eyes. And a woman always got soft and friendly—and trusting—afterward. Which is exactly what he needed. But getting angry at himself for letting her go pointed out just how much of a fool she was turning him into.

The saner thought was that he needed to stay far away from her. He'd been managing to do just that, knew very well she was trouble in more ways than one even before her father convinced him of it. Yet he still couldn't get her out of his mind, had found himself thinking of her at all times of the day. He did want her. There was no denying that. He just couldn't have her, and he needed to keep that fact uppermost in his mind.

They could *not* be left alone again. Today proved he couldn't keep his hands off her when they were. The only way to make sure she stopped tempting him like that was to give her the truths she wanted so she'd stop seeking him out. So he went up on deck where he expected to find her. She was there, looking calm and composed. He wasn't, so he decided not to approach her yet and moved to the stern of the ship and took out the extra spyglass Artie had found for him. The first mate was there, too, doing the same thing.

Yesterday Nathan had seen the captain surveying the ocean with a spyglass as well. But James hadn't mentioned the ship that had been trailing them the night the stowaway had escaped, and it hadn't been sighted since then. He'd surprised Nathan by volunteering information of a different sort, saying, "There's a Yank aboard named Boyd Anderson who you might want to have a chat with. Spends a few days seasick every voyage, which is why you might not have noticed him yet. But he can steer you to the people you need to discuss your plan with after we arrive. Might save you some time."

"Appreciate it, Captain."

"Don't mention it. Some Yanks do come in handy occasionally—good God, I need to bite my own tongue."

And he'd left with that odd statement.

Now, Artie lowered his own spyglass and, noticing Nathan, asked, "You've been watching for them, too, mate?"

"Curiosity compels me to."

Artie nodded. "No further sightings. They either got what they were after, gave up—or they know where *The Maiden George* is heading, so they don't need to keep us in view." Then he grumbled, "The day was when we would've circled behind and boarded them—or blasted them out of the water."

"Really?"

The first mate snapped his mouth shut and marched off, obviously unwilling to elaborate—or realizing he shouldn't have said that. Nathan turned to pursue the subject, but spotted Judith instead. She wasn't looking his way but was watching the fencing match between her cousins on the main deck. Leaning against the rail, her back to it, her arms crossed, her red-gold locks were whisked about her shoulders and back by the wind. She was so engrossed in the match that she might not even know he'd come on deck. He could keep it that way—if his feet didn't have a will of their own.

He stopped two feet away from her and watched the fencers for a few minutes. It immediately became apparent that Jacqueline Malory wasn't just amusing herself; she actually knew how to use that thin rapier in her hand. The lunges and feints, the quick responses, she wasn't giving Andrássy much of a chance to do anything other than defend himself.

Incredulous, Nathan asked, "Just what sort of tutors did you girls have?"

"Normal ones."

"Normal for whom? Pirates?"

Judith burst out laughing.

He glanced at her. "What was funny about that?"

"You'd have to know the particulars," she replied, still grinning. "So tell me, when you were a child, what did you want to be when you grew up?"

"Is that a trick question I shouldn't be falling for?"

"No, but when Jack played that wishing game, she decided she wanted to be a pirate. Of course, she's outgrown that notion. Thankfully."

"Are you sure?"

"Yes, quite."

"Yet it appears she mastered one of the skills of the job."

Judith giggled. "I know."

"Did you as well?"

"Goodness, no. We shared the same tutors since we live close enough to. We merely altered the weeks and subjects, one week at my house for literature, geography, and several languages, then the next week at her house for history, mathematics, even a smattering of political science, then my house again, et cetera. We just differed in our personal curriculum. She was interested in fencing, pugilism, and becoming a crack shot, all of which her father was happy to teach her. I was interested in needlepoint and learning to play an assortment of musical instruments. And you?"

"The rudiments of a general education taught at a local church. But I don't believe that she took up pugilism. There'd be no point, since it's not something she could ever make use of."

He caught the smile on Judith's face, which she wasn't directing at him since she'd yet to glance his way even once. Then she confided, "I would agree with you if I hadn't seen her in the ring with her older brother. Jeremy can easily hold his own in a fight. He is like a younger version of my father, but she was still able to beat him. Speed and a few tricks can counter size and brawn." Then Judith laughed. "Of course that only works once. Onto her tricks, Jeremy didn't let her get away with it twice."

Jack might be a few inches taller than Judy, but Nathan still couldn't picture what she had just described. But it did make him wonder if Judith might be good at lying, too, or just good at exaggerating. She still wouldn't look at him. Didn't trust herself? He started to smirk but ended up groaning to himself. He *had* to stop thinking she was as attracted to him as he was to her. It might even just be a ruse on her part to get him to confirm her suspicions. And why didn't he think of that sooner?

A pretty older woman appeared on the quarterdeck, elegantly clad in a hooded, green velvet cloak that she no doubt wore to protect her coiffure from the wind.

"Your aunt George?"

"Yes," Judith replied.

Noting the woman's serene expression as she watched the fencing, he said, "She doesn't mind her daughter's antics?"

"D'you really think she could be unaware of the lessons Jack had from her father? Of course she doesn't mind. She's proud of all of Jack's accomplishments, from never missing what she aims at with a pistol to her grace in a waltz—speaking of which, do you know how to waltz?"

Startled by the question, he quickly turned to look at her and saw she *still* wasn't looking at him. It was starting to annoy him. "Why would I? If you're going to dance, it should be fun."

"You think waltzing isn't fun?"

"Course it isn't, it's just what you nabobs do to make sure you don't work up a sweat. I've seen it. There's nothing fun about it."

"You won't think so after I teach you how. We'll have the lesson here on the deck."

He snorted. "Not bleedin' likely. You can't single me out like that."

"I won't. I'll get Jack involved and a few other sailors, so it will merely appear as if we're just amusing ourselves to counter the boredom of the voyage."

"Do whatever you like, but you can count me out of nonsense like that."

"On the contrary, I'm going to call in my beck-and-call

card and insist you learn some manners—at least how to treat a lady. We're merely going to start with the waltz."

"Why? Once I'm off this ship, I'll never be around ladies again, so your lessons will be pointless. And besides, d'you think I'm not aware that a lady is never left alone with a man? That she has a chaperone at all times? Maybe it's you who needs some lessons, darlin'."

"Our circumstances are—unusual. Or would you rather I ask my questions in front of an audience?"

"You're doing a good job of pretending I'm invisible right now, aren't you? We're talking and we're not alone. Keep it that way and I won't think you're seeking me out for more—"

"Stop it!" she cut in with a hiss. "The things you say, you *know* they are inappropriate."

He chuckled. "But it doesn't appear that we need to be alone for me to say them. Or would you like me to leave until you have someone else standing here with us? An actual chaperone? Like you're supposed to have?"

He probably shouldn't put her on the spot like this. She might be blushing now, but she was unpredictable, too, and adept at turning the tables on him.

"I wasn't suggesting the lessons on proper etiquette begin immediately," she said stiffly. "In fact, right now you're going to tell me why you looked so sad the night I thought you were a ghost."

"We're back to that?"

"Yes, we are, and no evasion this time."

Chapter Twenty-Four

"Answer me," Judith demanded when Nathan stood there without saying a word.

He said instead, "I wonder what Artie and Henry are arguing about."

"You're changing the subject?" she said incredulously. "Really?"

"Yes, really."

Exasperated, she followed his gaze. "You've been on the ship long enough to know those two are always arguing about something. It means nothing. They actually enjoy it. What you may not know is they are not only *The Maiden George*'s first mates, but Uncle James's butlers at his house in London. Yes, they share that job, too. They're also best friends, though at times, like now, it appears otherwise. They used to sail with my uncle. When he retired from the sea—"

"He used to sail regularly?"

"When he was young, yes, for about ten years. But as I was saying, Artie and Henry retired from the sea with him and became his butlers."

"Two butlers? Is that normal?"

"Not at all normal. But my uncle James isn't a conformist. Artie and Henry were going to draw straws to see who'd be first mate this trip, then decided to just share this job, too. Now—"

Nathan interrupted with the guess "The captain used to be a pirate, didn't he?"

She gasped. "How—did you arrive at such a ridiculous notion?"

"Something I heard Artie say about blasting things out of the water in their day. And you just admitted your cousin aspired to be like her father."

"I said nothing of the sort! Do *not* put words in my mouth."

She couldn't believe he'd guessed so accurately, but that was one thing about her family that was kept strictly in the family and was going to remain that way. James's days of being Captain Hawke, gentleman pirate, as cousin Regina liked to refer to his former profession, were long since over. He'd even faked Hawke's death when he finally returned to England to make peace with his brothers, though that run-in with the pirate Lacross a while back had let a few of his old cronies know he was still quite alive and well. But Nathan wasn't going to be told any of that.

She demanded, "So you think of pirates instead of the military? Yes, of course, a smuggler would."

"Keep your voice down."

"Then don't make statements designed to enrage me. If you want to know about my uncle, ask him yourself—if you dare be that bold. But first, you're going to answer me. Why were you sad the night we first met?"

He sighed. "I wasn't. Disappointed, yes, and if I'm admitting things, a little angry, too. My maternal grandmother had just passed on. I didn't know her well, hadn't even seen her since I was a tyke. She lived alone in London, I lived with my parents in Cornwall. My father and she didn't get along, and she wanted nothing more to do with us after my mother died. So I was surprised when her solicitor tracked me down to hand me a deed to that property."

"Are you saying you actually *do* own the manor?"

"I told you that when you were a child. If I *had* been there this other night when you intruded yet again, I would have done the same thing—simply told you to get out, that you were trespassing."

"I'm to believe this *now*? You had your chance to make the claim of ownership when I asked before. You didn't because it's obviously not true."

"It's a bleedin' wreck of a house."

"One that comes with a lot of land. My cousin Derek would even pay you a fortune for it, so you'd never have to work again."

"Maybe I don't want to sell it."

"Maybe because you don't really own it!"

He suddenly raised a brow at her. "Why so angry, darlin'? Because you found another trespasser in that house, or because you didn't find me when you hoped you would? Are you angry that I'm not your ghost?"

She almost sputtered, but took a quick, deep breath instead. She wasn't even sure why she'd just gotten so angry. Merely because he hadn't confirmed sooner that he was related to Mildred Winstock, who was an aristocrat by birth?

But he wasn't waiting for her to answer him. He continued with a shrug, "It's nothing to be proud of or boast about that I own a house that's falling apart."

"You didn't know it was a ruin until that night, did you?" she guessed.

He barked a short, bitter laugh before he said, "No, I actually went there to take up residence. It was just after the fight I had with my father, which I've already mentioned to you."

"Which led to your leaving Cornwall, yes, but you never said what that fight was about."

"I'd rather not talk about that. It's painful enough that I never saw my father again before he died."

Was that true, or was he just being evasive again? She glanced at him to check the expression on his face and got distracted by how handsome he was. He wasn't wearing a bandanna now, and with the sun shining brightly, his hair looked pure white again as the wind blew it every which way, including across his face, which he didn't seem to even notice.

Something in his expression was angry, but mixed with melancholy, too, which compelled her to finally say, "I'm sorry."

"So am I. At the time, I was angry enough to break ties with him and live on my own, but only because I thought my grandmother had left me the means to do so. What a joke that turned out to be."

"Surely not intentional."

"No, I doubt she ever stepped foot in that house herself and didn't realize she was leaving me nothing but a shambles. It had belonged to my grandmother's grandmother, but according to my mum, my grandmother had been born in London, raised in London, and never left London. It was probably just a nice excuse for why my grandmother never came to visit us in Cornwall, instead of telling me the truth, that the old bird hated my father."

Judith was inclined to believe him, which warned her she probably shouldn't. He might be making all this up to elicit her sympathy. He hadn't admitted to owning the house the first time they'd spoken on the ship. And he hadn't mentioned it in any of their earlier conversations. Then she realized she could confirm whether what he'd just told her about the house was true.

"What was your grandmother's name?"

"Doesn't matter."

"Actually, it does. I know who the last owner of record was. If you don't, then—"

He glanced at her sharply and demanded, "Are you this suspicious with everyone?"

"Just smugglers," she said without inflection. "And I notice you're not offering up a name."

He snorted. "Mildred Winstock. And now you can tell me how you know my grandmother."

She was surprised how relieved she was to have proof that he was telling her the truth. Now their earlier encounters in Hampshire were beginning to make sense to her. His owning the house explained the lock on the door and his claiming to know the house better than she did, even the cot that he'd added. Only his telling her not to say she'd seen him there was odd. And his accosting her. That wasn't how a property owner behaved. Or that he didn't want the lantern lit again so she could see who he was. So try as she might to exonerate him in her mind, she still couldn't, not when so many clues pointed to illegal activities.

"I didn't know your grandmother," she explained. "My cousin Derek tracked down the identity of the last owner of record so he could buy the house."

"Why?"

She was hesitant to tell Nathan the truth, but he had to realize what an eyesore his property was, sitting next to a grand ducal mansion. So she said in a roundabout way, "He wants to give it a proper burial."

"It's still standing."

"Barely."

"I know better'n anyone the condition it's in, but I'm not selling it just so your lordly cousin can tear it down. It's the only thing I have left from my mother's side."

She tried to sound cheerful for him as she suggested, "Then repair it."

"I intend to."

"Really?"

"Why do you sound surprised? It's the only reason I mastered carpentry."

Her eyes widened. Derek would probably donate whatever Nathan needed, anything that would improve the view from the back of his home. "You've had five years to get started. If it's a matter of materials—"

"It was, but not anymore. I've been stockpiling what's needed, stashing materials in that hidden room so no one would run off with them when I'm not there. I just wasn't in a hurry to get started with the repairs until recently. I did some work on the roof, I just haven't tiled it yet. I could redo it all in cheap slate, but slate doesn't belong on a house like that."

"You want to match the clay tiles that are currently on it?"

He nodded. "What's left of them. Just didn't realize how expensive clay is. And didn't expect this trip to add to the delay."

"What changed recently to prompt you to start repairing the house?"

"I'm not alone anymore."

Her eyes flared. "You have a *wife*!?"

He burst out laughing. It drew a few eyes their way, Georgina's and Jack's in particular. Jack even slipped up because of it, giving Andrássy his first chance to take the offensive. Jack's sound of exasperation could be heard across the deck.

Nathan noticed, too, and said uncomfortably, "I should leave."

"What you *should* have done was tell me you're married *prior* to kissing me," Judith said furiously. "I *despise* unfaithful husbands!"

He raised a surprised brow at her, but only briefly. He was still glancing about the deck to gauge the damage done from the attention she'd drawn to them. But he said, "That's a bit heated for an assumption, darlin'. Jealous?"

"Not in the least!"

"Then stop yelling at me and look away," he warned, but then suddenly hissed, "Bleedin' hell. Meet me up in the crow's nest tonight and I'll explain why you're mistaken. But I'm not staying for this."

This was James and Anthony. They had just appeared on the quarterdeck and were standing with Georgina now, one on each side of her. But neither was watching the fencing match. They were looking directly at Judith and Nathan instead.

Chapter Twenty-Five

NATHAN DID ABANDON SHIP, as it were, returning belowdecks again. Judith couldn't do the same, not if she wanted to put out the fire before it started. If anyone was going to tear Nathan apart for being *married*, it would be her, not her father. So she pulled up a bright smile, waved at her father, and joined him on the quarterdeck. And did a good job of hiding her fury.

Her father didn't. He was scowling even as he put an arm around her shoulders. "What were you doing with that chap?"

"Debating whether to toss him overboard."

"I'll kill him if he insulted you."

She rolled her eyes. "You say that about every man I talk to. But I was joking, so there's no need for you to kill anyone this trip. He was just shocked by Jack's display of fencing skill. I was merely explaining why and how she came by it."

"None of his bloody business."

"I thought we agreed you weren't going to hate every man I meet. Mother even assured me you wouldn't."

That was pulling out the trump card, and it seemed to

work. Anthony relaxed a little, even chuckled. But Georgina, having heard them, remarked, "Quite a handsome fellow, this one, isn't he?"

"And you noticed this why, George?" James asked.

Georgina laughed. "Am I to pretend to be blind?"

Judith jumped in, "Handsome, but sorely lacking in manners. Still, he's rather interesting."

Anthony looked over Georgina's head to say to his brother, "Blister it, James, did you tell *everyone* about his unusual mission?"

"Only you, old boy," James said, then proceeded to tell his wife about it.

Anthony peered down at Judith and demanded, "Just how did you find out?"

She didn't deny it. "You think his commission to track down ship-stealing thieves is the only thing interesting about him? Yes, I've spoken to him before today, which was when I found out he owns that big old house behind the Wrighton estate. You know the story of it, don't you?"

"Don't believe so."

"I do," Georgina put in. "It was built for the old duke's mistress, wasn't it, and given to her to lure—er, that is, it was a bribe?"

"Incentive, yes," Judith concurred. "She was gentry and a widow, but the duke wanted her closer to him than London, where he'd met and fallen in love with her. Derek found all that out when he tried to buy the property. Mr. Tremayne is the woman's great-great-grandson."

"So he's gentry?"

"Doesn't matter," Anthony insisted in a mumble.

"Course it does," Georgina said, giving Judith a wink.

"A dashing captain *and* a landowner of note, perhaps you should let this one run its course, Tony."

To which Anthony snarled, "James, kindly ask George to *butt out.*"

James merely laughed. Judith took a moment to glance up at the crow's nest, so high in the rigging. Several rope ladders were attached to it, but still, she was *not* going to climb up there tonight. In fact, she didn't care if she ever saw Nathan Tremayne again. But she wanted that to be her decision, not her father's.

So before he warned her off, she told him, "I'm just bored and he's interesting, it's no more'n that. I'm not like Jack, who manages to find dozens of ways to have fun on a ship—steering it, climbing rigging, even fencing."

"Have I been ignoring you, poppet?" Anthony asked in concern.

She smiled. "No, of course not, and you don't need to entertain me. You don't often have Katey to yourself like you do now while Boyd is indisposed. I do understand."

"Doesn't mean you can't join us when Jack isn't by your side."

She giggled, reminding him, "And how often do you think that is?"

Anthony rolled his eyes.

That's when Jacqueline bounded up to them. Out of breath, she hooked her arm through Judith's to drag her away, yelling back, "Time to change for dinner!"

It wasn't, not quite, but no one protested since Jack obviously needed a bath after her exertions. But as soon as they were out of hearing, Jack asked, "Did I rescue you? Do say I did!"

"Possibly. At least, Father didn't get around yet to forbidding me to speak to Nathan again."

"As much as he'll try to, you can't let him whittle down your options, Judy. I'm sure to be in the same boat someday, so we have to stick together on this."

"I know."

But Judith did suddenly realize, much too late, that in trying to explain to Anthony why she might be interested in Nathan other than romantically, she'd broken the Bargain with him. Well, not exactly, not if Jack didn't hear that he owned the ruin and put two and two together to conclude that Nathan was their ex-ghost. But she should probably warn Nathan—the devil she would. The way he'd warned her he was married?

Still incensed over that, it wasn't a good time to hear Jack say, "I'm so thrilled for you. He's incredible looking, isn't he?"

"Yes."

"And daring. Chasing after a stolen ship is going to be dangerous."

"Yes."

"Feel free to volunteer more'n yeses."

"He's going to inform the authorities, so he'll have help. It might not be dangerous a'tall."

"Or he might not come back alive."

"Jack!"

"Worried about him already? That smacks of a little more'n smitten," Jack teased.

"No, and, no, in fact, he's got some explaining to do," Judith retorted. "My conversation with him was cut short when our fathers arrived on deck, so I'm going to meet Nathan after dinner to finish it."

"Explaining about what?"

"I'll tell you afterwards. Don't want you going after him with your rapier in hand."

Jacqueline raised a brow. "Sounds like you've already thought of doing that yourself. You're actually angry with him, aren't you?"

"A little. Very well, a lot. But don't try to drag it out of me when it could just be a complete misunderstanding. I don't want you getting the wrong impression based on an assumption."

"Like you have?" Jack guessed. "Goodness, if you're touchy about the slightest things, you *are* smitten. Confess that at least."

Judith didn't, but not answering at all convinced Jack she was right, so at least she didn't get in a huff about not being told everything immediately.

And at least Nathan wasn't mentioned that night at dinner, either. But Boyd was responsible for that. Finally making an appearance, the Yank was back in good health and therefore fair game for James and Anthony. Boyd wasn't just James's brother-in-law, he was also Anthony's son-in-law, so of all the Andersons, he was doubly entrenched in the family. Which didn't stop them one little bit from ribbing him mercilessly throughout the dinner about his seasickness.

"If you need another week in bed, Yank, be assured we'll get along without you," James said. "Won't even notice your absence."

Boyd's malady used to cause him acute embarrassment, shipowner that he was. But he was so used to being the butt of the Malorys' jokes that he took them in stride these days, following the example of his brother Warren, who also came under the gun from these two and either laughed along with them or ignored them. It tended to work.

But James gave ground tonight for another reason. Andrássy was flirting with Jacqueline a little too openly, complimenting her on everything from her hair, her dress—Nettie had won the battle tonight—to her fencing skill. Jack was amused by it. James wasn't. While the ladies might have thought Andrássy had been quite brave to want to defend the family during the stowaway incident, even if he had misjudged the situation, James wasn't going to overlook that Andrássy's interference had given the stowaway the opportunity to escape.

Judith knew that her uncle had had doubts about Andrássy before, but after Andrássy had cost him the answers he wanted, even if unintentionally, any chance of James's warming to their newest cousin had probably been lost.

But Judith didn't spend much time thinking about it, not with her rendezvous with Nathan fast approaching. She didn't even yet wonder why his being married was a worse crime in her mind than his smuggling was. But a while later, she would climb up to the crow's nest to find out what he had to say about it.

Chapter Twenty-Six

JUDITH DRESSED FOR THIS excursion in her ship's togs, even braided her hair to make sure it didn't get in her way during the climb. She'd also left her shoes in her cabin, thinking bare feet would allow for better purchase on the rope rungs. But when she stood by the rope ladder and put her hand on it, she couldn't take that first step. She didn't have to look up to find out how high that crow's nest was. Were the answers she wanted really worth such a daunting climb? The ladder wasn't even steady! It was swaying so much it moved right out of her loose grip.

She stepped back, changing her mind, only to see Nathan drop down to the deck next to her, which explained why the ladder had been swaying.

"Didn't actually think you'd take me up on my suggestion of a tryst in the crow's nest, darlin'."

She was relieved he was on deck instead. "Now that you're here we—"

"Come on." He took her hands and placed them on the ladder and moved in so close behind her that she had nowhere to go but up. "I have the watch tonight and I can't do my job from down here."

She glanced back. "Then why did you come down?"

"Did you really think I'd let you make this climb alone?"

Actually, she'd expected to have to climb up herself and had assumed he wouldn't even know she was there until she arrived up top. But he must have been watching for her.

He added, "And miss a chance to be your hero and catch you if you should fall—into my arms?"

He'd just added a teasing note to his gallantry. She wondered if he was embarrassed to show her he had this chivalrous side. But she started climbing. She wasn't the least bit nervous now, not with him behind her. And he didn't touch her again, probably afraid it might startle her into slipping—until they reached the nest and she felt his hand on her derriere, giving her a push to get her over the edge.

The crow's nest was shaped like a big tub. Some nests were just flat platforms, some were mere rounded frames, and others were rounded and made of solid wood with planked sides such as this one.

"I'd already volunteered for the watch tonight, or I wouldn't have put you through the ordeal of climbing that ladder," he said as he followed her over the rim.

She stood up and gasped softly at the view. "Oh, my."

The full moon tonight looked so much bigger from up here and was incredibly beautiful. Not long over the horizon, it was still quite huge. Seen from this unobstructed vantage point, with its wavy reflection off the water, it was breathtaking, even highly romantic. She got her mind off that thought rather quickly and turned to Nathan.

But he was still gazing at the moon. "This is why I took the watch when it's not one of my duties."

"What if there had been too many clouds tonight instead?"

He looked at her before he said, "That's the chance you take to see something this beautiful."

She felt warmth in her cheeks, and inside her, too. She couldn't let him distract her with flattery, if that's what his comment was. "I believe you have something to tell me?"

"That I'm not married? I'm not and I've no plans to be. I'm not sure how you came to that conclusion from what I said earlier."

"Because *not alone anymore* doesn't imply family, it implies recent acquisition of family, which tends to mean getting oneself a spouse."

"Not always and not in my case. My sister and her husband died last year in a carriage accident. They had two young daughters that his family didn't want, so I have the care of them now."

For once he wasn't evading answers, but she certainly hadn't expected this one, or to be so relieved that he wasn't married that she was almost giddy from it. "How old are your nieces?"

"Clarissa is seven, Abbie is nine. They're all I have left now in the way of family, and I intend to give them a proper home as soon as I can. But in the meantime, I found a nice couple to look after them. You might even know them." He explained where the girls were, ending with "Ironic, isn't it, that they're currently living in a house your uncle owns?"

"Uncle James only bought that property so he would have a place to store his ship away from the crowded docks of London. But, no, I don't know his caretakers. And why didn't you mention your nieces earlier?"

"My responsibilities are not your concern. Besides, you were painting me only one color—black."

Reminded of that, she retorted, "I haven't seen any shades of gray yet. In fact, I find it irresponsible that you didn't give up smuggling when you became your nieces' guardian."

She was prompting him to deny it, but he didn't. He looked away toward the moon. And she immediately regretted sounding so condemning when she didn't know *all* the particulars.

He might have good reasons for not abandoning what he'd been doing prior to becoming the girls' guardian. Other obligations or debts, or perhaps he simply couldn't afford to quit yet if he'd been putting all of his money into materials for that ruined house. Or he could simply be addicted to the excitement and danger of smuggling, knowing it would mean prison or worse if he was caught. And she shouldn't be angry any longer now that he'd told her he wasn't married. If it was true. Good God, was she ever going to just believe him without wondering if he was lying to her?

"I'm not going to apologize—" she started.

"Course not. Nabobs never do."

"You think *that* excuses you?"

He glanced her way in confusion. "What?"

"It's been established that *you're* gentry. If you think that puts you above the law—"

His laugh was genuine. "Third son of a third son and so far back, no one remembers the lord who used to be in our family. No, I'm not gentry, darlin', and don't wish to be. Call me a blackguard all you want, but don't call me a nabob."

"Actually, you don't have a choice when it comes to family."

He snorted. "If you don't know who your ancestors are, if you can't name them, then it don't matter."

"It's a matter of record—somewhere. You just haven't looked."

"Maybe because it's not something I need or want to know."

Frustrated by his attitude, she remarked on the obvious. "You seem to have a distinct animosity toward the nobility. Why is that?"

"That, darlin', is none of your business."

"This is how you hold up your end of our Bargain?"

"My opinions and sentiments aren't part of our Bargain."

"Well, if you're going to skirt the rules, you might as well know I let it slip to my family that you own the manor house. Not that we met there. And Jack doesn't know yet, so she hasn't made the connection between you and our ghost . . . and the smuggler who accosted me."

"But if it's mentioned to her, she will?"

Judith winced. "Probably."

"You don't keep secrets very well, do you?"

He didn't sound angry, merely disappointed, making her feel awful now. And chilled. She'd cooled off enough from the climb to feel the chill, so she sat down in the crow's nest to get out of the wind. Over the rim of the nest she could still see most of the moon. And Nathan's silhouette in front of it.

"I didn't do it deliberately. Why does it matter if my father, aunt, and uncle know you own the ruined house?"

With the moon behind him now and so bright, she couldn't see his face when he turned to her. He sat down next to her before he said, "I don't want your family seeing me as an equal whether I am or not. I don't make friends with aristocrats."

"It must be extremely difficult, your having to deal with me, then, isn't it?"

"Oh, no. *You*, darlin', are about as big an exception as there can be."

Mollified—well, much more than that actually, after what he'd just said—she felt a sense of anticipation rise within her. They were sitting so close, not actually touching, but she could feel heat radiating from him. It made her a little breathless, a little nervous, too, to be up here alone with him. He was so unpredictable.

To distract herself *and* him, she said, "Tell me more about your nieces. What are they like?"

She saw a shadow of a smile as he said, "Clarissa is exuberant and affectionate. She took after my sister and me with light blond hair. Abbie's hair is a darker blond and she's more the proper little lady. But both girls love ribbons and are always asking me to bring them some. Turn around for a moment."

She wasn't sure why she did as he asked, possibly because she was enjoying hearing him talk about his nieces. But it was her own ribbon he was after. She could tell it was gone as her braid started to unravel.

"Sometimes the girls like to wear a ribbon on this side of their head." He leaned forward and kissed the right side of Judith's head. "Other times they prefer this side." He kissed the other side of her head. "But sometimes they wear the ribbon around their neck, pretending it's a necklace."

She gasped softly when she felt his fingers, so lightly, brush across her throat just before his lips pressed against the side of her neck and not briefly this time. The sensation was so delightfully tingly, she closed her eyes and bent her head to the side to give him better access.

"I figured this would be the least likely place that I'd be tempted to kiss you," he suddenly said, then added with a sigh, "I was wrong."

Her eyes flared wide, but he was already drawing her across his lap to capture her lips with his. Cradled there, her head resting against his arm, he worked the magic she'd twice succumbed to—and sparked the desire she now recognized, too. Her own. She'd spent so much time with him, too often staring at his long, magnificent body. That first day in the hold when he'd been half-naked had stirred up primitive urges in her more strongly than she'd realized. The far too many inappropriate remarks he'd made that had shocked her came back to her now, playing havoc with her innocence. She slipped an arm around his neck and wrapped her other arm around his back as she moved her legs so that she was straddling him. She did all this without thinking while his tongue parted her lips for a deeper kiss.

He groaned. She barely heard it over the pounding of her heart. His hand was caressing her along her thigh, around her derriere, provoking a rush of warm, delicious sensations that she felt too keenly. The material of her britches was so thin, it was as if it weren't there! It was why she'd felt chilled, which wasn't the case now, far from it. But when he cupped her breast, she moaned with pleasure as a wave of almost unbearable heat surged through her. He'd popped a button to get inside her shirt and under her chemise. But she didn't care. All she could think about was arching into his strong hand, gripping his shoulders even more tightly.

She kissed him with abandon, letting her tongue duel with his as both of his hands now claimed her breasts, kneading them gently. She almost screamed when he used a finger of each hand to circle her nipples, teasing her with the softest of touches and making her wild for more. All of her reactions were out of her control. If she had any thought at all, it was a hope that this night wouldn't end.

"You are the sweetest kind of trouble I've ever met, darlin'."

His hands moved to her derriere as he started kissing her again, deeper and then more deeply, and she realized he'd pulled down her britches. The feel of his callused fingers on the softest of her skin had her writhing in his lap, moaning with pleasure as he hardened beneath her.

But some things could still shock her innocent sensibilities, and feeling his fingers move between her legs did just that. She broke the kiss with a startled gasp and pulled back to gaze into his burning emerald eyes. They couldn't look away from each other, and Judith felt she finally knew what it meant to be intimate with a man. He leaned forward and kissed her lightly on the lips as he pulled up her britches.

"I won't apologize for wanting you, but this isn't the place for it. Too cold and not soft enough for you. Give me a moment and I'll help you down the ladder."

She said nothing, but she had to disagree. With a moon like the one shining down on them, it was a romantic place for kissing—and everything else they'd done. And irrationally, she felt some regret now for having stopped him.

Chapter Twenty-Seven

NETTIE WAS LEAVING JUDITH'S cabin, having just finished helping Judith dress that morning. Catherine arrived before the door closed, Judith's yellow ball gown draped over her arm and, by the looks of it, nicely hemmed now. Nettie had tried to put the finishing touches on Judith's wardrobe, but Nettie MacDonald didn't see well enough these days to do such intricate work, so Judith had stopped her and had decided to take Catherine up on her offer to do some sewing for her. Catherine had already finished three dresses. She spent a few hours every day in Judith's cabin, working on Judith's come-out wardrobe. And Andrássy hadn't been exaggerating about her skill with a needle. Her work was so fine that Jack was even considering asking Catherine to re-hem her own ball gowns.

Catherine had joined the family at the last few dinners in James's cabin and would probably continue to dine with them for the duration of the voyage. Her behavior had been polite and so pleasant that Judith wasn't the only one who wondered if Andrássy hadn't only exaggerated his stepsister's shortcomings, but had deliberately given them the wrong impression of her. While they believed that she might have rebelled in her earlier years against being thrust into a family she didn't want, which was understandable, her behavior indicated that she'd outgrown that resentment.

Judith turned to Catherine now and suggested, "Why don't you join us on deck right now? We're going to conduct some dancing lessons. It will be fun."

"Surely you already know how to dance?"

Judith giggled. "Of course. Jack and I are going to teach the crew."

Catherine smiled. "Thank you for the offer, but I confess I'm not very fond of dancing. Truly, I am happiest with a needle in hand, so you go ahead without me."

Judith shrugged. "Make yourself comfortable then, either here or with Georgina. She did invite you to spend your days with her."

"Yes, I sat with her yesterday . . . well, until your uncle came in. He makes me nervous, I'm not sure why."

"He has that effect on a lot of people. You just have to get used to him. But Jack's waiting on deck for me, so I must run now."

She didn't run, but she certainly had the urge to. Two days had passed since she'd seen Nathan. She'd done the avoiding this time, staying close to one member of her family or another so if she did see him, she wouldn't be able to talk to him. But enough time had passed for her embarrassment over what had happened in the crow's nest to have ebbed. He'd carried her down from the nest that night on his back. Insisted, mentioning that he didn't want her abraded palms on his conscience. She hadn't complained about the soreness, but figured he'd guessed that her palms stung because sailors were familiar with rope burn.

He'd only made one inappropriate comment on the way

down, telling her in a cheeky tone, "I've dreamed of having your legs wrapped tightly around me, but I enjoyed it more when we were sitting in the crow's nest."

She might have slapped him if she hadn't had her arms around his neck in a choke hold. The man wasn't accustomed to being around gently bred ladies. But two days without seeing him had left her feeling a little bereft, so she'd had a note delivered to him last night, telling him what time to present himself on deck this morning. She didn't mention why, not when he'd made it clear he didn't want dancing lessons.

Jacqueline was already there teaching two sailors to hum a tune. She'd called in three others as well, and even Artie had come over to find out what she was doing. Judith's intention wasn't to single Nathan out, and Jack knew that. The size of the group would assure him of that—if he showed up.

Judith laughed as she joined them, asking Jack, "Is that going to work?"

"Course it will. Besides, there isn't a single musical instrument aboard, so we've no other choice. You do recognize the song, yes?"

Judith answered by humming along while she carefully surveyed the decks without seeming to and even glanced up in the rigging. But there was no sign of Nathan. Jack was ready for a demonstration and grabbed Judith to waltz with her. Jack had even worn her pants so there would be no confusion over who was assuming the role of the man for the lesson.

"Pay attention to the position of the hands," Jacqueline told her audience, "and the distance you must maintain from your partner."

They danced a bit before Judith was forced to whisper, "You were supposed to lead, not make us a bungling pair with neither of us leading. Let's try it this way instead."

Judith let go of Jack and, with her arms still up in the appropriate positions, began twirling about by herself. She even closed her eyes for a moment, imagining that she was dancing with Nathan. But that just brought forth some annoyance because she had expected to dance with him, and he wasn't cooperating by showing up.

Behind her, Jack said, "Artie, you've seen enough waltzing to know how it's done. Come show your men."

"Don't even—" Artie started to balk.

But Jacqueline cut in, "Don't force me to get my father for this demonstration."

"He wouldn't," Artie snickered.

"He would for me. Of course, he'd still be annoyed about having to participate, and he'd take that out on everyone else afterwards."

Artie grabbed Jack's waist and began twirling her, if a little rambunctiously. But Jack started laughing. She was having fun. So was Artie after a few moments. And then Judith spotted Nathan watching from a distance, arms crossed as he leaned against the railing. She waved him over. He didn't budge. If she had to go get him, that *would* single him out. But Jack noticed him, too, and bounded over to him and dragged him forward, starting a lesson with him.

Judith was satisfied to watch them, avidly actually, so she was startled when Andrássy was suddenly dancing her around the deck. His engaging grin kept her from being annoyed with his presumption that she wouldn't mind.

"You should have let me know you needed a partner," he

said, showing her there wasn't much difference between the English waltz and the European version.

"We're not dancing just to dance, we're teaching the crew. But since you're here, we can demonstrate how refined and elegant this dance can be. My father and aunt have been keeping you company?"

"I have enjoyed learning the card games favored in your country. Your father is brutal at chess, though."

"I know." She grinned. "He taught me."

"I could use some lessons on how to beat him, if you are willing."

"Perhaps later today. But I've been meaning to ask you about Catherine. She's been most helpful, even sweet, a far cry from what you led us to expect."

"I apologize. Sibling squabbles perhaps made me sound harsher than I intended. She can indeed be charming when she tries, and I'm delighted she's presenting her best qualities on this trip."

Judith held her tongue, trying not to read too much into that about-face. She had to remind herself that she'd been on Andrássy's side to begin with when Jack and James hadn't been, so she didn't want to start doubting him now. And it was easy enough to believe that Andrássy had only given them the wrong impression due to a recent squabble with his stepsister.

But then he added, "I confess I was more worried that she would become testy simply due to boredom than anything else, but you have come to our rescue in that regard, and for that we both thank you. She is never more content and calm than when she is sewing."

Jack had released Nathan and grabbed another sailor. Nathan didn't stay to watch, though, was walking away.

Judith stopped dancing with Andrássy to go after him, telling her cousin, "Thank you for the dance, but I need to get back to our task before these men are called back to work."

She thought she could stop Nathan by skirting around in front of him, but he started to put up his hands to move her aside. Without a word, too. And he looked annoyed, even impatient. Or was he jealous? Jealous? Over Andrássy?

She quickly took his hand instead and thrust it out to her right with hers, then draped her other wrist over his upper arm. "Show me what Jack just taught you."

"No."

She grit her teeth. "This was all for *your* benefit. Don't disappoint me."

He just stared down at her for a long moment. But she could see in his green eyes that he was relenting, before he said, "You looked silly when you were dancing by yourself."

She tried not to grin. "I'm not out to impress, I'm here to teach. And now that we have your hands in the right places—"

"Not the right places for me. Just my opinion, darlin', but I'd much rather be touching—"

"Lesson number one." She leaned a speck closer and hissed, "Keep your risqué thoughts in your head, *not* on your lips."

She started them off. He quickly took the lead, making her wonder if he had done this before, until he said, "If I step on your toes, are you going to cry?"

"It wouldn't be the first time, but a gentleman doesn't usually wear such heavy boots, so do try not to."

But he got back to her previous remark, saying, "I thought you favored honesty."

"I do, just not the sort that might only be shared by married couples."

"So what you're saying is I'd have to marry you before I could speak my mind?"

He was teasing, but she still missed a step. "I see you *do* understand."

He shook his head. "Too extreme. I'll suffer the blushes instead, and yours are too pretty not to see them often."

"So you're choosing to be incorrigible? Never mind, no need to answer what's obvious. But one thing a waltz allows is *polite* conversation while dancing. Let's see if you can keep track of your feet and talk at the same time, shall we?"

He chuckled. "Isn't that what we were doing?"

"The operative word is *polite*."

"Very well, what did you want to discuss politely?"

"What will you do with the manor after it's repaired?"

He raised a brow. "You're allowed to scratch nerves but I'm not?"

"This isn't a touchy subject."

"It is for me."

She sighed, deciding now wasn't the time to persist in her questioning of him, so she was surprised when he added, "I'm going to live in it with my nieces."

"While you work as a carpenter again in Southampton?"

"No, the house comes with land. I was thinking I might try my hand at farming."

She winced for her cousin Derek, knowing he wouldn't like a farm in his backyard any more than a ruin. But she didn't quite believe Nathan, either. A farmer? She just couldn't picture it. Of course, a man in his position wouldn't need to plow fields himself. Gentlemen farmers hired workers. But she was sure he'd meant tilling the land himself.

So she said, "You're right, the house comes with a lot of land, the tract stretching to the east. Have you considered building houses on it that you could rent out? The income would support you very well."

He appeared surprised by her suggestion. "That's something I would never have thought to do."

She grinned. "Broadening your horizons, am I? Then it's a good thing you met me."

He snorted. "When you're nothing but trouble? And you've spent too much time teaching me something I already know."

She blinked. "The waltz? But you said—"

He laughed as he let go of her. "I'm a quick learner, darlin'. It only took a few minutes for me to figure it out."

"Selective learning," she humphed as he sauntered away.

Chapter Twenty-Eight

THE TWO TO FOUR weeks Nathan had mentioned to Corky that the trip could take hadn't seemed like such a long voyage to him before they'd set sail, but it did now. Of course, like Corky, he'd never sailed so far from land before. Crossing the Channel between France and England on his runs was nothing compared to an Atlantic crossing. So he hadn't known what this sort of isolation was going to be like. Now he did, and it was hell with such a desirable woman as Judith aboard—a woman who wouldn't leave him alone.

She was dangerous to him in so many ways. She'd gotten him to open up. He couldn't remember ever saying so much about himself to anyone else before. She made him want more for himself. She made him wish their circumstances weren't so different. But the worst thing was that knowing he couldn't have her didn't stop him from wanting her.

He picked his times on deck carefully now, first making sure she wasn't there. But he had been trying to find Boyd Anderson alone for several days now, without having to disturb the man in his cabin. Today he finally saw him, not alone, but on deck.

"The captain suggested I speak with you, Mr. Anderson, if you have a few minutes?"

The woman Boyd was with said, "It's a little too windy for me up here today. I'm going to return to the family."

"You have a beautiful wife," Nathan said as they both watched her walk away.

Boyd turned back to him with a smile. "I know." But then his eyes were drawn to Nathan's waist. "Ask whatever you like as long as you tell me what you have crawling around in your shirt."

Nathan laughed and pulled out the kitten. "It *was* sleeping."

"You weren't going to toss it over the side, were you? They're valuable aboard."

"Not this size they aren't, but no. I found it strolling down the corridor by itself. I looked for its mother for a while, but she's hidden her litter well."

Boyd was still staring at the kitten, curled up now in the palm of Nathan's hand. "I know Artie brought his tomcat along, but I didn't think he was such a romantic that he'd bring along female companionship for him."

"I'd have to agree with that assessment." Nathan grinned. "It's more likely a female jumped aboard on the southern coast, long before we sailed, to have kits this size."

"Well, good luck finding the mother. But don't let my wife see that tiny thing before you do, or she'll want to adopt it. Women can get silly when it comes to adorable babies. Now, I'm sure you didn't want to speak to me about lost kittens?"

"No. The captain, as well as the first mate, both steered me to you. Artie said you're as American as one can be, and I'm going to need American assistance after we dock."

"How so?"

"Are you familiar with the town of New London?"

"It's maybe a half day's ride up the coast from Bridgeport. It's a whaling town and one of our competitors."

"For whaling?"

"No, shipbuilding. My family has owned a shipyard for longer than I can remember. We don't just build ships to add to our fleet, we build by commission as well."

"Would you know if any of those competitors only claim to build ships?"

Boyd laughed. "That's an odd question."

"Not odd when you hear the rest of what I have to say." Nathan explained his situation, ending with "I didn't know the thieves are operating out of a whaling town. The thought of them overhauling *The Pearl* into a whaler turns my stomach. I need to find her before she's sold."

Boyd was shaking his head, his expression incredulous. "A decade of stealing ships right under the noses of the English? I wonder . . ."

"What?"

"Skylark had a ship disappear out of Plymouth harbor in England four years ago. We thought it merely departed ahead of schedule, and when the ship and captain were never seen again, we had to conclude they ran into trouble on the seas."

"If your vessel was one of the stolen prizes, they may have killed your captain if he was still aboard when they took it. The thieves killed a man when they stole mine, so they don't care if anyone gets hurt. But the information I have is that they only steal English ships."

"You can't tell the difference with ours. We got out of the habit of keeping our colors up in English ports after we dock. Damned lot of rubbish gets tossed on our decks in the middle of the night if we flaunt that we are Americans. Old grudges not forgotten on both sides, apparently."

"But your vessel could have been lost at sea as you surmised. You don't know that it's related."

"We don't know that it isn't. Regardless, while it's probably nothing that can ever be verified, the people you've described still need to be stopped. I don't know anyone in the town government of New London personally, but I have an old friend who settled there who would. John Hubbard and I go way back, and he owes me a favor."

"I'll be sure to look him up then."

"*We* will," Boyd corrected. "I'm going with you."

Chapter Twenty-Nine

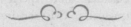

FINDING BOTH CATHERINE AND Andrássy in her cabin disconcerted Judith a bit when she returned there to change her clothes. A sailor hurrying past her had dropped a bucket of water, which had splashed all over her. The sailor had apologized profusely, but she understood his haste and sudden clumsiness. He'd probably just noticed the storm heading their way and had been startled by the sudden crack of thunder.

Nonetheless, she smiled at her cousin and his stepsister and said, "Time to batten down, as they're saying topside."

"And that means?" Andrássy asked.

Judith laughed. "I'm not really sure. But if you haven't noticed yet, there's a nasty storm bearing down on us. So you should put away everything in your cabins that might fall when the ship starts rolling and make sure your lanterns are secured and extinguished."

"But I can't work in the dark," Catherine said, annoyed.

Judith ignored the urge to roll her eyes. "A storm isn't the best time to be plying a needle, I would think. Besides, we're all meeting in my uncle's cabin for an early meal. They might be putting out the fire in the galley oven if the weather becomes extreme, so it could be our last hot meal until the storm passes. And do hurry. It's going to be upon us soon."

She realized the moment Catherine was gone that she should have asked her to wait a moment to help her into another dress. Getting out of the one she was wearing proved more difficult than she'd expected. At least one fastener tore as she struggled to twist the dress around to reach the others. With Nettie already warned about the storm and helping to secure the galley, and Jack in the captain's cabin already, getting into another dress was impossible.

She had no choice but to don Jack's favorite garb. At least she got into the britches and shirt in half the time it would take to put on a dress. And in only a few moments she had grabbed everything that was lying about the room and dropped it all into one of her trunks. She finally doused the two lanterns Catherine had been using, grabbed a cloak in case it was already raining, and hurried back to the main deck, which she had to traverse to reach James's cabin under the quarterdeck.

The storm was imminent; the only thing that hadn't yet arrived was the rain. Strong gusts were already upon them, the crew working swiftly to rope down anything that wasn't secure and to lower the sails. A laugh from overhead drew her eyes and made her pause. Nathan was hanging on to the mainmast, working in tandem with another sailor to tie down one of the bigger sails. His shirt had been blown loose from his britches and was flapping about as wildly as his hair, but he looked exhilarated, completely unconcerned about the dangerous storm that would soon overtake the ship.

"You like storms, do you?" she shouted up at him.

He looked alarmed when he saw her and immediately dropped down to the deck next to her. "Why aren't you inside?"

"I will be in a moment. Do you?"

He'd already taken her arm to usher her straight to the captain's cabin. "Love them—at least at sea. On land, I wouldn't even notice. Here, it's a fight against the elements, with Mother Nature cracking her whip, and there's never a certainty who will win in the end. Now—"

The wave cut him off, a huge one that suddenly washed over the deck, knocking them both off their feet. But it actually carried Judith with it. She screamed, her arms flailing wildly, trying desperately to find something to grab onto. She heard her uncle shout her name, but he wasn't close enough to reach her before . . . oh, God, not into the water! She wasn't that good a swimmer, would drown before anyone could reach her in the churning water surrounding the ship.

All of that flashed through her mind before she felt a hand on her foot. Spitting out water, she raised her head to see that she was only mere inches from the side of the ship, which was tipped precariously low to the water. She quickly closed her eyes as water rushed over her face, as the wave receded. Her heart was still slamming in her chest when she opened her eyes and saw water draining through the slats of the railing. As high as the railings were, she might not have washed over the side, but she'd almost been smashed against them. That could have killed her or, at the least, seriously hurt her.

She found out who had saved her when Nathan picked her up in his arms. "That was too bleedin' close."

"Are you all right, Judy?" James asked from beside them.

Nathan *still* didn't set her down! He was holding her so tightly to his chest she could hear the pounding of his heart.

With her uncle peering down at her with a concerned look, she quickly said in a trembling voice, "Yes, I'm fine now."

"Get her inside, Tremayne," James said briskly before he started shouting orders to the crew again.

Nathan carried her up to the quarterdeck. "If you leave his cabin—just don't. You've been splashed enough for one day."

Splashed? Then he'd seen the mishap with the bucket? But she hadn't noticed him on deck and she'd looked for him. She always looked. It was becoming quite annoying how easily he managed to avoid her within the relatively small confines of the ship.

But he didn't give her a chance to ask about it; in fact, she barely had enough time to say, "Thank you—for keeping me on board," before he set her down to open the door to James's cabin and closed it again the moment she was inside.

Anthony immediately noticed she was soaked and walked over to her. "Are you all right? What happened? It's not raining yet."

"No, it's not, but I was splashed by a little ocean spray." Judith grinned slightly to alleviate his concern.

Georgina rose from her chair. "Come with me, Judy. I'll find you something dry to wear."

She nodded and followed her aunt to the bedroom section of the cabin. She wasn't going to mention what had happened when Katey, Catherine, and even Andrássy already looked worried, and the worst of the storm hadn't even arrived yet. She changed quickly with Georgina's help, then spent a few minutes drying her hair with a towel before she braided it again and joined her family to wait out the storm.

Jacqueline nodded at her, but was already playing a game of whist with her mother, Katey, and Boyd at one of the card tables.

Anthony had been waiting for Judith to start up a game at the other table with Andrássy and Catherine and called her over. "Where have you been? What delayed you, poppet?"

"I had trouble changing." It was a pet peeve that she couldn't dress or undress herself without help. "One of these days high fashion will take into account a shortage of maids."

"I wouldn't count on it," Catherine said with a slight smile before her expression turned tense again.

Andrássy didn't seem relaxed either. Neither Benedek had experienced a storm at sea before. Judith hadn't either. Her first voyage had been smooth all the way. Georgina looked anxious, too, but then James was still on deck and she wouldn't relax until he joined them. Jack was her usual exuberant self as if she weren't even aware of the storm. Boyd seemed calm, apparently only concerned about Katey, whose hand he was holding.

Judith wasn't worried about the storm anymore, even though she'd almost been swept away in it. Her outlook didn't change even when the ship started rolling and dipping. Witnessing Nathan's attitude toward the storm had given her an odd sort of calm now that she was safe and dry in the cabin. But at one moment the table tipped so sharply that the cards slid halfway across it before the ship righted itself—and her mind flew to Nathan, hoping he was holding on during pitches like that. But she merely had to remind herself that *he* was having fun out there and, with so many years at sea, would know what precautions to take.

The card games, which were supposed to take people's minds off the weather, succeeded for the most part. Boyd, an old hand at sailing, assured them that the more violent a storm was, the quicker it would blow past them. Judith didn't find that particularly reassuring, but it held true. The storm was strong enough to pass over them in under an hour, leaving behind a gentle spring rain that didn't last long either.

There was cause for celebration afterward. Nothing had got damaged and the strong winds preceding the storm had pushed them ahead of course, even though the sails had been down during the rough weather. But celebration meant extra wine at lunch and again at dinner. So Judith was feeling quite sleepy by the time she retired for the night. Wearing a dress once again and waiting for Nettie to arrive to help her out of it, she lay back on her bed and was almost asleep when she heard the knock at the door.

"You don't need to knock," she called out to Nettie.

"I think I do" came back in a low baritone.

With a gasp, Judith flew off the bed and to the door to yank it open. Nathan stood there, his clothes neat and dry and his hair combed back but still wet, though apparently from a bath. He looked a little abashed, though she couldn't imagine why until she noticed one of his arms was behind his back, as if he was hiding something from her.

But her eyes went to his when he asked, "You weathered the storm all right?"

Had he really come to ask that so many hours after the

storm had ended? "Yes, quite, but I think I have you to thank for that, too. After seeing how much you were enjoying yourself out in the midst of it, I didn't find it nearly as frightening as I thought I would."

"So you weren't frightened *for* me?"

She wasn't going to admit that she had briefly been or that she'd sought out Artie the moment the rain stopped to ask if all hands were accounted for. She raised a brow instead to say, "Are you fishing for a declaration of concern?"

"A bit too obvious, am I?" he said with a grin.

"A little. Now, what have you there that you appear to be hiding?"

"Come closer and you can see," he suggested with a roguish lift of his brows.

"Or you can just show me," she retorted.

"But that's not as fun."

The man was incorrigible. He wasn't trying to conceal the humor in his eyes, either. She was no stranger to teasing, her family being quite prone to it, but this sort of teasing wasn't at all the same and too closely resembled flirting of the more rakish sort. It flustered her. It made her blush. At times it made her feel positively giddy. Tonight she fought the urge to simply laugh, which warned her she might be getting too used to Nathan's risqué form of teasing.

But then she felt his hand lift hers and the sudden warmth he placed in her palm. She glanced down and blinked at the white ball of fur she was now holding, then laughed a moment later when it uncurled and she realized what it was. Looking up at her was the most distinctive little face, with silver streaks fanning across its cheeks and up its brow, large, green eyes rimmed in black as if painted with kohl, and a black button of a nose. More silver streaks were on its bushy tail, but otherwise, it was all white.

She couldn't take her eyes off it, even as she wondered aloud, "And what am I supposed to do with a newborn kitten?"

"Feed it, pet it—love it. You know, what you usually do with adorable things."

That answer sounded a little too personal, as if he weren't talking about the kitten at all. And she did find his green eyes back on her when she glanced up at him.

She had to clear her throat to say, "Of course I'll keep it, if you'll promise to bring me fresh milk each day from that dairy cow in the hold."

He wasn't expecting to hear that. "You want *me* to milk a cow?"

She grinned. "Did you think you wouldn't have to do that if you took up farming? Farms usually do keep livestock on hand."

He snorted, but he didn't refuse the stipulation. Not that she would give him back the little gift if he did. It was too late for that. And she was sure he'd figure out soon enough that he could get the milk from the galley after someone else had milked the cow.

"And what have ye there, hinney?" Nettie asked as she finally arrived.

"A new addition to my cabin."

That Nettie immediately looked Nathan up and down after that answer had them both laughing. But the old girl took the kitten from Judith and held it up for examination. "Och, what a bonny-looking wee one. I'll fetch some grain from the galley fer a box that it'll be needing."

"Sand works, too," Nathan mentioned. "And we've

plenty of that barreled for ballast. I'll bring you a few buckets full tomorrow."

Nettie entered the cabin with the kitten cuddled in her arms. Judith took a moment to tell Nathan, "Thank you for the gift."

He shook his head. "It's not a gift, but a favor you're doing me, taking it off my hands."

"You don't like cats?"

"Never gave them much thought, but I was starting to like that one a little too much, after caring for it for the last few days."

"Ah, and it's not a manly pet, is it?" she guessed.

"You really think that would matter to me? I've just got things to do once we land and can't be taking a kitten along, so better to get rid of it now. And you're the only one I could be sure would give it proper care."

"Sure, are you? Why?"

"Because I've never met anyone as kind as you are, darlin'. So take good care of our kitten."

She gasped after that sank in. "*Our* kitten? I'm not just babysitting it. It's mine now!"

But whether he'd heard her or not was debatable, since he'd already walked away.

Chapter Thirty

JACQUELINE WAS HAVING ANOTHER match with Andrássy on the main deck this morning. Judith was watching them from the quarterdeck. It was such a warm spring day her aunt and sister had come out to join her, standing on either side of her.

"How's Nettie's cold, any better yet?" Georgina asked Judith.

"Her sniffles are abating, but she had a fever last night, so at least she's agreed to stay abed now. Catherine offered to finish my last gown in Nettie's room to keep her company, and I'll be sitting with her this afternoon."

"Not too close," Katey warned. "Can't have you catching a cold, too, when you'll probably be at your first ball before week's end."

Then Georgina remarked casually, "I haven't seen your young man since he thrust you into the cabin the day of the storm."

Neither had Judith, at least not enough to suit her. And she'd thought she had come up with the perfect plan to make sure she did see him every day for the remainder of the trip. The milk she'd asked him to deliver for the kitten.

But twice now she'd returned to her cabin to find fresh milk already there, and Nettie wasn't the one bringing it. Once Nettie answered the door and took the bowl from him, then promptly closed it again with a mere "Thank ye, laddie." Just one time was Judith actually alone in the cabin when he showed up, yesterday, their twelfth day at sea.

She'd just changed into her ship's togs, which she was resigned to wearing for a few days until Nettie recovered, when Nathan had knocked on the door. He'd handed the bowl of milk to Judith and brushed past her to enter the cabin without a by-your-leave. Without even making sure first she was alone! And he went straight to the kitten.

Picking it up and setting it in his palm, which it fit in with room to spare, his hand was so big, he'd asked, "What did you name it?"

"I didn't."

"Why not?"

"Because I couldn't tell what it is. Do you know?"

"Never bothered to check. I was just calling it Puss."

"And I've just been calling it Kitten."

He flipped the kitten over to examine it, then laughed. "I can't tell either. Something neutral then for a name?"

"Such as?"

"Furball? By the looks of it, it's going to have longer hair than normal."

She shook her head. "I'd take exception to that name if I were a female kitten."

He glanced at her, but if he'd been about to say something, he didn't. He seemed to be caught by her eyes instead. It was a long moment before he said, "You have incredible eyes," then spoiled the compliment by adding, "It's too bad your father has them, too."

She grinned. "Are you going to tell me I remind you of my father?"

"No, he reminds me of you."

"You've had more words with him?"

"Just nasty looks. But I'm not fueling that fire by being seen with you again."

Having said that, he left before she could think of a reason to extend the visit. She went to the door to call after him, "What about Silver for a name?"

"That'll do," he replied without looking back.

So frustrating, and the trip *was* almost over. Three to five more days depending on the winds, she'd been told last night at dinner. She had the feeling once they docked, she'd never see Nathan again. Yet she still wasn't completely certain that he wasn't a criminal. Well, obviously she was leaning toward not, or she would never have formed this tentative bond of friendship with him.

She could trust him to protect her if she needed protecting. That said a lot. She could trust him not to endanger her family anymore—if he'd been doing that. Yes, they had become friends—of a sort. And he probably knew by now that she wouldn't turn him in if he did admit he was a smuggler. But was he really going to go back to that career if he *did* get his ship back? When he had two young nieces depending on him? She should ask him that at least—if she was ever alone with him again.

Georgina, still waiting for a reply to her remark, added, "Would you like me to invite him to dinner?"

"Good God, no—and he's not my young man."

"Really? I got quite a different impression the day you spoke of him, that you were forming an attachment."

"No, I—no."

"Haven't made up your mind?"

"My father doesn't like him. Putting them in the same room isn't a good idea."

"Who are we talking about?" Katey wanted to know.

"Nathan Tremayne," Georgina answered. "Have you met him yet?"

"Briefly. Boyd is quite looking forward to assisting him. In fact, he intends to desert me as soon as we land and hie off to New London with the chap. What about James?"

Georgina laughed. "Oh, I've no doubt he'd love to get involved in that. He'd much prefer to jump into a fight of any sort than attend parties—if the parties weren't for Jack and Judy. Boyd shouldn't miss them either."

"I don't think he expects to be gone long," Katey said. "A few days at the most."

Listening to them, Judith realized that what Nathan had told her about chasing down his ship had to be true. Why make up a tale like that and enlist others' aid if it wasn't? In fact, most everything he'd said about himself was probably true. But had he ever clearly stated that he wasn't a smuggler? No, she didn't recall his being clear about it one way or the other, just evasive.

Later that night, she checked on Nettie once more before she retired, but the old girl was fast asleep so she didn't disturb her. Entering her own cabin a few minutes later, already pulling off the ribbon that held back her hair, she was halfway across the room before she noticed she wasn't alone and came to an abrupt halt. Nathan was there, slouched down in the reading chair, his head slightly tilted, a lock of hair over one eye, his hands folded across his belly, fingers entwined. He was sleeping! And the kitten was smack in the middle of his chest, stretched in a classic upright pose, legs bent, head up, eyes closed. She could hear it purring from across the room.

Incredulous, she sat on the edge of her bed and just stared at them, so much feeling suddenly welling up in her that tears nearly came to her eyes. The two of them made such a heartwarming picture, sharing contentment, love, and trust. The kitten had obviously made its choice about which human it wanted. She was going to have to give it back to Nathan, perhaps when he was done with his business in America. She knew where in England she could find him to do so. So perhaps this trip wouldn't be the last she ever saw of him. She found that thought more than comforting.

She was loath to disturb them and didn't do so immediately. The light next to Nathan wasn't bright. It merely gave the cabin a soft glow, but it allowed for a thorough scrutiny. It was breathtaking how handsome he was. She'd been entranced by his appearance even when she'd thought him a ghost. But as a flesh-and-blood man he could stir her in uncounted ways. Sleeping, he looked endearingly boyish. Awake, he was fascinating in just how masculine he was in size and strength. He was roguish, for sure. Outrageous, too. Yet, if he did ever behave in a gentlemanly manner, she'd probably tell him to stop it. Had she really gotten so accustomed to him with all his rough edges?

With a sigh, she finally approached and carefully picked up the kitten and set it down by the milk Nathan had brought tonight. Then she gently nudged his shoulder and moved back, in case he lashed out when he was awakened, as some men did. But his eyes opened gradually, looked at his chest first, where the kitten had been, then landed on her and opened wider.

He sat forward and stretched before he said somewhat abashed, "Sorry. I thought I'd be out of here long before you finished your dinner."

"The purring probably lulled you to sleep. It is such a pleasant sound. So you're still avoiding me?"

"When I have to fight myself tooth and nail to keep my hands off you, I thought it best."

Trust him to say something designed to make her blush. True or not, he grinned when the blush arrived, causing her to point out, "That's hardly adhering to our Bargain."

He raised a brow. "I'd think you'd be out of questions by now."

"Not quite. For instance, having told me you're responsible for two little girls who have only you to depend on, are you going to give up smuggling for them?"

"You *still* haven't let go of that notion?" he said, clearly exasperated. "If I ever was a criminal, I'm not one now. I'm going to retrieve my ship or die trying. What I do with her afterwards I haven't decided. But I promise you there's no noose waiting for me in England or anywhere else."

"I believe you."

He was suddenly looking at her in a completely different way. He stood up, cupped her cheeks in his large hands. "Do you really?"

"Yes."

He took her by surprise, hugging her. In relief? Possibly. But when she looked up at him, something else entered his expression. What happened next seemed a natural explosion of the senses. He didn't just kiss her, he brought her up to his mouth, lifting her off the floor, wrapping her legs around his waist to keep her there, pulling her so tightly to him she felt engulfed by his masculinity. And thrilled beyond measure. She'd been wanting this more than she realized, wanting to feel him like this, to embrace his passion and revel in it.

She wrapped one arm around his neck and slid her other hand up through his hair, gripping a handful as she returned his kiss with a fervency she scarcely recognized in herself. She didn't even realize he'd walked them to the bed until he laid her down on it. But she held on tight, dragging him down with her, unwilling to let him go for even a moment. Feeling him hard between her legs was so unexpected that a groan of desire escaped her. He moved off her so quickly, she might as well have burned him.

He was halfway off the bed when she realized he was leaving her and said, "Don't go."

She didn't want the kissing to end. He must have thought she meant something else because he glanced back at her with such yearning, and at that moment she realized she did. She smiled slightly. He made a sound as if he were in pain as he gave in.

He came back and straddled her hips so he could easily remove her shirt. It still wasn't easy. The chemise that followed was. Then came the blush and the moment of indecision. He was watching her, his eyes locked to hers as his hands began to explore what he'd uncovered. She was mesmerized by the desire she saw, then by what she felt, so tender at first, then the kneading, fanning the fire, then the flick of his finger against her nipple that sent shocks clear to her core. She wanted, needed to touch him, too, but all she could reach was his thighs, spread apart, one on each side of her.

She caressed them while he literally tore out of his shirt. She heard the rips and almost laughed. He moved off the bed to step out of his pants, but was back in a moment, at her side now, much better. She could reach his shoulders, his neck, his hair. It felt like silk against her chest when he leaned down to fill his mouth with her breast. She gasped at the heat that rushed through her body. Oh, God, the swirl of his tongue against her nipple before he sucked hard drew gasps from her, evoked another groan. He didn't pull away this time. Now, he seemed to know the sounds she was making were expressions of pleasure, not a plea to desist.

He was taking his time now, caressing her breasts and stomach, her neck and arms, as he kissed her, wanting to know every part of her that he could. Her shoes and britches came off so gradually she barely noticed because far too many other sensations were surprising and delighting her. Riddled with calluses, his hands weren't soft. But his lips were. They felt like molten velvet as they moved over her body. But the two opposite sensations—one excitingly rough and the other seductively soft—had such an amazing effect, arousing her and soothing her by turns, fanning her passion even hotter.

He rolled over to his back, taking her with him and placing her on top of him. She liked the position she was in with her knees resting on either side of him because it gave her better access to his wide chest, where she could feel the muscles ripple beneath her fingertips. She was delighted to discover that his nipples were just as sensitive as hers. But he didn't let her stay there for long. He flipped her onto her back again. He bent one of her legs at the knee and she did the same with the other as he slid his chest up hers for a deep, penetrating kiss that seemed to draw moans from her soul.

His voice was raspy as he said, "You can't imagine how

often I've thought of this, nigh every bleedin' minute, but nothing in my wildest dreams could have prepared me for what you make me feel. Do you feel it?"

With his mouth hot on her neck again, sending involuntary tremors throughout her body, she could barely think much less answer. But she gasped out, "What I feel is—akin to joy—"

He leaned up with a grin. "Really?"

"And so much frustration I just want to choke you!"

"You know why you have that urge?"

"Yes, I believe I do."

"Then have at me, darlin'. Or better yet . . ."

His idea of "better" was to entwine his fingers with hers and kiss her hard just before he entered her. This is what she'd been dying for. If she cried out, it was lost in his kiss, but she didn't think she did. Their joining was too smooth, too quickly done, and far too welcome. And with that thick heat filling her, she didn't move, just wanted to savor how deeply satisfying it felt. He accommodated her, holding himself perfectly still except for his mouth moving over hers. All he was doing now was kissing her deeply but tenderly.

So sweet of him to do that, but she'd had her moment to relish him and now every nerve in her body was clamoring for more. Her muscles flexed around him. He began to move, thrusting slowly into her at first, but she gave him every clue that that wasn't enough. Her grip on his shoulders tightened as she moved with him now, wildly as if she were being pushed toward some unknown precipice. But when it arrived, that indescribable burst of ecstasy, washing over her in waves, throbbing in her heart and loins, she merely held on tightly and rode out the storm until it vanquished him as completely as it did her.

His breathing rasped by her ear, his face dropped to the mattress over her shoulder. He was still trembling. Feeling it brought a smile to her lips. But when he finally rose up, he moved up toward the head of the bed, drawing her with him. With all that cavorting across the mattress, they hadn't been anywhere near the pillows until now.

With his arm around her and her cheek resting on the side of his chest, he assured her, "I'll go before dawn. Let me just hold you for a while."

In answer, she put her leg over his. She didn't want to talk. She'd never felt so deeply satisfied and—happy. Yes, happy. That was the glow she was basking in.

So she was almost asleep when she heard him say, "I'm never going to forget you. I want you to at least know that."

Beautifully said, but it sounded like a good-bye. It probably was. She knew these were stolen moments. But he didn't know she now had every intention of seeing him again when this trip was over.

Chapter Thirty-One

"Since when do *you* sleep the day away?" Jacqueline complained as she plopped down on the bed.

Judith curled into a ball, turning away from Jack and pulling the blanket up to her neck. "On those rare occasions when sleep eludes me, of course. Now go away."

"But—"

"A few more hours or I'll be yawning all day."

"Fine, but I'll be back if you're late for luncheon," Jack said, and flounced out of the room.

As soon as the door closed, the kitten jumped up on the bed and tickled Judith's nose with its whiskers. "Shoo. I'm not getting attached to you if I'm giving you back to him."

The kitten didn't obey, just settled down on the pillow next to hers. Judith hadn't been asleep. She had been awake for several hours. She had just been too content with her dreamy thoughts to want to get up yet. She could have spent the entire day in bed just thinking about last night. She should at least have gotten dressed, though, before someone showed up. Explaining to Jack why she was naked wouldn't have been easy when their cabins weren't overly warm.

She should probably have some regrets that she'd stepped so far beyond the pale, but she didn't. Not one. But she did wish Nathan had still been there when she woke. Actually, she wished he could be beside her every morning when she woke. But that required a commitment he wasn't interested in making. She shied away from that thought. Anything was possible and she wasn't done with Nathan Tremayne yet.

She rose and dressed quickly before Catherine made an appearance, too. She couldn't help smiling when she found her clothes from yesterday scattered about the floor. Jack was rather messy in that regard so it wasn't likely that she had noticed. Nettie would have. Judith was so neat she actually folded her dirty clothes before putting them in the pile for washing. And she might have to do the washing herself if Nettie didn't recover soon.

Catherine did indeed arrive before Judith vacated the room and went right to the wardrobe to put away the final gown she had finished. Judith was making her bed, but gave her a cheery smile. She hoped that wasn't going to be a problem today, not being able to stop smiling, even when she was alone.

Catherine paused for a moment to ask, "Are we sure this is the last gown? Your maid said it was, but she was sneezing when she said it, so she might not have checked all your trunks."

"I'll need a sailor to move the top chests so I can check the lower ones," Judith said.

She knew just the one to ask. Another smile, this one quite brilliant. But she had no *reason* to smile over what she'd just said. This bubbly happiness she couldn't seem to tamp down *was* going to be a problem.

Catherine nodded. "Which evening gown are you going to wear for the last dinner? I'm surprised your family wants to dress formally for it."

"The yellow and cream I think." Judith had put that one away yesterday, so it was still fresh in her mind.

"You have jewelry to complement it? If not, I have an amber pendant you can wear."

Judith chuckled. "I have every color gem there is, but I'm not sure if I brought my amber. Since we've had no reason to wear jewelry thus far, I can't remember everything I threw into my jewelry box for the trip."

"I can check if you like. Where do you keep it?"

Judith laughed again. "I'm not sure of that either! It's in one of the trunks. You didn't see it when you were taking the gowns out?"

"Your maid has been putting the ones that still needed work in your wardrobe for me, which is where I have been hanging the gowns I finished so she could put them back in your trunks."

"I'll find it when—"

"You there!" Catherine called to a sailor who was passing by in the corridor. "We could use your help, if you please." Turning to Judith, she said, "You look for your jewel box while I make sure all the gowns are indeed done."

Judith sighed. So much for getting Nathan back in her room with a legitimate excuse. She easily spotted her jewelry box in the third trunk she opened. But when she opened the box, she drew in her breath. "They're gone!"

Catherine, still bent over a trunk, said, "Who is, dear?"

"My jewelry, all of it!"

Actually, not all. She was relieved to see her most valued possession was wedged in a corner of the box, the tiny grass ring Jack had made her when they were children. Jack had one, too. They'd spent all day making them for each other. They had worn them for months until the rings had started to unravel and Judith had put hers away to preserve it. Even though it was too small to wear anymore, it was still precious to her. And, thankfully, worthless to a thief.

But everything else that had been in the box was worth a fortune because Roslynn had gone quite overboard in ordering extravagant jewelry for Judith's come-out. Her mother's bane was that her husband never allowed her to contribute any part of her large fortune to their living expenses. Anthony insisted on paying for everything. So she spoiled her children with gifts they didn't need, but it made her happy to do so.

Catherine peered over Judith's shoulder at the empty box. "Could the jewelry have spilled out in the trunk? Perhaps during the storm?"

"Actually, one trunk did slide off the pile that day. It got dented, but it was latched so it didn't open."

Judith dug into the trunk to check. It only took a moment. The jewel box had been filled to the brim because of the three large tiaras in it that took up so much room, and two tiered necklaces in hard settings that wouldn't bend. Any one of those would be easy to spot among the clothes. But just to be absolutely sure, she took every single gown out of the trunk and even shook them. No jewelry fell to the floor.

Judith sighed. Catherine put an arm around her shoulder. "Don't assume the worst yet," she said encouragingly. "Ask your maid first. She might have moved your jewelry for some reason. Servants that old sometimes forget to tell you what they've done."

Judith shook her head. "No, Nettie might be old but her mind is as sharp as a tack. I've been robbed. You might want to check your jewelry as well. I doubt I was singled out for this."

Catherine gasped. "But I can't afford to replace my jewelry! Go tell your uncle immediately. The ship will have to be searched to find the culprit and recover everything he took before we land. He can hide it, but it's still on board somewhere."

Judith nodded. At least she didn't have to worry about smiling any more today.

Chapter Thirty-Two

JUDITH RAN TO THE captain's cabin, but James wasn't there, so her father, who was playing chess with Andrássy, sent a sailor to fetch him. Jacqueline, red-faced with anger—that *would* be her first reaction—ran out immediately to check her cabin. Katey followed to check hers. Georgina quickly determined that her jewel box hadn't been touched, but no one expected her jewelry to have been stolen because the captain's cabin was never empty.

"Could this have happened at home before we sailed?" Anthony speculated.

"I don't see how," Judith said. "My trunks were packed and delivered to the ship the night before we sailed, and our servants handled that. And all of my trunks were locked and were still locked when I got to my cabin. I carried the key. And I didn't actually unlock my trunks until later that day, after we were out to sea."

"So you haven't opened your jewel box since we've been aboard? Until today that is?" her father asked.

"No, there was no reason to."

"What baubles did you bring along for the trip?"

"Too many. All the full sets Mother just had made for me, diamonds, sapphires, emeralds—"

"Good God, she didn't!"

"Yes, of course she did. And I packed the pearl tiara you gave me, the choker Jaime—"

"I'll get you another tiara, poppet."

"But I remember your giving me that one on my sixteenth birthday, and how pleased I was to have my first grown-up piece—"

Anthony hugged her tightly. "Baubles can be stolen, love, but memories can't be taken away. You'll always have that one."

She gave him a teary smile but it didn't make her feel any better.

Catherine rushed in, going straight to her brother, crying, "They took everything, Andrássy! Everything of value I had left. Do something!"

Andrássy appeared embarrassed by his stepsister's overwrought state, but he put his arms around her to comfort her. "I'll buy you some other trinkets."

"You can't replace my mother's brooch. You have to find it!"

Jacqueline burst in next, snarling, "I'm going to gullet whoever did this!"

"So yours are gone, too?" Georgina asked.

"Every last bloody jewel. This is going to *ruin* our come-out. Without proper glitter, a ball gown is just another dress. I am *so* furious!"

"Of course you are, dearest," Georgina said soothingly. "And you'll wear my jewelry if it comes to that."

But Jack wasn't easily appeased, huffing, "No offense, Mama, but your baubles are *old-fashioned*."

Georgina rolled her eyes. "Jewelry is *never* old-fashioned."

Katey came in next with Boyd and, with a sigh, said, "Mine are gone, too."

Anthony exclaimed, "Does *no* one lock their bloody door except me?"

Katey, the only one who had been robbed and did not appear upset about it, said, "Goodness, no, whatever for? It's a private ship filled with family."

"And a thief."

"Well, yes, obviously."

Andrássy, still trying to comfort Catherine, who was crying, asked, "Could it have been that stowaway?"

"No," Katey replied. "My jewelry was all still accounted for after that incident."

Judith dried her eyes with a handkerchief Georgina had given her and went over to Catherine. Judith felt bad for her. The rest of them could easily replace their losses. Judith and Katey had their own wealth, and Jack had eight uncles and two adoring parents who would fill her jewelry box to the brim again. But Catherine was dependent on Andrássy, who supported both of them with his inheritance. He was going to America to rid himself of his stepsister so Judith doubted he would willingly incur the expense of replacing all of Catherine's stolen jewelry.

Judith slipped her arm around Catherine's waist and took her aside, pointing out, "All isn't lost yet. It's an outrage that this happened, but our possessions are still on the ship somewhere, and no one is getting off it yet. And thanks to you, we found out much sooner than we might have, so there's plenty of time to find what was taken before we dock."

"You're right, of course. I shouldn't have let myself get so emotional. It's just that the broach is all I have left from my mother. I'll be devastated if I don't get it back."

"But you will, I promise."

"What happened?" James asked as he walked into the room, but too many of them started to talk at once, so he bellowed, "George!"

Georgina tsked at his tone and asked, "What took you so long?"

"Artie had trouble tracking me down, since I was up in the crow's nest. He said one of my crew has turned into a jewel thief?"

"I would guess the opposite, that our thief pretended to be a sailor. It was too neatly done, and too thorough. Aside from myself, *all* the women in this room were robbed, and none of them realized it until Judith found her jewel box empty a quarter of an hour ago, and they went to check theirs. That doesn't smack of a sailor acting on impulse. That's *four* different cabins snuck into, James."

Judith saw her uncle's gaze drift over to Catherine and then to Andrássy. Catherine must have noticed that James was looking at her because she leaned closer to Judith and whispered, "I didn't do it, I swear! I know Andrássy told your family I was rebellious when I first arrived at his home. He might even have mentioned that I used to take things in anger to get back at my mother, but I was just a child then, for God's sake, and I never took *any*thing of value. I—I can't imagine why he would even mention it, it was so long ago."

Judith couldn't either, for that matter, if Andrássy had actually told a member of her family that—unless he had done it to deliberately plant a seed of suspicion in his mind. For this? Good God, was Andrássy even who he said he was? They knew he was living off an inheritance only because he'd told them that. And James and Jack had both had doubts about him. Judith had staunchly defended him, but it wouldn't be the first time she had misjudged someone's character. Look how wrong she'd been about Nathan.

"It's been determined that at least some of the thefts occurred within the last week," Georgina was saying.

"Within the last four days, actually," Katey clarified. "I'm sure that's how long it's been since I took my amethyst earrings out of my jewelry box to wear to dinner. They simply go too well with that lilac dress I wore the other night. You'll have to replace them, Boyd."

"No," Boyd said, but quickly added with a chuckle, "I'd much rather find you the originals and I will."

"Indeed," James agreed. "All of the missing jewelry will be found before we dock. I want all of the baggage searched, and every inch of your cabins scrutinized. And because one tends to overlook things in familiar surroundings, I want a fresh set of eyes in every room, so you take Boyd and Katey's room, Tony. Boyd will take Andrássy's, and, Andrássy, you take Tony's room. Katey, you take Catherine's room. Jack and Judy, you switch with each other. Catherine, you can help my wife, since this is the largest of the cabins. Look into every nook and cranny, dear ones. The thief might be hiding his plunder where we'd least expect to find it."

"Do we at least get to eat first?" Anthony asked, only half joking.

James stared at his brother but didn't relent. "No meals until I have the culprit in my brig. If any of you missed breakfast, as my dear brother obviously did, stop by the galley before you begin. Once you finish the rooms, join me to help with the rest of the ship. If the first sweep doesn't yield results, then we will do it again. Before day's end, I'm bloody well going to know who dared to commit robbery on my ship."

Chapter Thirty-Three

"I'M BEGINNING TO ENJOY this." Jacqueline grinned as she lifted a small wooden carving of an elephant out of a crewman's locker. "It feels like we're on a treasure hunt, doesn't it?"

Judith, who was next to her, sorting through another locker, said, "Don't you mean scavenger hunt?"

"Considering what was stolen, I don't believe I do. You know, all combined, that jewelry is probably worth a king's ransom. Yours alone would be!"

Judith didn't blush or try to make excuses for her mother's extravagance. Everyone in the family knew how carried away Roslynn could get whenever she found something to spend her money on.

Judith had hoped to find Nathan working with James's group in the crew's quarters when she and Jack joined her uncle there after completing their search of each other's cabin. But although James had divided the crew who weren't actually manning the ship into two groups—one searching the cargo hold with Artie supervising, and the other assigned to the main deck and the battery deck with Henry in charge, James didn't trust any of the sailors to search the crew's quarters because he considered it the most likely hiding place for the jewels.

Working alone there, James hadn't made much progress, so he was glad to have Jack and Judy's help, and later Anthony's, too, when he joined them, although Anthony was mostly distracting James with his suspicions about who had robbed them. Boyd was at the other end of this deck working his way toward them. They didn't need to rip open the mattresses in the large bunkroom because the mattresses were thin enough that any jewelry that might have been sewn inside them could be detected by touch.

Boyd entered the crew's quarters and spoke with James. A few moments later, James called the girls over to him. "Boyd just found this," James said, holding up an amber ring. "He says it's not Katey's. Do either of you recognize it?"

Judith did. The amber ring went with her amber locket and bracelet. So she had brought her amber after all. It wasn't nearly as expensive as her other sets, but still beautifully made, especially the oval locket, which was circled with tiny seed pearls.

Her father had come over to have a look at the ring and answered for her, "That's Judy's ring. Gave her the amber m'self. The other pieces weren't with it?"

"No," James said, and nodded to Boyd, who left immediately. James didn't exactly look relieved by the discovery and told the girls, "I need to let George know she can stop keeping an eye on Catherine. I believe we're done here for the time being, so you might as well come along."

"You suspected her, too?" Jack asked, keeping up with him. "*I* did."

Judith tsked, but James agreed, "Her—or her brother.

Why do you think I sent you all to different cabins? It was to keep them out of theirs."

"Well, don't let *her* know you suspected her," Judith said quickly as she followed behind them. "She felt bad enough when you only *looked* at her earlier." Then, a little red-cheeked, she added, "Though I confess I did have a moment's doubt about Andrássy."

"Where this was found doesn't implicate either of them," James said.

"So a sailor got greedy?" Jack guessed.

"Or planned this well in advance," James replied. "But we'll find out soon enough. Boyd is having him brought to my cabin."

Judith was frowning before they reached James's cabin. If the ring hadn't been found in the crew's quarters or a specific locker, how did he know whom to bring in for questioning?

"George, *really?*" James complained the moment he entered his cabin to find her rifling through his desk, the papers on top of it all scattered.

She glanced up to give him a sweet smile. "I was running out of places to look, m'dear."

"You can stop looking."

Catherine, standing in front of the bank of windows, turned to ask him hopefully, "So am I exonerated?"

Judith was surprised that Catherine would actually ask that. So was James. Judith didn't think she'd ever seen her uncle look discomfited, but at that moment he did. He merely said, "Of course."

Anthony sat down on one of the sofas, stretched his arms over the back, and asked, "So who is our culprit? I've a mind to tear him limb from limb just for sneaking into Judy's room, much less for stealing from her."

James tsked. "He'll need to be in one piece when we turn him over to the authorities when we dock."

"Then just a few minutes with him. Really, James, you can't tell me you aren't just as incensed that the blighter would dare—"

"Course I am."

Anthony rolled his eyes at that calm reply. He should have known getting James to show what he was feeling was next to impossible. He'd tried, and failed, often enough in the past.

Boyd, looking grim now, returned with Katey, and they both joined Anthony on the sofa. Boyd had seemed the least disturbed of all the family members when he'd learned about the robbery. After so many years at sea, he traveled with nothing of real value that couldn't easily be replaced, and he had tried to convince Katey to do the same. So it was odd that he now seemed more disturbed than anyone else. Georgina noticed it, too, and moved over to perch on the arm of the sofa next to her brother to quietly question him.

Jack was standing next to Judy and leaned closer to her to whisper, "Who do you think it is?"

"I'm more curious to know why your father hasn't given us a name yet."

"Because we wouldn't recognize it if he did. Do you know all the names of the crew? I surely don't."

"Of course, I didn't think of that," Judith whispered back, then sighed. "I'm letting my suspicions run amok today. This is all so disturbing."

"Worse than that," Jack growled low. "We've never been robbed before, neither of us. I bloody well don't like how it feels."

"But the thief has been caught and we will soon have our jewels back. You shouldn't still be so angry."

"Can't help it," Jack mumbled.

Artie arrived, four sailors with him. Nathan was one of them. Judith's pulse picked up at the mere sight of him, but she was overcome with shyness, too, after what they had done last night. She still cast him a smile, but it faltered when she saw how tight-lipped he was. And he hadn't noticed her yet. He was staring at James, as were the other sailors.

James walked over to the sailors and held out the amber ring. "Recognize this?"

He didn't seem to be asking any one of them in particular, yet Nathan answered, "Why would I? I'm not your thief."

"Yet it was found under your bed. Dropped it by accident, did you? Didn't hear it fall and roll out of sight? Rather careless, that."

Judith blanched, every bit of color gone from her face. She was too shocked to remain quiet. "My God, a smuggler *and* a jewel thief! How *could* you?!"

Nathan didn't reply, but his emerald eyes weren't so lovely when they narrowed in anger. They were downright menacing instead. Because he'd been found out obviously. She was going to be furious as soon as she stopped feeling like crying.

"A what?" more than one person asked.

Catherine's timing couldn't have been worse when she added, "That's the man who entered your cabin, Judith, with a bowl of milk for that kitten you adopted. He was quite surprised that the room wasn't empty when he found me there working on your gowns."

Judith was even more horrified to realize Nathan had probably robbed her before last night and had *still* made love to her. Icing for his cake? Or was that so she'd defend him in case this very thing happened? He'd had plenty of opportunity these last four days to rob them. She'd given him that because of the kitten. Had he used the animal as a ploy, in case he got caught alone in her room? It was a perfect excuse, wasn't it? And she'd played right into his hand, insisting he bring her milk. And last night he hadn't said he wasn't a criminal, only that *if* he had been, he wasn't one now. The man played with words, and they'd *all* been burned because she was gullible enough to trust him!

"Why didn't you tell us he was a smuggler?" James asked her.

Judith's cheeks turned bright red as she was forced to confess, "Because it was just a suspicion. I thought I could keep an eye on him and ferret out the truth."

"He tried to buy your silence, didn't he?" Georgina said gently. "By toying with your affections?"

"Seducing me into silence, you mean?"

"Well—yes."

"I'll kill him!" Anthony snarled, and shot off the sofa.

"Wait!" one of the other sailors said.

But James was already grappling with his brother. "Not *now*, Tony. Jewelry first—then you can kill him if you've still a mind to."

The other sailor spoke up again, this time in a tone of disgust. "You nabobs are a bleedin' odd lot. Nate's no thief. I can vouch for that."

James pushed Anthony back before he turned to the man. "How?"

"I'm his first mate," the man said proudly.

"Are you now?" James said, and then to Nathan, "And how many more of my crew were previously yours?"

Nathan looked beyond furious, so it was just as well the other two sailors were holding him now by the arms. "Just Corky, and leave him out of this."

"It makes sense that you'd have an accomplice, a lookout, as it were. Lock them both up," James said to Artie. "The ladies don't need to be present for the questioning."

Chapter Thirty-Four

"Just let me at him for a bit," Anthony said to his brother as he paced the floor of the captain's cabin. "I'll get the location of his hiding place out of him."

James raised a brow at him. "I thought you were done with that grudge."

"He robbed my daughter. It's back in spades." Anthony looked over his shoulder at Judith, who was sitting on the sofa between Georgina and Jack, being consoled by them.

James's arms were crossed and he was leaning back against the door in a relaxed stance. But he was obviously blocking the exit, his not-so-subtle way of letting Anthony know James wasn't going to let him rip anyone apart just yet.

James said, "Artie is getting the rest of the ship searched, though considering our thief is a carpenter able to create his own hiding places, that's likely a useless endeavor. But I'm still going to give Tremayne a few hours to figure out that the only way he's not going to rot in an American prison is if he cooperates by returning the jewels and appealing to our mercy."

"No mercy, James," Anthony warned. "Jewels back or

not, he's still a thief and deserves to rot. *And* he's a smuggler. He'll be lucky if he ever gets out of prison."

James chuckled. "The Yanks aren't going to imprison him for thumbing his nose at English revenuers. They're more apt to pat him on the back for that. Besides, our smugglers aren't a cutthroat lot, they're merely a result of high taxes, protesters as it were. You could even say they are revolutionaries. They've taken up the gauntlet to help others. Jewel thieves are a different breed. They steal just to help themselves—or when they have no other choice."

"What the deuce does that mean?"

"Kindly recall that Danny, *my* daughter-in-law and your niece by marriage, was a thief. So you are aware that extraordinary circumstances can force someone to do something they'd rather not do."

Anthony snorted. "That is *not* the case here. The man's not a pauper. He's got his own bloody ship and a rich property in Hampshire."

"Exactly."

"Eh? Now what are you getting at?"

"Settle on one or the other, Tony, not both. If he's the thief—"

"If?!"

"Then everything else he's said about himself is likely a lie," James continued. "Consider this, a thief who gets easy access to wealthy people's homes because he is a carpenter. He hears about our trip and that four wealthy families will be on board *and* a carpenter is needed. Rich pickings all in one place. Sounds like a thief's dream come true, doesn't it? And free passage to a new continent where he can rob some more before he returns home to England. All plausible. But what isn't plausible is that he's gentry *and* a thief. The man's a damn good liar though. You realize he would never have come under suspicion if that ring hadn't fallen out of his stash without his noticing before he hid the rest. Foiled by a bit of carelessness. Bloody rotten luck, that."

"Makes me sick to my stomach that he lied about *The Pearl*," Boyd put in as he came over to join them. "Well, a ship he even invented a name for. And, no, I'm not seasick again," he added testily before one of his two standard ribbers thought to mention it. "I was looking forward to helping him recover his ship in New London."

"Am I the only one who wasn't gulled by him?" Anthony demanded.

"Give it a rest, Tony," James said. "Tremayne—if that's his real name—is not a stupid man. He wouldn't have done what *you're* thinking."

Anthony didn't deny his other suspicions. "Wouldn't he? He had the gall to rob her, so I can't believe that's not all he stole from her."

"Ask her," James said simply.

"The devil I will," Anthony replied uncomfortably, glancing behind him at Judith on the sofa. "That would be Roslynn's department and she's not—"

"George," James called out. "Ask her!"

"George doesn't know what we are discussing," Anthony hissed.

"Course she does," James replied. "You mean to say Ros can't read your mind as easily as George reads mine?"

Judith had heard them well enough. When her father was angry, he was rarely quiet about it. "The only thing he seduced out of me was my friendship—and trust," she said hollowly. "He convinced me of his innocence when he's not the least bit innocent. I should have followed my instincts. I *never* should have trusted him."

"It's not your fault, sweetheart," Georgina assured her. "He fed you a tale designed to appeal to your kind nature, so of course you'd believe him." Georgina added pointedly to James, "We all did. And he's had enough time to stew. Wrap this up, James, so we can put it behind us."

The ship's brig was more a cooling-off room for members of the crew who got into fights or just needed a mild reprimand. It wasn't set up for an extended stay. It could only be called a brig because its door was made of iron bars. It was actually a tiny room, one of four, in the hallway by the galley, where the cook had been storing sacks of grain.

Corky was using one of the smaller sacks as a pillow for his head, not that either of them was sleeping. Two narrow shelves or benches were built into the walls on either side of the five-foot-square room. But what they couldn't be called were cots. Yet they'd have to serve as such. There was nowhere else they could sleep other than on the floor.

There wasn't even room enough to pace in, though Nathan felt more like smashing his fist through a wall. He'd never been so angry at a woman in his life. The rest of them had behaved no differently from what he'd expect of nabobs, but Judith? After what they'd shared, how could she think he'd steal from her? From her! Being falsely accused didn't even compare to what he felt over that betrayal. But it was his own fault for trusting an aristocrat. Now he might have to spend the rest of his life in prison because of that error in judgment.

"I'd like to know who set you up so we know who to keelhaul afterwards."

Corky wasn't taking their incarceration seriously yet, but then his attitude was based on their innocence and the certainty that they'd be released with profuse apologies as soon as the real thief was caught. But there was evidence, which meant people were not going to look any further when they believed they already had their man.

"I don't think there's going to be an afterwards, at least, not for me," Nathan said, gripping the bars in front of him and giving them a hard shake, but he got no satisfying rattle out of them. "You, they'll have to let go. They don't imprison men for confessing to friendship."

"At least Artie left us a lantern. Surprised he did, after that angry look he gave you. Speaking of which, have you made an enemy you failed to mention?"

"Other than Lord Anthony, you mean? No, not that I know of. And as much as I don't like that lord, he wouldn't set me up by placing a missing ring under my bed. He's more direct, favoring revenge with his fists."

"He prefers Sir Anthony."

Nathan turned around. "Who does?"

"Sir Anthony does. He's the son of a marquis, so of course that *makes* him a lord, but according to the second first mate, he prefers to be called Sir Anthony, since he actually earned that title himself."

"I don't give a bleedin' damn what he prefers." Nathan sat on the bench across from Corky. "I was more likely picked as the culprit because aside from the two first mates, I'm the only other member of the crew who claimed a bed away from the main quarters. Planting that bauble in the communal area wouldn't have fingered anyone in particular as the thief. But planting it in my room points a finger directly at me."

"I've gotten to know the men," Corky said in a thoughtful tone. "Was feeling them out to see if any might want to join us on the trip home. Never would have guessed one of them could be cunning this way, much less be a bleedin' jewel nabber. If I had to make a guess—"

"Don't bother. Nothing short of finding the trinkets *on* someone else is going to get me out of this. Quiet!" Nathan cautioned, standing up and gripping the bars again when he heard footsteps. "Someone's coming."

"Or just passing by on their way to the galley," Corky said with a snort. "You'd think they'd put a brig in the bowels of the bleedin' ship, not close enough to the galley that we can smell food cooking."

Nathan didn't reply when he saw the captain was paying them a visit. Malory glanced around to locate where the key was hung before he continued down the hall. Nathan almost laughed. Where could he go if he could reach the key? But he couldn't. Even with a shoe to give him an extra foot's extension, he couldn't stretch to the front of the little hallway. But the captain's not knowing where the key was hung proved this room wasn't used often. Nathan wouldn't be surprised if Malory had had to get directions to it.

James stopped in front of the cell. His expression wasn't indicative of his mood, but his words were. "I'm disappointed in you."

"The feeling is bleedin' well mutual. Anyone could have put that ring under my bed and you know it. Obviously the thief did. The real one. Yet here I sit, framed for something I didn't do. A smuggler does *not* a thief make—not that I'm confessing to either charge."

"Let's be clear, Tremayne. It doesn't matter to me what you used to do, only what you've been doing since you boarded my ship. All that remains now is for you to fess up to where you've hidden the rest of the jewelry."

"So you've already searched everyone on board?"

"And the point of that would be? What was taken was from four separate jewelry boxes, and some of it quite bulky—necklaces and tiaras that don't bend, far too much bulk to conceal on a person."

"I've never stolen anything in my life, but if I did, I sure as hell wouldn't be dumb enough to hide it on a ship that hasn't sighted land yet. I would have waited until an escape was within view."

"But you're a carpenter, dear boy."

"So?"

"So who better to fashion a hiding place? You could have built a cubbyhole in any wall, floor, or ceiling and concealed it from view. A simple task for a carpenter of your skill. I'm going to be quite annoyed if I have to rip my ship apart to find your cubbyhole. Exceedingly so."

"I would be, too."

James actually laughed at that reply. "Yes, I suppose you would be—if you were telling the truth. Unfortunately, my family has been robbed, so I'm not inclined to believe the number one suspect just now. Proof, on the other hand, speaks for itself. I'll give you some time to think about your current situation, but not too long. I expect to see land tomorrow north of our destination, so we could be in Bridgeport late tomorrow night. Volunteer the location so the jewelry can be recovered and I might be able to calm my family down enough to let you go."

Nathan snorted. "We both know that's not happening *if* I'm guilty, but since I'm not, I can't very well tell you where the stash is, now can I?"

James shrugged. "Who knows what my family's sentiments will be once the jewels are recovered. But right now I know exactly what they are, and it's just your blood they want."

"You mean your brother does."

"Well, yes, that goes without saying. You managed to inveigle his daughter's trust. If you went a step further and bedded her just to get her on your side for this bit of pilfering, I'd kill you m'self. Did you?"

"You think I would say so after that statement?"

"I suppose not."

"Why don't you just ask her?"

"Oh, we did. But the darling chit has a way with words that can boggle the mind. If she gave a definitive answer, I'd have to say it only seemed so."

Corky joined Nathan at the bars. "If you'd stop barking up the wrong tree, Cap'n, you might open your eyes to other motives. Grudges, revenge, even jealousy, or just simple anger. I've seen a man break a priceless heirloom in a rage. Deliberately. And cry like a baby afterwards. And wouldn't take much to toss a sack of baubles over the rail, now would it? They'd be gone in an instant. Too late to regret doing it. You see my point?"

"You're talking about a fortune, a bloody king's ransom. No one in their right mind—"

"Exactly. Who's in their right mind when they're enraged, eh?"

The captain was shaking his head. Corky gave him a look of contempt and sat back down. Nathan hadn't thought of motives yet, but he did now.

"My friend's suggestions are a little far-fetched, but here's one that isn't. There was a stowaway who didn't have time to do any obvious damage, but was picked up by a ship that was on our arse. That was planned, and being so, one or more of the crew could have been in league with them all along. Just because there hasn't been another sighting of that ship doesn't mean it's not still following us."

"To hurt me or my family?"

"No, for what you just admitted is a king's ransom. That stowaway could have put the jewels in a crate that could float and lowered it over the side and then signaled that ship to look for it. The jewelry could very well be on that ship. That's what they were after all along."

"Or you could be the one in league with them and could have done exactly that," James said as he walked away.

"This nonsense is going to cost me my ship, damnit!" Nathan growled after him. "No bleedin' baubles would be worth that to me!"

He waited for a reply but there was none, which had him furiously shaking the bars again. Still not even a little rattle from them. He and Corky weren't getting out of that cell. His ship was going to end up sold. He was going to see the inside of a prison despite his pardon. Even if the Malorys didn't have an enemy out there on the high seas, they had one now aboard their ship.

Chapter Thirty-Five

"YOU CAN'T FOOL ME," Jacqueline said as she joined Judith at the rail. "Didn't touch your food last night or this morning. Haven't even remarked on the land you're staring at. You're still heartbroken, aren't you?"

Am I? Judith wondered. Is *that* what I'm feeling? She was still somewhat in shock and utterly disillusioned, and she'd cried herself to sleep last night. Her eyes were quite red from it. But then not even a full day had passed since Nathan had been apprehended as a jewel thief.

"I'm not saying I am, but will it ever go away?" Judith replied.

"Course it will."

"How do you know? You've never felt heartbroken."

"Because it stands to reason, don't it? Half the world would be in tears if it doesn't."

"I highly doubt half the world—"

"A quarter then, but if you want specifics, didn't your sister fancy herself in love with young Lord Gilbert last winter? She certainly cried for several hours over him. And not two days later she was happy as a lark singing the praises of Lord Thomas instead."

"Jaime was barely sixteen. She's allowed to float in and out of love until she figures out what it really is—which she hasn't done yet. She's too young—"

"So have you figured it out?"

"I just feel so betrayed. He led me to believe we were friends, then he robbed me, us, all of us."

"Friends and lovers?"

"Jack!"

But while Judith's cheeks had turned pink with a blush, Jacqueline was rarely embarrassed by any subject and wasn't dropping this one. "You wouldn't make love without telling me about it, would you? I don't think I could forgive you for keeping *that* a secret from me."

"I—wouldn't."

It wasn't a lie, it wasn't! She'd tell Jack eventually. She just couldn't bear to yet when the mere thought of just how close she'd gotten to Nathan made this pain even worse. It was clouding her mind and squeezing at her heart.

So she was completely broadsided when Jack said, "But you didn't tell me he was our ghost."

Judith actually groaned. Jack wasn't going to forgive her, ever, for the secrets she'd kept from her.

"You guessed?"

"Not a'tall," Jack replied in a tone that sounded hurt. "The hair so blond it looks white didn't give it away. Others have hair that color. But after you excused yourself from dinner last night, I heard my mother whisper to my father that at least he's not Derek's neighbor after all, and wasn't that the worst crime, his impersonating gentry? So I asked what she meant by that and she explained. Suddenly your immediate fascination with Nathan Tremayne made sense."

"He asked me to keep that secret and now I know why,

because it was just another lie. He doesn't own that house. He was just hiding smuggled goods there. I told you about my suspicions when we were visiting Derek and his family."

"So he's the smuggler you saw the night before we left Hampshire?"

"I didn't actually *see* him that night. But when I saw him on the ship and recognized him as our ex-ghost, something he said made me realize he was the man who had been at the ruined house behaving so suspiciously. I accused him of being a smuggler. He denied it, of course, and promised a full explanation if I'd hold off saying anything about it."

"It's not exactly a high crime," Jack pointed out. "Some people even consider smugglers folk heroes, you know. I mean, how would you feel if you couldn't afford a cup of tea anymore when you've been drinking it all your life?"

"I know. And that's the only reason I held my tongue."

Jack snorted. "I suppose how handsome he is had nothing to do with it. Or that you've fancied yourself in love with his ghost all these years?"

"Only his handsomeness—maybe."

"There's no maybe about that. He was fascinating to you back then and still is. Of course you could lay claim that he compromised you whether he did or not—if you want him for a husband. That might be the only way to keep him out of prison—*if* you want him for a husband."

"You're repeating yourself."

"Some things bear repeating. Prison can ruin a man. The time to save him would be now."

Already suffering from heartache and now overwhelmed by guilt, Judith suddenly burst out, "We *did* make love."

"I know."

Judith gasped. "No, you didn't!"

"I bloody well did," Jack retorted. "Think I didn't notice that silly grin you couldn't keep off your lips yesterday
morning? Think I haven't seen that countless times on the
women in our family? Even my mother, for Pete's sake, gets
that look after she and my father—"

"I get the point."

"I'll wait until you get over your heartbreak to insist that
you share every detail, but not a minute longer. I can't believe you kept *any* of this from me. *Me!*"

Judith winced. "I know. He tricked me into keeping
silent. I was trying to get at the truth, and agreeing to his
terms seemed to be the only way I could. But I realize now
all I did was give him time to make up an elaborate tale I
would believe."

"One you *wanted* to believe, you mean."

"Well, yes. And time to convince me he could be
trusted. That's the worst of it. I can't believe I trusted him!"

"Good God, don't cry again! Forget I said a word. We're
not saving that blighter. Prison's too good for him!"

Jacqueline said no more, just put her arm around Judith's waist and squeezed. The wind quickly dried her tears.
She continued to gaze at the coastline, which she figured
was in one of the states north of Connecticut. She didn't
care. She'd lost interest in this trip, lost her appetite, too, as
Jack had pointed out. All she could focus on was the abys-
mal pain that was overwhelming her.

She had thought about confronting Nathan. This morning she'd even gone down to the corridor that led to the
improvised brig. She didn't go any farther than that because
she had started crying again. It was too soon to talk to him
without screaming or crying, and what could he say to her
to explain why he'd stolen from her? She wouldn't believe

him anyway, could never believe him again, he'd lied to her about so much.

She couldn't stop thinking of him, though. The image of Nathan and the kitten asleep together in her cabin, so adorable, so—innocent—was stuck in her mind. Of course, even murderers could love their pets. His affection for a kitten did *not* make him innocent of anything. But it had been so heartwarming, seeing him like that. It had made her draw conclusions she wished she could now forget.

Her uncle James had said it wasn't plausible that Nathan was gentry *and* a thief. He should also have pointed out that Nathan's being a smuggler and a thief wasn't plausible either. Why would a thief smuggle when smuggling wasn't nearly as profitable as stealing? He couldn't be both. But he certainly wasn't adept at thievery when he'd carelessly left evidence behind. Was this his first attempt at it? Or had he been coerced into it, his nieces threatened . . .

She groaned to herself, aware that she was searching for reasons for him to be innocent because the thought of his going to prison made her sick to her stomach. No matter what he'd done, that single thought filled her with dread, as if she were the one facing such a dire future. Is that why she felt so miserable? Maybe it wasn't heartbreak she was experiencing, just gut-wrenching compassion for a friend. A supposed friend. No, he wasn't a bloody friend, damnit.

"I wonder what town that is," Jack said. "I'm going to read the charts and dig out my uncle Thomas's map to find out. Have you seen the one he gave my father? It's a map of the entire east coast of America and well enough drawn that my father didn't immediately toss it out simply because an Anderson drew it." Jack laughed. "Cartography might only be a hobby for Thomas, but he's quite meticulous at it."

Judith took a closer look at the town that had sparked Jacqueline's curiosity. She could see single-story houses, a church steeple, a few short docks with only fishing boats tied to them. *The Maiden George* was close enough to shore that she could make out some people waving at them, or more likely waving at the children swimming in the water.

Her eyes flared wide. A strong man could easily swim to shore from this distance. She didn't have to marry Nathan to save him from prison. She just had to let him out of his cell.

She hurried after Jack to have a look at that map herself. James had said they'd reach Bridgeport sometime between midnight and dawn. They would still get a good night's sleep since he didn't plan to dock the ship until daylight. So she could do it anytime after they were anchored in the harbor or even before that, if she could figure out where they were along the coast.

At least that sick feeling of dread had gone away, now that she had a positive plan. She did have a few second thoughts, though. The jewelry still hadn't been found. Her family would be furious at her for helping Nathan to escape. Jack was the only one who would understand why she had to do it. But when she snuck down to the brig late that night, she found it empty. Nathan was already gone.

Chapter Thirty-Six

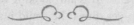

Late at night the weather was more than brisk in Connecticut—if they were even in that state. Clothes soaking wet, tired from the long swim to shore, Nathan and Corky were shivering as they walked up the beach toward the lights of the one place in town that appeared to still be open that late, a tavern.

Nathan still couldn't believe they were free. The set of circumstances was astounding. A noise had woken him in the middle of the night by mere chance. Even so, he almost went back to sleep before he noticed the door to the brig was open. Then, forgetting how narrow his makeshift bed was, he nearly fell to the floor getting up so fast to make sure he wasn't dreaming it. The door was open, but no one was in the hallway, so he didn't know whom he ought to thank for it. Most likely one of the crew who knew he was getting a raw deal from the Malorys. Or the actual thief, who regretted framing him?

In either case, he and Corky had bid *The Maiden George* farewell in quick order. They didn't even consider gathering their belongings first. They dove straight over the side and swam toward the lights onshore.

"Tell me you had coins in your pocket when we were tossed in the brig," Corky said hopefully. "A strong drink would be more'n welcome right now."

"My pockets are as empty as yours."

Corky groaned. "Wet, cold, no money, no belongings that we could trade, and a powerful local family will soon be trying to recapture us. This ain't looking too good, Cap'n."

No, it wasn't—yet. But if he could just get to *The Pearl* as soon as possible, their immediate problem would be solved because he knew something about the ship that no one else was aware of, not even Corky. At least, he hoped no one else knew it yet. But if they weren't even in the right state . . .

Nathan dredged up an encouraging tone for his friend. "We'll be fine as soon as we get to New London."

"Aye, the Yank's friend will help us."

Nathan shook his head. "We lost that opportunity when we got thrown in Malory's brig. We can't take the chance now that John Hubbard will simply believe us if we arrive without decent clothes and no letter of introduction from Boyd Anderson, which Anderson didn't bother to write since he planned to come with us. Hubbard would likely send a message to the Andersons to confirm our story first."

"As I said, this ain't looking good," Corky mumbled.

"Stop worrying. I have an alternative plan, but we need directions first, and I'm not waiting till morning to get them. Come on."

They entered the tavern. Aside from the skinny barkeep and one barmaid well past her prime, there were maybe a dozen customers, half of them lined up at the bar. While the sudden warmth in the room was welcome, Nathan wasn't there to waste time.

"Evening, mates," he said loud enough to draw every eye in the room to him and Corky.

All conversation and rowdiness stopped abruptly until one muscular young fellow at the bar demanded, "Who the hell are you?"

"Come to wash the floor, did you?" someone else snickered.

That started the laughter. Well, Nathan had to concede they did look ridiculous with their hair and clothes so soaking wet that puddles were forming at their feet, and not even a jacket to ward off the cold night air.

"If you can point us in the direction of New London, we'll be on our way," Nathan said.

But that caused even more laughter and a couple replies. "You're in the middle of it."

This was New London? But that couldn't just be a lucky coincidence. Someone on the Malory ship must have intentionally opened the brig door as the ship approached the town he intended to visit.

But before Nathan had a chance to ask about the shady shipyard and its owner, whose name Commander Burdis had given him, the big fellow came over to him and shoved Nathan's shoulder, hard enough that a slighter man would have fallen. Nathan stood his ground, but the man's aggressive stance didn't alter.

Nathan was shoved again as the man said, "We don't welcome strangers in our town, least of all suspicious Brits who show up all wet in the middle of the night."

Someone else with a grudge against England or just a

local troublemaker? Nathan wished he'd thought to tone down his accent, if he even could. But tonight was a perfect opportunity to reach his first goal, so he wasn't about to leave without directions to the shipyard.

He quickly decided to try to nip this man's aggression in the bud and hoped the crowd wouldn't rally to help their friend. "We're not here to cause trouble," Nathan said as he planted a fist in the man's belly, following up with a blow to his chin that knocked him to the floor. "Really we aren't."

Unfortunately, the fellow quickly jumped to his feet. He was big, even had a few inches on Nathan, and he exuded confidence, was even grinning now. But Nathan couldn't afford to lose when this tavern was a prime place to get some help, maybe even the men for the crew he would need for the trip home. That wasn't going to happen if he lost or backed down from this fight.

Nathan hoped for a charge he could easily avoid or take advantage of, but his antagonist wasn't unskilled and tried a few punches just to test Nathan's reflexes. Nathan did the same. For a few minutes neither of them was getting anywhere.

Already tired from the long swim, Nathan knew he wouldn't have the stamina to outlast the man if they continued to cautiously test each other's mettle. So the moment the man broke through his guard with a solid punch to Nathan's chest, Nathan came up with a backhanded left fist to the side of the man's head and leapt up to slam a quick right-handed blow to the man's jaw. With Nathan putting his full weight behind it, the fellow dropped to the floor again.

"*Really* we aren't here to cause trouble," Nathan repeated, and, willing to roll the dice, offered the man he'd decked a hand up this time.

The man stared at Nathan's hand and a moment later laughed and took it. Nathan introduced himself. His former antagonist told him his name was Charlie and ordered Nathan a whiskey, which Nathan passed on to Corky. He then asked the group at large if anyone there was familiar with Henry Bostwick and his shipyard. He got more responses than he expected.

"I worked for him a few years back, but the work wasn't constant and he shorted my wages to boot, so I didn't hire on again," Charlie said.

Someone else said, "Shorted my wages, too, and no excuse for it neither, when he auctions off ships three to four times a year. Course, buying them old and just bringing them here and prettying 'em up, he's only making half what he could."

"Don't make excuses for him, Paulie. My brother swears Bostwick is up to no good. There's been other ships he sells privately, and who knows the difference when that yard is all closed up like it is."

"Is this how Bostwick explains not actually building ships from scratch?" Nathan asked.

"He builds new ones, too, he just pulls the crew off 'em to work on the old ones when they show up, so it can take years for a new one to get finished. But that's how he's always done it, far as I know," Paulie said with a shrug.

"Always wondered how he manages to find so many ships," Charlie said. "The few I've seen come in over the years weren't actually old, so he would have had to pay a high price for them. How's he make a profit that way?"

"He makes a profit because he's not buying them, he's stealing them out of English ports," Nathan replied.

Someone laughed. "Is he now?"

Nathan stiffened, wondering if that was going to be everyone's sentiment, and asked the man, "You know something about that?"

"I know some of the ships brought in were indeed British. Had a peek at the logbooks before they were burned. But who cares?"

"I understand why you might not find his business practices objectionable, but I do, since I have reason to believe the ship he currently has in his yard belongs to me."

The man just shrugged and turned back to his drink. Charlie asked Nathan, "Is that why you're here?"

"Yes. To retrieve my ship and get the local authorities to put Henry Bostwick and his ring of thieves out of business."

"Good luck with that," someone snickered. "The word of a Brit against a local man of business?"

"There are a few things I know about my ship that Bostwick wouldn't know and hopefully hasn't discovered, but I need to find out if she's here first. Can someone take me there—now?"

"Why would we do that?" Paulie asked. "There's guard dogs let loose at night inside the outer fence, and any ship on the property is closed up in the big shed where they're worked on. There's no way you're getting in there to see anything."

There was a round of agreement with that assessment. But with the likelihood that *The Pearl* was still in New London, Nathan wasn't going to wait until morning to find out. His ship had to still be here. She was over twenty years seasoned. It would take a while to sand her down to give her the look and smell of a new vessel. That had been his only hope, actually. The time it would take to polish her.

"I'll pay handsomely to see my ship tonight," Nathan offered.

"Let's see some coins, Brit."

Nathan ignored that. "And I'm going to need a crew for the return trip to England. I'll wager some of you who aren't in your beds at this hour could use the work."

Some laughed over that remark, confirming it. But the same doubting Thomas called out, "Show us a ship before you go hiring a crew."

Corky warned in an urgent whisper at Nathan's side, "You're promising what we don't have!"

"Trust me" was all Nathan whispered back.

It was actually Charlie who downed the rest of his drink and volunteered, "I'll take you."

Nathan smiled and, grabbing Corky, followed the big man out of the tavern.

A while later, they approached Bostwick's shipyard on the shore. The fenced-in yard to the side of the big shed had plenty of space to build ships in, but it was empty except for a few piles of lumber and the roaming dogs. Was the shed there so that work wouldn't have to stop during the harsh winter months—or to hide whatever was going on inside it? But it wasn't tall enough to accommodate masted ships unless the ground in the work area had been dug out.

"Corky, stay on this side of the fence to distract the dogs if I can't get the front door opened quickly enough," Nathan said.

"No reason for the door to be locked if there are guards inside, and I know there's at least one," Charlie said. "I live near here. I've seen him come out to patrol the place at night."

Nathan nodded and amended for Corky, "Follow if the door's open, distract if it's not. Charlie—"

"Let's do this," the big man said, and hopped the fence before Nathan could finish.

Nathan grinned and followed. Unfortunately, the door was locked. But it was old. He could break it down easily, but that would immediately alert the guards, and the dogs. And they didn't know how many armed guards they would have to contend with.

"Kick it in?" Charlie asked.

"No, let's try pushing first, quietly," Nathan whispered. "It won't take much for the hinges to give way, but the dogs are going to get our scent soon, so we need to do this fast."

They both put their shoulders to the door and shoved, but it didn't give way quickly enough. A dog started growling—too close. Nathan didn't have to think about it; he raised his foot to kick the door in, but it suddenly opened before he could.

The guard that stood there looked so surprised to find them in front of him that he was slow in raising his rifle. Nathan grabbed it from him and smashed the butt of the rifle against the man's head. Fortunately, he didn't have to do it twice because Charlie was already shoving Nathan out of the way so he could close the door on the dog. It barked now on the other side of the door, but only for a moment. Corky must have figured out some way to distract it.

Around the shed on this upper level was a walkway, ending at an office on the other side. The windowed office looked down on the main area, which was indeed much lower. A light in the office revealed two more guards sitting at a table. A ship was below them in the center of the shed, but the large area was too dark for Nathan to tell anything other than that the ship was the same size as *The Pearl*. If it was in a trench, he could probably sail it out at high tide once the two enormous barnlike doors of the shed had been opened.

"Do we take out the other guards?" Charlie asked.

"That might lead to shots being fired, which I would as soon avoid. I just need to board the ship to confirm it's mine, and I think we can do that without their noticing. Come on."

Two sets of stairs led down to the work area, one by the office, one by the front door. Nathan led the way down and hurried up the long ramp to the ship.

"Hide here and keep an eye on that office," he told Charlie as they reached the main deck. "Let me know if the guards come out of it."

It took Nathan only a few moments to find what he was looking for: the concealed compartment he'd built in the deck below the wheel. He had to resist the urge to laugh aloud when he found all his money still in it. Bostwick hadn't found it. Nathan's initials carved in the hold probably hadn't been noticed either, but the compartment was all the proof he needed that the ship was his.

Once the two were outside again and back over the fence, Corky came running toward them. "Well?"

"They were nice enough to remove *The Pearl*'s barnacles for us."

Corky gave a hoot of laughter before he held up his bare foot. "I had to give up my boot to get that dog interested in something other than you."

Nathan patted his shirt where he'd stuffed his smuggling profits. "We'll get new clothes in the morning."

Charlie spoke up, "I'd like to sign on for your crew, but

I still don't see how you're gonna get your ship back. There's no way the authorities will believe a Brit who's accusing an American of stealing ships."

"Who is Bostwick's biggest competitor?" Nathan asked.

"That would be Cornelius Allan. Why?"

Nathan grinned. "Because he'll believe me."

Chapter Thirty-Seven

THOMAS, GEORGINA'S THIRD-OLDEST brother, was waiting on the docks for them, having just received word that *The Maiden George* had been sighted. Jack was waving at him from the deck, but she laughed when she saw how many carriages and wagons were pulling up behind him.

"I wonder if my uncle expects more Malorys than we have on board?"

"Isn't he the most practical of the Andersons?" Judith replied. "Easier to dismiss carriages than to find more if they're needed. And I can't wait to set my feet on land again!"

"Don't pretend you didn't enjoy the trip—most of it, anyway."

Judith didn't reply. She'd asked Jacqueline not to mention Nathan to her again. It was bad enough that everyone else was talking about him this morning, speculating about his escape. She didn't report it, but one of the crew did when the family was sharing a quick breakfast before James maneuvered the ship to the docks. Of course more than a few eyes had turned to her at the news. She had been able to say honestly that she hadn't done it and just kept to herself that she would have let him out of the brig if someone else hadn't had the same idea and beat her to it.

With Silver snug in Judith's arms, she and Jacqueline were the first down the ramp. Georgina's three other brothers arrived at the docks before the rest of the family debarked. Georgina introduced Catherine and Andrássy to them, briefly mentioning Andrássy's connection to the Malorys.

Andrássy was quick to assure the Andersons, "My sister and I will not impose on you. We will be continuing our journey immediately."

Georgina protested, but surprisingly, so did Catherine. "Actually, I would like to accept their invitation to enjoy some of the festivities. Please agree, Andrássy. It's been so long since I've been to a ball."

For a moment, Andrássy glared angrily at his stepsister for putting him on the spot like that, but gentleman that he was, he politely said, "Very well. We can stay for a few days."

A while later, Judith and Jacqueline were seated in a comfortable open carriage, riding with their parents to the Andersons' redbrick mansion not far from town. Four of the Anderson brothers on horseback, two on each side, escorted them so they could continue speaking with Georgina on the way.

James, glancing to either side at the in-laws he least favored, remarked, "Why does it feel like I'm riding to the gallows, George?"

"Location, m'dear," Georgina answered with a grin. "Will you ever forgive them for wanting to hang you here?"

"Course not," James mumbled.

"Thought you'd need reinforcements, James?" Drew said on their left, looking at Anthony.

"My brother wouldn't let his daughter come alone," James replied.

"Well, we're delighted to see *her* again. You, on the other hand . . ." Drew laughed and rode ahead.

"Can I kill just a few of them while we're here, George?" James asked his wife. "I'll be gentle."

Georgina tsked. "That sort of killing is never gentle. And you promised you'd behave."

"No, I promised to suffer in silence."

"Well, no one expects you to do *that*. But you knew they'd get in a few licks, being on the home front, as it were. Don't begrudge them that when you and Tony are unrelenting when they visit us in London."

When they pulled up to the Anderson mansion, Amy ran out to greet them. "Was it a smooth trip? Everyone in good health?"

James raised a brow. "You expected otherwise, puss?"

Amy blushed, confessing, "Well, I did think something might go wrong, but you know what a worrier I am."

"Something did go wrong," Anthony put in. "The ladies were all robbed of their jewelry, every last bauble."

"That's all?" Amy looked relieved, but quickly amended, "Well, it could have been worse."

A few of them rolled their eyes at Amy.

James said, "I do need to return to town, and now's a good time while the ladies get settled. I'd like to hire a few local carpenters to pry open parts of *The Maiden George* to see if the jewels are hidden somewhere on the ship. Several searches produced no results."

"Aren't you forgetting something?" Anthony asked, giving James a pointed look. "We also need to inform the local authorities that we caught the thieves, but they escaped from the ship last night. They'll be easy to find with their British accents and lack of money, as long as the search starts immediately."

Judith felt her heart sink. Nathan was going to be a fugitive now?

"These new boots are damned comfortable," Corky said, not for the first time. "I could get used to togs like this."

"You do look more presentable than usual," Nathan said with a grin.

He'd gotten them rooms at the local hotel last night. Hot baths, some decent food, and a few stops this morning for new clothes had them both looking like local businessmen as they waited in Cornelius Allan's office for the shipbuilder to join them. He was a well-respected citizen, successful businessman, and Henry Bostwick's main competitor, so Nathan was counting on Mr. Allan's *wanting* to believe him when he presented his case against Bostwick.

The middle-aged man looked hopeful when he arrived and said, "My manager just informed me that you claim to have proof that Henry Bostwick is a thief? This better not be a joke, young man, because I haven't heard such delightful slander in ages."

"It's very much the truth," Nathan assured Mr. Allan. "I confirmed last night that the ship he is refurbishing in his shipyard right now is mine. When his men stole it, a man was killed. But one of his men was also captured. The information gleaned was that Bostwick and his ring of thieves have been stealing ships from English ports for the last decade. It might have started as revenge against the British, but it's turned too profitable for that to be his only excuse anymore. Understandably, my government wants his operation closed down—and I want my ship back."

"An interesting story," Cornelius said. "But you understand why your word alone won't be good enough? No offense—Treemay, was it?"

"Nathan Tremayne, and none taken."

"Well, it's no secret that I detest Henry Bostwick. He's been a thorn in my side for years. He doesn't just undercut my prices, he's ridiculously secretive, enclosing his entire yard the way he did. But he claims to buy the ships he refurbishes, and while I would love to see the records of those purchases, I've never found a viable reason to ask him to produce them for inspection."

Nathan smiled at the older man. "Until now. If he has any records, they are bound to be fake. But he's gotten away with this for so long, I doubt he even bothers to cover his tracks with records."

"So why have you come to me with this story?" Allan laughed. "Other than the enemy of my enemy is my friend."

"Because as a respectable member of your community, your support could get this wrapped up quickly, perhaps even today. And I did mention I have the proof you would need to do so. There are two things about my ship that no one knows but me. I carved my initials in the hold when I was a child because my father had just told me his ship would be mine one day and I wanted to put my mark on it. But I didn't want my father to notice, so I carved them on the backside of one of the beams nearest the hull. Even if Bostwick has had the hold painted, the painter wouldn't have noticed those initials to sand them down first. I also built a secret compartment on *The Pearl* that Bostwick hasn't found."

"Nor would he, if he merely bought an old ship. But the initials do sound promising."

"There's more. I've also spoken with some of the local men who've worked for Bostwick in the past. A few of them have actually seen some of the ships that were snuck onto his property in the dead of night. They are willing to testify they were British ships, not American ones, and that he passed them off as being newly built when he sold them. That was from just a handful of men. There are probably others in town who will have more to say about his illegal activities. But since the locals also say that Bostwick actually does build a ship every so often, don't give him a chance to say he bought mine. Simply demand to see the purchase document before he has a chance to say anything. If he doesn't yet have a falsified document to show you, then he might make the claim that he built my ship. If he does that, you'll then have him red-handed, because he can't show you where the ship's secret compartment is, whereas I can."

Cornelius Allan grinned with a good deal of relish. "You got me on board when you mentioned local witnesses. But tell me, after all this obvious thought you've put into bringing Bostwick to justice—not that I'm complaining, mind you—you appear to be in quite a hurry to see it done. Is there another reason you bear him a grudge?"

Nathan chuckled. "Stealing my ship isn't enough? No, I've just been away from home too long. I'm eager to return with my ship, and with an official document attesting that these thieves have been put out of business." Of course he couldn't add, *Before the Malorys show up with the law to arrest me, which could be as soon as today.*

Chapter Thirty-Eight

JUDITH AND JACQUELINE WERE enjoying an exhilarating ride that morning, ending with a race back to the house. Judith won, but their groom hadn't been able to keep up, which was why Jacqueline was laughing as they dismounted in front of the house.

"I'm so looking forward to seeing Quintin again tonight," Jacqueline confided as they handed their reins to the tardy groom.

"First name already?" Judith replied. Jack had met the young man at Amy's soiree last night.

Jack grinned. "Yes. He's delightful, charming and funny—and I hope he'll try to kiss me tonight."

"On your second meeting?!"

"I'll wager he does." Jack grinned widely. "Yanks aren't as concerned with propriety as Englishmen, and besides, he knows I'm not going to be here for long, so an accelerated courtship is quite in order. *You* keep that in mind and start enjoying yourself. This is our third day here and I've barely seen a smile out of you!"

"I've just been distracted."

"Is *that* what you want to call it? You need to forget

about that bounder who's going to be in jail soon and get into the spirit of the festivities. Honestly, Judy, you should be excited about meeting Raymond Denison at the ball tonight instead of worrying about a man you'll probably never see again. Amy confided in me that she's sure you'll adore Denison."

"If she bet on it, I might have to ring her neck."

Jack rolled her eyes. "She wouldn't do that."

Catherine suddenly called out to them, and they turned to see her walking toward them on the road from town. "If you wanted some fresh air, you could have joined us for our ride," Jack said as Catherine reached them.

"Thank you, but I'm not very good with horses. And I needed to visit the shops in town for some trimmings to spruce up my dress for tonight. I didn't actually pack a ball gown for this trip, but it doesn't take much to turn a dress into one."

It didn't? Judith thought. Well, maybe not for someone as skilled with a needle as Catherine was. Catherine and Andrássy were still at odds, too. He might have relented on staying a few more days before they continued their journey, but he obviously wasn't pleased about it. They'd even been seen arguing in whispers.

The girls followed Catherine inside. Servants were rushing around, getting the house ready for the ball, with Amy in the hall calling out orders. She looked frazzled, but she wanted everything to be perfect for her first ball.

Catherine excused herself to go upstairs. Amy joined the girls and with a nod toward Catherine said, "I have a funny feeling about that woman."

Jack laughed. "Many people do. Judy is the only one who really likes her."

"That's not true," Judith said in Catherine's defense. "Your mother does, too."

Jack snorted. "My mother is too gracious to show what she *really* thinks."

"I saw her talking with a young man in town yesterday," Amy mentioned. "A bit too familiarly for a first meeting. Does she have friends in Bridgeport?"

"That isn't likely," Judith replied. "She hasn't been in America since she was a child."

Jack snickered, guessing, "Maybe she found herself a beau our first day here while the rest of us were settling in. You know she could be more worldly and experienced with men than we thought."

Upstairs, Andrássy slipped quietly into Catherine's room. He didn't expect to find her packing. "Going somewhere, Sister, without telling me? I thought you weren't ready to leave Bridgeport yet."

She swung around in surprise. "We're both leaving tomorrow as agreed. There's no reason to wait until the last minute to pack."

His eyes narrowed in anger. "You're lying. You're planning to sneak off without me."

He grabbed her and tried to kiss her, but she shoved him back. "Stop it! I warned you there'd be no more of that when you began the role I hired you for. And you've played that role superbly, but it ends tomorrow when we go our separate ways. Nothing has changed from the original plan, Andy."

"You already changed that plan by sticking around when we were supposed to leave as soon as we docked. So you could sneak off without giving me my cut?"

She tsked and tossed him a small bag. "Satisfied now?"

He opened the bag, saw the jewelry on top, and stuck it in his pocket. But it still made no sense that she was risking everything by delaying their departure.

Then his eyes widened. "You're not going to carry out your friend's lunatic plan, are you? It failed once and you can't risk it again, not here with so much family around. Your father will be happy enough with the fortune in jewels you stole for him. You assured me he would be."

"I know my father. He won't be happy unless he gets *everything*!"

"I won't let you do it!"

"If you say or do anything to stop me, I'll tell the Malorys who you really are and that it was *your* idea to steal the jewels, that you forced me to help you!"

"They'll never believe you. They love me, consider me one of their own. I've played my role well."

"Oh, they'll believe me all right. I got the jewels off the ship by sewing them into the hems of my dresses, but I also sewed a few into your clothes, and I won't tell you which items in your extensive wardrobe are currently serving as jewel cases. But I *will* tell the Malorys if you insist on ruining this evening for me." Then Catherine added more sweetly, "I've so been looking forward to my first American ball."

Chapter Thirty-Nine

NETTIE FINISHED PREPARING JUDITH for the ball, then hurried off to help Jacqueline with her hair, too. Judith remained sitting at the vanity in her room, staring in the mirror at the necklace around her neck. Nettie had helped her put it on, but had left the matching bracelet and rings for Judith to don herself. She had borrowed the jewelry from Amy, but it didn't matter who owned it. She had a feeling that anytime she ever put on jewelry again, she would be reminded of Nathan.

She gasped when she suddenly saw his reflection in her mirror standing right behind her as if the thought had conjured him. She touched the glass, but it wasn't her imagination. He *was* there. She knocked over her velvet-padded stool, she stood up so fast, in time to see him angrily toss a handful of gold coins behind him on her bed.

She had no idea if he'd used the door or one of the open windows to get in here, but if he was discovered . . . "You shouldn't be here."

"I couldn't leave the country without setting the record straight. I didn't steal your jewelry. I don't need anything from you Malorys."

He'd risked getting caught to tell her that? She could have pointed out that his having money could merely mean he'd already sold some of the jewelry. It proved nothing, and yet she didn't need proof. She'd known, deep down, that he couldn't be guilty, at least not of stealing from her.

Still incredulous that he was even there *and* looking so angry, she asked hesitantly, "Have you been hiding in Bridgeport all this time?"

"No, I've been busy getting my ship back."

"So you really own one?"

She shouldn't have said that! He sounded even angrier when he replied, "*The Pearl* is real and I've almost finished putting a crew together for her. She's anchored just a few miles east of here."

"And after you have a full crew?"

"I'll be heading home to Hampshire."

"So you really own that house?"

"Did you only *pretend* to believe me?"

She winced at his tone, as sharp as it was. Everything she said seemed to make him angrier, but she couldn't help it, she was so nervous—for him. Her father was just down the hall, could stop by at any moment to collect her to go downstairs. She should warn Nathan to leave, but she didn't want him to leave! How could she have a single clear thought with him standing so close to her?

She searched desperately for a subject that wouldn't strike a nerve with him. "Are you looking forward to seeing your nieces again?"

His expression softened slightly. "Of course."

She tried to further lighten his mood. "Did you remember to get them some ribbons?"

It didn't work. He was suddenly glowering at her, what

was on *his* mind finding voice. "How could you believe I stole from you?"

"I was shocked by the robberies, and you never did directly deny that you're a smuggler. You were always so cryptic or evasive whenever I asked. So I didn't know what to think, but when I calmed down, I realized you couldn't have done something that awful. But you must admit how bad it looked. It had even occurred to me briefly, as it did to members of my family, that you'd been paying attention to me because you wanted to keep me quiet about my suspicions that you were a smuggler, and so you could gain access to my cabin and help yourself to my jewels."

"Underestimating your own attractiveness, aren't you? Let me give you a little advice as you begin your come-out season, darlin'. You are one woman who doesn't need to worry about ulterior motives in the men you meet. You're as fickle and pretentious as all those other aristocratic women, but never doubt that you're beautiful."

His tone was so scathing she was completely surprised when he grabbed her by the shoulders and pulled her up against him. His mouth claimed hers in a deep, angry kiss that conveyed even more depth of feeling than his words had expressed. But Judith didn't care why Nathan was kissing her so passionately, only that he was. Her heart soared as everything she felt for him was drawn to the surface. But he gave her no chance to reciprocate, no time to even put her arms around him! He simply let go of her and walked away.

"Happy husband-hunting, darlin'," he tossed over his shoulder before he climbed onto the ledge of one of the windows and actually leapt toward a nearby tree.

Judith ran to the window to make sure he didn't get injured in that jump. She saw him just before he dropped the last few feet from the tree to the ground and disappeared into the darkness.

Judith moved back into her room and picked up the vanity stool she'd knocked over. She caught her reflection in the mirror and laughed at the silly grin she was wearing. He'd come to find her before he left the country, even climbed a tree for her! He was angry, yes, still hated her family, true, but she didn't care. At least she still had a chance with him, and if he didn't find her in England, she'd find him. Finally she had something to look forward to.

Chapter Forty

THE RECEIVING LINE AT the ball was long with so many Andersons and Malorys present. Clinton stood at the head of the line with Georgina and Jacqueline next to him so he could introduce his niece to old friends of the family's. The Willards, who were renowned for hosting their own balls each winter, came through first.

Reverend Teal was next and paused to say to James, "I'm delighted to see you and Georgina are still married." When James had shown up bruised and battered at the private marriage ceremony that Teal had been asked to perform all those years ago, the reverend had been quite sure that James had been forced to participate, so his remark tonight was genuine.

"We tried to undo that, Reverend," Warren said on James's right. "Really we did. Unfortunately, James couldn't be coerced twice."

James raised a golden brow at Warren. This Anderson used to have the worse temper of the lot, had tried to hang James. But Warren's temperament had changed completely when he married Amy, so much so that James couldn't get a rise out of him no matter how often he'd tried over the years.

"Feeling brave on the home front, are you?" James said drily to his brother-in-law. "If I'd known that's all it took, I would have visited more often."

Warren grinned. "Like hell you would have. It's too bad you didn't figure out a way to avoid this. We hoped—er, *thought* you would!"

"The thought of taking on you and your brothers again at the scene of your brief triumph was too much to resist, dear boy, I assure you. Of course, George will insist it be one-on-one this time—not five on one."

"She won't allow it and you know it," Warren rejoined confidently.

"We can wait until she goes to bed."

But Georgina overheard that and leaned forward to tell her second-oldest brother, "Don't bait him, Warren. James has promised me that he'll be on his best behavior tonight."

"More's the pity," James said, waiting only until Georgina turned away to jab Warren with his elbow, hard. "But do take this up again tomorrow, Yank."

Once the last guest arrived, James and Anthony took to the floor with their daughters to start the ball off. Their dark formalwear was the perfect foil to the girls' sparkling gowns, Jack in pink silk, Judy in pale blue. Drew and Warren joined Georgina on the side of the floor.

"He actually knows how to dance?"

"Shut up, Drew," Georgina said without glancing at him, wiping away a tear as she watched her husband and daughter twirling by.

"But you must admit, this is just *so* not like him," Warren said on her other side.

"Tonight it is. He'll do anything for Jack, including

adhering to traditions he would otherwise thumb his nose at—including bringing us here."

"*That* was writ in blood long ago," Drew reminded her.

Georgina rolled her eyes. "Remember who you're talking about, as if something James said on the day of Jack's birth, when he was so overwhelmed with emotion, would make a jot of difference now—particularly considering *who* he said it to."

Drew laughed. "*James* overwhelmed?"

She tried to swat his shoulder, but Drew was adept at staying out of his sister's reach when he saw it coming. "It was Jack who wanted to come," she told them. "She didn't want to disappoint you, so we came."

Warren put an arm around her waist and squeezed. "We know how much he loves her, Georgie."

On the dance floor, Jacqueline was having nearly the same thought as her uncles. "I didn't expect this, you know."

James smiled. "Didn't you?"

"As if I don't know how much you hate dancing? You could have claimed a sprained foot. I would have backed you up and helped you hobble around."

"Hobble? Me?" He rolled his eyes before he stressed, "*And* I don't sprain feet. But I am exactly where I want to be, m'dear. Besides, now these young bucks know who they have to get past to get to you."

She beamed a smile at him, whether he was serious or not. Dancing past them, Judith was smiling at her father, too, which made Anthony comment, "Your mood seems remarkably improved, poppet. I hope it's not because one of these Yanks has caught your eye already."

She laughed at his less than subtle attempt at slyness. "D'you really think I'd mention it if they did?"

"I promise I won't kill him."

He said it with a grin, which she returned. "I know you won't. But, no, no one here has caught my interest yet."

"Not even young Denison? Amy was so sure you'd like him."

Raymond Denison was supposed to be there tonight, but she couldn't recall having met him yet. "He wasn't able to come to the soiree last night. Perhaps he couldn't make it to the ball, either."

"Judy!" Anthony said, looking at her incredulously. "He gave you three compliments in the receiving line. If he had spouted one more, I was going to forcibly move him along. You really don't recall?"

She blushed slightly, but then grinned. "I was probably distracted, remembering Mama's admonishment to enjoy myself here without falling in love with an American. But if you want me to form an interest in Mr. Denison, you can take me to meet him again as soon as we finish this dance."

"Bite your tongue. If he wasn't memorable enough for you, we'll keep it at that."

She did meet Raymond Denison later, though, and danced with him. He appeared to be quite the catch. Jacqueline even pouted that he was more handsome than her Quintin. Judith wasn't sure if she was teasing. But Raymond was the equivalent of an English gentleman, an American man of leisure. His family apparently owned long-established businesses not just in Connecticut but all over New England, and he was the young heir to it all. He was amusing. She laughed quite a bit with him, much more than with the other young men she danced with. But she had a feeling even bad humor would have made her laugh tonight, she was feeling so bubbly inside. And no matter whom she danced with, she wished it were Nathan instead. . . .

Amy was ecstatic. As the evening wound down, she'd received so many compliments it was clear her first gala event was a resounding success. Even her first attempt at matchmaking appeared to have worked. She said to Jacqueline when she joined her at the refreshment table after dancing with Andrássy, "Judy seems quite taken with Raymond Denison. Have you noticed how often she's laughed with him tonight?"

Jack grinned. "Like Jaime, it just took a new man for her to stop lamenting over the wrong one."

"Then she said something to you about Raymond?"

"She hasn't stopped dancing long enough for me to ask!"

"If you mean Judith, I quite agree," Catherine said as she stepped up to them. "I was hoping to get her opinion about this wonderful man I've met."

"Who?" Amy asked, but amended with a laugh, "I'll ask again later! I must find out why the champagne is running low."

"But the night is almost over!" Jacqueline called after her cousin, not wanting to be left alone with Catherine, but Amy didn't pause as she hurried off.

"Will you join me in the garden for a moment to meet him?" Catherine continued. "I just want to see what another young woman thinks of him before I consider delaying my trip even longer—because of him."

"Is this the man you met in town while shopping?" Jack asked.

"Why, yes, it is."

"Then why don't you bring him inside?"

"Because he wasn't invited. But we danced in the garden. That was quite romantic. I'm surprised you haven't tried it with your young man."

Now *that* was a sore subject. Jacqueline had twice tried to get Quintin out to the garden tonight, but both times he got distracted by one of his many friends. Maybe if she disappeared for a while, he'd get the idea. So she agreed to accompany Catherine, but spotting Quintin, she still waved at him so he could see where she was going.

The terrace was well lit with the pretty lanterns Amy had decorated it with for the ball, but that light didn't extend far. The extensive garden did have old lampposts though, interspersed along the many paths. But a few had gone out, leaving long stretches of darkness between them. Catherine kept moving deeper into the garden.

"For a party crasher, he's doing a good job of staying out of sight," Jacqueline remarked impatiently.

"He *must* still be here," Catherine whispered beside her. "I assured him I would return."

The man suddenly stepped out of the shadows and smiled at Jacqueline. She drew in her breath. He was handsome, very handsome. Black-haired, dark-eyed, wearing a double-tiered greatcoat and an oddly shaped hat with feathers drooping off to the side of it. She guessed that Catherine didn't want an opinion about him at all. She just wanted to show off that she'd found the most handsome man in Bridgeport!

But Catherine suddenly whispered, "Hurry!"

That broke through Jacqueline's momentary surprise. With a frown, she turned toward Catherine, only to get a gag shoved in her mouth and a steely arm clamped over her chest. But she also saw Andrássy running toward them, his sword in hand. Thank goodness! Whatever Catherine was up to, her brother wasn't going to let her get away with it.

"Let Jack go, Catherine!" Andrássy ordered furiously. "I warned you—"

Jacqueline's eyes flared as someone else snuck up behind Andrássy and hit him over the head. The sword fell to the ground. So did Andrássy, and he didn't move again. They'd killed him?! But it was the last thing she saw. Without a word from these men, she was bundled up and carried away.

Chapter Forty-One

JUDITH JOINED GEORGINA, AMY, and Gabrielle, who were standing near the entrance. There might be a few more waltzes, but most of the guests had already departed, and Judith had had quite enough dancing for one night.

"Well, how was it, your first official ball?" Georgina asked, putting an arm around her.

"I'll probably have sore feet in the morning." Judith grinned. "And where's Jack gone off to? Surely not to bed yet?"

"Not without telling me, she wouldn't."

"Like you, she was dancing most of the night," Gabrielle said. "But I haven't seen her lately, now that you mention it."

"The last I saw her, she was with Catherine at the refreshment tables, but that was quite some time ago," Amy replied.

Judith glanced about the room again. "I don't see Catherine, either."

"Nor Andrássy, for that matter," Georgina said, beginning to frown.

"Those two wouldn't sneak off tonight without saying their good-byes, would they?" Amy asked.

But Georgina was a little more than concerned now. "Never mind them, start looking for Jack. I'll send the men to search the grounds."

Judith groaned and hurried upstairs with Gabby to check the bedrooms. Jack was probably in the garden getting the kiss she'd wanted from Quintin, and she would be mortified when their fathers found her there. And it would be Judith's fault. She should have looked for Jack there first.

Jack's bedroom was empty, as Judith figured it would be. Gabrielle met her in the corridor to say Catherine's belongings were all still in her room, and Gabby hurried downstairs to report that. Judith started to follow her, but thought she better check on Andrássy first. As fond of Jack as he was, he might know where she was or at least where his stepsister was. Catherine's absence might be a matter of concern after Jack was found.

But Andrássy's room was empty, too, his trunks still there. An envelope propped up on his bureau was odd enough for her to grab it along with the little velvet pouch pushed against it that was holding it upright. James's name was on the envelope. Perhaps Andrássy and his sister did sneak off, after all, and this was their farewell note? But without their belongings?

She hurried downstairs just as her father and uncle were coming in from the garden—without Jack. She felt a pang of fear, seeing how worried they looked. Clinton was informing them, "I've sent for the militia, James. We'll search the entire town and beyond if we have to, but we'll find her."

"You might want to read this first, Uncle James." Judith handed him the envelope. "I thought it was only a farewell note from Andrássy that he left in his room for us to find tomorrow morning, but it could be more than that."

James opened the letter and started reading it.

Anthony complained, "Blister it, James, don't keep us in suspense. Read the bloody thing out loud."

James ignored Anthony until he finished reading. His rage was apparent, the more so because he said not a word, but he handed the letter to his brother. Anthony was about to simply read it silently, too, but Georgina snatched it out of his hand and read it aloud to everyone:

> *The only reason you are reading this is because I have failed to stop my former lover Catherine's plot to abduct Jacqueline. I never wanted this to happen, but she and her accomplices are determined to commit this foul deed to please her father. You will receive a ransom note tomorrow by post. No, I am not who I said I am. I am a professional actor who foolishly fell under her spell. She hired me to aid her in her plot because I do actually have Gypsy blood and she wanted me to pass myself off as your relative. I helped her steal the jewelry, but I am leaving my portion of it here to prove I am a man of honor. No harm will come to Jacqueline. I will see to that and to making my amends to the Malory family the next time we meet.*

Georgina had started crying before she finished.

Anthony was the first to respond; "Dead men can't make amends."

A round of angry agreement followed that statement.

"This must be what I had a premonition about," Amy said miserably. "I knew something bad was going to happen, but I thought it was the theft when you told me about it. I should have known it would be something worse than that."

Judith was so shocked by Andrássy's revelations, she almost forgot about the pouch, but she handed it to James now. "This was with the letter."

He opened it and emptied the contents into his hand. No more than a few pieces of cheap costume jewelry rolled out along with a lot of stones added for weight.

Anthony snorted, "Of course he's not a Malory. He's too stupid. She gave him little more than a pile of rocks in payment."

"And he has stunningly bad taste in women," James added, referring to Catherine.

Judith felt hollow inside. She'd befriended Catherine, defended Andrássy! "I believed them without question, but you didn't, Uncle James. You had doubts from the beginning."

"His only proof of being related to us having been destroyed in a fire was too convenient, leaving just his word, and a stranger's word isn't good enough when it comes to my family. It would have been easy enough to learn about the Stephanoff side of the family, particularly in Haverston, where people still remember Anastasia."

"Can we even trust what he's written?" Katey asked. "After all, he's a Gypsy."

"Perhaps not even that is true," Boyd said to his wife.

But just then someone ran in and yelled that the ships in Bridgeport harbor were under attack. James left immediately, everyone else following as quickly as the horses could be saddled or hitched, the ladies in the carriage, the rest on horseback. What they found in the harbor defied description. *The Maiden George* was tilted on her side, the wharf she'd been tied to demolished under her as she sank into it. The ship on the other side of that wharf was also starting to tilt in the other direction. There didn't appear to be a single ship along the docks that wasn't sinking. It was as if the entire area had been fired upon, yet there were no fires and no ships out in the harbor to account for so much destruction.

James was actually walking on the side of his ship, looking for the hole that had sunk her. One of his crew swam out of the hold to report, "A sawed and pried-loose plank, Cap'n, just as you suspected. Had to be done earlier tonight and underwater, which is why the watch saw nothing amiss until it was too late."

James leapt ashore and told Anthony, "I sent Artie to wake the postmaster. If Catherine and her cronies didn't want us to get their ransom note until tomorrow, it could have a clue in it about where they're taking Jack."

"Out to sea, obviously, or they wouldn't have sunk our means to give quick chase," Boyd said.

"Possibly," Warren replied, "or that's just what they want us to think."

But someone suddenly yelled, "Look there!"

A ship was coming into view, moving out from behind a bend just beyond the outskirts of town. It was heading out to the middle of the Sound—and the ocean beyond. James started swearing. Judith thought she saw a woman on the deck, but it was too dark to be sure.

But Henry was on hand and had his spyglass. He handed it to James. "That's Catherine."

It was infuriating to just watch them sail away with no way to stop them. James wasn't the only one swearing now. Then Artie returned with the ransom note. James read it aloud this time:

> *Come to St. Kitts if you want to obtain your daughter's release. You will be contacted there with further instructions. It will be a simple exchange, you for your daughter.*

James snarled to no one in particular, "They want me, why the bloody hell didn't they just take me?"

"Speaking from experience," Warren said cautiously, "you're not an easy target to take by any means. Whoever wants you apparently knows that."

"But why make Uncle James travel so far for this?" Judith exclaimed. "Why not do the exchange right here?"

"Because James can gather an army here," Georgina said, quietly crying again. "They obviously want him isolated, which means—"

Georgina couldn't finish that thought, but Judith could fill in the blanks. Money wasn't being demanded as it had been when she'd been kidnapped as a child. They wanted James specifically, which could only mean one thing. They planned to kill him.

"But this makes no sense," Boyd put in. "They want you to follow but take away your means to?"

"They obviously don't want a sea battle, likely aren't prepared for one."

"Neither were you," Boyd replied.

"But that wouldn't stop me from ramming them out of the bloody water."

"Not with Jack on board you won't," Georgina admonished even as she put her arms around James.

James conceded that point, correcting, "Or from boarding them."

Judith couldn't bear it, knowing how frightened Jack must be, remembering her own terror when she'd been abducted right out of Hyde Park. Watching her aunt and uncle, she knew they were just as frightened. James just dealt with it differently from most people. He'd move heaven and earth to get his daughter back—and demolish anything that stood in his way. She *knew* he'd rescue Jack. But at what cost to himself? His only real chance was to get to Jack before her abductors reached their destination.

She moved over to speak with Artie for a few moments before Clinton approached James to assure him, "We might be able to find you a ship before yours is seaworthy again. I'll send men tonight to the other harbors along the Sound. We probably won't find a new one, but I'm sure we can locate a captain willing to sell his. It still won't be soon enough for you to catch up to them."

"I can't count on that," James said. "I bloody well wouldn't sell my ship for a rescue that means nothing to me, so I don't expect anyone else to."

"No, but you'd help," Georgina said. "You've done it before."

"In either case, I'll rouse our shipyard employees to get to work immediately on your ship," Thomas offered. The calmest of all the Anderson brothers, even he looked grim tonight.

James nodded, but Warren added as Thomas left, "It's

still going to take several days or more. It won't be the first time I've assisted in dry-docking a ship, though it's much easier to do at our shipyard. Everything needed will have to be hauled here. We'll just need to dismantle the wharf to make room. As soon as the tools get here, we can get started on that."

Drew remarked, "You instead of money, James? You know who that sounds like, don't you?"

James shook his head. "Lacross is in prison for life. It's not him."

"Are you sure? How do you know he didn't scheme his way out? And don't forget a few of his men escaped that night we rescued Gabby's father. One might be trying to get revenge for Lacross."

James snorted. "That was too many years ago, Drew. Besides, you really think that pirate had any friends? Most of his men were coerced to work for him toward the end, your father-in-law included. This was Catherine's doing, for *her* father, whoever he is."

Drew conceded with some exasperation, "It was just a thought. I don't like not knowing exactly what we're up against."

"Neither do I," James said, then peered at Drew's wife. "I don't suppose your father was planning to attend this reunion and is just late getting here?"

"I'm sorry, James, no," Gabrielle replied. "He got his hands on a new treasure map recently, which means we won't see him for months."

James was reaching an explosive point, being foiled at every turn. He started ripping up the wharf with his bare hands long before the workers got there. It was painful watching him as the hours passed, because he knew—they all did—that tomorrow would be too late for him to catch up with Catherine and her cohorts before they reached St. Kitts. Even if a ship *could* be bought, it wouldn't happen soon enough.

And then *The Pearl* sailed into the harbor.

Chapter Forty-Two

"Of all the bloody nerve," Anthony was saying while he held Judith protectively close to him. "Sail in as bold as you please when he expects a noose to be waiting for him here?"

At least half of them had moved down the dock to where *The Pearl* was being directed to an empty slip. James had confirmed Nathan was on the ship after he put his spyglass away, but he said to his brother, "Kindly remember that's no longer the case. Stop grousing about one thing when it's another thing that's got your dander up. And do *not* antagonize him. I need that ship, preferably with his cooperation."

Judith didn't understand why Nathan was even here. She'd sent Artie to find him up the coast, hoping Nathan would be willing to help with Jack's rescue. But Artie had returned just as *The Pearl* was sighted to tell her that he hadn't been in time, that Nathan had already sailed.

She searched for Nathan on the decks, but all she could see were men in unusual uniforms who looked nothing like sailors. "He's brought the military with him?"

"Looks like some of our local militia boys," Clinton confirmed, recognizing one of them.

"Ha!" Anthony crowed. "So he's spent the last few days in chains after all."

"You better hope not—for James's sake."

"Why?"

"Because right now your brother has a ship *and* a captain on hand to negotiate with, which is much more than he had a few minutes ago. But if this captain is under arrest, then his ship will be locked down until after a trial."

"That won't stop my brother, Yank."

"You might want to remember this is Georgina's hometown. He won't want to be outlawed from it."

With a hard stare from James, Anthony held his tongue for the moment. One of the militiamen jumped down to the dock to tie off the ship. James and Boyd went to help him when it appeared he wasn't sure how to do it. A wide ramp was dropped for debarking. But before any of them could board the ship, a few horses were led off, already saddled, then the militia followed.

Anthony stopped one of them. "Is Nathan Tremayne under arrest?"

The man actually laughed. "Arrest? The man's a hero. He helped New London take down a band of thieves who were operating right under their noses for a damned decade."

Well, that explained why Nathan was bold enough to sail into Bridgeport, Judith thought. He didn't just have the local militia on his side, he had them with him!

"Tony, for the *last* time . . ."

That's all James said, but it had Anthony snarling, "I get it. So he told the truth about his ship being stolen. That changes nothing—"

"Then give it a little more thought, because it does."

"A welcoming committee? I'm touched."

They turned. Nathan was standing at the top of the ramp, arms crossed, tone icy. He looked ready for a fight. And Judith couldn't take her eyes off him.

"I'd like a word, Tremayne," James said as he moved halfway up the ramp.

Nathan didn't change his stance or step aside from blocking the way onto *The Pearl*, didn't even acknowledge that he'd heard James. But he was staring at Judith now, who still stood with Anthony's arm tight around her.

James, glancing between them, asked, "What did you come here for?"

Nathan's eyes moved back to James. "New London is full of whalers. Hard to get a full crew there that doesn't want to be off chasing whales instead and I've been trying for two days. These militiamen figured I'd have better luck in their town, getting the last few men I need, even offered to help get us this far by way of thanks."

"So you're just here for a crew?"

"Just that. Disappointed I'm not in chains instead?"

"Not a'tall. We found out who stole the jewelry tonight, but that's not all she's guilty of. I need your ship to take us to the Caribbean. I'll—"

Nathan's harsh laugh cut him off. "I'm not helping you bleedin' Malorys after what you did to me."

"That's—unfortunate—considering you were assisted out of that predicament by someone on my ship."

Nathan gave James a long, hard look. Whether he read anything into that statement was unclear. Judith did. So did Anthony, who was swearing under his breath now.

But Nathan's next question wasn't odd, since they were all still wearing their evening apparel. "You're having a ball on the docks tonight?" A glance down the pier. "Or a war? What happened here?"

"My daughter has been abducted. The bastards went out of their way to make sure I couldn't follow immediately."

"Judy's cousin Jack?"

James again glanced between Nathan and Judith, who were staring at each other, before he made the decision easier for Nathan by saying, "I'll pay you thrice what your ship is even worth."

"Some things don't have a price," Nathan said angrily.

James took another step forward. "You really don't want to know the extent I will go to, to get my daughter back. Take my offer, Tremayne. It's more than fair, and it even leaves you to captain your ship, which isn't actually how I'd prefer it, but I can be reasonable."

"As long as you get what you want?"

"Quite right."

Nathan didn't answer for a moment, which was better than another outright refusal. But Boyd came forward to sweeten the offer, saying, "I'll even throw in a full cargo, once you return us here. Give you a taste of the trader's life—if you haven't tried that yet."

"Us?"

"My brothers and I. Jacqueline is our niece. While we're not incredibly fond of our brother-in-law, we'd rather he not be exchanged for Jack. So we need to recover her before that happens."

"*You're* the ransom?" Nathan said to James.

"Yes."

"Our—your mystery ship?"

"Undetermined, but possible."

Nathan glanced down at the dock at so many expectant faces staring back at him. His eyes lingered the longest on Judith, again, but he stiffened when he stared at Anthony.

Yet he told James, "Come aboard, alone, if you want to hear *my* terms."

Judith let out her breath in relief. Nathan was agreeing, just with stipulations. Which was fine. At least he was going to help! But of course he was. He had his own agenda, might still be furious with all of them, but he had a good heart. And as long as *The Pearl* got under way soon, it still had a chance to catch up with that ship before it even reached the Caribbean, so both Jack *and* James could come out of this unscathed.

On the ship, Nathan led James to the center of the deck, where they couldn't be seen from the dock. James had already guessed: "I suppose you don't want my brother to come along?"

"Correct. He isn't setting foot on my ship—ever."

"If that's all it takes—"

"That's not all. You can bring only three Andersons with you. Counting you, that's the number of men I still need to round out my crew. You can choose, but you might want to check if one of them can cook."

James rolled his eyes. "So we're agreed?"

"If you can supply my new cabin boy—Judith."

James went very still. "And I was so hoping I wouldn't have to kill you."

"That's not negotiable. And don't be a hypocrite. I overheard Artie teasing your wife about the time she acted as *your* cabin boy, when you knew she was a female but she thought you weren't aware of it."

"I ended up *marrying* her," James growled.

"Beside the bleedin' point. Those are my terms, Viscount Ryding."

James didn't answer for a long moment. He finally said, "You have a cabin for her?"

"Yes, one. The rest of you will have to sleep with the crew."

"Then let's be clear. If she agrees to this nonsense, and the decision must be hers, you don't touch her, not even by accident. I'll need your word on that."

"Agreed. But if you're leaving it up to her, you might remind her of the Bargain she struck with me—tit for tat is owed."

James just narrowed his eyes before he left the ship. He pulled Judith aside to explain Nathan's demands and what he'd said about their Bargain. Anthony joined them before she could give her answer.

"Well?" Anthony asked. "Are we going or is he still sulking over a few hours in your brig?"

"His terms are, you don't go—but Judy does."

"Like hell she does!" Anthony snarled. "This isn't a bloody pleasure jaunt. She stays here with the rest of the women."

"I've already accepted his terms."

Judith put her hand on her father's arm. "I was going to insist on it myself," she said, not even sure if that was a lie. "This is Jack we're talking about. I'm going. I'll just gather a few things and be back before the supplies are loaded."

She started to leave, but heard behind her, "Damnit, James, why didn't you just toss him in the water and take his bloody ship?"

"Because his chums are still here, who hail him a hero and have the authority to gather the entire town against us.

We aren't getting Jack back if we're tossed in jail instead. Judy will be fine under my protection."

Would she? She'd seen the anger in Nathan's eyes. He might have kissed her earlier tonight, given her such hope because of it, but he was still so furious with her. And she couldn't see that ending, not when he'd just included *her* in his terms to help them. Tit for tat? Or just payback for her and her family's accusing him of something he didn't do?

Chapter Forty-Three

"YOU MISSED A SPOT."

"This floor isn't even dirty!"

"Because you're keeping it that way."

Nathan couldn't take his eyes off Judith as she angrily stood up with her bucket and came over to the side of his desk where he was pointing. Getting back on her hands and knees, she grabbed the rag out of the water and slapped it hard enough on the floor for the water to splash in his direction.

"If you wanted to polish my boots, you should have said so." He turned in his chair so she could reach his feet.

She glared up at him. "Enjoying yourself, aren't you—a little too much?"

He grinned. "Actually, yes."

He'd been embarrassed when she'd first entered his cabin the morning after they'd sailed from Bridgeport. It had none of the luxuries she was used to and barely any furniture. He couldn't imagine what she'd thought of it. *The Pearl* was three-masted like her uncle's ship, but not as long and not as wide. His cabin might be located in the same part of the ship as the captain's cabin on *The Maiden*

George, but it wasn't even half the size. His father hadn't slept in his cabin, merely used it as a chart room and a place to dine with Corky—and Nathan, when he was aboard. Nathan had turned the cabin into his personal quarters and had added a hammock, which was where he slept. One of Bostwick's men in New London had put a cot in it, an alteration that Nathan didn't mind.

Nathan didn't know the three Andersons, Warren, Thomas, and Drew, whom James had picked to accompany them. He would have preferred for Boyd to join them, but he recalled James saying that Boyd would be useless for half of the voyage because of his seasickness. James and the three Anderson brothers were pulling their weight, though Nathan had caught all of them giving orders to the other sailors, or starting to before they remembered they weren't in command on this voyage. For men who'd been captains for most of their lives, it was a hard habit to break.

The first morning at sea Judith had made his bed, dusted his desk, swept his floor, and fetched his breakfast, all without saying a word. She didn't castigate him for putting her in the position of a servant, she didn't demand to know why he'd done that, and she displayed no resentment either. She had seemed more the martyr, willing to do whatever it took to rescue her cousin. She'd even appeared a little grateful to him for helping them with the rescue mission. But Nathan didn't want her gratitude. Although he was keeping his anger in check, he still felt plenty of it—especially, toward her.

He'd trusted her. That's why the rancor wouldn't go away. He'd never trusted anyone quite like that, when the odds warned that he shouldn't. She'd even made him look at nabobs differently, showing him they weren't all heartless snobs the way Angie's in-laws had been. Only to prove in the end that he'd been right all along.

Corky had given up his cabin for her. *The Pearl* only had three of them, and the Anderson brothers had claimed the other. Nathan didn't know where James was sleeping, but he wouldn't be surprised if it was in the corridor outside Judith's cabin, or even on the floor inside it. Nathan had given his word he wouldn't touch her and he wouldn't, but James was still helping him to keep his word.

The man never knocked when he entered Nathan's cabin and made no bones about deliberately failing to do so, unless he knew Judith wasn't in there. *Then* he knocked. But when she was in the cabin and Nathan was, too, James showed up once or twice. Unexpectedly. Quietly. He didn't even provide an excuse for it! Nathan found it annoying, but he wasn't fool enough to ask him to stop it, when he knew very well he'd crossed the line with his terms. It had been a moment of madness that James would no doubt make him pay for as soon as James had his daughter back.

Ironically, Nathan shouldn't even be here. He could have checked in other towns for more sailors to hire for his crew instead of the town Judith was in. He should have been on his way back to England and his own nieces, instead of embroiling himself in Malory family problems. If only he didn't know Jacqueline, gutsy, brazen, funny—and Judith's dearest friend. He could have said no if he'd never met Jack or hadn't seen that pleading look in Judith's eyes there on the dock. . . .

And Judith hadn't remained the silent martyr for long. Her testiness had showed up the first time he ordered her to do something she wasn't expecting to have to do, such as washing his clothes or scrubbing his floor again today when she'd just done it yesterday.

"This isn't tit for tat a'tall," she pointed out now. "I barely asked anything of you."

"But you could have, darlin'. You can't imagine how many sleepless nights I had, thinking of all the ways you could have taken advantage of me."

She blushed furiously. He relented and put his feet back under his desk before she actually reached for them. But he couldn't keep his eyes off her as she began scrubbing around the corner of his desk. Beautiful as she was in a dress or a gown, she looked quite fetching in her boyish garb, which was all she'd been wearing on his ship. Right now he had a glorious view of her derriere, which was outlined nicely by her britches as she leaned forward to swab the floor. It was getting harder and harder for him not to touch her, particularly when he saw her in such an alluring pose and she got so close he could smell her, as she was now. He had to be a masochist to put himself through this when he still wanted her so much, just so he could squeeze out a few more days with her before they parted and he never saw her again.

Glancing up at him again, she suddenly asked, "Who let you out of the brig?"

Pleased that she was still curious about him, but angry because of the subject she'd just raised, he realized she was doing it again, stirring contradictory emotions in him. But he wasn't surprised. She had no idea of the depth of emotion she'd tapped in him. He'd never given her a clue about his feelings, not even that amazing night when he'd made love to her. But the truth was, he was afraid he'd fallen in love with her. That there was no hope for a future with her and had never been fueled his anger.

"I wasn't awake to see who it was, but it obviously wasn't you," he said bitterly.

She started to reply, but changed her mind, started to again, but again closed her mouth.

His brows snapped together as he watched her. "What?!"

She glanced down at the floor and said so quietly he barely heard it, "I was going to."

"Going to what?"

"Let you out. I waited until everyone was asleep. I waited too long. You were already gone."

He snorted. "How convenient for you to say so now."

Her cobalt eyes rounded in surprise as they met his again. "You don't believe me?"

"Why would I?"

"Perhaps because I've never lied to you? I've lied *for* you, but never to you, well, at least nothing of import that I can recall."

"Import? What does that even mean?"

She shrugged. "I might have lied about members of my family, but family secrets are family secrets, you understand, and they are not to be revealed except by those members involved and at their discretion. Certainly not at my discretion. You, on the other hand, lied to me. Or are you going to maintain at this late point that you were never a smuggler?"

"D'you really think I'd answer that? You, darlin', can't be trusted."

She stiffened, obviously insulted, but he couldn't miss the hurt that briefly flickered in her eyes, too, which twisted his gut. He started to reach for her, but caught himself at the last second. That damned promise . . . And like clockwork, James opened the door—and frowned when he didn't immediately see Judith.

But she stood up, guessing who had arrived without knocking, and with her bucket in hand, told Nathan stiffly, "The floor is finished and it's time for your lunch."

She hurried out of the room without glancing at her uncle, but James didn't leave with her. He came forward slowly, his ominous demeanor predicting payback might be coming sooner rather than later.

"I know this isn't your fight, Tremayne, which is why your terms were outrageous—"

"No dire predictions, please. I'm not abusing her in the least. And you are mistaken. I was compelled to come along."

"Oh? I didn't realize I was so persuasive."

Nathan barked a laugh. "You aren't. But my reasons are my own. As long as nothing happens to this"—he picked up a document from his desk drawer and dropped it back in—"then when I return to England isn't an issue."

"And that piece of paper is?"

"Proof that I accomplished my mission."

"I'm all the proof you need, old boy. Or in case I don't survive this, my family is."

"No offense, Lord Malory, but I prefer the document that was demanded of me."

"I begin to see . . . stipulation for a pardon?"

Nathan laughed again. "You are amazing. Your deductive reasoning astounds."

"So you don't care to own up to why you need a pardon? You don't need to. I've led an eventful life, seen more things than I ever cared to. Even though you will be sailing home with your ship, the fact that you must still deliver written proof that you accomplished your goal speaks for itself. You're aiming for a promotion or a pardon, and since you aren't a military man . . ." James sauntered back to the door, but paused a moment to glance back. "I liked you from the start. Decking my brother, for whatever reason, took guts. I hope I'm not going to have to end up killing you."

Nathan leaned forward. "Did *you* let me out of the brig on your ship?"

James's expression didn't change, not even a little. It was annoyingly devoid of emotion of any sort. "That would mean you owe me a favor, wouldn't it?"

"You aren't going to answer?"

"Me? Do good deeds?" James laughed as he left the cabin.

Nathan stared at the door for a moment, frustrated. That was a detestable habit Malory had, of leaving things up in the air like that. Of course he hadn't done the deed, when he was the one who'd put Nathan in that brig in the first place. The Malorys now knew that Catherine was their thief, but they hadn't known it when they were all on *The Maiden George*. Nathan was *not* going to look for a reason to be beholden to that man. He much preferred it the other way around.

Chapter Forty-Four

FOUR DAYS OUT AND they still hadn't sighted the ship they were trying to catch. James had said it could take upward of a week to reach St. Kitts, less only if they were lucky with the currents and the wind. They'd been sure that overtaking Catherine's ship en route would be the only way to rescue Jack without a loss of life—on their side. But obviously the other ship's head start was an advantage they couldn't overcome, so an alternative plan had to be considered.

To that end Judith had a purpose other than delivering Nathan's breakfast when she arrived at his cabin this morning. He was standing at his desk, but he immediately glanced at her, his eyes lingering for a long moment, before he looked down again at the charts that were spread out on his desk. James's charts of the Caribbean. They had been soaking wet when Artie had fetched them from *The Maiden George* before they had sailed. But now that they had dried out, they were still readable.

"Only one plate again?" Nathan said before she could broach her subject. "You don't follow orders very well, do you?"

She smiled. "Eating with you isn't appropriate—while I'm acting as your servant."

"I'm not releasing you from your job as my cabin boy."

"Did I ask you to?"

"No, you didn't—and why haven't you?"

She was surprised. This was the first time he'd revealed that her complete compliance with his demand might have baffled him. But she would never admit how thrilled she'd been to be included in his terms. She'd been a little nervous at first, but that hadn't lasted long when it became clear that he only wanted her to perform the customary chores of a cabin boy. He had no way of knowing that the work she was doing actually made her feel as if she was helping in a small way to get Jack back.

In answer, she said, "So you could tell me no? That's quite all right, thank you." Then she quickly mentioned, "We're getting close to St. Kitts. Strategy needs to be discussed with my family. I suggested we have dinner tonight here in your cabin so you could be included."

He raised a brow. "A little presumptuous of you, wasn't it?"

She gave him an innocent look. "You don't want to be included?"

"With *you* serving dinner? I can imagine how well that will go over with your family. How many of them will I have to fight off before they get around to discussing anything?"

"I won't rub their faces in your orneriness. Tonight I'll eat with you."

He laughed. "Is that what I am? Ornery?"

"Better than acknowledging that you're getting revenge against me."

"Never that, darlin'."

"Then what would you call it?"

"A simple need for a cabin boy."

She twisted her lips in annoyance that he wasn't any more willing to tell her his real reason for making her his servant than she was willing to say why she didn't mind. She went over to make his bed. She could *feel* his eyes still on her. It was almost as if he were actually touching her. And why didn't he?! Yes, he'd promised her uncle he wouldn't, and James had assured her that he and his brothers-in-law would mutiny if Nathan did, but she'd never expected Nathan to adhere to his word so literally.

Then he suddenly said, "I woke up this morning with a crick in my neck that isn't going away. Come over here and see if you can work it out."

Her eyes flared wide. She straightened and turned slowly to find him sitting at his desk now. She asked carefully, "What about your promise to my uncle?"

"I'm not breaking it. Your uncle said I can't touch you, but he didn't prohibit you from touching me."

Her stomach fluttered at the thought, but she was worried about getting that close to him, worried that she couldn't do what he'd asked without touching him the way she wanted to touch him. Her breathing quickened before she even reached him. When she stood behind him, staring down at his wide shoulders, she felt a rush of warmth and desire for him. She had to pretend it wasn't *him* she was touching. She closed her eyes and tried that, taking care to keep her fingers on his shirt.

"I can barely feel you." He rose from the chair, turned toward her, and starting unbuttoning his shirt.

Judith groaned to herself yet couldn't take her eyes off him, and when he removed his shirt and hung it over the back of the chair, her gaze roamed from his muscular chest down to his belt buckle.

"Now, try it again." When she looked up, she saw a half grin on his face. He was enjoying this!

Judith took a deep breath, deciding to make him as uncomfortable as she was in this intimate situation he'd concocted. She put her fingers on the soft skin of his neck and rhythmically moved them up and down, and then lower to the tops of his shoulders. His hair brushing against the backs of her hands was so sensual she almost gasped at the sensation! While she might have started out stroking him, soon she was kneading his shoulders, deeply massaging them, then lightening her touch to a caress. She heard him groan and then sigh. Soon she was lost in her ministrations, which were clearly giving him pleasure, lost in thoughts of what could happen next. . . . She leaned forward and asked, "Can you feel me now?"

"This wasn't—" Nathan shot out of the chair. "Leave. Now!"

Judith ran out of there, straight to her own cabin, and stayed there until the flush left her cheeks and her hands stopped trembling. Contradictory man! She hoped his sore neck got worse—no, she didn't. Or did he even have a sore neck? He'd sounded a little smug when he'd told her she could touch him. Had it just been a ploy that had backfired on him? That thought had her feeling a little smug now. But she didn't return to his cabin before dinner—with her family.

That could have turned out much worse than it did, but the Andersons were actually neutral where Nathan was concerned, even though Judith was their brother Boyd's sister-in-law and Georgina's niece. Judith had seen to that by assuring them she didn't mind helping with the "cause."

But Nathan's cabin wasn't exactly designed for guests. His table only sat four and was so filled with the food that arrived that no one tried to eat at the table. And the discussion had already begun.

Thomas and his brother Drew were leaning against one wall as they ate. Warren, James, and Judith used three of the chairs, while Nathan remained behind his desk.

"You can't just turn yourself over to them," Thomas was saying to James. "When we get there, we must find out where they're holding Jacqueline *before* they know we're there."

"Dock elsewhere?" Drew suggested.

"That won't be necessary," Warren put in. "Catherine is the only one who will recognize any of us, but she won't know this ship."

"Enter the town disguised then?" Thomas said.

Warren nodded. "Long enough to find one of them that we can question."

"When Jack might not even be there?" James said.

"What are you thinking?" Warren asked.

"They are directing me there just for further instructions. That doesn't mean that's where they are going."

"And what's the point of that?" Thomas asked.

"To get me on a different ship—alone."

"Don't do it, James," Thomas warned. "You can't just give them the only leverage we have. You."

"I still think if you can figure out who Catherine's father is, then we can ascertain how to foil him," Drew insisted. "Think, man. Who wants revenge against you so badly they'd go to this much trouble to get it?"

"We already ruled *him* out, and it's pointless speculating. I stepped on too many toes in my day, yours included. I can't honestly count the number of enemies I have on this side of the world."

"Yet most of them think Hawke is dead," Warren reminded James. "That alone narrows it down."

"Who's Hawke?" Nathan asked.

Silence greeted that question, but a few Andersons glanced at James to see if he would answer—or lay into Warren for mentioning that name. But James stared at Nathan for a long moment before he said, "It was a name I used to go by when I sailed these waters years ago."

"When you were a pirate?" Nathan persisted.

Worse silence. Tense silence. Judith groaned to herself, almost blurting out that *she* didn't tell Nathan that. But James actually laughed. "Like you were a smuggler?"

Nathan snorted. "Touché."

"But I *am* the black sheep of my family," James continued. "And for a time I felt compelled to protect them from my antics by using a false name. Couldn't give them more reasons to disown me, you understand, when they already had so many."

Nathan tipped his head to that vague reply. "Then might I point out that you're overlooking the obvious? If you're going to sneak around St. Kitts, grab Catherine while you're at it. Then you have a more palatable exchange."

There was full agreement with that idea. But James also pointed out, "That's if her ship is even there. They might merely have someone planted there to direct me elsewhere. But we have contingencies now, so we are at least prepared for numerous outcomes."

Chapter Forty-Five

CATHERINE WAS STEWING. IT wasn't the first time she'd felt frustrated on *his* ship. She wanted him. It would have been nice to add the bonus of a passionate interlude to the real reason she'd convinced her father to send her along on this venture. With such a lengthy voyage to England and back, she'd been so sure she could seduce the captain. But she'd found out too late that he despised her father, and because of it, he could barely tolerate her presence on his ship. She *should* have known that, but her father never told her anything!

"I thought these men were yours, but they don't seem to like you," Andrew said as he joined her on the deck.

"Shut up. You shouldn't even be here."

"Then why am I?"

"Do you really need to ask, after you took that silly moral high ground? I couldn't trust you not to spill your guts to the Malorys before we sailed."

He quickly changed the subject from that reminder. "Where are we going?"

"After St. Kitts? To another island, one so small it doesn't even have a name. You won't like it though."

"Why not?"

"Pirates," Catherine said smugly.

"So that's who these men are?"

She snorted. "Do they look like pirates to you?"

"Actually . . ." he said warily, glancing around the deck.

She chuckled. "That's just the flamboyance of the Caribbean, nothing more. These aren't my father's men."

"So *you* hired them?"

"No, but the captain does my father's bidding. He was tasked with getting Jacqueline. Amassing a fortune in jewels for Father was the only reason he let me go along on this venture. He thinks I'm as incompetent as his other bastards. This was a test for me, one he was sure I'd fail. But I haven't failed. I even helped with the captain's mission, so now Father will know I can be an asset to him. He won't send me away ever again."

"You barely know the man. Didn't it take you most of your life to find him? Why do you even want to impress him?"

"He's my father! The only real family I have left."

"But since you were not tasked with kidnapping Jacqueline, you could let her go."

"Don't be absurd. She—"

"Has the captain's full attention. You think I haven't noticed how you look at him—like you used to look at me."

Her eyes narrowed on him. "They were going to keep you locked up. Don't make me regret letting you out."

"I'm only pointing out the obvious. You want him, but you're not going to get him with a beauty like Jacqueline aboard—kept locked in his cabin. He hasn't let her out once. Do you even know if she's all right?"

"Of course she's all right. She's his *precious* cargo,"

Catherine said scathingly, turning to glare at the locked door Andrew had mentioned.

"I still don't understand why you snuck their man aboard *The Maiden George* when they were following us to Bridgeport anyway. What was the point of that?"

"You ask too many questions," she mumbled.

"You don't even know why, do you?" he guessed.

"It was the captain's doing. I'd already devised a way—you—to get *me* on that ship that was about to sail with a fortune in jewelry on it. They tried to get to Jacqueline before the Malorys sailed, without success. The captain didn't want to waste time following the Malorys to America if he could get Jacqueline off that ship a few days out of England."

"He even had his man drug her, didn't he? She kept saying how tired she felt the first few days at sea. That smacks of desperation when stealing her off that ship could only have saved a week or two of time."

She shrugged. "*He* thought the timing was important. He didn't say why, so don't ask me! He's so closemouthed I don't even know his damned name."

Andrew was incredulous. "But he works for your father."

"My father doesn't tell anyone anything they don't need to know, about his men or anything else."

The captain suddenly left his cabin, slamming the door, looking furious.

"What's wrong?" Catherine asked.

"She won't eat. Not once has she touched her food, and we're four days out. Her belly cries, but she refuses!"

The food *was* horrible compared to what they'd had aboard *The Maiden George*, dry, flavorless, half the time burnt, but that wouldn't be causing Jacqueline's rebellion.

As handsome as this man was, she was amazed he hadn't cajoled the girl into being reasonable. So captor and prisoner weren't getting along at all? That eased her jealousy a little, but not enough.

"Let me talk to her," Catherine suggested. "I'll get her to cooperate if I can see her—alone."

"When you led her out to me in that garden? She thinks you're one of us."

"Did you tell her that?"

"I've told her nothing."

"Then I can convince her to at least eat."

He started to deny the request, but then nodded stiffly and extended his arm with a flourish toward the door. She expected Jacqueline to still be wearing her ball gown, but when she entered the cabin, she found the girl wearing one of *his* long shirts and nothing else! She stared at bare legs from the knees down and saw red. Had they made love?

Jacqueline was standing at the windows that faced behind the ship, not a full bank of them, just two, but with clear, clean glass. Hoping to see her father's ship appear, no doubt. Back stiff, arms crossed, she turned at the sound of the door's opening with eyes blazing. And the anger didn't dissipate at the sight of Catherine.

"What do *you* want?" Jack demanded.

"My lover isn't happy with you, Jacqueline."

"Your *what*?"

"He didn't mention our relationship?"

"Are you mad? How can you consort with that bastard? They're going to kill my father!"

Catherine tsked. "Whatever happens, you won't be able to help, will you? Not if you're so weak you can barely stand up because of this childish refusal to eat."

Jacqueline marched over to the captain's desk, where a plate of food had been left, untouched. Catherine smiled, anticipating the captain's gratitude for her success in making Jacqueline behave reasonably. But the girl didn't lift the plate to eat from it. Catherine ran out of the cabin, but not before the plate came flying after her to break on the deck and make quite a mess.

She smiled to herself, despite the scowl the captain was now giving her. She could not care less if Jacqueline ate before she was delivered. She didn't need to be in good health when the exchange was made.

Andrew noticed Catherine's smirk as she sauntered away. He took a chance and approached the captain himself. "That was a mistake, you know. Jack has never liked Catherine. She wouldn't listen to anything she had to say, but she'll listen to me. I guarantee if you let me speak to her, she'll start eating her meals."

"You have until more food arrives and not a moment more."

Andrew nodded. Catherine hadn't bothered to close the door. He peeked around it to make sure Jack wasn't ready to throw something else before he rushed inside. But she wasn't happy to see him, either.

"You, too, Andrássy?" Jack snarled.

He gave her a weak smile. "It's actually Andrew, but there's no time to explain. You know I'm not part of *this*," he whispered urgently. "But I might be able to help you escape."

"I've thought of nothing other than escape—when I'm not thinking of ways to kill *him*. But how? He keeps me tied at night, the door locked in the day."

He nodded toward the two windows. "Use a blanket to

break those, as quietly as you can. I will knock three times on the door to let you know when we are nearing the harbor at St. Kitts. That's when you must do it and quickly, while the captain is distracted by docking the ship and the noise in the harbor. But you must eat in the meantime, or you won't have the strength to do this."

"Catherine said nearly the same thing, just without mentioning escape, so how can I trust you?"

"I'm only going to give you the signal, Jack. The rest is up to you. But once you escape, I would advise you to hide and stay hidden until these people give up and go away."

"And if they don't leave?"

"Do you really think they will stay and face your father without you in hand?"

She grinned for the first time. "No, that wouldn't be very smart of them."

Two days later, they reached St. Kitts late in the morning. Andrew had given his signal to Jacqueline, but since he was not allowed to debark and the captain's cabin was locked, he had no way of knowing yet if she had successfully escaped. The captain went ashore to arrange for a go-between. The exchange wouldn't happen here. They just wanted to make sure that James Malory wasn't going to arrive with a flotilla of ships before he was directed to the next and final location. But by the time the captain returned and gave the order to sail again, Jacqueline had been gone for several hours. They might even have sailed without knowing that if the captain hadn't gone straight to his cabin when he got back.

Of course he was in a panic when he saw that Jacqueline had escaped. He began to send his men to search the docks nearby. Catherine approached him quickly. "Call them back," she warned. "There's no time to waste here now that your hostage is gone and her father could arrive at any moment."

"He won't. I sank every ship in their harbor."

"You underestimate him if you don't think Malory would have found another ship within hours. We need to report to my father right away. The fortune I am bringing him will lessen the blow of your failure—or I could lie for you."

"Lie?"

She coyly put a hand on his arm. "I can tell him she jumped ship and drowned. That there was nothing you could do. You will of course assure him that you will leave immediately to obtain another Malory to use as a hostage instead. His wife, perhaps, while she's still in America. Or you can return here to try and catch Malory yourself while he's looking for his daughter, though I do assure you that isn't likely to go well—for you. But in either case, I insist you return me to my father now. You can't risk losing the fortune I went to great risk to get for him, by allowing me to be discovered here."

Andrew was close enough to have heard most of that and note how annoyed Catherine was when the captain didn't answer her either way. But they did pull up anchor and depart in haste. Andrew looked longingly at the shore as they left, wondering if he should dare to jump overboard. But Catherine would probably send the ship back for him. He knew too much now. And Jack couldn't come out of hiding until they'd gone. So he didn't jump and just hoped he wasn't making an even bigger mistake than he'd made when he'd succumbed to Catherine's wiles.

Their final destination was only a few hours away. The tiny island was overgrown with plants and tall palms. It didn't look inhabited, yet two other ships were anchored there in the aqua waters. The only building that could be seen from the ship was the top of an ancient, crumbling fort. There was no dock. They rowed ashore and started climbing a steep, sandy hill. At the top, a small village of huts was spread out in a clearing in the jungle. Inside the fort, near the huts, was a new building, a big one, which is where they headed.

Catherine was obviously happy and excited to be home, particularly since she'd succeeded in her own task, and she ran ahead of them to crow to her father about it. The captain, having failed in his task, looked distinctly worried, which infected Andrew to the point that his feet stopped moving.

He called after the captain, "I'll just wait on your ship, if it's all the same to you."

The man turned. "You aren't my guest, you're hers, and she would have left you in St. Kitts if she was done with you. Come along."

"But—is her father actually dangerous?"

The captain took Andrew's arm to get him moving again. "Yes. But if you still have her protection, then you have nothing to worry about. Just try not to draw his attention to yourself, and if you can't, address him respectfully as Captain Lacross."

They entered a big, open room that contained large, long tables and resembled a medieval great hall. The balcony in the back had rooms off it upstairs and below. But this main room was where men were gathered. Catherine was hugging an older man who had stood up at one of the long tables.

But then she turned and pointed an accusing finger at Andrew. "Daddy, he helped Malory's daughter escape!" Then she pointed at the handsome captain. "And your captain took no steps to prevent it!"

Chapter Forty-Six

DREW KNEW ST. KITTS well; his father-in-law lived here. But most of Drew's brothers knew it, too, since the well-populated island had long been on Skylark's trade route. The plan was for all the Andersons to debark immediately to begin scouring the town and asking questions. It wasn't necessary. Jack was standing on the dock waiting on them, wearing her soaking-wet ball gown and barefoot.

James didn't wait for the ship to be tied off nor the ramp to be dropped, he simply jumped to the dock and gathered Jack into his arms. And ushered her onto the ship the moment the ramp was dropped. They still didn't know what they had to deal with. He wanted her out of harm's way before they did.

Jack was passed around; everyone needed a hug, and now they were all damp from her gown.

Judith got hers last and didn't want to let Jack go, whispering, "I was *so* frightened for you, Jack!"

"I was fine," Jack replied with a short laugh. "Enraged, but fine."

"Were you simply let go, or did you escape?" James wanted to know.

"I broke a window and jumped into the water just as they were docking."

"But you're still dripping. Did this only just happen? Are they still here looking for you?" The gleam of battle had entered James's green eyes. He was only waiting on her answer before he charged off to find her abductors.

"That was a few hours ago. I swam behind the other ships moored here. I had hoped one would be a Skylark vessel, but it appeared not. And I was hesitant to cross the dock looking like this, which could have gained too much notice, and someone might have led them in whatever direction I took. So I just stayed in the water, hiding behind the last ship down at the end of the pier. I was still floating there when I saw them just sail off without me about an hour ago."

"Uncle James, please," Judith interceded. "If they are gone, can I at least get Jack into some dry clothes before we hear what happened?"

James nodded. "Of course. Bring her to Tremayne's cabin when you are done."

"Tremayne?" Jack asked as Judith led her below to her cabin.

"This is his ship and not really designed for passengers, but he showed up in the nick of time and agreed to assist in your rescue. They'd disabled *The Maiden George*."

"Yes, I know, I heard all about it," Jack said with disgust. Judith tossed a pair of breeches and a shirt on the cot for her. "Oh, thank God, I was afraid you were going to hand me one of your dainty dresses."

Judith laughed as Jack stripped out of the wet gown and petticoats. It seemed like forever since Judith had been able to laugh. "How on earth did you swim in that? Your legs didn't get tangled?"

"I tied the skirt up first, sort of like swaddling, and just dropped it before I climbed out of the water. It left me tired though . . . well, my limbs are. You can't imagine how exhausting it is to try to stay afloat in one place for over an hour."

Such mundane subjects when Judith had so many questions she was nearly bursting with them. But she didn't want Jack to have to repeat herself, so she held her tongue.

But Jack wanted to know, "So you've forgiven him?"

"It doesn't matter, when he hasn't forgiven me."

Jack winced for her. "Well, don't fret it. He'll come to his senses if you want him to."

"Oh?" Judith managed a grin. "Wishful thinking will do it, will it?"

"Not a'tall! But a nudge or two will, so we'll figure something out—after we get home. I do want to go home, Judy. I don't like this part of the world anymore."

Judith nodded as she hurried Jack to Nathan's cabin. Kidnapping, sunk ships—heartache. Judith would just as soon go home, too.

The only one sitting was Nathan, behind his desk. He glanced at Judith as she arrived, even stared at her for a long moment before he gave Jack a slight smile in greeting. But then he just stared pensively at a long-tipped pen he was winding through his fingers, as if he had no interest in this reunion.

He'd told Judith before they'd arrived that he was releasing her from her duties because he knew she'd want to spend every moment with Jack as soon as they got her back. Magnanimous of him, but she didn't want to be released! She'd hoped they'd have enough time together for her to breach his defenses. She'd been so encouraged every time he laughed or smiled at her. But then that stiffness would sneak back into his demeanor, the obvious anger just under the surface, and she was afraid whatever they'd had between them was truly gone. She couldn't even blame him when she'd accused him of stealing as quickly as her family had. How did you forgive someone for thinking the worst of you?

"Did they hurt you?" James asked carefully as he approached Jack.

"No, just my pride. I was captured too easily."

James smiled as he hugged her to him fiercely. "Do you know what he has against me? Why he did this?"

"The captain who took me? He doesn't even know you, he works for someone else. Never even gave me his name, so I gave him one. Bastard. You can refer to him like that. I certainly did."

Quite a few smiled over Jack's disparagement. James wasn't one of them. "Why were you kept in the captain's cabin?"

Jack blushed. "How did you—?"

"It's the only cabin on a ship that would have a window big enough for you to escape from."

"He pretended I had a choice, there or his brig. When I chose the brig, he just laughed. He didn't want his *prize* to suffer deprivation. But nothing untoward happened—other than me trying to kill him. And then Andrássy—well, it's actually Andrew—he helped me escape. It was his idea to go out the window and he gave me a signal when the time was right for it."

"So it appears he told the truth then," James said.

"About what?"

"He left us a letter of confession. He admitted he's no

relation to us, that Catherine hired him to pretend to be one just to get them on *The Maiden George* so they could steal the jewelry."

"*They* did it?" Jack asked in surprise.

A few embarrassed eyes went to Nathan. His expression was no longer pensive or detached. His eyes moved over the room and ended on Judith. His anger was definitely back.

But James and Jack weren't watching this byplay, and Jack said to her father, "I knew this wouldn't surprise you, that they were impostors. You didn't trust them from the start."

"No, but the theft wasn't enough for Catherine. Andrew suspected she was going to abduct you, too. Instead of warning us before it happened, he foolishly thought he could stop it."

"He did try, actually, but he got knocked out. I didn't even know they'd taken him, too, until he was allowed to see me one time on the ship, which was when he assured me he'd help me escape. I really wish Catherine would get blamed for that, but she probably won't be. She and Bastard are quite chummy. *Very* chummy, if you get my drift."

Judith gave Jack an odd look. That had been said quite scathingly. But then Jack hugged her father again and added, "I just want to go home."

Nathan stood up. "I'll begin departure."

But James stopped him. "I need to go ashore first, Captain Tremayne. I won't be long."

Drew followed James out of the cabin. "You think some of them might still be here?"

"If they are, they'd be the proverbial needle and would take too long to ferret out in a town this size. However, first instinct is usually the accurate one, so come along and

take me to your Skylark office here. I want to arrange for
someone you trust to find out if our mutual nemesis is still
in prison and send me word. I would like him crossed off
the list, or not, before I return to settle this."

"I hope you will include me in your numbers when
you do."

"Itching for a fight, Yank?"

"I don't like how this played out. None of us do. Lacross
or not, they stepped over the line when they took our Jack."

Chapter Forty-Seven

—◦6◦2◦—

"JUDITH MALORY, I INSIST. If you don't tell me what's wrong *this* minute . . ."

They'd just finished breakfast together. Whenever her mother used her full name *and* that tone, Judith knew she was in trouble. But she just didn't want to talk about Nathan, didn't know where he was, didn't know if she'd ever see him again. Of course that didn't stop her from looking for him every place she went.

Roslynn had been given a full account of the trip, so she even knew who Nathan was and had nothing but good things to say about him, how he'd changed his plans and sailed to the Caribbean to find Jack. She had also expressed regret at how shabbily he'd been treated by the Malorys, her husband in particular.

"You should be asking Jack that," Judith replied to her mother. "She's been behaving most odd. She is angry more often than not for no apparent reason."

"No, I *know* you. I've caught those sad looks when you think no one is watching. Are you just worried about Jack? Did you fancy one of the men you met in Bridgeport? Or are you disappointed Lord Cullen got engaged before the

Season even began here? That was so unexpected," Roslynn complained. "But that cast on his foot got him far too much sympathy from the ladies—"

Judith cut in tonelessly, "I assure you I'm not lamenting over the Scotsman."

She was worried about Jack, but she was equally worried about her father. Finding out that Nathan was innocent, that he'd been so wrong about him, didn't sit well with Anthony Malory a'tall. He did apologize when Nathan returned them to Bridgeport. It had been an exceedingly embarrassing moment for him that Judith had watched from afar. Or her father's foul mood could be a result of the tiff her parents were having. She didn't even want to know what that was about. Or it could simply be because she had half a dozen young lords aggressively courting her. Two of them had even whispered to her that they were going to ask for permission to marry her—from her mother.

Ordinarily Judith would have laughed at their admissions of which parent they preferred to approach. She hadn't told them not to, but only because she didn't want to have to explain why. She would tell her mother instead. Actually, she ought to sit both her parents down and have a talk with them. But not today. She had a recital to attend this afternoon, a dinner tonight, a ball tomorrow. A Season in London was a whirlwind of activities.

So Judith was appalled with herself when she suddenly burst out, "I found out what love is like, Mama. It's horrible. I hate it!"

"Only if— Who would dare not return your feelings?" Roslynn demanded hotly, but then she guessed, "Oh, good God, your father was right? You got attached to that young man from the ship, Nathan Tremayne? But Tony didn't say it was serious!"

"Because it's not—not anymore. He couldn't forgive me for doubting him. I can't even blame him for that. But we were mismatched from the start, never meant to be. I'm beginning to accept that. Well, I have to, don't I?"

"Not if you don't want to, sweetheart. Or do I need to point out that you should never *ever* say never. Or perhaps I need to remind you that your father and I didn't marry for love. He merely made the ultimate sacrifice of his bachelorhood to protect me from my cousin Geordie. Tony was the worst rake in London, with the exception of his brother James, of course, so I was sure it would *never* work. Look how wrong I was. So tell me more about Mr. Tremayne. . . ."

Mere blocks away in the West End of town, Nathan was hiding around the corner of a building, waiting. He wasn't alone. Arnold Burdis leaned against the wall next to him, six of his men lined up beyond him. Nathan thought he heard a wagon pulling up to the back entrance of the tavern, but when he peeked, there was nothing there. It was just sounds from the street out front that he'd heard.

This was one of three fancy taverns in this wealthy part of London. Commander Burdis had groups of men posted at the other two, and single men watching four other establishments that weren't quite as fancy, but still in the general area. If normal deliveries weren't made in the mornings, they wouldn't even be there yet. But Nathan had a feeling Grigg would be that bold. Night deliveries, with the tavern filled with nabobs, might draw suspicions. But Nathan and Burdis had been doing this for a week now, ever since Nathan got back to England and reported to the commander—and confided what he'd learned before he'd sailed from Grigg's man.

He was beginning to think Grigg's man had lied about those London deliveries. Yet everything the man had said that night had made sense. Why would smugglers come to London except to do business? Why wouldn't Grigg hit this lucrative market after finding it nearly risk-free? His runs across the Channel would be much quicker, and he'd avoid the heavily patrolled southern coast. And revenuers didn't police the city. They might keep an eye on the docks, but the city was too big. And they weren't expecting smuggled goods to get in by land routes.

"Are you sure this plan will actually bear fruit?" Burdis asked, not for the first time.

"This tavern is almost out of brandy. They are charging exorbitantly high prices for what little they have left. Last night I went in and ordered a glass. When I commented on the price, I was told to stop complaining, that they'd be getting a shipment soon."

"Yes, yes, I know it looks promising, but—"

"You didn't have to come along."

"You mean you hoped I wouldn't. But the man's got to hang, Nathan, publicly, legally. I can't let you just have at him."

"But he'll be hung for smuggling, not for killing my father," Nathan growled.

"Does it really matter why he hangs, as long as he hangs?"

It mattered, but obviously only to Nathan. Grigg had caused the rift between Nathan and Jory, made them part ways with anger, and killed Jory before Nathan could fix that, before he could tell Jory how sorry he was for leaving the way he did.

"You still going to that ball tomorrow night that I arranged for you?"

The commander's attitude toward Nathan had changed quite a bit after Nathan returned to England, almost as if they were friends now. Having "worked together," as it were, and successfully, Nathan wasn't even surprised. But he'd found it useful, having friends with connections, when he'd got it into his head to enter *her* world.

Which had been a crazy notion to begin with, and since he didn't even know if Judith would be at the ball, he said, "I don't know."

"My tailor didn't come through for you in time?"

"He did. I'm just having second thoughts about it."

"I had to call in a huge favor someone owed me to get you that invitation. What the devil d'you mean, you don't know?"

"Just that. I'm not so sure it's a good idea now, to see her again."

Arnold, who hadn't questioned why Nathan had wanted to attend a ball in London, rolled his eyes. "So it's a woman. That's what I had to promise my life away for? I should have known."

"Your life?" Nathan said with a chuckle.

"You can't believe what that hostess is capable of demanding in return. If I wasn't already married, she might even demand that I propose marriage to her. She's a widow."

As exaggerations went, that one had to be a whopper.

Nathan should never have asked the favor. He just didn't like the way his relationship with Judith had ended. At least that was the excuse he'd convinced himself of. He'd behaved like an ass. He knew it better than anyone else. But he wasn't used to these feelings she had stirred up in him. They were driving him crazy. She had given him no clue about how she felt about him. The sadness he'd seen in her eyes was as likely to have been disgust as disappointment. During the entire trip back to Bridgeport, he'd never seen her alone. She'd always been with Jack or her uncle. She wore her family like a shield. That damned, infuriating family . . .

Her father did apologize, but how sincere could an apology be when a threat was laced into it? "You might be innocent on one count, but not all," Anthony had added that day. "I know what you did. Stay away from my daughter. I won't warn you again."

Nathan might have demanded an explanation if his first thought hadn't been that the man knew he'd bedded his daughter. But saner reasoning later suggested Anthony couldn't know that. Nathan was still alive, after all.

But not every member of her family was hostile to him. Her American uncles weren't bad sorts at all. Boyd had been true to his word. He had rounded up a crew and a full cargo for Nathan and had even suggested where he could sell it quickly, in Ipswich or Newport, for the best prices. Nathan hadn't declined it when a free cargo would turn quite a tidy sum. But he was almost feeling rich now since James Malory had also come through with the handsome fee he'd promised him for his help.

It was nearing noon. Burdis would be taking his break soon but would resume surveillance again that evening. He'd been doubtful of a morning delivery from the start, was still sure the smugglers would prefer to operate in the shadows of night. Nathan knew Burdis was just here now to humor him.

"I'm going to have to start bringing a chair for this mission," Arnold said, only half joking.

Nathan started to laugh, but stopped at the sound of another wagon nearby. He glanced around the corner again. A slow, satisfied grin spread across his lips. A wagon was approaching the tavern's back entrance. Three men were on the perch, another three in the back sitting on crates. It didn't take that many men to make deliveries.

"He's here," Nathan warned in low tones. "And with enough men to stave off trouble. He obviously doesn't take risks with a load this big."

"You're sure it's him?"

"I've only seen him once. But Hammett Grigg has a face you can't forget. He's got his top man with him, too, Mr. Olivey."

"I want his ship as well," Arnold reminded Nathan.

"I'm sure you can persuade one of them to take you to it afterward—if any of them are left alive. So we're handling this as we discussed?"

"We discussed *not* killing them, as I recall," Arnold grumbled, and sent half his men around the tavern to come up on the other side of it. He wanted no one escaping. "Go ahead and distract them. If you can manage a confession, I'll add murder to his list of charges. If it looks like he'd rather just shoot you, get out of the bloody way."

"Yes, Mother," Nathan said drily, and stepped around the corner.

The wagon was just coming to a stop with all six men still in it. Nathan walked to the front of the wagon and patted one of the horses as he positioned himself between the two animals. The reins were within his reach, but he'd have to lean forward to make sure he got both of them. The wagon was the only way Grigg and his men might still escape, simply by charging forward down the alley. But Nathan knew grabbing the reins was too aggressive a step to take just yet.

Olivey noticed him first and nudged Grigg. The older man glared at him. "You again? You Tremaynes are a bleedin' bane," Hammett said, drawing a pistol.

"There's no need for weapons," Nathan replied calmly. "Killing my father wasn't enough for you?"

"Who says I did that?" Hammett smirked.

"One of your men."

"Like hell," Hammett began, but then he laughed. "Jory horned in on a couple of my buyers and wouldn't let me go near your sister, preferring that damned nabob. He had it coming. And now you do, too."

"My sister? You bastard—"

The shot was fired. Nathan dodged, then leapt for the reins, yanking them out of Olivey's hands. Grigg had used an old pistol with only one charge, but now he was reaching for another tucked in his pants.

Arnold's voice rang out clearly as he moved in with his men, "You will cease and desist! In the name of King William, I am placing you under arrest for stealing from the Crown with the crime of smuggling—and for the murder of one Jory Tremayne."

The revenuers behind the wagon had already come forward, their rifles aimed at Grigg's men. The three in the back of the vehicle didn't reach for theirs. The third man on the perch jumped down and ran to the tavern's back door, but it was locked. A shot to his leg made sure he didn't try anything else. Nathan started to calm the horses, worried they still might bolt from the noise, but they'd merely raised their heads, well trained or used to loud noises. He still quickly used the reins to hobble one of them for now. Olivey had immediately raised his hands. Grigg did so slowly now. He still might reach for the pistols tucked in his pants, but with so many rifles pointed at him, that was doubtful.

Nathan headed toward Grigg, but Arnold yanked him back as someone else got Grigg down from the wagon and confiscated his weapons. "We have his confession. The charges now include murder."

That bleedin' well didn't help. "Just give me five minutes alone with him," Nathan asked.

But Arnold knew him by now. "Out of the question. I can't hang a dead man."

"One minute, just one."

It took a moment, but Arnold nodded reluctantly, saying, "But not a second longer."

Grigg put up his fists when he realized what was about to happen. But he wasn't a fighter. His style was to shoot someone in the back, send his men to do it, or fight dirty. He tried dirty, drawing a concealed knife while he was bent over from Nathan's first punch. But whatever had hold of Nathan, it didn't include caution. He lunged for the knife the moment he saw it, grabbed it, and tossed it aside. Grigg's attempts were pathetic after that. Nathan even allowed one of Grigg's wild swings to land, just to make the fight *feel* fair for himself, but it wasn't. He got no satisfaction in beating the man unconscious, not when the first blow to his face knocked him out. It didn't even take a minute.

Chapter Forty-Eight

JUDITH AND JACK GOT to ride alone to the ball in one coach, their parents following in the other. Jack's armed escort—all four of them—was with the girls, though, and had been with Jack ever since they'd returned to London. Although the men dressed in livery, they were too big and brawny to look like servants. James had insisted on the guards, and they were going to remain with his daughter indefinitely. Judith thought that could be why Jack's moods were far from sterling. She wouldn't like being hemmed in.

She glanced at Jack, who was staring out the window. They both sparkled tonight. Jack's gown was dark pink silk, but a layer of white chiffon over it created an appropriate pastel color. Even her jewelry was pink, rose quartz mixed with diamonds.

Judith's gown was new, ordered the day after they got home, even though she already had a half dozen others she hadn't yet worn. But she didn't object when shopping calmed her mother, and Roslynn had needed calming after learning what had happened. The new gown was Judith's favorite color, pale blue. Half of her wardrobe was that color. But she'd boldly picked a much darker blue for the edges, a mere inch. Roslynn didn't complain when she saw how the color matched Judith's eyes. And of course Roslynn had seen to buying Judith more jewelry immediately, too. So her gown was complemented by sapphires tonight.

"You look magnificent tonight, Jack. I wish I could wear pink like you, but Mother thinks it makes me look wan— are you listening?"

"What?"

Judith sighed. "I wish you'd tell me what's wrong. You're either distracted or snapping at me over something—more *often* snapping. If your eyes were red, too, I'd think you're going through what I went through with Nathan. You aren't, are you?"

Jack snorted. "Believe me, when I fall in love I'll know it. And *you'll* know it. Everyone will, because I'll drag him straight to the altar, kicking and screaming if I have to— well, my father will see to that."

Judith couldn't help chuckling over the image that created. "Very well. I was just worried you might have gotten overly attached to Quintin."

"I might have, if we'd had more time together, but no. Bastard cut that short."

Jack was *still* calling her abductor by that name, and she usually got angry every time he was mentioned. Not just snappish, but really angry. But Jack's tone had been even just then, so Judith wasn't going to press it, when anger was the last thing Jack should be taking to a ball.

Instead Judith said, "And any of these new lords who've been courting you since we got back?"

"Not yet, but we're in no hurry, remember?"

How could she forget that? They weren't supposed to fall in love anytime soon, either, but so much for well-laid plans. So she took another guess, nodding toward the roof of the coach where the escort was riding. "You hate these precautions, don't you?"

"My guards? No, actually, they're nice enough chaps."

Judith was running out of ideas, so she tried her mother's tactic. "Jacqueline Malory, you're going to tell me *right* now what's been bothering you. I insist!"

Jack snorted again. Judith was encouraged. Jack's snorting was normal. "I don't like being so helpless, as I was during—it's made me hate being a woman!"

Judith was taken aback. She would never have guessed *that* could be the problem, and yet she should have. Jack was always so in control, always in the lead, always sure of herself and her capabilities. To have lost that control, even for a little while, would have hit her hard.

But Judith replied pragmatically, "Nonsense. D'you think a man really would have fared better? A man would merely have been knocked out and dragged off, instead of being carried off. And he would have been bound before he woke. Truly, Jack, men can be rendered just as helpless in such a situation. But—is that really all that's been bothering you?"

Jack wrung her hands in indecision, then admitted, "No."

"Then what?"

"I didn't tell my father everything." When Judith's eyes rounded, Jack added, "No, nothing like that. But there was another note, the original one penned by Bastard's boss. When I found it, I accused Bastard of not leaving any note at all, so my father would have no idea what happened to me. I could have killed him that day. Actually, I tried to. But he assured me that Catherine had sent a more polite version of the original one."

Eyes still round, Judith said, "A polite kidnapper? Are you serious?"

Jack actually grinned for a moment. "I had that exact thought at the time, you know." But then she wrung her hands again. "I was afraid that if I told my father about it, it would stir an old memory for him, and he'd know exactly whose idea it was to abduct me and where to go to find him. The original note from Bastard's boss implied he would. And I don't want my father to go after him, at least not when they are expecting him to. I couldn't bear it if *my* words led him into a trap."

"Don't you think you should let your father decide the matter?"

"I'll tell him, after enough time has passed for his anger to wane a bit so that he doesn't hie off and get himself killed."

"But it's been weeks since we got home."

"I know, and maybe Bastard has warned his boss to change the location of his lair and this can all just be forgotten."

"Is that who you're trying to protect?" Judith asked carefully.

"Gads, no, *he* should be drawn and quartered!" Jack spat out.

Judith sighed. "It's your choice, Jack. I just hope this decision doesn't come back to haunt you someday."

"You can't imagine how much I've been agonizing over this. The indecision was making me furious with myself. But I've never been so afraid for my father before. They were going to control him through *me*! Kill him because of *me*! I *am* going to tell him, whether it helps or not, but after the Season is over. Besides, by then he'll probably have more information. Uncle Clinton assured him that all the Skylark captains who pass down that way will keep an eye out for Catherine, Andrew, and Bastard. Something is sure to come of that."

Judith didn't usually disagree with Jack but she tsked now, "I hesitate to say it, but I think you should simply have more faith in your father. As long as he doesn't have the rescue of loved ones to contend with, he won't be restrained. And you know how that works out."

Jack grinned, then laughed. "Yes, I know. I'm just making sure it does happen that way, by letting enough time pass so whoever did this won't be expecting him. That's all, Judy. I just want my father to have a better fighting chance. And I did consider how torn up he'd be if he missed my Season just to wrap this up."

That was sound reasoning, so Judith said no more on the subject. And Jack obviously felt better for having made a clean breast of it. She was still smiling when they arrived at the ball.

Chapter Forty-Nine

LADY SPENCER'S BALL WASN'T the first of the Season. They'd missed that one due to their detour to the Caribbean, which had delayed their return to London by a week. It wasn't the second ball, either, but at least they'd managed to attend that one, with a mere one day's notice, which was why Judith had so many suitors already. But she'd hoped she might actually enjoy this third ball. Nasty thing, hope, when it didn't stand a chance in hell . . .

Jack's suitors converged on her immediately, but then Georgina had held James back when they arrived, so the young bucks hadn't yet noticed that Jack's father was in attendance. Georgina had insisted on taking this precaution. Because James was such a social recluse, rumors about him of the dastardly sort had always abounded and were still whispered to this day. He simply never gave the *ton* a chance to get to know him and never would. Georgina had had to hold him back at their first ball, too, so Jack would at least be able to meet a few young men before he was noticed. James was actually amused by his wife's ploy.

Judith didn't face the same challenge on entering the ballroom with her parents. The only rumors that had ever circulated about her father concerned his having been a notorious rake and having had his share of duels because of it, most of which were long forgotten. It was still well-known that he was a master in the ring, but what young buck didn't know that when they had all at one time or another visited Knighton's Hall to witness firsthand his renowned skill.

Judith knew it was simply her father's demeanor that gave young men pause about approaching her—whenever Roslynn didn't have her eye on him, urging him to smile or at least keep a neutral expression on his face. But at the first ball, Roslynn had managed quite well to keep Anthony from scaring away every man who approached Judith, and Roslynn had been overly nice to all of them as well, which was why Judith already had a handful of suitors. They came forward tonight, just more slowly since Anthony was still at her side.

But an elbow was discreetly jabbed in Anthony's ribs as his wife whispered, "Behave. Be cordial. Be their bluidy best friend."

"Now *that's* going too far, sweetheart, 'dced it is," Anthony complained. "But I'll give the first option a try if you'll stop frying me—and put your brogue away."

The byplay was brief but long enough for Addison Tyler to whisk Judith onto the dance floor with a relieved laugh. "Gad, I thought she'd never distract him."

With barely ten minutes passed since she'd entered the ballroom, she knew that was a gross exaggeration. But Addison was still smiling, so it was obviously intended to be. Firstborn of an earl, Addison would eventually inherit that title. With blond hair, dark gray eyes, and a handsome visage, he knew he was quite the catch this Season. The ladies did, too. Quite a few had set their caps for him before Jack and Judith had arrived home. Judith knew a good number of the debutantes, those who lived in London with whom she and Jack had socialized while growing up, and she'd been snubbed by a few of them as if she'd stolen Addison Tyler away from them.

"Does your father hate me for some reason?" Lord Tyler asked as he glided her smoothly in the current waltz.

"No, he hates you all equally."

"So he's that sort of father, eh? Can't bear to let you go?"

"Something like that."

Addison was one of the two young lords who had already decided that they wanted to marry her. Hadley Dunning was the other. They'd both called on her every day this week at the appropriate midmorning hour. They weren't the only two who had done so. But Addison was behaving somewhat aggressively toward her other suitors, too, as if he'd staked his claim and they ought to know it and back off. Some harsh words had even passed between him and Lord Dunning at the recital yesterday. The hostess had expressed concern they were going to come to blows right there in her music room. Judith doubted that they would have done so because they knew each other well. But their hostess had still asked them to leave.

Addison hadn't apologized for that yet, might not think he ought to. Roslynn had been amused that men were fighting over Judith already. Anthony didn't know because he had taken his own aggression to the ring yesterday afternoon.

"But at least your mum is nice enough."

Nice enough? What the deuce did he think, that it was him and her against her parents? But then she groaned to herself. She was looking for a reason not to like him, wasn't she? Yet she'd favored him from the start, but only because he was the most handsome of the lot. Yet having gotten to know him better, she still found him acceptable. A little carefree, a little too bold, quite the flirt. But he hadn't made her laugh, not once.

She actually liked Lord Dunning more. Hadley wasn't quite as handsome as Addison, but he was definitely more amusing, and she needed some humor in her life right now. And he was much more friendly. He was actually trying to get to know her and wasn't attempting to immediately sweep her off her feet as Addison was doing. But she wasn't going to be rushed into a decision, and she was feeling rushed, by both of them. That had to stop. The Season had barely begun.

So she held her tongue, waited for the apology that didn't come, and managed a smile when Addison escorted her back to her parents. But he blocked Hadley from getting close enough to her to ask for the next dance. Deliberately. There was even a slight shove.

Which prompted Anthony to say, "I'm good at cracking heads together. If I have to behave, you bloody well do, too."

His saying that with a tight smile kept Roslynn's hackles from rising. In fact, as soon as Hadley Dunning led Judith onto the floor, she whispered to her husband, "Lord Tyler's jealousy might be amusing, but not if it gets out of hand."

"Say no more, m'dear. I'll—"

"Oh, no, you won't." Roslynn knew exactly what Anthony was itching to do. "If they want to fight over Judy, let them. We can only hope they will not do it at one of these large events—actually, I suppose it wouldn't hurt for you to discreetly say a few words to him, just to help tone it down—if you can do that without laying a hand on him. If it scares him off, so be it. It's not as if she favors him or anyone else here."

"Music to my ears," Anthony said with a *very* genuine smile.

They were still whispering, but only because two more of Judith's beaux were lingering with them instead of moving off to find a partner for the current waltz. Inconvenient, but these young bucks had made *their* choice and didn't want to miss catching Judith for the next dance.

"You should be asking yourself why your daughter isn't thrilled with any of these young lords," Roslynn warned.

"I already know why. She and Jack made a pact. They're not getting hitched this year. Thank God."

"That's not why and I think you know it. She's in love with someone else. I just haven't met him yet."

"An infatuation, that's all that was, and it was nipped in the bud. She's over it."

"I happen to know otherwise. And it's high time I met Mr. Tremayne."

"I'm happy to say he's gone and good riddance."

"Are you now?" she said sternly. "Happy? That your daughter isn't?"

He snorted. "Look at her, Ros. She's laughing. Does it look like she's pining over that blighter?"

"She hides her feelings well, but she confided in me. So let me ask you this. *Would* you stand in the way of her happiness?" He didn't answer, so she added, "You should track him down for her."

He actually laughed. "No, I will not. We're not interfering for one simple reason. The man doesn't want her. If he did, he'd be here asking me for her hand before someone else does, but he's not, is he?"

"Because you obviously don't like him and he knows it."

Anthony shook his head, disagreeing, "No, he's actually not afraid of me, Ros, not even a little. That's the one thing I *do* like about him."

"That's some progress." She smiled.

He rolled his eyes. "One sterling quality does not make him acceptable to me as a son-in-law."

"No man is *ever* going to be acceptable to you for our daughter. I'm not even surprised this is turning out to be so difficult. But you have to think of Judy, not yourself. You knew this day would come."

"But it hasn't come yet. I repeat, he doesn't want her, and she'll just have to—"

"Would that be him?" Roslynn suddenly asked, nodding toward the entrance at a handsome man with white-blond hair.

Anthony hissed, "Of all the bloody nerve."

"Well, you *did* say he wasn't afraid of you," Roslynn smirked.

Chapter Fifty

JUDITH SAW NATHAN THE moment he entered the ballroom only because her eyes kept venturing in that direction, hoping he would. But when he did, it took her a moment to believe it. Dressed in black evening attire tailored to perfection, blond hair queued back for the occasion, he fit right in as if he belonged here. Well, didn't he? He had the credentials to be here, but how had he finagled an invitation? He must have one, she supposed, to have gotten through the door.

As if she cared how he'd managed it. He was here! Her heart was already racing with anticipation. He'd come to his senses, finally. He'd come to find her. But to do it this boldly? When he could have just come to her home? He would have been let in. Every day since she'd been back, she'd warned the butler to expect him, then had dealt with the disappointment when he didn't show up.

Their eyes met across the room, but she couldn't hold the look because she was still dancing with Hadley. But the moment the music ended, she hurried back to her mother to make herself available for Nathan to approach her. Her father was conspicuously absent. Thankfully! But then she noted Anthony on the edge of the room. He'd gone to join forces with James. Those two had better *not* chase Nathan off, not tonight. Tonight was going to be magical now, the veritable highlight of her Season, of her life, for that matter. Nathan would make it so.

Roslynn wasn't alone. The two beaux Judith hadn't danced with yet were still waiting for her, and two others had joined them, one she knew, one she didn't. Three of them asked to have the next dance, which she promptly declined. Yet they didn't leave!

Roslynn whispered to her, "I suggested they find other partners while they wait for a turn on the floor with you, but I think their feet have grown roots."

Judith was flattered, but right now it was quite vexing. Would Nathan even come forward with so many lords presently vying for her attention? She couldn't see where he'd gone.

But then Roslynn said in an even lower tone, "Perhaps you are thirsty? Lady Spencer has laid out extensive refreshments to suit everyone's tastes."

Judith guessed, "You saw him?"

"Your father confirmed your Mr. Tremayne is here, yes." Roslynn added with a grin, "I'll hold down the fort and tender your excuses."

Judith beamed a smile at her mother and started toward the other side of the room. But she'd barely gone ten feet before she saw Nathan dancing by with someone else. She stopped as it dawned on her that he might not be here to see her at all. This could merely be his introduction to high society, a means to an end, since he intended to take his guardianship of his nieces more seriously. Just planning ahead for the connections he would need when his nieces came of age? Or was he just making sure that Anthony would leave him alone if he devoted his attention elsewhere for the moment? Or worse, making sure that *she* knew he was done with her. But in any case, she didn't like his tactics, not one little bit.

She returned to her beaux and said to the newcomer, "We haven't met. Shall we rectify that with a dance?"

He didn't decline, even though he hadn't asked her for one when he'd had the chance. "I'm Robert Mactear," he said once he began to waltz with her. "I was just paying my respects tae yer muther. She's vera good friends wi' mine."

She heard no more than the name, which sounded familiar, for her eyes and attention were elsewhere. Nathan passed within a few feet of her. The pretty chit he was dancing with was talking his ear off. He appeared raptly interested in her every word.

"She had a handful o' invitations sent tae me long afore this Season started. I ken she had high hopes for us."

Judith blinked. "You and I?"

Had her mother *really* looked for another Scotsman when Ian Cullen got snatched up by another debutante? But this would have been while Judith was in America— before her mother knew about Nathan.

"Aye," Robert confirmed it. "I had tae return tae London on business, so I thought I should let yer muther know I'm already taken, well, as soon as my lass says yes tae me."

She might have laughed. Roslynn was simply *not* destined to be a matchmaker. But she grouched instead, "So am I, though *my* lad appears to want to ignore me tonight."

"In that case, ye might want tae laugh and pretend yer flirting wi' me? Just tae nudge him a wee bit. I know from experience how bluidy well that works."

She did laugh. "You're a good sport, Robert."

A while later Jack found her and asked, "What the devil is *he* doing here?"

"Causing a stir," Judith said. "The ladies can't take their eyes off him, if you haven't noticed."

Jack peered at her. "You've obviously noticed. Why don't you just tell him how you feel?"

"That's not how it's done."

Jack's brows shot together. "You're joking, right? That's how *we* do it."

No, that might be what Jack would do, but Judith wasn't nearly that bold. She wished she were, though, and visited the refreshment tables a few times to see if that might give her more courage, but it didn't. It did allow her to flirt outrageously with her beaux though, per Robert's suggestion, but that didn't help either. Nathan didn't notice because he was too busy dancing with every debutante but her. Bloody blighter, he was going to take his anger to the grave?

But when she saw him heading for the exit, she actually ran across the room to stop him. "You're leaving? Really? Without a bloody word to me?"

He turned. "Yes. This is your world, darlin'. Not mine."

She didn't know what to say to that, but it was coming back, that pain in her chest, constricting her heart, squeezing. Yet, he seemed to be waiting for her to say *something*, but all she could do was stare at him, at his handsome face that she hadn't seen for nearly a month, the bruise on his cheek that was barely discernible, but *she* noticed it, the tight line of his lips, his stiff jaw, and the intense emotion in his eyes. Hot or cold? She couldn't tell!

But the only words she managed were "What's that bruise from?"

"Unfinished business finally put to rest."

"And is that your only unfin—?"

The question died off. He'd walked away and right out of the ballroom! Oh, God, why did she flirt so hard with the other men? Had he just given up because of it?

She got through the rest of the night. More champagne helped, perhaps too much champagne because she was aware of being a little foxed when she found herself in bed and didn't even remember the ride home.

But she went right to sleep that night. She was sure she was still foxed when she heard *his* voice, felt *his* hand on her cheek, a touch that healed all her wounds. But of course she wasn't sleeping.

Now she was wide-awake. "How did you get in here?"

"Through your window." He was still caressing her cheek. Like their kitten, she felt the need to lean toward his hand and tilted her head slightly so she could. "It's not the first time I've stood below it."

That surprised her. "But how could you know which was mine?"

"Earlier this week I found one of your kitchen maids out back and convinced her that I wanted to throw pebbles at your window to get your attention. She was happy to point it out to me. She thought I was one of your many swains trying to impress you with a private serenade."

The idea of him singing to her made her giggle. "You wouldn't have."

Enough moonlight was in the room that she could see his smile. "No, I wouldn't."

"You could have just come to the front door."

"Knowing your father, I couldn't. But I threw some pebbles tonight, so many of them I was afraid the glass would break. You just didn't hear them."

Damned champagne—no, she was glad the noise didn't wake her, glad that he must have found the ladder leaning against the apple tree in their garden. But why did he? What little he'd said at the ball suggested she'd never see him again, certainly not like *this*.

"What are you doing here?" she asked breathlessly.

"Tell me you didn't expect me."

"No, I didn't."

"Deep down, you did."

She didn't correct him again, yet he'd assumed something that wasn't so, while she'd been crushed by his seeming indifference tonight, sure he was still angry. Had they both fallen prey to false assumptions? When mere actions could speak much louder, as his were doing right now?

But remembering that hurt, she said, "We should have spoken at the ball, at least, more'n we did."

"I thought we would. I even thought we would dance. But when I got there, I was a bit stunned by how beautiful you looked—and how perfectly you fit in that glittering room. And I was afraid I would kiss you, right there in front of everyone, if we—"

She sat up immediately to kiss him, cutting off his words. It's what she'd wanted to do from the moment she'd heard his voice. He'd been at the ball, for her. He'd come here tonight for her. She didn't need to hear another word. But she needed to feel again what only he could make her feel. She'd longed for this, cried for this, for him. She ought to take him to task for that, but not now when he was showing her the depth of his feeling, crushing her to his chest, devouring her lips.

So when he pushed her back to her pillow, she could have cried, until she heard, "Give me a moment, darlin', please. I don't want to hurt you, but you can't imagine how much I want you."

She understood. She could have said the same thing. But she didn't want a moment. "Take a deep, calming breath if you must, just do it quickly," she insisted, *demanded*.

He laughed shakily, saying, "That worked, your silly humor."

It was no time to tell him she wasn't joking. But he stood up and shrugged out of his evening jacket, then took off his cravat and shirt. She kicked her covers away so she could kneel on the side of the bed in front of him. Within close reach of him, she slid her hands over his bare skin. So fascinating to all her senses. He had such a magnificent body, perfectly proportioned, big, lean, rock hard. Just looking at him had always affected her on a primal level she never quite understood. But right now, he was the flame and she was the moth, finding him a lure that was impossible to resist, and her body was on fire for him.

He was undressing quickly, yet not fast enough for her. Her nails scraped over his nipples, not intentionally, yet she heard the groan. Arrested, she wasn't sure what she'd just done to him, caused him pain or pleasure? But she tossed off her loose nightgown to find out and scraped her own nipple to feel what he'd just felt . . . oh, God!

He said it aloud, "Oh, God," as he tumbled her backward on the bed.

They rolled together. She laughed and ending up beneath him, gave him a brilliant smile. He appeared transfixed by it. She was caught by his eyes and the wealth of feeling in them. He loved her! She wished he'd say so, but she was content just seeing it. His lips were gentle on her now, her face, her shoulders, her neck. His love for her was in every touch. Even when he entered her a while later, it was with such tender care. They were like two pieces of a whole that were meant to rejoin, fitting together perfectly.

The ecstasy arrived for her first and rather quickly. She hoped it wouldn't always be so, because reaching that pinnacle was half the pleasure. Perhaps she could persuade him to make love to her again. But the champagne caught up with her as she finished the thought and nodded off.

"I want to marry you—if I can have you without your family." Nathan was only half joking, yet she didn't respond. "Judy?"

He sighed when he realized she was already asleep. Or pretending to be, and that would be his answer, wouldn't it? No, he was done with doubts, had experienced far too many when it came to her. He dressed, kissed her brow, and slipped out the way he'd come in. It was her turn now. If she wanted him in her life, she knew where she could find him to let him know.

Chapter Fifty-One

JUDITH WOKE WITH A smile and a nasty headache. The headache went away as the morning progressed; the smile stayed. It had been a magical night, just not at the ball. It would be nice if she could remember it in more detail, but her joy was still overflowing. She ought to caution herself that she'd felt this way before after the first time Nathan and she had made love, but she didn't. This was different. This time she was sure Nathan loved her.

Jacqueline showed up midmorning instead of staying home to receive her own callers, which wasn't unusual. Jack didn't have the patience for *all* the formalities of a Season. But she still couldn't escape all of her beaux. Having been told where she'd gone, some of them followed her to Judith's house, so the parlor on Park Lane was quite crowded today. Which was why it took so long for Jack to find a moment alone with Judith.

When she did, Jack observed, "You seem quite chipper today, though I have to admit that *was* a splendid ball, wasn't it?"

"No, but it was a splendid night."

"I thought you went home angry?"

Judith didn't reply to that, grinning excitedly instead. "I've made a decision. You were right. I should have told Nathan long ago how I feel about him and I will, just as soon as I see him again."

"He barely said two words to you last night. D'you really think that's going to happen?"

"Yes, for the simple reason that he made quite an impression last night on the *ton*. He's no doubt on everyone's lips this morning."

Jack glanced over her shoulder, then nodded with a short. "He's definitely on *their* lips."

"So every hostess is going to want to include him now."

"They might want to, but no one will know where to send invitations!"

"But I do." Judith grinned. "And I'll make sure they do."

"You're going to break our pact to wait, aren't you?" Jack said with a sour look.

Judith hugged her tightly. "I have to. You will, too, once you feel this way. It's the most glorious thing, Jack, really it is."

"Just so you know, if he hurts you again, I'll do the same to him."

Judith laughed. "So will I!"

She canceled her engagement for that afternoon so she could go through all of her own invitations and jot brief notes to each hostess. She gave his address in care of Derek, so she sent her cousin a note, too, to deliver them to the ruin. She even added the postscript "It will be repaired soon!"

Of course Nathan might not go straight to Hampshire. He might be staying somewhere in town until he could declare his intentions to her. But in that case he'd finagle his own invitations, just as he'd done last night. So she did expect to see him again, and soon. The only thing she didn't expect was for him to call on her on Park Lane. He'd made it perfectly clear that he didn't want to run into her father. But he could come through the window again. . . .

Her confidence started to wane by the end of the week. She didn't get despondent, though. She got determined instead. She confided in Jack about what she was going to do. Jack merely cautioned her not to go alone. So they found her parents in the dining room that morning, and just in time. Anthony had just stood up to leave. His habit was to escape the house before the callers arrived.

"Sit down, please," Judith requested. "And don't worry, the house is now officially back to normal."

"Did a few months fly by without my noticing?" Anthony said drily as he resumed his seat.

Judith might have laughed at his quip if she weren't putting the cart before the horse, as it were. "No, but I am henceforth declining all callers, well, except—no, he won't, and we know *why* he—" Before she got any more tongue-tied, she declared firmly, "I've canceled all my engagements, too. The Season is over for me."

Roslynn might have had some warning, but she still exclaimed, "Judy! It's barely begun!"

"But there's no point, Mama, when I already know who I'm going to marry."

Judith was looking at her father as she said it. He didn't ask her who, merely said, "I don't suppose he intends to ask my permission first?"

"And risk a resounding no?"

"But has he even asked you yet?"

"No, but he will, just as soon as I get to Hampshire. Will you take me?"

He didn't answer. He looked at Jack and asked, "Are you responsible for the courage in her words?"

Jack grinned cheekily. "No, actually, I just wanted to watch."

Anthony snorted. "Minx."

He didn't look angry, and it was usually quite easy to tell when he was. Judith still held her breath as he stood up and came over to put his hands on her shoulders.

"Is he who you really want, poppet?"

"More than anything."

"That's quite a lot. And since I've already had my brow beaten quite enough lately, I suppose I should summon the coach."

She gave a delighted cry and hugged him, but he wasn't quite done. "Of course, if he should disappoint you, I'll want to know why."

At least her father didn't say he'd kill him. One hurdle down, the bigger one to go. . . .

Chapter Fifty-Two

THE RUIN LOOKED THE same from a distance . . . well, except for the roof, which appeared to be finished, and all in clay tiles, too. But as Judith got closer, she saw that many of the windows had been replaced as well, perhaps all of them. Nathan had obviously been busy this week. Too busy to open the invitations she'd arranged to have forwarded to him? Or had he deliberately ignored those?

The front door was wide-open. So were the new windows. As she stepped inside, she noticed that a nice breeze was circulating. The entrance hall and the parlor hadn't changed much, but at least the cobwebs were gone and the staircase had new boards, all but one, which Nathan was still hammering in place.

His shirtsleeves were rolled up, his tool belt strapped to his hips. And he was wearing knee-high Hessian boots? She almost laughed. Did he not realize he shouldn't be working in such fancy footwear? But he probably found them too comfortable to resist. He'd obviously done some shopping while in London. Or collected the rest of his wardrobe that he'd left in England when he sailed.

She'd been filled with such determination and resolve.

Why the deuce was she suddenly so nervous now that she was here? But she didn't have much time. Her father was allowing her a brief visit alone with Nathan, but warned if she took too long, he'd come to find out why. Did he really think they'd make love in a crumbling old ruin? Well, rake that he used to be, he probably thought exactly that.

She carefully stepped inside because he'd replaced some of the rotted floorboards in the foyer, but not all.

"Are your nieces here with you? I've looked forward to meeting them."

He glanced back, straightened, and came down the stairs without taking his eyes off her. "They'll be remaining with Peggy and Alf, your uncle James's caretakers, until the house is fit for them."

"You mean until it's finished?"

"No, just until it's no longer a danger to curious children. Which won't be much longer. The attic and the first floor sustained the worst of the weather damage. The second floor hasn't needed nearly as much work. The girls' rooms are already done."

She was surprised. "And furnished?"

"Well, no. And I've still got to paint or wallpaper them and figure out what to put on the new floorboards."

"You don't think they'd like to be a part of that? Watch the progress? Make choices for their own rooms? They could stay with my cousins next door in the meantime. They've got an army of servants to watch over them, including my cousin Cheryl's old nanny. And Derek's cook makes such wonderful desserts. They'd be thrilled."

His brow furrowed with a frown. "Too thrilled. I don't want them getting used to a grand mansion like that because then they might be disappointed with the home I'm giving them."

Judith knew his nieces would be delighted with this manor once she added her touch to it, but she didn't say that. He was annoyed enough with her suggestion to finally take his eyes off her face—and notice the kitten in her arms. She'd brought it as an excuse to visit him—if she ended up needing one.

"I never expected to see it again." He couldn't help smiling at the furball. "Figured you would have found it a home by now."

"Bite your tongue. Silver is quite entrenched. And *it* has been determined to be a he by my mother."

His eyes came back to hers. "Why did you bring him?"

"I know you only gave him up because you had nowhere to keep him while you finished your business in America. I thought we might share Silver, now that you appear to be staying in England for the time being."

"Share?"

"We can—figure something out." She looked away.

Her nervousness had just shot through the roof. This wasn't exactly how she had expected this meeting to go. Why wasn't she in his arms already? Or was he as nervous as she was?

She set Silver down on the floor. He didn't wander off, just started licking his paws. Nathan might have picked him up, but he followed her instead when she walked over to the room she'd first met him in—when she'd thought he was a ghost. And had, more recently, been kissed by him. He never did confirm that he was a smuggler. Still, she was sure he used to be one, but hoped he was done with that part of his life.

The room looked the same with blankets hanging over the windows and a rumpled cot in it. But the blankets looked clean. She guessed he simply preferred this old study for now to a moldering master bedroom upstairs.

"Show me the hidden room."

She wasn't sure he would, yet he moved past her to one of the decorative wooden strips spaced several feet apart on each wall to cover the seams of the old wallpaper. One had a switch on the side of it.

"A bookcase used to hide this," he explained as a panel opened in the wall next to him. "It was empty, the books likely stolen, and wasn't worth keeping, so I used it for firewood long ago. Then I noticed the latch when I was here one day, trying to see how easily I could punch my fist through these walls."

She grinned. That must have been one of his angry-at-the-house days. She went over to peer inside the room. The decent-size space was filled to the brim with stacks of lumber and other supplies—and an open case of brandy up front, a few bottles missing from it.

"Ahha!" she couldn't help saying.

He laughed behind her. "When *The Pearl* became mine, her crew expected me to continue in my father's footsteps. Smuggling I knew how to do. Merchant trading is much more involved, and I didn't know the first thing about finding markets that would turn a profit instead of a loss, or making contacts for cargoes. I do now, thanks to the Andersons."

She swung around. "So you're going to try legitimate sailing?"

He shook his head. "I'm actually thinking of hiring a captain and sending *The Pearl* to join the Skylark fleet, which was Boyd's suggestion. They already know all the markets and have all the necessary contacts."

"And you'll turn a tidy profit from that while you—farm?"

He laughed again. "No, I think I'm more partial to your idea of building a few rental cottages. After the house is done, of course."

They were talking about such inconsequential things while she . . . "I don't have much time." She hurried back to the main room to make sure her father hadn't yet arrived.

He followed her and put his hands on her shoulders to keep her there. "I was going to give you two weeks."

"Two weeks for what?"

"Before I returned to London for your answer. But I'm not exactly partial to climbing through windows, so I'm glad it only took one week for you to bring it to me. But if you heard my question, I'd like a chance to rephrase it."

"I'm pretty sure I would have answered if I'd heard one," she said breathlessly, her heart starting to soar. "When—did I miss it?"

"Last week, and thank God you don't know what I'm talking about."

She swung around with a gasp. "Excuse me?"

"I mucked it up, darlin'. You would have been too angry to say yes."

He obviously wasn't talking about what she hoped he was, if she would have been disturbed by what he'd said. She'd rather not get angry with him ever again, so she wasn't going to ask him to repeat whatever he'd mucked up.

Instead she said, "About that rephrasing?"

He grinned and put his arms around her. "I'd get on my knees for this, but I don't trust these floorboards to risk—"

"Yes!" she squealed, and threw her arms around his neck.

He leaned back with a chuckle. "You're supposed to wait for the question."

"Go ahead, but my answer is still going to be yes." She smiled.

"So you guessed that I love you?"

She grinned. "It's nice to hear it, but I had my suspicions."

"Did you now? And that I want to marry you?"

"That I wasn't so sure about—until now."

"I do, darlin'," he said tenderly. "It was agony fighting with you, and for that you can't imagine how sorry I am. But it's even more agony being apart from you, and it didn't take long to find that out."

"I don't feel whole without you either. I've loved you for so long." She giggled happily. "Even when I thought you were a ghost."

"I was never—never mind. Just tell me how soon we can marry. Today can't be soon enough for me."

"My mother will want to arrange it. We can't deny her that."

"If you insist."

"And you should probably formally ask—"

His hands cupped her cheeks, his words brushed her lips. "Will you marry me, Judith Malory?"

"I meant ask my father."

He groaned, placing his forehead against hers. "I would do anything for you, but you must know I'd rather be shot than ask his permission—"

"Then it's a good thing I've already given it," Anthony said from the open front door.

Nathan immediately stepped back from Judith to

demand, "How long have you been standing there, Sir Anthony?"

Anthony was leaning against the doorframe, relaxed, as he replied drolly, "Long enough." But then he straightened. "Just so you know, Tremayne, the only thing I had against you was that my baby was falling in love with you. I wasn't ready to accept that yet, it was too bloody soon, but I've had it beaten into me that there's no accounting for *when*, merely that it's happened. So you've my blessing, for what it's worth. But if you ever hurt her or make her cry again, I'll bloody well kill you—just so we're clear on that."

Judith was grinning. "Go away, Papa, we were about to kiss."

"No, we weren't," Nathan assured Anthony.

Judith grabbed the front of Nathan's shirt. "Yes, we were."

She started it, but he soon forgot they had an audience, embracing her fully, kissing her deeply. But she couldn't quite lose herself with a *parent* in the room. She didn't let go of him though, just ended the kiss so she could lay her cheek on his chest, a happy smile on her lips.

"Is he gone?" Nathan whispered after a moment.

She bit back a giggle to peer around his shoulder. "Yes. You *will* get used to him, you know. You'll probably even become great friends."

"Somehow I don't see that ever happening. But as long as he doesn't visit us too often."

"He might, at least for a while. He'll want to see for himself that I'm going to be blissfully happy here. He's not going to just take my word for it. But it won't take long for him to believe it."

"But he won't want to reside in this house when he visits, will he?"

"Probably."

"Then I won't repair the guest rooms."

"Wait—"

"No."

"But there's something you don't know about me. I'm rich, and I don't mean my family is. I have my own money and a lot of it."

"And why does that warrant a 'wait'?"

"Because you have to promise me you won't be like my father. He refuses to let my mother spend any of her own money on things that are needed. It quite infuriates her."

"You had me at 'don't be like your father.' I bleedin' well *won't* be like him."

"So I can decorate our house?"

"I love the sound of *our*. Yes, to your heart's content, darlin'. As if I know anything about decorating."

"And furnish it?"

"Don't press your luck."

She laughed. Compromising with him was going to be fun. She brought his lips back to hers to prove it.

Continue reading for an exclusive excerpt from

WILDFIRE IN HIS ARMS

Johanna Lindsey

Coming June 2015 from Gallery Books

THE SOFT CREAK OF the wood floor woke him. Degan opened his eyes to see Max Dawson tiptoeing out the door with his saddlebags in hand, coat donned and hat on. Degan's failing to check the pile of leaves the outlaw had been using as a mattress proved just how tired he'd been after tying up his prisoner. Any number of things could have been hidden under it. Obviously a knife.

"I wouldn't if I were you," Degan growled.

The boy still did, bolting out the door. Degan swore and gave chase, nearly tripping over the saddlebags that had been dropped just outside the door. He didn't draw his gun even with such a clear target in the moonlight. He'd never shot a man in the back and wasn't going to start now. And he had a feeling Dawson was too desperate to stop at the threat of a gun right now, even if it was fired.

The boy didn't head for his horse. Turning the animal around in the small cave where it was hidden would waste too much time. He was simply running down the hill for freedom, zigzagging through the trees, probably hoping Degan would lose sight of him so he could hide, then double back for his mount. It might have worked. There were enough trees to hide behind. But the kid was short and Degan's legs were long.

He got a handful of the long doeskin coat that was flapping behind the boy and yanked on it. That should have stopped him, but Dawson slipped his arms out of it, leaving the coat in Degan's hand while he kept on running. Degan tossed it aside and closed the distance between them again. He got his hand on Dawson's vest this time, but damned if the kid didn't do it again, slipping his arms out of it so Degan was left with just the stiff leather—and the sound of the kid's laughter floating back at him. So Dawson had planned that one, unbuttoning the garment as he ran? Incredible! This was starting to feel like a joke with Degan as the punch line.

He hadn't chased anyone like this since he was a child playing with his younger siblings. Since coming West, he'd never encountered a situation where he *had* to chase anyone. Though his gun could put a stop to this nonsense, he still didn't draw it. But he wasn't falling for Dawson's tactics again when the kid was probably already unbuttoning his shirt for a third slip.

"Give it up, fancy man!" Max yelled without looking back. "You ain't catching me!"

Degan tackled the boy to the ground. It probably knocked the breath out of him, considering their weight difference. The kid was so still now it might even have knocked him out. Or was he thinking up some other trick? Degan was done playing children's games.

Dawson's tan hat had rolled farther down the hill when they'd hit the ground. Degan got off the boy, grabbing a handful of spiky blond hair, pulling Max to his feet. The kid came up swinging his fists. Degan shoved him back to the ground and, getting down on one knee, held him there at arm's length while he searched for the knife the kid had used to cut the ropes. The boy was resisting with fists and knees now. The fists couldn't reach Degan's face and he barely felt them as they struck his chest, but the knees jabbing him in his side were getting annoying. And then Max changed tactics and just tried to get Degan's hand off his belly, but that didn't work either.

"I could have slit your throat while you slept but I didn't!" Max snarled at him.

"Two points for you, kid."

"For your life? That's a hundred damn points if you ask me!"

"I'm not asking."

The knife wasn't in the boy's belt, so it was probably in one of his boots. Degan figured he could either knock the kid out and carry him back to the shack to find it or risk getting a boot in his face if he removed the footwear here. For all the trouble Dawson had caused him, Degan opted for the knockout, and he was in a good position to deliver the blow with one hand still holding Dawson down.

But Max saw the punch coming and used all the strength he had left to avoid it, trying to turn on his side and covering his head with both arms. With the sudden movement Degan's palm slid up a few inches and touched something soft. That brought Degan to his feet fast.

"What the . . . ?"

The kid was still cowering on the ground—like a girl. Oh, hell no. There must be a money pouch or something else strapped to Dawson's chest that would account for what he'd felt. He was *not* dealing with a damn girl.

"Get up," Degan growled.

The kid rose with a wary look. Degan clamped his fingers around the back of Max's neck and, keeping him at arm's length in front of him, walked him back up the hill. He didn't collect the discarded garments they passed on the way. His thoughts were bordering on furious, which was disconcerting since he hadn't been this angry in years.

He shoved Max into the shack before he let go. The lantern was still burning. There was fear in Max's dark eyes now. About damn time.

"This is what is going to happen now," Degan said in a low tone. "You are going to remove your shirt."

"The hell I will!" Max backed away from Degan until the wall got in the way.

"If I have to do it, there won't be any buttons left on your shirt. If it's the only shirt you've got, too bad. I'm not interested in you, just what's under your shirt."

"So I've got a pair, so what? You don't need to see them when you already felt—"

"No more pretenses for you or assumptions for me, kid. Show me or I show myself. Your choice."

Degan saw a flash of blue in the dark eyes that were glaring murderously at him. He might have been startled by the appealing hue if he wasn't so angry and frustrated himself. If Max was a girl, what the hell was he going to do with her?

The shirt was unbuttoned very slowly. If there weren't still murder in her eyes, he'd think she was trying to entice him. She pulled one edge of the black shirt to the side, revealing a breast. It wasn't large, but decently plump and incredibly beautiful to his eyes, which warned him he'd been a fool to go so long without having a woman. She started to uncover her other breast. He must have been staring too long. If she hadn't been trying to seduce him to begin with, he was sure she was now. He ought to take her up on the offer to show her what happened when she played with fire. Not that she would get what she wanted from him.

He turned around. "Cover yourself."

Whether she did or didn't, she leapt at his back, slamming both fists into it before yelling, "Happy now, you son'bitch! Doesn't change a damn thing and you know it!"

Didn't it? Degan wondered. Maybe not. Max Dawson, female, was still an outlaw wanted for murder and bank robbery. What would his friend U.S. Marshal John Hayes do under these circumstances? His job, of course, and that was to apprehend and bring in the individual so a court of law could decide the matter of guilt or innocence.

The fists pounding on his back didn't budge him, and since he was blocking the shack's only exit, he didn't turn around right away to confront her. He'd give her time to button up her shirt and himself time to get the image of her breasts out of his mind. When he did turn, she was pacing back and forth across the shack's measly eight feet of space, kicking the cut ropes, kicking the pile of leaves, the only two things on that side of the shack to kick.

The lantern was in the front corner to Degan's right, the coil of rope to his left, but she didn't go near them. She was staying away from him now, as far as she could get. It was a good thing he'd brought a long coil of rope. He was going to have to use the rest of it now.

"Take your boots off," he said.

She stopped to give him another glare before she sat down hard and reached for one of her boots. "Sure! Why not? This shack doesn't stink enough already?"

Two knives fell to the floor when the first boot came off. A third fell with the second boot. Degan shook his head incredulously. He knew one of those knives had been stashed under the leaves because she wouldn't have been able to reach her boots when she'd been tied up. She definitely took precautions, carrying so many weapons.

He looked at her feet and saw dingy gray socks with holes. He wondered if she ever willingly took her boots off. He wondered if she ever bathed for that matter. He figured she must because she didn't smell bad. But she obviously hadn't washed in the last day since the rain. Her mud-caked dirty face was like a mask, and not a pretty one. Did she know how she looked? Did she even have a mirror?

He could see the two curves under her shirt, now that he knew to look for them. The stiff leather vest she'd been wearing earlier had acted as a corset, flattening and concealing what was under it. He should go pick up her things that were scattered down the hill and get her back into that vest. But he was still having trouble coming to terms with the fact that there was a female beneath that rough, muddy exterior. His eyes roamed over her. Her loose black shirt was tucked into loose black pants, leaving her waist and hips undefined. She'd chosen the right clothing to hide her womanly shape. He never would have believed Max Dawson was a woman if he hadn't seen her breasts.

He picked up the three knives and tossed them outside before he said, "You can put your boots back on, but stay where you are."

"You're all heart, fancy man," she replied scathingly.

He picked up one of the pieces of rope on the floor, one long enough to bind her hands behind her back. He couldn't bring himself to hog-tie her again, but he knew just tying her hands wasn't enough to keep her from trying to escape again. So he got the remainder of the coil of rope and wrapped it around her arms and torso to keep her arms confined to her sides. Then he hauled her to the back wall and sat her down so she could lean against it.

"I take it back," she snarled. "No heart at all."

"Shut up," he said tonelessly. "It's this or I tie you to a tree outside."

"I'll take the tree if it means I don't have to be in this room with you."

"I wasn't offering a choice."

He started to sit down next to her so he could finish securing her with the rope, but he reconsidered. If he tied their ankles together they would be sitting side by side and she might lean against him when she fell asleep and rub some of that dried mud on his jacket. He went outside to get his canteen of water. He offered her a drink first, which she took grudgingly, then removed the bandana from her neck and thoroughly wet it. She tried to avoid the cloth as it came toward her face, but she didn't have room to maneuver and fell over on her side. He dragged her back up so he could finish his work.

"I'll need that back before you take me in," she said.

He held up the bandana to show her how dirty it was. "It has to be washed first."

"I don't care what it looks like," she insisted. "I have a specific use for it, and it's not to protect my face during dust storms."

"I can guess."

"No you can't. I use it to cover up the fact that I don't have a lump in my throat like you do."

"Yes, I've already figured that out. And that lump has a name."

"Like I care what it's called? Just put it back around my neck."

"You can do that in the morning when it's dry."

He draped the cloth over the peg in the wall. When he

turned back to sit next to her, he paused. He'd done his best not to look at what he'd been cleaning, but it was hard to miss now. He didn't castigate himself for not seeing it sooner. He'd come across too many late-blooming boys for a girlish face to have warned him, even if hers hadn't been so dirty. Well, maybe not. With the mud and dirt gone, she was a little too pretty now.